IN

LAMAR GILES

SCHOLASTIC INC.

All rights reserved. Published by Scholastic Inc., *Publishers since 1920.* SCHOLASTIC and associated logos are trademarks and/or registered trademarks of Scholastic Inc.

ISBN 978-1-338-53899-1

10 9 8 7 6 5 4 3 2 1   19 20 21 22 23

Printed in the U.S.A. 23
First printing 2019

Book design by Phil Falco and Carol Ly

For Jody, an unsung hero

Still me, till they kill me.

—TUPAC, "HOLLER IF YA HEAR ME"

KYA

I did not kill Paris Secord.

I should've told the two police officers staring at me from across the table, though they hadn't asked. There'd been other questions about the night, I answered as honestly as I could—as honestly as felt smart. Yet, I wanted to state, unequivocally, that I was not the murderer here. Sweat made my shirt sticky, like a licked envelope, even though the tiny room was cold.

"You go to Cooke High?" Detective Barker asked.

Through my damp shirt, I clutched the oblong charm that dangled from a nylon necklace and rested against my chest. "Yes."

"My daughter was an Eagle. Class of '97." He dragged a finger down the sheet in the open folder before him. How did he have a paper about me, and this? "Sophomore?"

"I'll be a senior in the fall."

I did NOT kill Paris Secord. Even rehearsing it in my head it seemed too loud, too fake. I did not KILL Par—

"If I understand the situation correctly, your friend Paris was a DJ known for throwing impromptu parties in unsanctioned locations?"

"Pop-ups. Yeah. Not so much these days."

"Something changed with her?"

"She got busy. With her music production." My hands kneaded into each other, worked invisible dough between them.

"Help me understand that a bit more. I'm an old guy. That means what exactly?"

"She made songs. The beats, sometimes lyrics, but not always. She made it all sound good together."

"This was more than a hobby?"

"She had a song go viral some time ago. Then she did it again. And again. Bigger artists have been wanting to work with her. I heard J. Cole had some interest."

"You heard?" One of the detective's bushy eyebrows lifted. "Not from her?"

"No." There hadn't been many meaningful conversations between us lately. That last real talk was just mean. More name-calling than career updates. I had a feeling some of this stuff they knew already. How could they not? Paris was famous. Maybe not that get-mobbed-in-the-mall kind of fame. Not yet. Her name rang out in Virginia, and with music heads in general. She was on her way.

And now she wasn't.

My hands kept working, even though I willed them to stop. Nothing was in my control that evening. Not even my own body.

I pressed my palms flat against the table. *Stay!* I shouted inside my skull, only slightly more convincing than my silent assertion of innocence. The camera just above the interrogation room door caught every bit of me acting weird while answering the simplest questions. When the cops rewatched this video, I'd look guilty. If they ever played it before a jury, I'd look guilty times twelve.

"Is there something you want to tell us?" Barker said. He was dark-skinned, like me, with matted black-and-white grandpa hair that looked like he'd been rolling in baby powder and coal dust. He'd smiled when he walked me into the room, and I remembered wondering if they'd found a black man who smiled so I'd forget that badge on his belt and say something wrong. Were his simple questions *meant* to make me act weird, like a trap?

I DID NOT KILL Paris Secord.

"Hey, hey, Kya." His hands raised, palms facing me, a sign of peace. His smile twitched away. He looked as frightened as I felt. "I only asked because you were moving your lips a moment ago."

Moving my lips. I mouthed words when I got nervous. I'd probably mouthed *jury*; an expert lip reader might tell them I was already thinking of a way to trick the jury because I was 100 percent guilty.

His partner—a silent, youngish white policeman who was scary in a way I was used to—burst into the room, making me yelp. He held a box of Kleenex. Only then did my vision blur from accumulated tears that spilled over. I accepted the tissues and oh God, Paris was gone.

Staying quiet was the smart move. They hadn't arrested me. They never read me those rights cops read criminals on TV. I didn't know if that was a good or bad thing. I only knew that silence was always advised. How many movies had a lawyer yelling at their innocent client to keep their mouth shut? But there was the thing I needed to say. Out loud, once, and make it sound true. "I did not—"

Something crashed just outside the interrogation room. Shrieking curses followed. A general sense of panic soured the air inside the Ocean Shore Police Department's Second Precinct.

Barker and his partner rushed from the room, joining a couple of uniformed officers trying to contain the destructive lunatic who should be in here, handcuffed. Maybe muzzled too.

I did not kill Paris Secord. Had absolutely nothing to do with her death.

Could all her so-called friends say the same?

FUSE

"She is not dead! Stop saying that!"

The cop was a liar. He was . . . giving false testimony or whatever. A lying hater with a crappy toy-store badge, and I threw a stapler at his head for saying that stupidness. Didn't he know DJ ParSec was *immortal*?

He ducked. The stapler crashed into the wall behind him, denting it. How could he say something so . . . *nasty*? How was he *allowed*?

I reached for my back pocket out of habit. Planned on blowing him up on every platform I had access to. Insta. Snap. YouTube. I'd rip the audio for SoundCloud, and even post it on Facebook so old people could see how . . . how . . . *corrupt* this cop was. This whole department. I'd have a quarter of a million likes by noon tomorrow. Easy. Except my phone wasn't where it was supposed to be.

I'd given it to someone earlier, a sure sign of how insanely nightmarish this all was. Handed it over to someone who wanted my dad's number from the emergency contacts because I wouldn't talk. Wouldn't walk on my own until someone said *shock* and *hospital* and I knew I'd end up at Sentara where Mom was doing rounds. "No hospital!" I'd managed, and they brought me here.

Lieutenant Liar held his hands at chest level, fingers curled, ready to grab me. "Calm down," he said.

Calm down? I thought, in rhythm, to the infectious melody of my homegirl's smash track that people were singing all the way in China!

Calm down? Uh-uh. When they say calm down, we turn up! TURN! UP!

ParSec wasn't gone. She couldn't be.

While I was distracted, Liar Cop wrapped me up at the shoulder so all I could do was kick, then he lifted me so those kicks only hit air. "Lemme go! Lemme go!"

Two cops emerged from a door I hadn't noticed. One was white and tall and handsome like he could be in one of those superhero movies. The other was black and old, with a Santa tummy.

A third person emerged from that other room, and I went limp. It was the first I'd seen of her since they separated us at the warehouse and drove us off in different cars. She was as tall as the superhero cop, but gangly, too loose. As if her clothes were missized, or she was missing key bones and was held together by muscle and skin only.

Her eyes were red, her badly applied makeup smudged from crying. Like she had a right. I directed all my venom, every bit of rage, and grief, and guilt, and disbelief, and violence at her. "What did you do, you . . . you *street trash giraffe?*"

Kya Caine's face twisted, her lips peeled back, flashing slick teeth. ParSec's self-proclaimed *first* best friend snarled and slipped between all the officers who should've been protecting me.

Her punch connected with my left eye. A solid *POP!* A white explosion of pain that washed out the room for a hot second.

The cop who held me cursed, dropped me. My vision flooded back when my butt connected with the floor. Kya stood over me, a thousand feet tall. All three cops wrapped up her limbs then, maybe saving me from a kick to the ribs.

Beyond the tussle, another flash. From a camera phone. A quick burst from a young guy who'd been carrying files from somewhere to somewhere else. He swore under his breath, obviously not intending for the flash to go off. Yet the cops paid it no mind, too worried about a girl fight in the office pool. I watched camera boy with my good eye; he pocketed the phone, kept moving.

A throbbing pulse consumed the left side of my face, confused my senses. I half hurt, half heard, only catching some of the nasty things Kya shouted.

"Ask her!" she said. "Ask her why Paris didn't want to see her!"

Wait. No. Was she trying to say *I* had something to do with what happened? Like she had any clue what was going on between me and ParSec. Was this psycho trying to blame—?

"Stop it!" said Black Santa Cop. His voice boomed and froze the room. "Both of you are working on an overnight stay if you don't pull it together. Given what you've been through, I'd rather you get to sleep in your own beds. But test me if you want."

He stared me down, and I flinched. I wanted my own bed.

Kya stopped bucking against the men who held her.

A tired-looking woman with glasses and gray streaks in her hair rounded a corner. "Detective Barker, guardians are here."

Black Santa—Barker—said, "For which one?"

"Both."

"Thank God." Barker motioned my way. "The wounded one first."

The pity in his voice shamed me into lowering my hand and exposing my swelling eye. Liar Cop tucked a hand into the armpit of my leather jacket, gently, an offer of help. I shook him off and got up on my own, glaring at Kya like I was Mad-Eye Moody. We. Weren't. Finished.

She *didn't* flinch.

Things between us—all three of us—were bad before. I welcomed this new, enhanced anger and the pain that came with it. It was better than everything else I was trying not to feel. Or remember.

Like that sheet of sticky, dark blood over half of ParSec's face. How she'd been a rag doll, arms spread wide, across the turntables. Almost religious. Her eyes bulged, the right one deep red where white should be, like something in that side of her head had exploded, the other staring at a crowd no one in this world could see.

I choked back something between a sob and shriek.

Detective Barker positioned himself strategically between Kya and me, and soon we were in a corridor, walking through doors with steel-mesh windows embedded in them. The last door required a hand signal from the detective. Someone monitoring the corner-mounted camera registered the gesture, and an angry buzz accompanied the released lock. On the other side, a harshly lit lobby where my dad sprang from a cracked vinyl chair.

"Fatima!" His attention was on my eye. The shadows over his face darkened. Before I could answer, he sidestepped me and was in Barker's face. "Which one of you put your hands on my daughter?"

"Mr. Fallon," Barker began, monotone. "It's—"

"I want your name, badge number, your supervisor's name . . . You know what, I want a list of everyone working in this building tonight."

He kept ranting, so concerned with discovering who dared assault his daughter that he'd forgotten I was right there and really wanted to go home. I knew better to interrupt him, though. So his voice became a drone, and my focus shifted to the other person present.

A tall woman in a short sequined dress, fishnet stockings, and a light jacket with a fake fur collar. Her hair was curled, though the once-bouncy coils struggled in the night's humidity. She had on too much makeup that didn't look great with her annoyed expression. I got the impression Kya wasn't in for a great time when she was reunited with her mother.

Good.

"Let's go, Fatima!" Dad's heavy hand landed on my shoulder.

Barker said, "We'd like to set up some time for questions. After she's had some rest."

"You've got my number." Dad applied more pressure. "Move."

"My phone," I said, barely a whisper.

"What?" It was his back-talk tone. He was mad I wasn't silently obeying. He'd be more mad if I left a thousand-dollar cell phone here.

"I need my phone."

Dad's head whipped toward Barker, who cut off his next tirade with a wait-a-minute finger. The detective disappeared into the station. Leaving me alone with the worst cop in my life.

"What did you do this time, Fatima?" Dad asked, hushed. My personal judge and jury had already decided I was guilty of something.

Kya's mom was tight-lipped, alert. She awaited my confession too.

That angry buzz again. Barker returned, my unmistakable bedazzled purple phone in his hand. I took it and fled through the exit into the muggy night, my nostrils filling with the scent of the salt sea just a couple of blocks over. Paris *loved* that smell. She said it was inspiration like no other, was the reason why some of the biggest music stars came from right here, our state. She said Virginia music is the reason there's a saying about *it* being in the water. I knew that wasn't true, that saying was way older than us and our sound. Still, it felt true a lot over this last year. Felt true last night. True six hours ago. Before.

I thought I heard the waves crashing too. Knew deep down sound didn't carry *that* far. Not even Virginia sound.

Maybe it was life as I knew it, crashing.

And burning.

KYA

Mama didn't stand up when Detective Barker brought me through the exit door. The buzzing of the released lock jolted me, shooting electric pain from my probably sprained wrist to my shoulder.

Mama saw me wince, her head tilted, calm observation. If a second head sprouted from the side of my neck, she'd show just as much concern, at least while people were around. She was a master of the public poker face.

Barker walked me to her and did a good job of keeping his face from crinkling in the heavy perfume cloud surrounding her. He said, "Ms. Caine—"

That's when she stood. She was taller than me and the detective, and she liked looking down when handing out corrections. "Caine's her daddy's name. I'm a Stokes." She'd found the nicotine gum she'd been mining for in her bag and popped a stick in her mouth.

"Pardon me, Ms. Stokes."

"Cinda's fine."

An annoyed edge crept into his voice. "Cinda, then. I was hoping you'd be open to sitting with your daughter while we ask her a few questions about what happened tonight."

"Naw, my daughter ain't answering no questions."

Barker's head snapped back, as did mine. I hadn't expected such a matter-of-fact refusal from her. I wanted to hug her right there, but that's not what we do.

"Ma'am, a girl was found—"

She waved a hand in front of his face, rude but effective. "Save that ma'am mess. I know Paris dead, it's all on the news. I *saw* you bring that other girl out. When her daddy was getting on you about her eye"—Mama's gaze flicked to my limp, sore wrist, making connections, as sharp as she was loud—"you weren't worried about questions. You wanted them gone even though they probably gonna lawyer up before they speak on anything with you. But I'm supposed to be Boo-Boo the Fool letting you question my child with no *legal representation* so you can twist whatever she say?" Her voice sped up, rose, emphasized odd words, a performance. She turned her attention to me. "Tell me you ain't been in there running your mouth?"

"No, Mama."

"Come on, then!" Mama grabbed my hand, narrowed her eyes at the detective. "She's free to go, right?"

Sounding exhausted, Barker said, "She is. We will need to speak soon. With your lawyer if you prefer. I just need his name."

"You'll know when I do." With that, Mama dragged me out of the station, and I gulped warm night air greedily.

She didn't let my hand go until we reached our car. A 2002 silver Impala with rust on the passenger's side and a left lean thanks to bad suspension. Inside the car she started the engine—always a rough enterprise. I rolled my window down halfway—any farther, it would free-fall into the doorframe and need to be pried up—and tried for whatever fresh air I could manage before the yelling started. Mama's anger became formidable over small, private inconveniences. This would be a wrath of legend.

A block away from the police station, she began, and not as I expected. "Are you okay?"

Surprised and touched, I said, "Yes, Mama. I only found Paris. I was scared, but no one tried to hurt me. Whatever happened was over by the time I got there."

"You'd tell me if you were hurt or something?" She pointed with her chin. "The emergency room right up there."

"I'm fine." I wasn't. But this conversation was stranger than the circumstances that brought me to the police station in the first place. Mama asking if I needed emergency medical treatment was her emotional distance shrinking to its narrowest band. It was the equivalent of a loving and open parent sobbing through sloppy forehead kisses and loudly thanking God for my safety.

We passed under a couple of traffic lights and tears blurred the city lights into neon streaks that were prettier than what should've been allowed that night. Mama said, "Hey, you hush up that crying. We don't do that, Kya."

If anybody heard her say that, they might've thought Mama was cruel. But there was no edge in her voice, just direction. The same kind she'd given me since I was little. Only present what you want the world to see, and you don't want them to see you weak.

"I know she was your friend before," Mama went on, "and I ain't saying you shouldn't feel nothing, but don't forget how she went and got rich and treated you like she didn't know you from Eve."

"I . . ." What to say? That was the extent of the story Mama knew. I never told her everything. So I mopped dampness from my cheeks with my sleeve. "I'm sorry."

"You're fine. We'll figure it out."

I didn't know what *it* she was referring to.

She glanced over, changed the subject before I could dig. "That little girl at the police station, you pop her in the eye?"

"Yes, Mama."

"She had it coming?"

For a long time. "Yes, Mama."

"Good, then. Don't let no one disrespect you. Ever."

That was our thing. Cinda Stokes and Kya Caine would not be disrespected. Paris Secord getting famous and leaving her friends behind was the ultimate disrespect in Mama's eyes. She didn't say it, but I couldn't help wondering if she saw Paris getting her head busted in as . . . karma?

I still took my mama's hand and lavished in her not pulling away. As she said, we'd figure it out soon enough.

PARIS/DJ PARSEC

(24 MONTHS BEFORE)

This was it. I'd been working on this drum pattern all day.

Bom-bom-ba-ba-ba-tah! Bom-bom-ba-ba-ba-tah!

"When they say calm down, we TURN UP! When they say calm down, we TURN UP!" I mumbled the words. Lyrics? I didn't know. That part was for later. Right now, this beat was everything!

Bom-bom-ba-ba-ba-TAH!

That high hat accent on the end of that sequence . . . I liked it a lot.

Hunched over the ancient Casio keyboard, I looped my brand-new bass line. That keyboard with its circuitry guts exposed, a bunch of red, green, blue, white wires snaking to some other plastic box thing, was janky as anything. It did the job, though. The plastic box—a *something-something* converter, also janky—had its own singular cable running to the USB port of a slightly less ancient Dell laptop. There, a pirated version of my FL Studio production software kept the strained hard drive whirring like a blender mixing up this hotness. Now that I got the pattern down—

The laptop screen flickered.

No.

An ominous static line swept over my user interface, bottom to top, some ghost in the machine trying to squeegee away my work.

With the urgency of a soldier signaling his platoon of an incoming attack, I jabbed Ctrl+S, hoping for a quick save.

Nothing happened. Except more static. More signs of an impending crash.

No, no, no.

"Kya!"

She sprawled on Grandma's couch, gripping a coding book from the library at the ten-and-two position like she was driving it. She lowered the top edge, peered at me with her eyebrows raised.

"Yo, it's happening again," I said.

She heavy sighed, pawed for her favorite bookmark (because of course she had a favorite bookmark—no judgment, it *was* signed by Jacqueline Woodson), then gently wedged it into place because dog-earing pages was a sin in her particular smarty-art cult. All that care and attention to detail gave me palpitations because she wasn't caring for the details of my whole day's work.

"Kya! My beat."

She didn't move any faster, laying the book next to her glass of water. Swung her feet to the floor, where her thick socks likely offered more cushion and warmth than the thin, worn carpet. This chick had the nerve to yawn and cat-stretch. Hello, am I disturbing you?

"Look—"

She held up a halting hand. "Yell at me, and I will not save the day."

"But . . ." More screen flickers. I traced a finger across the track pad, and the cursor responded on a delay, jerking in squirrel leaps. "The last time this happened, we didn't move fast enough and . . ."

The screen froze. I rubbed my finger across the track pad as if scratching an electronic itch, and the cursor remained fixed. No delay, just still, a drawing of a cursor. I slammed my fist into the folding card table that was my music studio. "Can I yell at you now? You're too late."

"Hold the power button for a hard reboot."

"What's it matter now? It's gone."

"Just do it."

I did. Waited through all the you-didn't-shut-down-properly-last-time garbage, and a thousand years later I was able to reopen FL Studio, expecting—

It was there. Oh . . . Crap! It was there. "How did you do this, tech witch?"

She scowled. "I know you think it's empowering for us to call each other things like that. I don't, though. So stop. Also, I changed your autosave settings. New changes get uploaded to a free cloud account immediately."

The file I thought I'd lost forever was *right there*. I tapped my space bar.

Bom-bom-ba-ba-ba-tah! Bom-bom-ba-ba-ba-tah!

I flung myself on her, coiling her in my arms, while she screamed and squirmed and laughed. She was way longer than me, a living stick figure. I had girth on my side, my body swallowing her. We sank deep into couch cushions that were older than us.

"If you suffocate me," she shouted through laughs, "I can't fix my equipment."

"*My* equipment."

"I'll accept payment at any time."

"Girls." My grandma, reeking of Lipton Iced Tea and Bengay. "Have you lost your minds? Shut up all that racket. I'm trying to watch my stories."

"Sorry, Miss Elsie," Kya said, sounding way more respectful than her trifling tail really was.

"My bad, Grandma."

We positioned ourselves on the couch like proper young women, and when Grandma went back to watching TV rich folks cheat, and steal, and kill their long-lost twin uncles on those dumb soap operas, I got back to work, while Kya resumed her reading. That's how we were, sisters, despite what our birth certificates said. The loud one and the quiet one. That's how we'd always be. Maybe one day we'd write a song about it.

This song first, though.

FUSE

I would still be attending Cooke High, apparently. It was 5:00 a.m. on Thursday, and minds were made up.

For the entire weekend, and half the week after Kya and I found ParSec, there'd been a raging debate in the Fallon home. Listening through the walls, I found Dad fell firmly on the "No! She's not going back there!" side of the argument.

Mom, logical to the point of robot, explained, "There's too little time left in the school year. It makes more sense if she finished, then we enroll her somewhere else over the summer."

Nobody bothered to ask me.

Aside from my consent on the school thing, there were other items missing from the lingering Parental Kombat match—at least the parts I remembered when I wasn't crying hysterically:

1. Any sort of reconciliation around my best friend being brutally killed
2. The reporters harassing Security-Guy Greg at the gatehouse of our community
3. My inevitable conversation with Detective Barker
4. ParSec's funeral

Her funeral.

A thousand little needles pricked the back of my eyes, a familiar sensation by then. Tears were natural, being crushed was expected. "Purging the pain from your heart," Mom said, "is like getting the poison out of a snakebite."

I didn't know if those two things were alike at all. Mom was a doctor, who said things with authority and didn't like second opinions. I agreed because it was easier. Yes! Purge-crying! Though, this time, I blinked those tears away.

If I was going back to Cooke High in T-minus two hours, I couldn't lose a second on sobs. I had arrangements to make. Protections to put in place.

My only way to do that hinged on a crap laptop still running Windows 8.

The night I came home from the police station, Mom, in her infinite wisdom, took all my electronics—phone, tablet, smart-watch, and MacBook. "You heal by resting."

She didn't get that being unplugged was the opposite of restful. I couldn't relax knowing the interwebz were buzzing with articles, and blogs, and tweets, and snaps, and everything else about ParSec's death and music. The first night, I barely slept. Mostly because when I closed my eyes, I saw her. When my eyelids popped open, and I groped for my phone to get a little bit of comfort from our followers . . . it wasn't there. I begged Mom for my watch at least, but she just shook her head.

By Monday, I couldn't take it. I attempted sneaking into Dad's office while my parents were at work and logging on to his computer as a guest. No go. Suzanne, our housekeeper, only half-focused on her sweeping, mopping, and dusting, took on the extra title of Prison Guard for a temporary pay bump. She was to keep an eye on me during this "trying time."

My room became a cell where my captors only allowed access to sports news, MSNBC, and *Charmed* reruns on my wall-mounted TV. Desperate, I dug through a big Tupperware bin at the back of my closet filled with things that mostly embarrassed me now. Dolls, canisters of hard, cracked Play-Doh, and . . . an old computer from like two laptops ago.

Usually, Dad removed the hard drives and took them to the tech guys at his office for recycling. This one had slipped his grasp. The power cord was with it, and when I booted it, I had to sit through an hour and a half of updates, fearing I'd never see the desktop. Behold, miracles do happen. Shortly after Suzanne allowed me a ration of chicken salad and sweet tea, I had a functioning portal to the internet.

It was stupidly, ridiculously slow. I mean, frustrating to the point I wanted to toss it across the room. Once my desired webpage loaded, it became slightly less miserable.

Until I actually saw the page.

I hit Twitter first, which was, ugh. Using the native site, it took a minute for me to orient, but once I did, and got a look at the thousands of mentions I'd missed, my heart ached with a deep pain I'd been anticipating.

As I'd suspected, given the tragedy, and in my absence, #ParSecNation was in turmoil.

Custom Shoes for Ya! @SneakerHead1213
Mad love to a VA original gone too soon. #TURNUP #RIPParSec
#ParSecNation

Shyla the Don @757BoomBap
In tears right now. Rocking her SoundCloud all night long. She
did it for the culture. #RIPParSec #ParSecNation

Lost Without Her @PSLover

I bet the party in heaven is LIT right now. Best believe whoever
did this gonna burn tho.
#BoomBoomClick #RIPParSec #ParSecNation

James Flames Is the Name @LukeSkyRimmer

Why the good die so young? #RIPParSec #ParSecNation

And so on.

From the time I saw the first glut of comments, to the time Dad got home with a grocery-store rotisserie chicken and sides from the deli, I scrolled and read and—despite apprehension churning in the pit of my stomach—responded.

Regardless of where we'd left things the last time #ParSecNation heard from me, I was needed.

I thought carefully about what my first post to the hashtag in weeks would be. Typed things, deleted them, retyped with slightly different words. In the last year, I'd picked up some books on public relations and branding to better assist in DJ ParSec's meteoric rise, and I kept slipping back to the quick-tip bullets they provided. One of my favorites came to mind.

- **Be Bold. Let the World Know What You Believe In!**

Made perfect sense. It's what ParSec would've wanted. So I posted:

Fuse Is Heartbroken @FuseZilla14

When they say calm down, we TURN UP! @DJParSec wouldn't

want tears. She'd want jamz! Stream her latest now! #RIPParSec
#ParSecNation

The likes, retweets, and replies came fast and furious, a significant uptick after every painstakingly slow browser refresh. A lot of the responses were positive, @DJParSec fans from all over the world mirroring my sentiment. A lot of responses weren't.

More than I expected, if I was being honest.

I Spit Hot Fire @MicLord007
What kind of super groupie fronts like she still on the team
when @DJParSec been said bounce? Disrespect! @FuseZilla14
#ParSecNation

Randy B @RandalltheBarbarian
Somebody trying to get their follows up. You so thirsty.
@FuseZilla14 #supergroupie #ParSecNation

Lost Without Her @PSLover
Sooooo shady! @DJParSec already showed them receipts on
you. Now you all like, pour one out for the homie? Watch ur back!
#ParSecNation

One out of every four replies was something nasty. What slid into my DMs that first night—and ever since—ranged from obnoxious to terrifying. It didn't help that the dude who snapped a pic of me and Kya fighting at the police station posted the photo to a ParSec Nation forum, so it was now making the rounds, allowing the internet to be the internet, with strangers drawing all sorts of conclusions about my standing with ParSec in her last days.

The Trash Monster @TrollHunter99
You're Fuse, right? If I hooked jumper cables to a car battery and clamped them on to your fingers and toes . . . would you blow?
#ParSecNation

I blocked as many as I could until I was forced to hide the laptop and eat dinner with my parents. When they released me back to my room, there were too many messages to block. All flashing #ParSecNation or a variation of the hashtag that I kinda hated, even though it'd popped up way before . . . all this. #DarkNation

That bugged me almost as much as the threats. ParSec's music was party music, and ParSec Nation was a fun, enthusiastic fandom—by design (mine). Why incorporate "Dark"? That wasn't the brand ParSec and I created. It was disrespectful, if you asked me.

This snowballed Tuesday and Wednesday, and I couldn't look away. More than a few of those unfriendly Twitter accounts belonged to fellow Cooke High classmates.

Mom called from the hall, "Are you getting dressed? Ticktock."

"I am." I wasn't. A speedy shower and hasty wardrobe solutions weren't the issue.

The Nation—both the light and dark variety—needed to understand that if there was a ParSec "frenemy" to blame here, it wasn't me. I'd hoped this would blow over like most online beef did, but #ParSecNation was loyal. Loyal, and mistaken. Some guidance was in order.

Kya Caine didn't appear to have a Twitter account—which was, I don't know, quaint. So I just led with her initials.

Fuse Is Heartbroken @FuseZilla14
THREAD! 1/? #ParSecNation Some disturbing things about the #MadScientist we all know as KC have come to my attention . . .

KYA

Paris was the fourth Cooke High student to die this year. My fourth friend. And it's been so different this time.

Early this year, three boys—Phillip, Simon, and Jim—were riding together when Jim lost control of his car on Route 58. They weren't popular boys, making up the vast majority of our after-school coding club known as the Smart Ones. The club's shining achievement was an app called SoundChek that did okay numbers on Apple and Android platforms, pulling down an average of eight hundred bucks in ad click revenue monthly into the club's joint checking account. Money we planned to invest in tech stock, to one day finance college or a fortune-finding trip to Silicon Valley to become tech billionaires like our idols, who average people knew mostly as brand names. Airbnb, and Lyft, and Snap.

When my fellow "Tech-Necks" (a term coined by Simon, our branding-minded member) were killed, the principal told everyone in a PA announcement, saying each boy's full name to stone-faced reactions from nearly everyone in my homeroom. Me included.

It was only upon their tragic deaths that their classmates notified they existed at all.

Some doodled while "available grief services" were mentioned. Some did a poor job hiding their "who?" expressions while glancing to friends for some clue about dead kids they never knew. I went full thousand-yard stare during the truncated eulogy, as if the topic was the Magna Carta or frog dissections. Only present what you want the world to see.

With homecoming a week away, the Smart Ones were forgotten before the dirt covered their coffins.

As the sole survivor of the club, that hurt me in a way no one knew, or would likely care about if they did. That pain was freshly revived, given the school's reaction to Paris's demise.

How much grief, on average, does it take to break a person?

I tapped the question into my Notes app, almost losing my phone when the school bus bounced on a pothole. There's probably an equation that could calculate an answer. Jim could've done the math, giving me something to code. Phillip would've worked out monetization or, as he liked to put it, "how to get that shmoney!" Then Simon would've come through with the snazzy title, logo, and rollout plan.

Without any of them here, I was stuck with just the question. The latest in a long Smart Ones list of ideas and problems and wishes I'd started after they died.

I watched the "All Changes Saved" message flash in the header of my digital notepad, the whole time recognizing there might be something terribly wrong with maintaining a list of technical problems for your dead friends to solve. Like, maybe I wasn't handling this all so well.

How much grief does it take to break a person? Maybe, three to four friends' worth.

Just a guess.

For the last three days, there were multiple counselors on-site, time slots booked from school start to school end. A tribute

Tumblr—ParSec Love—started by a sophomore girl, typically known for her other salacious Cooke High gossip pages, who was quick enough and slick enough to become the top tribute page for the grieving, both domestic and abroad, gaining her valuable, valuable upperclassmen cred. She upgraded lunch tables and everything.

There wasn't a hall you could walk without sobs, soft and loud, battering you. Paris's fans repped in force, even if most only became fans as of this week. Guess that's what could be expected for Cooke High's most popular student who hadn't set foot in the school for, like, a year before . . . what happened, happened.

I'd been watching the group mourn unfold since Monday, back at school so soon not because I wanted to, but because no one got to sit in Mama's house doing nothing. Even if nothing = grieving.

My usual preferred presentation—invisibility—served me well in the hollow days after this "community tragedy" (Principal Corgis's words), when I fell into my classes like the school was a shifting box triggered by a periodic bell, and I only ended up wherever gravity dictated. Most people had forgotten any connection I had with Paris before "Calm Down, Turn Up!" blew, starting her ascent. So I didn't get ordering info on the airbrushed RIP tees featuring a distorted rendering of Paris's face in soft strokes that made her look more angelic than she would've liked, or the black DJ ParSec armbands. None of them knew that I'd seen what was left of Paris, the way she'd been discarded. I wasn't about to let anyone know, not even the counselors going for pointed eye contact each time I passed their table. Three days of successful avoidance. A new normal developed. So this morning's distinct "offness" troubled me.

Why was I suddenly seen?

Stepping off the bus, I started my initial locker trek and felt eyes, like rough feathers, brushing over my skin. When I glanced at my observers, they quickly flicked their attention elsewhere. A few held firm with smirks and scowls. My usually purposeful strides became cautious; the dull polished tiles now concealed landmines.

At my locker, hesitant to touch the combo lock, the feathery glances increased in pressure, became the sensation of sinking to the bottom of a pool. I checked the dial for glue, or spit, or worse. "Greasing your lock" was a Cooke High prank staple for reasons I didn't know and never wanted to investigate. There was no foreign residue present, best I could tell. Pinching the—dry, thank God—knob, I began the right-left-right procedure, when I heard a friend's voice.

Paris said, *"That VA sound, comin' 'round again!"*

I leapt back, terrified, my stomach in my shoes. The mean chuckles in the hall weren't loud enough to drown a dead girl's voice.

"We 'bout to take you for a spin!"

Bom-bom-ba-ba-ba-tah! Bom-bom-ba-ba-ba-tah!

I undid my lock quickly, yanked my flimsy metal locker door, and snatched the cheap Bluetooth speaker off the shelf inside. Or tried. This particular speaker was the pastel blue of an Easter egg, a kind meant to stick on the walls of showers or tubs for bathroom listening. The suction cup at its base cemented it in place, making me look more foolish as I grabbed it two-handed, attempting to break the seal.

Bom-bom-ba-ba-ba-tah! Bom-bom-ba-ba-ba-tah!

Tinny bass vibrated in my palms as Lil' Redu's opening rap verse began. *"They say they want us calmer, but we want drama . . ."*

The suction cup gave slowly, peeled gradually. A sudden quick release had me reeling back, colliding with one of the complicit witnesses, a beefy girl rocking a DJ ParSec memorial band on her bicep. As soon as our bodies met, she shoved me at my locker with instigating force. "Watch where you going, shady!"

Paris's song continued playing from my palm while I processed the insult. It was wrong somehow. Not: "Watch where you going, *clumsy!*" That *shady* was meaningful somehow, pointed. What did it mean exactly? Why was it pointed at me?

More laughs, more mean clowns grinning until their faces blurred together. Examining the speaker, I thumbed the proper button until an Android-like tone indicated a power-down. Already, phones were aimed, recording, waiting for a meltdown they wouldn't get.

Lifting my satchel's flap, I tucked the speaker inside, ignored heckling about how I was so poor I was gonna trade it for food. I gathered the books I'd actually come to my locker for.

With the show over, my "fans" churned, en route to wherever they were supposed to be with just a few minutes left until first bell. I weaved past them, hoping I could catch an empty bathroom to center myself before homeroom, to reinstate my invisibility. Turning a corner by the cafeteria, I ducked around some breakfast kids, while one girl approached from the opposite direction. When I tried to sidestep, she moved with me. Thinking it one of those awkward we-both-tried-to-avoid-each-other-and-it-didn't-work moments, I sidestepped again. As did she.

We were now in speaking range, my guard up, ready to—I don't know—*counter* if this was some kind of attack. I wasn't a real fighter, evident by my still-bandaged wrist from when I punched Fuse Fallon. But I wouldn't back down easily. Ever.

No fists from the gossip girl with the newly popular ParSec Love Tumblr, whose name escaped me.

She said, "You might want to check your Twitter."

A confusing statement, since I didn't mess with Twitter. I found the character limit silly and arbitrary. Before I could fully process what she meant, she added, "And transfer."

She left me with a sinking feeling and a pressing need to add an app to my phone.

FUSE

Didn't expect my reintroduction to Cooke High society to be warm exactly, but felt I would not be without a support system. After all, everyone who jammed to, and loved, ParSec's music was family. #ParSecNation, rise up! All day, every day. I could do this.

My actual family, Dad, didn't settle for a drop-off, given my extended absence. He marched me into the crowded main foyer, making my insides clench. We sailed past my whispering peers, down the administrative corridor, where student workers paused in their photocopying and stapling duties. More than a few of them wore some sort of DJ ParSec paraphernalia. Not official stuff, and I made a mental note to text Paula Klein about licensing concerns now that I had my phone back.

In the main office, Principal Corgis waited in a stiff stance, like he was the resource officer instead of the principal. Corgis's preferred mode of dress was golf-course-ready—pleated khakis and a polo shirt. This was in stark contrast to Dad's custom suits, hundred-dollar ties always cinched in huge knots, with gold and jeweled embellished cuff links, tie tacks, and such. Dad had commented on this a couple of times after PTA meetings, saying his tax dollars should afford better-dressed administrators.

"Mr. Fallon," Corgis said, hand extended, his cheeks and bald spot a rosy pink.

"Jim." Dad shook, then led Corgis and me into the principal's office.

I half expected Dad to pull a crazy disrespectful boss move and sit on the wrong side of the desk, in Corgis's leather ergonomic chair. My father reined in his alpha maleness and hovered next to the pair of chairs on the trouble side of the desk, waiting until Corgis and I took our seats before proving he wasn't a statue.

Corgis tapped keys, brightening the light emitting from his monitor, though it was turned in a way that didn't allow me a view of whatever he was looking at. Could've been my permanent record or Powerball. From what I'd heard of Corgis and his little gambling problem, probably Powerball.

He began, "Mr. Fallon, I'm glad Fatima is back. We—"

"Have a situation, Jim. I want to be frank about that."

Principal Corgis radiated cautious surprise. "Situation? What would that be exactly?"

"Obviously, Fatima won't be able to finish her high school career at Cooke. The school year, yes, but she will be transferring for her senior year."

Corgis pressed back into his seat, steepled his fingers. "Okay."

I read the novel hidden in that one-word answer. There were almost two thousand students at Cooke High. If I'd never come back *this year*, Corgis's day wouldn't have changed by a percent. Where was Dad going with this?

"That girl that got herself killed—"

"ParSe—Paris, Dad." My tongue had a wicked reflex that I wish I could deactivate.

Dad gave me the don't-interrupt-again side-eye. Continued. "She hung with hoodlums. Some of them go here. So-called 'rappers'"—the diamonds in his platinum wedding band glimmered as he made air quotes—"who really only write barely coherent poems about violence and debauchery. Under your roof. I've heard the school even encourages their activities."

Hypocrite hovered over my tongue, but I clenched my jaw and foiled its escape. Poems about violence and debauchery? Like he didn't grow up in the '80s and '90s singing along to rhythmic revolutionaries, proud gangsters, and player presidents. Those songs only told what people were really going through. They were journalism, not instructions. *He* told me that.

And heard from who? Not me, for sure. What had Dad been looking into these last few days?

Corgis didn't get it either. "I'm not following, Mr. Fallon."

"I know for a fact at least one of that dead girl's 'crew' leads some kind of slam music club here."

"Slam *poetry*." That reflex again. His side-eye came with a wicked dose of telepathy that time. The message: *You're only going to make this worse for yourself, but that's nothing new.*

My nickname, Fuse, wasn't one I took. It was given, by my dad. His "Little Short Fuse" because of the tantrums I'd throw as a child and the punishments those tiny blowups got me. But he was wrong here. ParSec didn't have a "crew," not the way he was trying to make it sound, like they planned casino heists in their spare time. And the poetry leader he was talking about was Shameik Larsen.

Crap.

"Seaside Poets," Corgis added, naming the demon Dad was trying to conjure. "It's faculty sponsored."

Dad's head tilted, shrewd. "So sanctioned by you?"

Corgis only managed to catch half of his flinch. "We have many official after-school programs."

"Do they all endanger your students?"

"Dad," I said, "slam poetry doesn't endanger anybody. That's not even the same thing ParSec did. You know that. You—"

He adjusted his tie knot, waiting for me to finish. Pointless arguments made with zeal were still pointless, as Mom would say.

Dad finally got to his point. "I don't care that the program exists and that you don't see anything wrong with it. I care about my daughter and that she is no longer in close proximity with the people involved in whatever resulted in a young girl's murder. There's, what, six weeks left in the school year? I'm going to ask that we make some alternate arrangements for Fatima."

My voice quaked. "What kind of alternate arrangements?"

Corgis, way too accommodating, probably anxious to have a noisy and powerful member of the Cooke High parental community gone, said, "What do you have in mind?"

Dad explained. Corgis nodded, with only the occasional question, and a final, "Unorthodox, but doable."

My assessment: horror.

■ ■

By the time Dad and Corgis settled on the *arrangements*, we were well into second period, and Dad complained about how he was late too. The difference being, when he strolled into his office, it would be with zero scrutiny. His various indentured marketing nerds would probably be scared to look away from their displays. Joys of being the boss. When I made my late entrance into Mrs. Jasper's American History class, with my principal escort, it was all eyes on me.

The room was dark when we entered, a projector shot a beam of light and levitating lint at a whiteboard-mounted screen. This particular slide featured a painting of a covered wagon moving among tan sands and tumbleweeds, with a header reading "Westward Expansion." Mrs. Jasper stopped talking, and Principal Corgis motioned to the light switch. "May I?"

Mrs. Jasper nodded, and Corgis flipped the overhead fluorescents on, waking a couple of beauty sleepers. One of the groggy travelers forced from the Dreamlands was the subject of Dad's earlier, misguided rant: Shameik.

His mouth stretched sideways in an exaggerated yawn, various creases in his sleeve had left a pattern on his dark brown cheek and temple from where he laid his head. His usually pristine fade seemed thicker and less attended to, his hairline as fuzzy as a rough sketch. His skin was dull, ashy. This was a different boy than the one I'd known. He was in the back row, next to my empty desk. He blinked, spotted me, and his mouth turned down. I wanted to go to him, hug him. And kick him. It was complicated. Thanks to Dad, my leash wasn't long enough for any of that.

Shameik held up his phone, pointed at the dark screen. Even without an app visible, I knew where he was going with the gesture. It was about my early morning tweets. He mouthed, *What did you do?*

A shrug was all I could manage.

Principal Corgis told our teacher, "A quick word?" Mrs. Jasper joined him in the hall.

Alone with my peers, shuffling my feet while they all stared, the room felt heavy, like gravity shifted.

About forty years later, Mrs. Jasper returned, motioning to the row where I usually sat. "Everyone shift back one seat, please." With confused grumbling as the initial response, Mrs. Jasper added, "Right now."

The relocation began, my classmates gathering their things to allow me access to the first desk in the row, my seat for the rest of the school year. In. Every. Class.

Like Principal Corgis told Dad, unorthodox, but doable.

Lunch would be worse. No more cafeteria . . . or as Dad called it when explaining his plans to Mom, "GenPop." I'd be eating either in the teachers' lounge or the in-school suspension room, depending on which was less populated.

With ParSec's murder, my bougie Dad converted the best public school in Ocean Shore, Virginia, into little more than a medium-security prison. With veiled threats to the principal, he'd gotten me thrown in the hole.

Settled into my new seat, the lights went out, and the monotone lecture resumed. A mere five minutes in, Lacey Barr reached from the desk behind me and lightly tapped my elbow, quickly followed with a folded paper square tumbling over my shoulder into my lap. I unfolded it between sheets of loose leaf in my binder, in case Mrs. Jasper's spider-sense went off, and found nearly unreadable chicken scratch that could've only come from one person.

Typically this exchange would've been done via text with our phones in our laps, and the brightness slider on its lowest setting. My sudden classroom repositioning forced us into a post-apocalyptic analog state.

Shameik had written:

Yo, I didn't think you were ever coming back. I was scared, Fuse. Nobody's saying anything about anything other than she's dead. Over and over, they sorry about her being <u>dead</u>, and we can go talk to the counselors about her being <u>dead</u>. And they're telling me they're sorry for my loss. Like, huh?

The only one I wanted to talk to is you! Were you there with ParSec? People saying that. And worse. Then those wild tweets you sent this morning. You really think Kya Caine set ParSec up?!

Look, I know you and me weren't in a good place last time we really hung out. We had a misunderstanding, that's all. Hit me back. Soon. I don't care how. ~S

I crumpled the paper in my fist. *The only one I wanted to talk to is you!*

Like the last time he wanted to "talk" to me went so good.

A return note—which likely would've been a bunch of curse words and a glob of nasty spit, in other words, everything Shameik deserved—wasn't a possibility when I was this visible. Mrs. Jasper would see it, confiscate it. I heard teachers used to read notes aloud before lock screens made text messages unreachable, and I didn't want more ParSec gossip getting out.

Then those wild tweets you sent this morning. You really think Kya Caine set ParSec up?!

Is that how he took it?

Not that I cared what Shameik thought about anything, but were other people taking it that way too? Is that what I really thought?

Honestly, I don't know that I thought much about anything beyond getting people to understand I didn't cause my friend's death. Change the narrative, another thing I read about in my marketing books.

So, people were pointing daggers at Kya now because of what I tweeted? Good.

She punched me, and I punched back.

Our fighting styles varied.

KYA

Fuse Is Heartbroken @FuseZilla14

THREAD! 1/? #ParSecNation Some disturbing things
about the #MadScientist we all know as KC have come to
my attention . . .

Fuse Is Heartbroken @FuseZilla14

2/? Y'all know me and @DJParSec butted heads from time to
time, as creatives do. That's how you get the art you love, it's
how you know where to find it. Trust me, @DJParSec and me
were a team . . .

Fuse Is Heartbroken @FuseZilla14

3/? But KC has always been on some different stuff. Like, a little
possessive if you ask me. Angry because she wasn't in the loop
like she used to be. And I think that's worth noting over the next
few weeks as more truth comes out. When @DJParSec spoke
on old friends changing up on her, welllll . . .

Fuse Is Heartbroken @FuseZilla14

4/? So all you non-crazy people out there think on this: an up-
and-coming artist, beloved by almost all (me included) gets got
under mysterious circumstances. Who should you look at first?
The person who's mad. The person who's off.

Fuse Is Heartbroken @FuseZilla14

5/? The person who was at the scene of the crime.

Fuse Is Heartbroken @FuseZilla14

6/6 Oh you didn't know that part? Well, welcome
to the Information Age, my friends. Do with it what
you will. Love y'all! #TurnUp

#ParSecNation

I was a statue on the toilet, the rim covered in five flimsy-thin seat liners. This was the second-floor girls' bathroom, where I'd missed the third-period bell to sign up for my own Twitter account—@KCappwiz—and see, exactly, why I suddenly had a target on my back. Now I knew.

Her last tweet was accompanied by a GIF. It was the basketball player Kobe Bryant of the Los Angeles Lakers, on the night of his final game, in home-court gold and purple, blowing a kiss to the crowd, and performing an epic mic drop. *MAMBA OUT!* flashed along the bottom of the animation. I somehow managed to super-impose another word in place of the catchphrase.

FUSE!

FUSE!

FUSE!

How could she throw me under the bus like that when she was at the crime scene too?

The GIF kept going, as they do, the loop hypnotizing. It was as if Kobe—no, Fuse, all of this was Fuse—were another snake, a cobra instead of a black mamba, eyes locked, swaying, hissing before the strike. Deadly in a different way, but venom was venom.

I had some too.

My analytical mind kicked in, the same way I organized to-do lists to maintain maximum efficiency day to day, the way I drew meticulous flowcharts before diving into any kind of coding or design project, the way I picked my clothes in the morning, factoring in outdoor temperature with the patterns of the school's erratic HVAC system. Failing to plan was planning to fail.

The likes and retweets on her rant were in the hundreds and climbing. A response, in kind, was due. Not on this platform with my bird's egg avatar and zero followers. @FuseZilla14 had over nine thousand followers (thanks to her loose, exaggerated connection to Paris, no doubt). I didn't have the troops to fight a war on that front.

I knew who did.

Quickly, I found the ParSec Love Tumblr, clicked the direct message icon, and thumbed out my SOS—

Hi, this is Kya Caine. We don't really know each other, but we should. I've got some DJ ParSec scoop that you and the rest of #ParSecNation need to hear. It's . . . killer.

■ ■

We were to meet after school in the empty cafeteria, at the very table where she now spent lunch periods schmoozing with the cliquiest of cliques. But I lingered at the door, peering through the porthole windows, cataloging her. I hadn't taken notice of her wardrobe when she'd advised me to check Twitter that morning. Now I sized her up the way Mama taught me when girls like this would've been my competition on the tiaras-and-talent circuit.

She wore a *We'll Always Turn Up for You, DJ ParSec* shirt that seemed to be of higher quality than the quick airbrushed numbers

I'd seen around the school. It was long-sleeved, thicker, almost a sweater despite the heat. She'd paired it with a denim skirt, pink heels, and a psychedelic neckerchief accenting everything. Her fingernails shimmered, so did her eye makeup. Her head was shaved on one side, while a thick mop of hair on top swooped in the other direction.

Her name was Florian Dominguez (something I learned from the signature of her email setting up this meeting) and she was mourner chic.

She perked up when I entered, opening the computer that had been dormant on the table, as if we were about to study. I approached cautiously, second-guessing myself.

Florian began working me immediately, typing while she talked. "It's smart to want your side of the story told. I promise you ParSec Love is the place to do it. My Tumblr is among the top-five DJ ParSec tribute sites, even with more launching every day. More importantly, I'm ParSec Nation. If she were still with us, Paris could tell you I was there in the early days, when she was spinning at house parties."

"Wouldn't you have been in middle school?"

She got sheepish and proud at once. "I might've tagged along with my older cousins after my mom went to sleep. It was worth it to hear the hottest DJ around."

I was regretting this already. I should've at least taken a seat where I could see her monitor. So I'd know what she was writing down. "You don't have to give me a sales pitch. I just want people to know what Fuse is implying is trash nonsense."

She peered over the top edge of her laptop. "What is she implying exactly?"

"I don't know. It's weird. Like she's trying to say I had something to do with what happened to Paris."

Her keys clacked. "You didn't find DJ ParSec's body?"

"I did. But so did Fuse. She was there first." Fuse's car had been the first thing I noticed when my Lyft pulled up. I watched her walk into the warehouse. Was halfway through the door myself, when I heard her scream.

Florian said, "Now that's interesting. It's something none of the other sites will have. That's not even in the news. What did she look like?"

"Fuse?"

"No. What did DJ ParSec look like when you found her?"

The question hit me like ice water. "Dead. She looked dead."

Those clacking keys again.

What the heck had I done coming to this digital ghoul? Half of me wanted to push away from the table and run from the school. The other half remembered what this long day had been like. Stares, and whispers, and low-key threats. No invisibility, no matter how much I wanted it. Because of Fuse's insinuations. "Are you going to write something that lets people know Fuse is being dishonest? I mean, I'm not on social media like that. People pay attention to your stuff."

"Absolutely."

I pulled out my phone and bookmarked her site. "Should I look for it soon? Like, by this evening?"

"Not so fast," she said, closing her laptop. "While this is a scoop for my page, it's also kind of a favor. If I'm being real, rumors probably drive traffic more than honest accounts, so just linking to Fuse's Twitter rant will get me traffic."

She let that hang and made me reach. "What do you want?"

"I hear there's going to be a secret memorial service for DJ ParSec this Saturday. You know anything about that?"

I knew a lot about that. "What if I did?"

"The only thing that drives traffic more than rumors is secrets. What are your photography skills like?"

PARIS/DJ PARSEC

(21 MONTHS BEFORE)

"Ohhhhhhh! It's at eight thousand plays, Kya. In two days." I clicked the refresh button, and the browser flashed white as my SoundCloud updated. I promptly lost my ish again when I saw the count jumped to 8,024. Pushing my chair back, I stood and did a little shimmy. While I danced, Kya sidestepped me, leaned toward the screen, and opened more tabs.

"What you doing?" I asked, still jamming.

"Checking the other aggregators we uploaded to. Deezer, Grooveshark."

She mumbled something about it being a pain to click through all the apps one by one like that—Little Miss Efficiency, missing the point again. Finally, she settled on what was actually important. "People like it."

Kya returned to the SoundCloud window, her cursor hovered over the heart icon, which had a count of six thousand plus, then she moused through the incremental in-the-moment comments like: FIRE! and BANGER! and THEM DRUMS THOUGH!

"It's not all praise," Kya said.

I stopped dancing. "Why are you being a butt right now? Don't kill my vibe."

"Don't be thin-skinned. The music is fine. People aren't as hype about the feature. You should keep that in mind for whatever you do next."

Kya highlighted the portion of the song that was all Lil' Redu's corny, shoot-'em-up verse. The part of the song getting the most negs.

SHOULD'VE PUT ME ON THE TRACK, I GOT BETTER BARS
THAN THIS.

THESE "RHYMES" KINDA KILL THIS SONG FOR ME.

IS "REDU" SHORT FOR "REDUNDANT"? DUDE SOUND LIKE
EVERYBODY EVER. #NoOriginality

It went on, clearer and clearer as Kya kept expanding the feedback. Basically she was saying, "Told ya so."

"He's not that bad," I said. People got mean when they were internet anonymous.

Kya said, "He's not that good either."

"I needed some vocals. It wasn't like you were going to do it, right?" I stared her punk tail down. What you got to say about that, Kya?

She shook her head and opened a different browser tab. "I've been looking over the analytics and comparing them to what a typical SoundCloud user does. Honestly, you're crushing it. Despite Lil' Redu."

"So, what else the dialysis—?"

"Analytics."

"Whatever. What's all that mean?"

Kya leaned back in my grandma's kitchen chair, fiddled with the little porcelain saltshaker that was shaped like a bluebird. "I think you want to maximize on the growing following somehow."

"Like, another song?

"Maybe. I guess."

That was where I knew Kya struggled. Her uncertainties came in doubles. She kept going, talking about things that *might* work. Everything she said seemed like she was pulling it out of the air. Put links to the SoundCloud on Insta, with some cover art. Send my track to the local radio station and see if they'd play it. Burn it to some thumb drives and hand them out to sketchy men in dark parking lots.

I don't know if she actually said any of those things. Only knew this wasn't her lane. So while she talked, I threw up a Bat-Signal on Twitter.

The Queen Is Here! @DJParSec
Yo, fam. I got this fire track that I'm trying to get the word out on. Anyone got LEGIT tips on world domination? DM only if you for real! #CalmDownTurnUp

Kya kept talking. "Maybe we could make a banner."

"How about we hit Five Guys for a burger. That seems like the move. Right?"

. .

A ripped brown bag turned dark by fries, grease, and vinegar divided our table. I pawed at the fries blindly while checking SoundCloud from my phone. Bit down on a hard, tasteless fry that cracked, then splintered in my mouth. Panicking, I spit the pieces onto the foil my burger had been wrapped in.

"That's a fork," Kya said.

What the——? With a bouquet of napkins, I swabbed drool from

my chin and made sure I didn't swallow any shards. "Where'd it come from?"

"While you were focused on your phone, I got up, refilled my tea, asked that nice man behind the counter for a fork. Then I put it where your hand was. It was like watching a Hungry Hungry Hippo snatch a marble."

"Are you crazy?"

"If all you were going to do was what you were already doing at your house, I could've just brought food back for you."

"I'm sorry. It's up to ten thousand plays, K. Forgive me for being a little excited about people liking my stuff."

"Don't make it seem like I'm not excited too. It's just . . . if being with someone feels like being alone, I'd just rather be alone. That way neither of us worry about being distracted. We could connect later, after you work on your thing and I work on mine.

That was news. "What thing are you working on?"

Her eyes flicked away, and she took a minute to answer. I don't know what she was annoyed about. Her attitude got on my nerves sometimes. She said, "The coding club at school—"

"You talking about them white-boy nerds you be around?"

A flung fry bounced off my chest. What? What I say?

"First of all, Jim's Korean. Second, what's that got to do with anything? We're working on some cool stuff."

My plays jumped to 10,200. "Whatever you're working on ain't this!"

Kya flinched. Parted her lips as if to say some other nonsense but knew better and stayed quiet.

"This is huge," I said. "Like first steps to something big. I can feel it."

She had that hurt look she got whenever I was too real with her. God. "Big for *both of us*, Kya. You're in on this too, even if you ain't *on* the track. Where I go, you go."

"Cool." She nibbled her burger.

Cool. That's settled, then. Refocusing on my phone, I swapped apps and checked my Twitter inbox. A solid thirty-plus messages were there. Mostly useless troll stuff that I blocked, and a few positive, if not totally feasible, offers to help me with my marketing. They were notes from people in New York, LA, one person from Australia (which got me hype all over again . . . AUSTRALIA!). Among them was a name I'd seen a few times before in some Cooke High–related threads—funny memes, various draggings. @FuseZilla14. Her message said:

Hey, DJ ParSec, we don't have classes together, but we both go to Cooke High and I've been to a couple parties where you were spinning. That new track you dropped is SO HOT! And I saw you looking for some help getting more listens. Let's connect, and I can tell you some thoughts I have. I know you're probably skeptical, but hear me out. Just think on these three words: personal music army.

Intrigued? (I know you are.)

All I need is a when and where.

~Fuse

Kya slurped her sweet tea down to the ice water. Said, "What you wanna do tonight? We could go bowling. Or see a movie."

"I don't know, Kya. My stomach's feeling funny. I might just go turn in early."

Her head bobbed. Tight, tense nods. "Oh, okay."

Was I not convincing? Oh well. She had her own thing to work on, right?

Focused on my phone, I gave Fuse Fallon the time and place she asked for.

FUSE

Friday night, 8:00 p.m. My bedroom.

My parents reinstated my rights to my MacBook and other devices. After a few unpleasant communications, even I had to question their decision.

There were the multiple missed texts from Shameik, intense and persistent in a way I'd hoped we'd moved past.

SHAMEIK

I've sent like a hundred texts. You just going to keep ignoring me?

SHAMEIK

I know you're getting them. I can see the little "read" message after each one.

SHAMEIK

It ain't right, Fuse. Who else am I supposed to talk to about what happened between her and me? And me and you?

ME

Stop! Okay? I can't do this yet.
Just, give me some time.

SHAMEIK
More time, you mean. Infinity? Is that
what you're going for?

I muted him. Thought about blocking him but knew if I was capable of that, I would've done it long before now.

That intensity made him the poet he was. His delivery like gut punches. What he crafted paired well with our mutual friend's music, even if what they did together never went public. That wasn't something I wanted or needed to get into that night.

Nothing in my inbox was as overtly ugly as the public jabs and private messages popping hourly on all of my social media. That was the nature of those platforms on a normal day. Some of it was vultures scavenging for anything newsworthy, and I'd expected that. Radio personalities from a couple of the local stations, a few podcasters, journalists wanting some scoop from someone close to ParSec. Winston Bell, a reporter from *MIXX* magazine, had been particularly persistent, having emailed almost daily since the night of. I flagged most of those for follow-up, not knowing if I ever actually would.

The worst emails, the ones I lingered on, were personal. The nastiness camouflaged in niceties and professionalism. Corporate shade from one of the best:

From: Paula Klein
To: F. Fallon
CC: HR (PK Music Group)
Subject: Ongoing SM Manager Duties

Fatima,

I hope this email finds you well. We're all still grieving over losing Paris—I'm barely sleeping. You're lucky to have your family to lean on in these difficult times. Cherish them, always.

Given the recent tragedy, I'm sorry to turn to business matters, but since we're closing out the current pay cycle, I wanted to make you aware of a change in roles. We have an outside firm taking over social media manager duties for the PK Music Group, therefore you won't be burdened with those responsibilities anymore. You'll still be paid for your work through the end of the month, but I'll need you to supply all username-password combinations for each of the social media platforms associated with the DJ ParSec brand. It seems they were changed at some point, and we don't currently have access here at the office.

If you can get that info to me by Monday, I'd be willing to add a $500 bonus to your final paycheck.

Hope to hear from you soon. Take care.

Paula Klein
Founder and CEO of the PK Music Group
Ocean Shore, VA

There was so much trash in that email. So much *Paula*. Last I checked, the PK Music Group consisted of exactly three people. Paula, ParSec, and me. So that "*we* have an outside firm" and "*we* don't currently have access here at the office" stuff was lies. It's just you and me now, you crooked old bag!

And cc'ing that crappy email to HR (PK Music Group)? Please. There's no human resources department in Paula's mildew-smelling apartment. ParSec and I *were* the human resources. She might've had a few more acts on her roster, but they came *after* us. We were the draw. This was more fake-it-till-you-make-it trickery Paula was good for. A way to paint this as inevitable, out of her control. Something different than what it really was. An opportunity to do what she'd wanted to do since she saw ParSec as money on demand and me as an unnecessary expense. Get rid of me.

I'd handled all of ParSec's social media since the SoundCloud days. I created #ParSecNation! So, what kind of "outside firm" was going to take over when what I built was there, but ParSec wasn't?

To be . . . *ousted*! By someone like Paula Kryptkeeper! It twisted my guts like spaghetti on a fork. Still, that wasn't enough to put me over the edge. The follow-up emails, though. The ones about ParSec's funeral . . .

I'd seen some buzz in the #ParSecNation feeds. A secret memorial service. Tomorrow. False, obviously, since *no one had told me.* That's what I wanted to think. Until I saw a single tweet getting liked and retweeted over and over.

PK Music Group @PKMusicGroup

In lieu of flowers for @DJParSec's memorial service, please consider donating to one of DJ ParSec's favorite charities (see links in replies below). It's what she would have wanted. #ParSecNation

So there was a service. As for those charities that ParSec would've wanted the Nation donating to, never heard of them. That was a back-of-my-mind concern. More pressing was my response to Paula's email.

From: F. Fallon
To: Paula Klein
Subject: Re: Ongoing SM Manager Duties

Where is ParSec's memorial? And what time?

It didn't take long. Paula's fake professionalism decreased by half.

From: Paula Klein
To: F. Fallon
Subject: Re: Ongoing SM Manager Duties

Fuse,

    I have a feeling that you know that's not happening. It's been determined, by all involved parties, that your presence would be a hindrance to the event. I'm sorry. Could you please send my username-password combinations ASAP? Thank you. Have a good evening.

~PK

What involved parties? What hindrance? She was my friend.

"Fatima," Mom called, fresh off a hospital shift, her stubby shadow legs blocking the light seeping beneath my bedroom door. "Have you eaten?"

Straining to steady my voice, I said a simple "Yeah."

"Well, come down in fifteen minutes if you want to watch a movie with Dad and me. It's his turn to pick, so I understand if you don't want to." A rare joke from her. She'd been trying to lighten things up around here.

"Sure." It was all I could manage without cracking. Couldn't stop looking at my emails.

Screw Paula. I went online and put out discreet feelers about the memorial service in some well-known #ParSecNation subreddits. Outside my window, a fat june bug rammed itself against the screen as if trying to get my attention, reminding me summer was near. For the first time in my life I wasn't looking forward to it. A whole season would be missing a piece this year, as would I.

The fifteen minutes Mom allotted for me to join movie night passed. Then another fifteen, then another hour. All that time, and I still had no idea where the service would be, and simply posting the question publicly wasn't an option. Then #ParSecNation would know just how out of the loop I was.

A new email notification popped.

From: Bell, Winston—MIXX mag
To: F. Fallon
Subject: Follow-up for DJ ParSec Feature

Fuse, hi! This is Winston, a journalist from—

That's all that showed in the little gray notification window that appeared in the upper right-hand corner of my screen. I might not have clicked on it any other time. As a general rule, I despised reporters. There was something about that "Fuse, hi!"— something I hadn't felt in so long. For whatever reason, minuscule, insignificant, petty—someone needed me.

When I opened the message, read it and all the others preceding it, I could've slapped myself for curving this guy so hard. The message said:

From: Bell, Winston—MIXX mag
To: F. Fallon
Subject: Follow-up for DJ ParSec

Fuse, hi! This is Winston, a journalist from *MIXX* magazine. We met a couple of times while I was working on the DJ ParSec story for our Summer Heat issue. First, my condolences, sincerely. I know how tight you two were. Second, and I apologize for this but, given the circumstances, I need to ask some critical follow-up questions. The timing is terrible, but if you have a moment at the memorial service tomorrow, I promise this will be relatively painless . . .

There was more to the message, of course. Things about the article that I didn't care about and did not dwell on. My response—drafted quickly and anxiously, as if this chance might disappear—was:

From: F. Fallon
To: Bell, Winston—MIXX mag
Subject: Re: Follow-up for DJ ParSec

Winston, can we meet before the service? Then, if it's okay, can I ride over with you?

KYA

Seven days ago was the last time I saw Paris. Seven days later and it's the last time I will ever see her. There was symmetry here, but no comfort. There was never a time I didn't find comfort in symmetry. I turned it over and over in my head, looked for flaws in the alignment. The memorial service was at three in the afternoon. I found her body closer to 7:00 p.m. last week, so the timing wasn't exact. That's . . . something.

In my Notes app, I added another inquiry to my Questions for the Smart Ones list:

Is there a fundamental design flaw, maybe a glitch, that accounts for good people dying young?

I put my phone away and my hand floated to the nylon necklace, anchored by a barely-there bulge beneath my dress. This charm was supposed to be an olive branch that, maybe, got Paris and me closer to what we once were. The thought didn't seem as naive last week as it did now. Since she died, it became part of my daily apparel. Wedged between my skin and the world. Penance.

Paris's grandma, Miss Elsie, squeezed my other hand. Spoke softly, exhausted. "Lord, Lord, Lord."

We were together in the back of a slow-moving limo that smelled of coconut air freshener. The leather seats had the oily sheen of fresh detailing and vacuum lines streaked the dark floor mats. I looked the part—black dress, dark shades, a black hat from Miss Elsie's own church-lady crown collection—but I wasn't supposed to be here. Mama and I never talked about the service, she never forbade me from going, but she would've. She won't react well when she finds out I went—and she will find out.

Some things are worth the consequences.

"Thank you for riding with me, child," Miss Elsie said.

Would she be so thankful if she'd known the way things were between Paris and me this time last year?

We weren't in Ocean Shore anymore, having crossed a bridge and taken a tunnel to the neighboring city, Portside. I'd only been there once or twice in my life. It was dreary, no sense that the ocean lapped sand just a little ways away. The only VA sounds here were traffic and wind. Paris would've hated it.

A divider descended, opening a porthole between us and the driver. He said, "We're here, ma'am."

Miss Elsie shook her head as if telling reality this version was unacceptable. I squeezed her hand back.

We pulled up to the curb between two orange cones outside of an ornate building. Not a church. A movie theater. The marquee protruded over the ticket booth like an overbite, the black block letters read: Private Event.

Crowds gathered across the street with their We Miss You, and Turn Up, and #ParSecNation signs. Being that they knew this address before I did, I supposed the secret was out.

The crowd wasn't overwhelming, though a few police officers maintained order. A pair of brown girls younger than me dabbed tears with tissues. One was stout, in baggy overalls with a striped shirt underneath, and earbuds snaking white wires to some device in her pocket. The other, scrawnier girl pushed glasses atop her head. Paris and I once looked like them, and a wave of sadness hit.

Then I spotted another spectator that shocked me from my sadness. My immediate thought: *Are the cops seeing this?*

A few yards from the pair of girls, behind more animated fans who waved signs, or volleyed for attention from whoever actually had access to the venue, was a featureless face. Smooth, white. No eyes, nose, or mouth, though the contours for all that were there.

Twisting in my seat, I intended to ask if Miss Elsie saw it too, but she was halfway out the door, on course for the theater entrance. When the driver finished helping her, he extended a hand to me. I coiled my fingers into his and stepped onto the sidewalk. Over the limo's polished roof, I searched for that creepy masked figure. They were gone.

■ ■

If the mourners across the street represented what Paris and I had been, then the attendees inside the theater represented what we never wanted to be. Old. Stiff. The adults who sat at separate tables—or in separate rooms—during Thanksgiving dinner and talked about the news. Who were these folks?

At a glance, I estimated seventy-five to a hundred people packed into the lobby. Enough to turn their combined conversations into something like reverb, so loud you'd have to nearly touch shoulders to hear or be heard by the person next to you. While some grinned through small talk in loose clusters, or munched meat, cheese, and fruit from a central snack bar, a photographer roamed, breaking up chats for group poses. Others hovered by golden columns at the lobby's less crowded corners, jotting down notes on little pads or holding their phones to another person's lips, recording their conversations. It didn't feel like any funeral I'd ever been to.

I hung at Miss Elsie's hip, like I once did with Mama, uncomfortably familiar with this kind of see-and-be-seen gathering from my pageant and talent search days. Back then, I knew the adults in the room were there to pick and judge. So it made even less sense I was feeling that vibe *here*.

Where was Paris's other family? There should be out-of-town cousins here. Aunts and uncles. All from Miss Elsie's side of the family because Paris's dad situation was worse than even *my* dad situation, but still. Where were other people from the neighborhood? People who'd grown up with Paris even if they'd lost touch with her since the music took over?

There were barely other *black* people.

At the center of the largest clique, visible by brightness alone, was a platinum-haired white woman in a pristine white pantsuit. Tall like me but with deep creases around her mouth, slashing her forehead, clutching the corners of each eye.

She excused herself from her worshippers and made her way to us, her arm extended for handshake. "You must be Paris's grandmother, Miss Secord."

Miss Elsie tilted her chin toward the hovering hand, as if examining it for germs, pinched the fingers quickly before pulling away. "Are you Ms. Paula Klein?"

"Paula is fine! I'm sorry that we're meeting under these circumstances."

Miss Elsie nodded curtly, seemed to take in the room. Could she be feeling the same anxiety about all of this that I was?

She said, "You and my granddaughter did what together, now?"

"I was her manager. Really, business partner. We had plans, Paris and I."

"It was her plan that you do"—Miss Elsie did another sweeping gaze of the room—"*this?*"

There was justifiable venom in that last word.

Paula Klein's expression didn't shift at all, though she flung poison too. "Since Paris was emancipated—"

Miss Elsie still held my hand, the reflexive squeeze cracked my knuckles.

"—arrangements fell to parties she designated. I had power of attorney in most of her business affairs, so I put together what I thought was tasteful. I apologize for not getting you involved sooner. It took me a while to find you."

Miss Elsie's chin dropped, her back heaved, quiet sobs. I looped my arm over her shoulder, reeled her to me. Our emotionless hostess observed how she'd broken Paris's only living relative at this ghoulish cocktail party. Paula's reaction—or lack thereof—was chilling. The neighborhood boys were more compassionate burning ants with broken glass and sunlight.

Paris's whole emancipated minor thing was something that never sat well with her grandma. Or me.

What did that matter now?

"Oh dear," Paula Klein said, switching her robotic face to the Concerned setting. "Please, come with. Let me get you some water."

Miss Elsie let Paula take her other hand without issue; there was no fight left in her. I might have held on tighter, fought for her, if my eyes weren't on the main entrance. As it was, my entire focus shifted away from the person in the most pain, to the one I wanted to cause pain. Miss Elsie's fingers slipped free, and I found myself locked in a stare-down with the girl I'd come to think of as my nemesis.

Fuse Fallon was in the building.

FUSE

Winston Bell's dreadlocks swayed as he walked me into the theater, the beads on the ends of select strands colliding, creating a cabasas-like clacking that his voice harmonized to naturally, giving his words a lyrical lilt. "After the service, maybe we can get a bite and talk. There's a great restaurant around the corner. Best chicken and waffles on the East Coast, I swear."

"Uh-huh."

His suit matched the wispy gray threaded through his beard and lion's-mane hair. Winston wore a white *Fugees Europe 1997* tour T-shirt underneath his suit coat, taking it out of the realm of strict funeral attire to the kind of outfit you could work or party in. That was his thing, like he was a dad and a little too attached to a scene meant for his kids.

Every time I'd seen him during those long, follow-you-around interviews with ParSec, he was always doing the "when I was your age," followed by some positive-to-negative comparison of his youth versus ours thing. It was harmless, but it got tired fast. Like on the car over.

"When I was your age, people actually read about the music," he'd said. "Real words by real aficionados. Slick glossy covers with dope photos and art. Not all this comments-section, typo-ridden blog stuff. *MIXX* magazine's managed to hang on, though. Grateful for that."

It was a short ride from the coffee shop I met him at in Norfolk. I'd purposely been late to our meeting and amped up my grief on the way so he'd back off with the questions. I'd give it to him, he wasn't letting me off easy. I'd actually considered living up to my end of our bargain despite my intense dislike for journalists. Until I saw her.

Kya Caine was here? How in the actual—?

Oh crap.

Sidestepping, I dipped into the shadowy recess between a tall fern and trio of men, as Paula caught sight of my ticket into this joint. She gave Winston a curt nod before shuffling some old lady away. Winston's head swiveled toward the spot I'd occupied a moment before, smirking, ready to talk my ear off some more, but his smile fell when he found empty air. I slipped around the men who'd become my camouflage.

I moved on, peeking between bodies to make sure Paula remained unaware of my presence. So far so good, but Kya tracked me like a nightmare stalker, rotating on her heels so she didn't lose me. Her punching hand flexed.

I posted up in a corner, a golden column between Kya and me. Relaxed a little, and wondered . . . why *hadn't* the service started already? This whole thing felt like Dad's holiday office parties. Hardly anybody even seemed sad.

If this was for ParSec, I mean, for real, why did the fans across the street seem to get it more than the people in here? Half of this lobby was old-old, jockeying for Paula's spot on the Iron and Fiber Throne. They weren't even playing ParSec's music, and I know she would've wanted that at her funeral. She'd told me herself.

There *was* a Muzak version of an old Anita Baker record playing. Don't get me wrong, Anita Baker's voice was *fire*—thanks for that fine bit of music education, once-cool Dad—just not as jazz-piano-and-saxophones without actual Anita Baker. Some dude over by Paula and the elderly lady actually tapped his foot to this atrocity.

Were Kya and I the youngest people here?

I thought so, and not only that . . . I did know these people. At least some of them.

All the leeches, and publicity hounds, and scandal creators. All the people ParSec expressed open disdain for, here to see her on her back. Forever. My hands shook; I dug my nails into the meatiest parts of my palms to stop the rage tremor. It'd be like if Batman died, and everyone at his funeral was the Joker. How were these people allowed here?

Easy. These were people who might make Paula Klein money someday. This was a networking event. One benefiting not just Paula.

Ugh. Lil' Redu was here.

Or, as I liked to call him, Lil' Wannabe Gangster Steaming Trash Monster.

He was a frail dude with only a few inches and pounds on me, who always smelled strongly of weed and cologne. Even though he was young—a high school dropout who would've graduated same time as me if he felt school was worth his time—his attendance here was just as mystifying as the old folks' home field trip filling this lobby. Despite being forever linked because of their collaboration on "Calm Down, Turn Up!" Lil' Redu and ParSec had hated each other lately.

He nudged his way toward me, clearing a wide path with the two girls flanking him, grinning, and said, "What up, *Lose* Fallon?" Then cackled at his own corny "joke." When his dates didn't laugh too, he flicked cold glances, reminding them of their obligations, and they chittered lightly.

My punching hand flexed. He proudly represented the worst, most exaggerated perceptions of hip-hop. The misogyny and stupid-dumb excess, from the gaudy chain on his neck, to the precious metal grill crammed in his mouth. In honor of ParSec's memory, I was happy continuing the tradition of hating this dude. "Oh, I see. You swapped *Fuse* for *lose* because they sound alike. Nice. It's almost like you're a rapper."

One of his escorts snort-laughed, genuine that time. His head snapped to her, silently scalding. Knowing how he rolled—ejecting people from his oversized entourage anytime they displeased him in the slightest—she'd probably need a ride home after this.

He tipped his too-big bulbous head forward so he peered over the rims of his Gucci shades. The combo of dark lenses and blood-shot eyes felt like he was looking at me four different ways, like spider eyes. "See you still got that smart mouth. Thought you was fired, though. You here to stuff some hors d'oeuvres in your purse?"

Hors d'oeuvres was a big word for this miscreant, and him com-menting on my employment situation rubbed me all kinds of raw. How'd he even know? "Why are *you* here? The last time you and ParSec spoke, you threatened to run her over with your truck."

"See"—he leaned in—"that's your problem. You always thought you knew more than you did. ParSec and I talked plenty. She still hadn't come around to seeing things my way, which was too bad. Unfortunately, she met her little tragedy before we could conclude our business. So that's what I'm here for. To discuss getting my masters back from someone more reasonable. And more alive."

Paula. The woman trying to wring every dime out of ParSec's corpse. That's how he knew I'd been booted from the PK Music

Group. She'd been holding court with Lil' Redu for . . . I don't even know. What the heck was going on here?

People stared. We weren't loud. It wasn't *a scene*. Our energy, though. It made the room skittish. Deer before an earthquake.

Paula slipped between guests, accompanied by a few dark-suited men. I spoke before she could. "I'm not here to cause trouble. Okay? I just want to see her one last time."

She didn't respond. She did greet Lil' Redu. "LR, good to see you. Unfortunate it had to happen under such circumstances."

He shook her hand. "Fo' sho'," he said.

Paula welcomed his girlfriends individually, taking her time getting around to me. Letting me squirm.

Finally she faced me. A simple "This is surprising. Let's walk."

She grabbed my tricep, pinching it in a way I wouldn't have allowed if I wasn't desperate to remain here. I endured, a test of will. One almost broken when Kya, not so subtle, raised her phone level with my face and took a photo. There was no flash, but I knew. And I wondered.

Thoughts of Kya flitted away as Paula steered me toward the exit. "I'll give you the usernames and passwords you asked for if you let me stay."

Her goon squad paced us. She gave them a tight nod, and we all stopped. Still inside. Still close to my friend.

I misinterpreted everything.

The lobby lights flickered dim-bright, dim-bright, five times, the way they did in playhouses shortly before a performance began.

ParSec's final show.

The crowd of strangers poured toward the auditorium, murmuring, almost cheerful. Though Paula was speaking, I wasn't hearing her. The screaming inside my own head was too loud. IT'S

NOT A PIXAR MOVIE! IT'S PARSEC! SHE SHOULDN'T BE HERE, BUT SHE IS, AND YOU DON'T HAVE THE RIGHT TO SMILE ABOUT IT!

One of those people was Kya, our eyes locked. She wasn't smiling. She was furious. Not at me. At them too.

Her stare was ice-cold.

For a hot second, we were like-minded. It passed. She linked arms with the elderly woman Paula had tended to before I became her most pressing problem. ParSec's grandma? I'd never met the woman myself, and I was getting the impression that wouldn't be changing today. The pair disappeared into the auditorium, and just over their shoulders, I caught the briefest glimpse of an ivory shell. The coffin.

Winston Bell got pulled along with the attendee current but took time to make a confused gesture, his palms toward the ceiling, mouthing, *What's happening?*

I didn't have a good answer.

". . . so you understand, then." Paula concluded a speech I hadn't heard at all.

"What?"

She glanced away, gathering herself. Determined to control her annoyance. "I said, I don't need those usernames and passwords anymore. We've made other arrangements. Fresh, official PK Music Group social media accounts meant to memorialize our girl properly. We've already got a contact at Twitter working on getting the prior fraudulent accounts taken down."

"We who?" The last of the lobby stragglers slipped into the auditorium. Paula's guards sealed them in. And me out.

"Not you, Fuse."

The guards moved in unison, flanking me but not touching me.

Paula said, "You're trespassing at a private function. I'm well within my rights to have you thrown out, and to notify one of the lovely police officers across the street of your unwanted presence. Is that the way this afternoon's going to go? A dozen YouTube videos of you being tossed into the back of a squad car? As I've recently been informed, you don't need more bad coverage."

Everything she said, I couldn't process. Her men hovered uncomfortably close, and I'd scream if they touched me. Maybe Paula knew that too. She said, "Back off a bit."

Her goons took two steps.

"Paula"—do not crack, voice—"I . . . I just want to see her one last time. Something different than what I actually saw in that warehouse. Please don't"—and I was begging, *begging freaking Paula Klein*—"make my last memory of her be a corpse flung across some turntables."

She glanced toward the ceiling, her head bobbing, considering. Like everything else she did, being decent required calculation. "Fuse, I know you actively campaigned for ParSec to fire me and find a different manager. I know you told her she didn't have as much money as she should have because of me. I know you, a schoolgirl strumpet who's good at finding Instagram followers, thought you could mess with my business and get away with it. So, no, you don't get to go in there. Though it shouldn't be that big of a deal"—she leaned in, whispering—"corpse on turntables, or corpse in a box, what's the real difference anyway? Bye, now."

She snapped her fingers, and her goons grabbed me by the armpits. I screamed, no one cared. They carried me out and set me down gently. Though I called them every horrid thing that popped in my head, they spared not a glance. The theater doors slammed shut.

Alone, noticing cops noticing me, I stopped my tirade. Phones were out across the street, undoubtedly snapping photos and video of me getting thrown from a place I should've been more than welcome. How did I get here?

With my shoulders hunched against the cold on that relatively warm day, I marched up the sidewalk, away from the crowd, my head turned to the ground, away from anyone looking to get social media hits off my misery. My tears were private, today of all days.

Around the corner, I passed a Print & Ship office store, the strong notes of pulp and cardboard wafting from its cracked door. A quick glance over my shoulder, and I spotted some ParSec fans in loose pursuit. Still on the far side of the intersection but angling to watch where I went with their eyes and phones. I sped up and cut through a parking lot midway up the block, spotting a sketchy alley running between the buildings. I made a sharp detour, hoping to discourage any other rude jerks who couldn't read body language (or who could, and thought a shamed Fuse Fallon was better clickbait).

In the dark recesses between buildings, my thoughts swirled. Deep, bottomless grief for missing her funeral. A vengeance-fueled blowtorch scorched the spiteful things Paula had said into my memory forever. She and I weren't done, not even close. Though one thing she said puzzled me more than the rest.

As I've recently been informed, you don't need more bad coverage.

Turning another corner, I saw the alley's end about thirty yards away, blocked by a dark van. Its sliding side door an open, hungry mouth, and nope, definitely not going that way because I've seen all the horror movies. Turning to escape, I found that option had been taken from me. A large dude in a white mask blocked my path.

An opaque sack slipped over my head.

Everyone had an if-it-were-me scenario. Thoughts about what you'd do in the face of a very specific danger. I had an if-it-were-me scenario for being kidnapped. It was all lies.

I hardly screamed at all.

PARIS/DJ PARSEC

(18 MONTHS BEFORE)

"Explain it to me again?"

Fuse left her director's chair, also known as my bed, and triggered her tripod's quick release lever, snapping her iPad off the mount. She rotated the screen and played back what she'd recorded.

She said, "Video drives online engagement better than anything. And you smashed this video, friend."

In the playback I wasn't doing much, just scratching and mixing at my turntables. It wasn't even a mix I'd thought up. Fuse had requested it, brought the records with her and everything. Real talk, her idea sounded corny when she'd first said it. But since we started connecting on my social media outreach a couple of months back, most of her ideas been on point. So I was like, whatever, if you say so. Now that I was hearing the final result, gotta admit, kinda fire.

It was a simple mix, really. Darth Vader's music from the original *Star Wars* soundtrack and an old-school hip-hop track by Queen Latifah and Monie Love called "Ladies First." I'd recognized the *Star Wars* music—who didn't?—just by being alive. I was a little embarrassed I hadn't heard "Ladies First" before. When I asked Fuse where she got it, and how she even knew to get it, she rolled her eyes and said, "My dad used to be cool."

Fuse shot me from the side, with a lot of zooming on my hands as I moved between the vinyl and the fader, making the two records sound like they were happily married.

She said, "We should shoot a couple more things. You talking about how you sped up 'The Imperial March' to match the up-tempo record. Maybe talk about the equipment a little."

My stomach clenched. "Naw. You should show something else. My setup looks crazy. All these mismatched pieces."

There were two different turntables, an old Technics 1200 I got from the pawn shop, and a Vestax PDX with droopy half-melted housing that I found in a dumpster behind a lounge that burned down about a year ago. The mixer Kya found online for like ten bucks because it didn't work . . . at least not until she got her hands on it.

"That's even better," Fuse said. "There will be a lot of people who can't afford top-of-the-line stuff. When they see what you do, it's going to be, I don't know, inspirational."

That word again. *Inspirational.* I made party music, but she'd been pushing hard on "growing my brand" into something "more robust" like that expensive spaghetti sauce Grandma buys.

On top of music videos—which we hadn't actually shot yet—Fuse wanted a series of how-to DJ videos *and* production videos that show the way I make songs: from when the idea first hits, to building the beat, to adding the vocals, to mastering the mix. Still, I said, "Half of music is about your rep. You don't think people will clown me over my gear looking homemade?"

"Maybe some. There are always trolls. Most will get it—that it paints you as, like, a genius who can make anything work."

"*I* made that work, though." Kya stood in my doorway on some ninja stealth stuff, pointing at the equipment she helped piece together. Her sudden appearance made me yelp.

There was a Nerf basketball on my desk. I threw it at her head—missed. "Announce yourself, fool. Rolling up in here like a ghost."

She said, "I'm here."

"I ain't know you were coming over."

"You never needed to know before."

Fuse didn't look up from her tablet, already editing the video file. "Hey, Kya."

Kya grunted.

Fuse tapped away from the newest video and a grid of thumbnails filled her screen. She flipped it so Kya and I could see, the good little presenter she was. "I figure for every hour we spend shooting quality video, we can leverage it into ten to twenty different artifacts for cross-promotion. Full videos on YouTube, a bunch of fifteen- to thirty-second snippets for Twitter and Instagram stories. Of course, the audio we can push through the normal channels. It's going to drive ParSec Nation wild."

"ParSec what?" Kya stepped fully into the room. Usually, she sat on my bed. There was still room—Fuse's frail tail don't take up no space—but Kya leaned on my closet door instead, her arms crossed. Her face tight.

I said, "Fuse, tell her what you did. It's sweet, K."

Fuse swiped away the video app, opened her social media dashboard full of rapidly scrolling columns of new posts from different platforms. "You know the BeyHive and you know Rihanna's Navy. There's Swifties, and Team Drizzy, and Selenators. All of those fandoms love their artists, and the artists love them back."

"Okay," said Kya.

"ParSec Nation is our dedicated fandom. I started the hashtag a few weeks ago and have been working with ParSec to distribute regular, hot content. The hashtag's usage has been on a steady incline. Every time someone shouts out the Nation, ParSec's message gets amplified."

Kya said, "Like a street team?"

"Eh. That concept's kind of prehistoric."

Kya's head snapped back. Fuse probably could've said that a little better.

She kept going, though. "I'm of the opinion that most artists don't use their fandoms to maximum effect. Let's be honest, Beyoncé could start the Purge with a tweet if she wanted. That is untapped power."

Kya immediately countered. "I'd bet Beyoncé doesn't 'start the Purge with a tweet' because she doesn't want murder and jail to mess up her brand. Is *brand* the right term? Not too prehistoric?"

Jeez, this was going south fast. I crossed the room, plucked the tablet from Fuse's grasp, and handed it to Kya. "Look."

Kya unfolded herself and took the tablet. Fuse was on her feet, floating at Kya's hip. "You can swipe left to see more—"

"I know how tablets work," Kya said.

Fuse threw up her hands and retreated to the turntables, where she took pics of the still records with her phone.

Kya and I stood together while she checked all the traffic #ParSecNation was getting. She nodded. Not super enthusiastic, but she was too smart not to get this.

"This from last week." I swiped to the specific tweet Fuse showed me when she first arrived.

ParSec The Don @DJParSec

If you at a party this weekend, and they ain't #Turnup with your fave #ParSecNation track, you need to have a chat with the DJ. #Makeanoffertheycantrefuse

Then I swiped to the column Fuse created that tracked all the combined uses of #ParSecNation and #Makeanoffertheycantrefuse. "The Nation really went in on this."

There were tons of selfies of #ParSecNation supporters crowding a DJ booth like some invading force, with posts like:

Da Bounce @JYeezy1428
Oh, she turned up. Believe that! #ParSecNation
#Makeanoffertheycantrefuse

And a Boomerang, looping the moment a bunch of partygoers tipped the DJ and all his equipment off the dais into a swimming pool glowing with purple lighting. The tweet saying:

Kung-Fu Kelly @KendrickFan4U
All you wack DJs out there be warned. He **didn't** take the offer. #ParSecNation #Makeanoffertheycantrefuse

Kya's head whipped on that one. "Paris, they just threw all of his equipment in a pool. That looks like a couple of CDJ-2000 multiplayers. A mixer. A *MacBook*. That's like eight grand worth of stuff ruined. You're okay with that?"

I wasn't. At first. Fuse flicked some subtle side-eye our way. She'd explained that we didn't *make* them do that. Didn't even suggest it. I got the sense she was done explaining her tactics to Kya, so I repeated what she'd told me. "We don't *control* people, K."

A different, calmer video might be in order. "Mostly this is what we're going for."

In it a glassy-eyed #ParSecNation fan bounced while shooting a selfie video from behind the DJ's table. He was with friends, having a good time, and more importantly to me, so was the DJ. My music—a new dance track, "Splitsville"—played to a jamming crowd. The cameraman shouted, "HE TOOK THE OFFER!"

Kya squinted like the video was fuzzy when it wasn't. She tapped the screen, jumping the video back ten seconds. "Who is that?"

I paused and she pointed, the figure I hadn't noticed before was barely in the frame. It was some old Friday the 13th dude hovering over the DJ, mask and all. Not a hockey mask. It was plain white, maybe even a little creepier than a hockey mask.

"Fuse?" I said, walking the tablet back to her.

Fuse frowned at the screen, tilted her chin down a bit. "Hmmm. I've seen those masks popping up in some posts. Not a ton. I think it's just coincidence, maybe some new fashion thing. Like fauxhawks."

"Fauxhawks?" Kya said. "Paris, I need to talk to you downstairs."

Here we go.

Fuse gave a mighty eye roll and turned her attention back to her device. Kya stomped past me and down the stairs, her footsteps like falling rocks. I was slow joining her, recognizing the signs of an oncoming Kya storm.

When I got to the living room, her hip was cocked. Her right foot tapped. She had the "are you serious?" look popping. Kya pointed up—through the ceiling, aiming at Fuse—and spoke in her whisper-yell voice. "Where did she even come from?"

I whisper-yelled too. "What you mean? She's been in school with us for years."

"No. Not with *us*. With her people. The rich kids who got dropped off in Audis and laughed at our clothes."

"Naw, Fuse won't ever like that." I remembered all those laughing faces. They were fuel on late nights when the music wasn't coming out right. I imagined those laughs drying up when they saw me and my crew stunting at the Grammys.

Kya said, "She doesn't even use your name, Paris. It's all ParSec this, ParSec that."

"Yo, don't Johnny Odom call Superman Superman?"

"Jimmy Olsen."

"Whatever. I ain't tell no lies, though. I like that she gets that my artist side and my at-home side ain't really different. It don't make me mad, why you salty?"

"You didn't come to school today. You told me you were sick. I came here to check on you. You seem fine to me."

Lord! "Look, my grandma gone all day with her sister and I didn't have any tests. We skipped to get this video shot, edited, and uploaded ASAP because Fuse and her people going skiing this weekend."

She went to a true whisper, her face turned away, like I was hard to look at, direct sun with no shades. "Do you hear yourself? You lied. To me!"

"Because you act like this."

Her mouth gaped, as if she had more to say (I'm sure she did), but her eyes flicked toward the staircase. Fuse was so petite the creaky stairs didn't make a sound beneath her. "I got what we need, ParSec. Seems like I should probably go. I'll email you about the schedule over the weekend. When things are less volatile."

Kya shook her head and disappeared into the kitchen. I stopped Fuse from letting herself out. "Hey, maybe not today, but I want y'all to work this out. I think you'll really like each other if y'all sit down and really talk."

Fuse glanced toward the kitchen, then met my eyes. "No thanks. You need new followers way more than I need new friends. I can't help if she's jealous. Can't let it slow us down either. I hope you get that." She peeled my hand off the doorknob. "Watch all your feeds this weekend. Major gains coming. Calm down . . ."

"Turn up," I said, with a boost of fake energy.

Fuse walked into daylight, and I went to finish the vibe-killing conversation with Kya. Only she was gone too. Escaped out the back door.

I didn't follow her.

KYA

Paris's service was . . . hard. And fake. Not what a funeral should be, and nothing in me believed she'd asked for this. No flowers, though I'd seen bouquets stacked five high on the street outside of Miss Elsie's house, along with teddy bears, and burned CDs, and other respectful tokens to Paris's fame. Here there were blown-up photos of Paris on tripods, though. Promotional shots from shows and music releases.

That Paula lady gave a eulogy about Paris's talent and revolutionary style that somehow didn't feel like it was really about Paris in the least. "Not many would've recognized the incredible package Paris Secord represented. I've prided myself on spotting the star power others missed, and she appreciated me for it." It felt like she was presenting an award. The coffin goes to . . .

The Fifth Street Baptist Church choir should've been here. That was Miss Elsie's church, a short drive from our neighborhood, where Paris got dragged every Sunday before she could call shots. There was no "Amazing Grace," no "His Eye Is on the Sparrow." Songs I'd heard at every funeral I'd ever been to in my entire life. Including Paris's mom's.

Instead, five white guys who had *boy band* written all over them sang—this was so crazy—"Over the Rainbow" from *The Wizard of Oz*. Huh?

Miss Elsie's breathing quickened. Her look, I'd seen it plenty, from the times Paris and I really crossed the line. Drawing on her walls as kids. Sneaking in late like we had homes big enough to make sneaking in feasible. She was angry. I was too.

We endured. The sermon from a Catholic priest named Father Cullen. Another selection, Frank Sinatra's "My Way" by the boy band that then doubled as pallbearers, carrying Paris's sealed coffin to a waiting hearse.

Paula Klein had programs printed. To continue the vast differences from any kind of funeral proceeding I was familiar with, there was no information about a burial site. We found out why as the vulture-like onlookers departed the theater.

Paula approached us in the emptying lobby, cutesy-waving to *her* guests. When we had her attention again, she said, "Miss Secord, something I didn't do was make burial arrangements. I thought you'd might want Paris to be with her mother."

"That's one thing you were right about," said Miss Elsie, a hint of gratefulness bleeding into her tone.

"If you have a preferred mortuary service, let me know."

Miss Elsie nodded, and Paula produced a tiny notepad and pen. They walked to the theater concession counter to scribble out the arrangements that I tried not to think about as handing off Paris's body, though if we were being honest . . .

Alone, in a nearly abandoned lobby, I took the opportunity to sneak my phone out, snapping pictures in quick bursts, honoring a deal I'd made with Florian. I sent them quickly, along with the pics I snuck before and during the "service," hoping the skeezy, dirty feeling I had over being a spy left quickly too. It didn't.

Maybe I was shady becoming Florian's secret agent. But I didn't get here on my own. Fuse started this pettiness with her tweets.

Though, judging by the way she got booted from this service, my brand of payback might not rank high among her priorities.

When I saw her having a hard time with Paula and the security, I'd wanted to savor it. But everything here was so, so wrong. Fuse was the only other person here who, at one time, seemed like an actual friend to Paris. Regardless of how everything went down, Paris shouldn't have less friends in attendance today.

Wonder where she ended up?

Miss Elsie returned, looking smaller than she did when the day started. "Let's go, child. Are you ready?"

She didn't have to ask me twice.

■ ■

The funeral home limo dropped us off on our street, inside Harding Home Estates, aka "the Home," and I saw Miss Elsie back to her unit. A yellow, weather-grimed town house in a row of weather-grimed town houses. They all used to be identical, inside and out, but a few years back whoever made the decisions replaced the siding so each unit was a different color. The row now looked like a series of children's building blocks stacked side by side. Ours was pink. It's the only improvement of the property I recalled in my entire life.

People—strangers, fans—had stopped hanging around several days ago, but their shrine remained. The gifts, the candles, poster-board signs. All those "Love you, ParSec" items that looked like trash since it rained the other day, soaking everything into a mushy mess. On my way to school this week, I'd seen the neighborhood motormouth Miss Sal out in the street fussing at Miss Elsie about how all that junk made the street look "ghetto." I hated that word and all its racist, classist implications. Kind of hated Miss Sal too.

When the limo pulled away, I spotted her in her living room window, blinds bent wide, staring.

Heavy sighing, Miss Elsie said, "I need to call the city to come clear this mess so that hateful witch will leave me alone. Probably cost money. Everything do."

I wasn't convinced I should leave her, but my phone had been buzzing for the last half hour with texts from Mama, several variations on "Where you at?" and "Call me. Now!" Plus, Paris's grandma wasn't one for forced charity.

"Go home," she said. "We both need rest, and I need some time to think."

Think of what, I didn't know and didn't dare ask. Knew better. I'd been well trained in recognizing "grown folks' business." If I was meant to know, she'd mean to tell me. "If you need anything, I'm right down the street . . ."

Miss Elsie cupped the back of my head. Short and wide like Paris, she tugged me into a stooping posture to kiss me on the cheek. "You always have been, child. At least I have one grand-daughter left."

My smile was tight, lips pinched. She had no idea that while she still considered me a granddaughter, Paris hadn't considered me much of a sister in those last days. Did Miss Elsie know I'd given Paris the same treatment back?

You're rotten on the inside, Paris.

Someone should throw you away.

I left, no goodbye. Hugging myself with one arm while rechecking all of Mama's texts. She was picking up an extra shift, wouldn't be home until late. Mama's hostess job at a restaurant on the boardwalk often left her too tired to be concerned with things other than payday. That worked for me. I began the walk home. Maybe she didn't have to know the details of my day.

I sent a preemptive text. Not a lie, since I had no reason to think I wouldn't make it to my door.

ME

I'm home.

MAMA

Now you are. Where you been all day?

ME

School stuff.

It wasn't a direct answer, so it couldn't be a blatant lie. Right?

There were seven units between Miss Elsie's house and mine, and the black van parked at the halfway mark only registered in my back brain. A low, dull ping, dismissed too easily. I was so oblivious. The perfect victim.

The van door wasn't well oiled. When I passed and it opened like a mouth, it was with a light scrape. I didn't even glance over my shoulder; my mind was on all the cameras at the memorial. Surely there'd been social media posts, stuff Mama could easily find if she put in any effort. What would I do then?

The quick footfalls behind me were hushed. The sound that finally got my attention was the grunting coming from inside the vehicle, like someone coughing through thick cloth. I turned—too late—to see two white masks rushing at me, duct tape stretched and ready.

The first strip pressed hard against my lips while one of my assailants wrapped me in a bear hug, pinning my arms. It was so fast, there was no time to feel fear. This was happening to someone else.

The two of them danced around me. More tape wrapped my wrists, then my ankles, with the speed of a spider entombing a fly in silk webbing. Then I was off my feet, bent at the waist on some man's shoulder, hoisted toward that gaping van door. Even then, the fear didn't register.

It came when I heard the tune they hummed. A Paris song. In perfect harmony.

Somehow that frightened me more than anything.

FUSE

My kidnappers totaled five. One in the driver's seat, four in the back of the van with me. All wearing familiar masks that I never expected to see this close.

They didn't openly threaten me. Since removing the sack from my head no one pointed a knife at my throat, or detailed the horrible things they'd do to me if I didn't comply. That's the thing about sitting in the back of a van, where the walls, roof, and floor were covered in foamy, ridged soundproofing. They didn't have to. I already knew what this crew was capable of.

As terrifying as this was—I'd never been so scared—having been with these monsters for a couple of hours now allowed me to calm down slightly. With my panic decreased by a percent, I remembered things Mom and Dad told me when I was much younger, should I ever find myself in this very situation. Pay attention. Look for opportunities to signal for help or escape.

We'd been sitting for a while, waiting on something.

Suddenly two of the four masks who'd been surrounding me for what felt like days jumped out of the van, while the remaining two angled their pale faces toward me. Were they watching me? Maybe. I couldn't see their eyes, so they could've been sleeping behind the facade. Though every time I flexed my wrists, or tried loosening the plastic ties restraining me, at least one mask would tilt, a gesture I read as, "Really, Fuse?"

Then I'd go still again.

This open door was the first real opportunity I'd had, even if it meant flinging myself through it and inchworming away. There were still two people between me and the exit, so that wasn't really happening. Maybe someone was close by, someone who'd find a nondescript black van creepy-strange, and human screaming even more so. So I tried it!

"Help! Help me!"

Because of my gag, it sounded like *MMMDMD! MMMDMD-MD!*

A mask—the smallest, most aggressive of the bunch—slammed a palm into my chest, pushing me back against the van wall. If anyone heard me, I couldn't tell, because the two who'd gone outside returned, humming, with a new passenger flung over one of their shoulders.

The newbie thumped next to me. One mask banged the ceiling with his fist, yelled, "Go, go!" as he resealed the door. We were in motion.

The new captive twisted into a seated position, stared at me with her face splayed in terror.

Kya?

KYA

Fuse?

I scooted closer, screaming unintelligibly through my taped lips that *we need to fight*. She flinched like I was attacking *her*.

The van lurched out of my neighborhood. Soon, we'd reach an intersection, and a right turn would take us toward a highway ramp. Then, who knew?

Bucking, trying to get her to do the same, I only drew the attention of a mask, who bopped me on the head with a rolled-up newspaper. Like I was a dog.

"Stop that!" she said, voice distorted by plastic covering her face. "We don't intend to hurt you. That's not what this particular meet and greet is about."

She was smaller than the others, her dark hoodie too baggy on her, while the muscles in her fit legs flexed through yoga pants. Her sneakers—white high-top Nike Air Force 1s—had loose laces, and the Looney Tunes character Bugs Bunny drawn on the right foot, while Elmer Fudd and his ever-ready shotgun took aim at the "wabbit" from the left. She'd opted for total comfort *and* style in the commission of her felonies. From that moment on, I thought of her as . . .

Elmyra Fudd said, "Good, you're calm now."

I wasn't, but there were four of them crowded back here with us, one drove. Loser odds even if our hands and feet were free.

Only impossible white guys—Tom Cruise and Captain America—in movies won those fights.

The van turned right. Accelerated to highway speeds.

"Get the gags off," she instructed. Her minions obeyed. One tore off my tape, along with some skin. Another undid the bandanna knot at the back of Fuse's head, and she hocked up some balled-up, spit-soggy cloth.

"Who are you?" I said.

Fuse only sighed and chewed her lip. Later, I'd understand it was because she already knew.

Elmyra Fudd said, "We're the Dark Nation."

FUSE

Oh. Crap.

Now that they'd admitted what I suspected, and I knew how crazy these lunatics could get, I couldn't stop squirming, trying to free myself of the zip ties around my wrists and ankle. We had to *do something*.

There was nothing to be done, though. Not physically. I think Kya got that. She remained still, her eyes bouncing from one assailant to the other. Their dark hoodies tugged up so their masks looked like chunks of moon floating in a starless sky.

#ParSecNation worked a certain way. They were fun, bold, relentless, all with one goal: serve DJ ParSec. I'd made them that way.

#DarkNation was a different animal altogether. A group I'd never intended. One that rose up like a weed, scary in their devotion to ParSec's songs. Ask the music blogger in San Diego who ended up in a marina tied to a boat's mast because she'd written a scathing diss of ParSec's entire catalog. Or the record executive who got his ribs broken in a New York nightclub for saying indie artists like ParSec and her fans were the death of music. They had been a problem when she was still around. Now that she was gone, how would the kingdom honor a dead queen?

All masks angled toward my futile gyrations. One of the males, his voice soft and high, said, "She thinks that's going to work?" He spoke to me, "Unless superstrength is part of your Super Groupie powers, you can stop now."

Kya, glaring, said, "Did you do this, Fuse?"

"Me?" I shook my bound wrists at her. "I'm not exactly flying first class here."

"Then what is this?"

The girl in the cartoon shoes said, "That, I can explain."

One of the male masks passed her a tablet. She woke it, turning her white mask a spectral blue in the glare, and tapped the screen. "Kya Sherée Caine and Fatima Alexis Fallon, also known as Fuse. Former friends of the incomparable DJ ParSec, both present at her murder scene."

"Wait, wait," I said. "We weren't 'present at her murder scene.' I mean, yes, we found her, but we weren't there when it happened. We didn't do it!"

Cartoon Shoes's mask tilted toward me. "That doesn't seem to be what you implied in your lengthy Twitter thread earlier this week."

She showed me my own words on her tablet. The subtle shade I tossed Kya's way. No outright accusation, just enough to . . . well . . . get us here.

Kya said, "You couldn't leave things alone, could you?"

Cartoon Shoes bopped Kya on the head with the rolled-up—something—she'd used earlier. "Ah, ah, ah. You're not much better on this front. Are you, Kya?"

The tablet turned toward Kya, but I still saw the screen. Cartoon Shoes swiped to a browser page. It was that ParSec Love Tumblr that girl at school ran. The latest post titled: "What We Don't Know About Fuse. UPDATED!"

Whoa. Hold up! There'd been a post about *me*? Up long enough that it required an update?

Suddenly Paula's *you don't need more bad coverage* made sense. I'd been too busy scamming Winston Bell for a way into the venue to pay attention to my mentions today.

My viewing angle was too severe, and the font was too small for me to read any of the text. The accompanying photo made it pretty clear what that "update" was about. It was me arguing with Paula and her security at today's memorial service. The pic Kya took on her way into the auditorium before I was thrown out.

Swinging my bound legs around so fast I almost tipped over, I threw a two-heeled kick toward Kya's chest. Must've telegraphed it, because a mask grabbed my calves before I connected, spun me back into a seated position. Cartoon Shoes bopped me on the head. "Stop it. Don't make this worse, Super Groupie."

Angry enough to tear a chunk out of Kya—what did that post even say?—but recognizing the insanity of everything, my patience wore thin. "Make what worse? What do you want?"

"Did one of you do it?" one of the bigger, gruffer masks asked. "Did one of you take her from us?"

Kya flinched at his heavy voice and possibly the implications of the questions. I might've jerked away too, if I wasn't so used to my dad asking gruff questions or yelling gruff things, suddenly, with no preamble. This wasn't so different than conversations at my house, with the exception of the kidnapping and restraints.

We were in ridiculous danger. There was something leading in the big boy's question. A plea. He wanted one of us to say yes, and then . . .

Didn't want to think about that part. Because, one thing I knew to be 100 percent true . . .

"I did not kill Paris Secord!" Kya shouted.

I pressed back into the padded van wall. There was so much force behind it, like she'd been storing it in her gut all week, waiting for the right moment to projectile vomit the words. After that, all masks turned to me, and I stuttered, "M-m-me neither. She was my friend."

Cartoon Shoes continued working her tablet. "Now we know that part's a lie. She wasn't friends with either of you over the last several weeks. That much we've pieced together from various sources."

"What sources?" Kya said, staring daggers at me.

Cartoon Shoes ignored her. "How did you both end up in the same room, at the same time, with her dead body if you didn't have anything to do with her murder, though? Who wants to go first?"

"I was there to apologize," Kya blurted out. "Okay? I'd been a jerk, and we had some problems, but I was still her best friend. She invited me to the party she was throwing, to fix things between us. I was going to apologize. When I got there, I found Fuse. Never got to give that apology."

Faint road noise and expectations filled the void left when she finished. The masks turned to me. My heartbeat seemed as loud as my voice when I said, "I was going to yell at her."

Cartoon Shoes was taken aback. "Really?"

"We were at odds because of all the control she'd handed over to that leech Paula Klein," I explained. "I got it, we were young and didn't have a ton of business experience. I probably could've found a way to monetize our online reach better. But there's older and more experienced, then there's *oldest* and skilled in the art of sketch. That's Paula. She drove a wedge between ParSec and me. Honestly, if I'd gotten the chance to have my say, I probably would've driven a deeper wedge between us. When I arrived, she was dead. Now I just wish I'd said I loved her." It hurt to admit that. Then it just hurt.

The masks turned from one to another in some form of silent communication I couldn't decipher. Like birds perched on a lamppost, conferring on bird matters. Their verdict took an eternity.

Finally Cartoon Shoes said, "Good enough. For now."

Thank God. They believed us. Though I had to wonder: When Kya told her side of the story, had she been lying too?

KYA

What I told the masks wasn't everything. Not even *most of the things.*

Did it even matter? The van hadn't changed direction. We were far away from where we'd started.

Elmyra Fudd said, "We'll have time to dig into your stories a bit more. For your sake, they better hold up. For the record, most of the Nation believes neither of you could've actually pulled off the killing. Your arms are too skinny."

"Our . . . *arms?* What kind of body-shaming crap is that?" Fuse was indignant.

Elmyra Fudd kept going. "This little parlay was always meant to be reconnaissance to feel you two out, see if you were up for the assignment."

"Assignment?" Fuse and I said at the same time.

"You two are like a set of bookends, aren't you? Good. You'll need to be in sync to give us what we want. We're going to explain some things to you. Some you may already know. Some, you'll want to dismiss. Don't. Are you ready?"

All of the aggression between Fuse and me had sloughed away. No matter how we felt about each other, we weren't the source of our immediate danger. We exchanged frantic looks. Both uncertain. Both scared. We had more to bond over in the last half hour than we'd ever had before. We nodded. Ready.

A dude mask spoke next. "We're huge DJ ParSec fans. I don't think there's been a more innovative music maker to arise this decade. I mean, she's like Missy Elliott, Timbaland, and the Neptunes built a time machine, scoured the future for genius sound, and brought her back with them. You know?" His tone was high, giddy. "If you doubt me, pay attention to the track she produced on Mic Drop's *Facepalm* album, her first ever. People focus on the bass line, but the most inspired part is that pop-sizzle sound in the hook. An actual fuse blowing! How'd she even record—"

Elmyra Fudd cleared her throat. Loud and exaggerated.

Not-So-Calm Dude took a deep breath and re-centered. He reined in his rant—which wasn't totally accurate. The song on the *Facepalm* album wasn't Paris's first production credit. She'd done indie tracks for all the neighborhood rappers, who mostly sucked but sounded better through her efforts. As for how she recorded that fuse-blowing sound, and most of the other odd accoutrements she dressed her music in? With my help. We learned those tricks together.

"My point," he continued, "we—the entire world—lost something priceless. There must be justice."

"Yet," Elmyra Fudd said, "history tells us, in a case like DJ ParSec's, justice is unlikely. Have you ever heard the name Adelaide Milton?"

The *whomp-whomp-whomp* rotation of tires over rough asphalt was the only agonizing sound while I searched my memory for the name, spoken like I *should* know it. The craziest part was I kind of did. It had the familiarity of a difficult word, one you could use but couldn't quite explain without a dictionary.

"I'm sorry," I said, *apologizing to my kidnappers.* "I don't know her."

Fuse said, "I do. She got kidnapped. Are you guys going for justice, or poetic justice? Because these." She shook her bonds.

Elmyra Fudd said, "Adelaide Milton, age five, was vacationing with her family here at the Ocean Shore boardwalk. Her mother turned her head for a split second, and little Adelaide was gone. She is trending on Twitter and Instagram right now. She's very pretty. Green eyes, strawberry-blond hair. In the last twenty-four hours, she's garnered roughly fourteen million more internet impressions than DJ ParSec, despite the best efforts of the Nation. Monday morning, barring any other major, worldwide developments, Adelaide's story will be featured in the first half hour of all the national news shows. No one plans to run a story on DJ ParSec."

That stung. Of course national news wouldn't care about our grief. Already rationalizing, I made the distinction between a dead big girl and a kidnapped little girl. "I don't understand what Adelaide Milton has to do with this. If she was kidnapped this weekend, with enough coverage, enough noise, maybe that little girl gets found."

"Adelaide Milton went missing five years ago. This is the anniversary."

Whomp-whomp-whomp.

"This weekend," said Elmyra Fudd, "three girls of color—two black girls, one Latina—have gone missing in southeastern Virginia."

"Five, if we count you two," said a male mask. The threat became an additional passenger.

"If you want to know what they look like, you can google them. That's probably the *only* way you'll know. The police effort to find them will amount to little more than paperwork. On a similar note, the detectives working DJ ParSec's case have already stalled.

No leads. They're not even looking at you two. Funny, considering murders are usually committed by people closest to the victim. Check out the case file for yourself. What little there is."

That rolled tube she'd bopped me with wasn't a newspaper, but a folder, thin, with very few papers inside. She dropped it between Fuse and me.

Frustrated, I said, "We already told you we didn't do it!"

"We heard you. But our demand is simple: Find out who did."

FUSE

Every mask was still, waiting for our reply.

I said, "That's just stupid."

"Fuse!" Kya said.

"What? They're the ones with kidnap equipment and access to police files. Why isn't the *Dark Nation* using their resources to honor their god? Leave us out of it and cut these stupid zip ties. My wrists hurt!"

The masks weren't angled on us anymore. They were angled on me.

Maybe not the best time for a tantrum.

Cartoon Shoes tapped her tablet screen. "Our masks won't work for this. The very nature of our anonymity and tactics would void any chance of on-the-level, legal repercussions for the sleaze who did this. For anything we do to stick, someone in our ranks would, eventually, need to expose themselves. That would certainly lead to other problems, being that in our zeal for DJ ParSec's music, we haven't always engaged in . . . *lawful* activities."

Kya said, "You're worried about lawful activities? You're kidnapping us right now."

"You're not the police. You're not lawyers, judges, or a jury. You can't stop us with paperwork and red tape. Also, I'mma keep it one hundred with you. Since the tragedy, you fill a void. You entertain us." She rotated the tablet so we could see. Located at some complicated URL was a web poll, animated so the wedges pulsed in time with "Calm Down, Turn Up!" flitting through the speakers.

#DARKNATION POLL
#SuperGroupie vs #MadScientist
Who You Got?

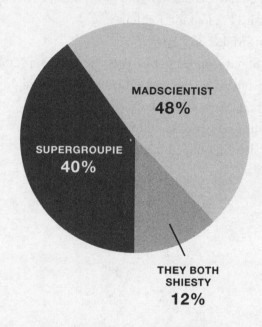

Under the chart was a still shot of us being restrained by police the night we found ParSec, taken by the jerk with the camera phone. Now I had an idea how they might've gotten a copy of the police's case file.

"How—?" I wasn't sure what I was even going to ask. How did they do this without me knowing? How were we supposed to do what they wanted? I lost my train of thought when Cartoon Shoes signaled to one of her minions, who slipped a sack over my head, blinding me.

"Stop that," Kya said. "Don't touch—"

She went quiet too.

"Relax." Cartoon Shoes's voice was muffled by the sack. "We're invested in keeping you safe. For now. That may change if you decide to get talkative about tonight's little parlay. Feel me? We're— what's the word I'm looking for, fellas?"

The Gruff Male said, "Shy."

Cartoon Shoes snapped her fingers. "Right. Don't embarrass us by trying to put us in the spotlight. Or else we might decide to invest elsewhere. Any other questions?"

I had nothing else to ask. Only wanted out.

The van slowed, stopped. Ride over.

KYA

The only senses I had were hearing and touch. In the sack, I couldn't smell anything but my SheaMoisture hair products, a yucca-and-plantain fog. Couldn't taste anything through my freshly retaped lips. And, of course, the only thing to be seen was bag.

The van door slid open, blasted us with night heat that made the sack on my head go from uncomfortable to suffocating. Claustrophobia that I didn't know I had kicked in. I bucked at my restraints involuntarily. My body insisted I be free.

Two masks lifted me quickly, carried me from the van, and stood me upright, leaned me against something cool and smooth. It didn't stop me from freaking.

"Stop moving," one of them said. The ties around my ankles got sliced. Then my hands were freed. "Count to ten before you take that bag off. Understand?"

I didn't say anything.

"You too." To Fuse, presumably.

I sensed motion. A sudden return of sanctified personal space. The van door slammed shut, the engine revved, I'd counted to eight as I heard it drive off quick, tires squealing. At ten, I yanked my bag off and found Fuse a few feet away, the hood of a car between us, already unbagged, and squinting after the vehicle, ripping tape from her mouth. "The license plate was covered in mud, I got nothing."

I peeled the tape off my mouth, or tried to. It took a couple of attempts to pry a corner free and do the painful yank. My hands were still shaking, but I willed them steady to ensure my necklace—thank God—remained where it should, with me. "That just happened."

Spinning in place, unsure of where we were, I spotted a bank and a coffee shop across the street. A comic book store and a pizza parlor. We were in an empty, poorly lit lot that seemed of no interest to the people in any of those businesses. If the Nation had dumped our corpses here, would they still be enjoying their calzones and lattes and Avengers comics while we rotted? This didn't feel like Ocean Shore. The smells weren't right, no salt in the air. "Where are we?"

"Norfolk," Fuse said, her voice as shaky as my hands. Before I asked how she knew, she produced a key fob from her pocket, thumbed a button. The car we'd been leaning on flashed its lights, the doors unlocked.

"Why's your car here?"

"I had to meet a guy before the memorial service. It's a long story that I don't feel like getting into." She stared over the roof, barely. She was the size of an action figure. "So I'm going home before another van full of psychos decides they'd appreciate my company." She opened the driver's side door.

I had a brief moment of panic that overrode the pride telling me not to ask the question. "Could I come too?"

"I unlocked all the doors, didn't I?"

Despite the snark, I got in. This car was way newer than what Mama drove. Almost everything was. Inside, it smelled like clean linen. Fuse pressed a button, and the engine came on, but I couldn't hear it over the blaring music. You know who.

It seemed to startle Fuse. She tapped the radio off. Lowered the windows and took us downtown, toward the highway, with wind roaring through the cabin too loudly for a conversation. Locating the switch, it took me a couple of times to actually roll my window up because my hands were shaking. I managed to complete the mission, cutting the mega-draft by half. "We should talk, don't you think?"

"I don't want to." With the controls in her door handle, she lowered my window again, and the wind slapped me like a hot hand.

Determined, I rolled the window back up. "They were outside my house, Fuse!"

Her head jerked, as if she were a bobblehead whose chin I plucked. "That's where they got you?"

"Right off the street."

"I—I'm sorry."

I almost said thank you, was close to being grateful. But, no. "You should be. Why'd you tell those lies about me on Twitter, you jerk?"

"I didn't lie. I just presented select facts."

"Select. Facts."

"You punched me in my face, Kya! What was that about?"

"I lost it a little, okay? You know what that night was like. But me punching you didn't draw a bunch of creepy lunatics to us, did it?"

"I—" She rolled her window up so we didn't have to yell at each other, even if we kind of wanted to. I noticed a tremor in her hand before she reestablished her grip on the wheel. "I didn't think it would get this bad, Kya. And what the heck did you say about me on that Tumblr?"

"Something that I didn't think would get this bad."

"Touché. People throw shade on the internet all the time, you know. It's not for real."

"Tonight felt very real."

She didn't argue. "I'm sorry, really. Okay?"

"Yeah, me too. Really."

We were on the highway by then, 264 East, toward Ocean Shore. Silent and scared.

I said, "Do you think they were serious about us, like, solving Paris's murder?"

"Name some things more serious than snatching humans into dark vans. There are a few. Not many."

The talking helped. And I meant my apology. Fuse was but a blip on my radar compared to the rough hands tossing me into the back of a van. Letting go of our pettiness felt like an important first step to normal after today's horrors.

Though there were still miles to go.

FUSE

We sailed into ParSec's old neighborhood at the residential-friendly twenty-five miles per hour. These homes—really a single large building, divided vertically, like sliced cake—seemed uncomfortable. Like everyone was being squeezed by everyone else. ParSec's old room had been stifling small whenever I visited. The one time she came to my house, she mentioned her room could fit in my dad's man cave "if she folded it right." I'd just smiled and shrugged because I hadn't known how to respond. Maybe I was a little embarrassed.

I knew the Cooke High population represented "several different tax brackets." Something Dad pointed out whenever I brought home less-than-stellar grades, or I didn't get excited by the phrase *Ivy League*. As if the range of classes—social, not academic—at school negatively impacted my performance and rational thinking.

ParSec came from one of those lower tax brackets. As did Kya, thus their close proximity.

How privileged would I be if I said any of this out loud?

"Over there," Kya said, motioning. We coasted to a stop. This was her street. Her home. The Dark Nation violated it. I didn't necessarily *like* Kya, but I felt her on this one. "You okay going in there?" I asked, with no plan if she said she wasn't.

"Mama's home. I'll be fine. As far as kidnappers go anyway." She popped her lock and opened the door, triggering the interior lights near where my ceiling met the windshield.

I flicked them off, still wanting to talk without feeling exposed. "Shameik Larsen. We'll want to get him involved."

"Involved?"

"Full disclosure: I created ParSec Nation. Those loonies back in the van aren't it. Kidnapping us was their first move, Kya. Do you want to know their second? I don't. Unless you have some genius plan I haven't considered, I imagine you're thinking the same thing I am."

She knew I wasn't wrong. "We're going to play."

"Until we have a better move, it's our only move. We put all that catty online beef aside for now. Plus . . ." This part, I didn't know how to really say. There was a silly hope to it that might sound dumb vocalized.

Kya, apparently, didn't have the same hang-up. "Adelaide Milton doesn't need our help."

And there it was. Somebody needed to remember what ParSec meant, and do something about it (in a way that wasn't Dark Nation crazy). "Do you know Shameik?"

"Enough to recognize him in the hall. What's he got to do with any of this?"

"Remember what Cartoon Shoes said about suspects being those closest to the victims?"

"Yeah."

"Shameik was ParSec's boyfriend."

There was more to it than that. But like back in the van, I was not forthcoming with the whole truth.

I hoped I never had to be.

PARIS/DJ PARSEC

(16 MONTHS BEFORE)

There were a lot of trash rappers and singers out there.

I didn't mean to be rude about it, and, you know, everyone's gotta start somewhere, but the reason I stopped letting people get on the mic at my parties was because almost everybody sucked. Sorry, not sorry.

Nothing killed a vibe like some fake deep MC talking a bunch of conspiracies about how the earth was really flat and wrong stuff about Egypt or whatever. Or some screechy, doing-too-much-with-her-notes vocalist woo-woo-wooing a song to three times its length. Lord help us all if any of those dumpster water artists wanted to battle each other, it was like watching two sloths race.

Lately when I spun, more people wanted on the mic. Like they were auditioning.

Word's out. Fuse and her internet magic meant most people knew I was on the come-up, and they wanted a piggyback ride to success. So the rule was hard: No rhymes when I spin. Period. As for the singers, I'd already heard the best Ocean Shore had to offer, and I wasn't settling for less. Keep it moving.

This party was in a neighborhood called Emerald Greens. Big houses on a golf course. Rich private-school kid with absentee parents hosting. Not a bad way to make coin on a Saturday night. Cooke High represented, a few of my more popular classmates snagging invites. Fuse was among them controlling the dance floor with boys and girls admiring.

Stepping up the mix, I faded in a new track from Omar Bless, a song called "Best Kept Secret" and a collective "Ohhhhhh" sounded throughout the house. More people crowded the dance floor, getting loose like I knew they would.

So I barely noticed the boy lurking all close to me while I worked.

"What's that do?" A bony, pointing finger hovered into my line of sight.

Sneering, I turned slowly, ready to give whoever violated the sanctity of my workplace the business. "Yo, dude, you need to step back."

But then his smile was the brightest thing in the dark room and his fresh haircut glistened in the colorful strobing party lights. Shameik Larsen. A CUTE-cute boy from my grade. Suddenly him invading my personal space wasn't such a big deal.

"If I turned that knob," he said, pointing to the channel 2 bass control, "would the party self-destruct or something?"

He reached like he was going to twist it. I smacked his hand. He snatched it back, grinning. Mostly, I was being playful, but there was a little bit of possessiveness that wanted my new equipment to remain untouched by all but me. I'd done a couple of production gigs thanks to the buzz off "Calm Down, Turn Up!" The money was enough to update my gear. No more mismatched turntables with a taped-together mixer. These days I was rocking with a Pioneer Rekordbox and a basic laptop. Not top-of-the-line, but functional, and miles ahead of what I was used to. He didn't need to know all that, though. So I said, "I'm not telling you trade secrets."

"Respect. I get it. You been killing all night."

"Thank you." Did he remember me from school? At all?

I cued Remy Ma and Fat Joe's "All the Way Up" remix, faded it in, and the crowd grooved approvingly. My guest nodded to the beat, then said, "What instrumentals you got?"

Ohhhhhh gawd. "Nobody raps when I spin."

"That works, because I ain't a rapper. I'm a poet."

"What you want a beat for, then?"

"Because I like reciting poems to music."

"Isn't that—?"

"Nope. Not rap. Not the way I do it."

"What way is that?"

"You should let me show you." He leaned toward my board again, bypassing the knobs he wasn't really curious about, and grabbed the mic that I kept on hand for ad-libbing when the party was really going. He bounced it in his palm, testing the weight. Really, testing *me*. "Well?"

That smile. That smell. That body. "What instrumental you want?"

"You know Common?"

I almost punched him in the chest, insulting me like that. "Of course."

"You got the intro to his *Be* album?"

"I can get it." The beauty of Wi-Fi. No music was out of reach.

I found it easily and faded "All the Way Up" into a jazzy old-school track: "Rebirth of Slick (Cool Like Dat)" by a group called Digable Planets, letting the crowd get used to the change of pace instead of abruptly interrupting the party and throwing dude to the wolves. I could tell from the confused looks most didn't know this song. I hadn't known it until Fuse brought me the vinyl for another video in our series. I caught her eye, she nodded, then started swaying with the nearest boy. As they'd done all night, the crowd followed her lead, and before long they were into the strumming bass guitar. As the hook neared its in end, I told the poet, "You're up, and you better be fire."

"Flames all day." He gripped the mic confidently by its housing, didn't smother the head the way a lot of amateurs do because they think it looks cool, when it actually muffles their voice. Kya would've appreciated that.

Suddenly there was a pit in my stomach. I hadn't seen Kya in a while except for school. Hadn't even thought of her much until now. Been busy. Distracted. So much happening.

Shameik stepped from behind my decks, put himself on full display, distracting me from Kya again. I faded in the beat he asked for.

"Yo," he said, booming through the speakers, as smooth as the horns on the track. "It's Shameik, but y'all knew that already."

His audience murmured positive confirmation. "Shameik!" some chick yelled from the crowd. I'm not sure he heard her, but I felt a sharp, jealous pang.

"I wanna talk about something that's been on my mind a lot these days," he said, easy, conversational, even though I could tell he was already performing.

"I saw this kid the other day / running, at play / and I got
shook when his shadow was as long as a man's / and his
hands weren't in plain sight / and a black-and-white patrol
car made a hard right / just to pass him, for once / should've
been good news . . . / I went inside to catch them easy
breaths / because the situation didn't go left / and yet . . ."

He went on like that, a blistering two-minute poem about police violence, and black fear, and mamas crying when their angelic sons became demons in the eyes of law enforcement. A few of the white kids got salty scowls and stomped away to other parts of the house, but whatever. His words outlasted them. And the beat; I forgot what the heck I was getting paid to do. Nothing was cued. I didn't run the instrumental back. I became a part of his audience too.

He finished his work a cappella. His speed, and cadence, and message ramping up to a hard-hitting crescendo, ending on a gut-punch line.

"That kid was me / what I might-a could-a be / if they had seen me for me, instead . . . of . . . pow!"

Silence, a few heartbeats' worth. Then thunderous clapping that he bowed to dramatically, before handing me my microphone. "Hot enough for you?"

Boy! If only you knew.

"Play something!" That was Fuse, reminding me of my actual function. I quickly cued some Cardi B and got the party going again. Then I returned to the most interesting thing in the room.

Shameik, tall, with wide shoulders and a tapered waist, looking like the letter *V*, leaned into my laptop, skimming titles of upcoming tracks. He pointed at something way down the playlist. "Why don't you play that next?"

"Ummmm, because I'm not. Thank you. I know what I'm doing here."

"Chill. I wasn't trying to tell you what to do. I'm trying to learn. Like, why do you put the list together like that? What's the madness to your method?"

"Her method is a trade secret," Fuse said, wedging her way behind the turntables and making my personal space way too crowded.

"Already told him that," I said, kind of wanting Fuse to leave.

She flashed me a sly look that I didn't like, then gave Shameik a once-over. "I know you," she said. "Seaside Poets, at school."

His head bounced. "Our name rings out."

Her sly look found me again, and I got a bad feeling. She said, "Hey, ParSec and me going to Waffle House after this. Want to come?"

He grinned. "Of course. Who don't like waffles?"

Fuse gave a curt nod, then leaned into me, whispered, "You can thank me later."

KYA

Sometimes a weekend could wipe the slate clean, turning Cooke High into a giant Etch A Sketch. Saturday grabbed one side, Sunday the other, and a mighty shake started Monday fresh. Traversing the halls, I could feel the school moving on from Paris. I thumb-typed another question in my phone.

Is it ever appropriate to think of your dead friends and not feel hurt?

There were no more grief counselors set up in the hall. Wardrobes reverted back to pre-Paris-memorial styles. No one craved forever sadness, some of us just got cursed with it. And new nightmares of white-masked monsters tossing me into vans that were really bottomless pits didn't help the recovery. Every time I closed my eyes that bag was back on my head, and eight showers later I still felt the tacky adhesive from the tape around my wrists.

Shoulder-deep in my locker, I considered my first order of business. My stomach fluttered over my after-school mission. I still had a whole day to get through. Biology and English and Precalc. I needed to get my mind right.

Emerging from my locker, I had that horror movie moment of shutting the door and finding a person materialized behind it. Florian. I looked down on Cooke High's tiny Tumblr maven in pink-framed glasses she probably didn't need. Tight, bright yellow top. Fresh denim with slashes at the knee. Blue-on-white Air Jordans and her nails sparkly with dope designs. So many colors, she looked like a bag of candy.

She beamed at me. Her new long-lost buddy. "We got *so many hits* this weekend. Your claims of Fuse and DJ ParSec having issues in the days prior, plus those memorial service pics you snapped, combined with images I pulled of Fuse getting tossed from the venue. So scandalous. I felt like TMZ." Florian turned her phone to show me likes and shares I didn't care about. "Look at that traffic. People are *crucifying* Fuse."

That landed like a strong kick. Not that I wasn't provoked, and I didn't feel guilty exactly. The news just didn't bring me the joy it would've three days ago.

I shut my locker, skirted around Florian, and mumbled, "Glad it worked out."

She stayed with me, orbiting. I had my own gravity today. "What else you got?"

"Nothing. There's nothing else to have."

"Seriously? No word on why Fuse is in protective custody all of a sudden?"

"You mean ISS. Why are you using cop talk?"

"So you do know something."

I'd been texting with Fuse constantly since our joint kidnapping. She explained how her dad micromanaged her school day. Class, isolated lunch, home. Thus the need for me to be her eyes and ears this afternoon. "I don't know any more than you."

"More pictures would be a nice boost for the site, Kya. Maybe of the coffin."

I stopped like I'd smacked into an invisible wall. "Where's your next class?"

Florian, oblivious, motioned back the way we'd come. "East wing."

I spun on my heels and reversed course toward the west wing. Out of the way but better than spending any more time with Florian.

"Wow. I can see you're not a Monday person. Later, then." She backed into the crowd, disappearing among our churning classmates, and I continued on to where I needed to be. Class, then lunch, then, according to Fuse, an after-school meeting to "get my poetry on."

■ ■

Seaside Poets met in Mr. Martin's Earth Science classroom. A strange place for engaging in poetry; the Layers of the Earth poster didn't seem all that inspirational to me. Maybe a more creative mind could find the linguistic beauty between the mantle and the crust. I lingered near the door. Mr. Martin, who had white earbuds screwed in while hunched over papers, didn't look up from his grading when I entered.

Shameik was front and center, sliding desks forward from their normal daytime placement. He spotted me and didn't offer much of a greeting.

When Fuse asked me if I knew him, I didn't lie, though I downplayed my awareness. Shameik was one of *those* boys. Attractive and tallish, he had most girls by five inches, though I had him by two. His haircut was always sharp, and angular at his temples. His eyes brown and his skin dark and smooth. He dressed well, spoke well, had all the traits that would make most girls at least think about whatever came out of his mouth.

Shameik was the kind of boy Paris once thought neither of us would ever have a chance with. I guess notoriety changed her mind.

"You looking for somebody?" he asked, but not in a friendly or helpful way.

"I was hoping I could have a word with you."

More people entered the room chatty and upbeat until they recognized me, then their voices flattened under the tension. I was seriously questioning Fuse's strategy here.

The latest Seaside Poet arrivals perched in random desks. Whether I'd be staying was still up in the air, so I didn't eye any particular spot.

Shameik saved me the trouble. He motioned to the middle desk among the five he'd arranged. "Have a seat."

I felt the stares as I made my way to the designated chair. Everyone else remained behind me, chatting about their own stuff, so being this close to Shameik felt personal, like having a conversation at a table in a crowded restaurant. Our space was our space.

Before I came here, Fuse had tried coaching me on things I should say in a volley of last-minute texts. Ways to make him trust me.

FUSE

Don't start out talking ParSec. Ask him about
Seaside Poets, slowly work your way to
where he was the night we found her. Should
be easy enough to check for lies.

FUSE

If he gets suspicious about why you're there,
say you knew the club meant a lot to her.

FUSE

It didn't. Not really but he liked to think it did.
They were funny like that.

ME

What do you mean "funny"?

FUSE

Face-to-face for that. Too deep to text.

Despite her tips, I felt clumsy at this spy game. Exposed. Especially when he said, "You want to talk about Paris."

"Ummmm." This was not the plan.

He turned away, uncapped a dry-erase marker from the tray at the base of Mr. Martin's whiteboard, and began writing numbers in a column.

More people spilled into the room. I'd heard Seaside Poets was a popular club, but I didn't know it was this popular. There were at least fifteen people present, and more coming.

"How'd you hear?" Shameik asked, before gazing past me and doing the pointing-and-mouthing-numbers thing people do when they're getting a head count but also want to look cool while getting a head count. He nodded, satisfied, then waited for his answer.

"Hear what?" I was supposed to be interrogating *him*.

"I thought you and Paris weren't really that cool anymore . . ." He made a dismissive waving gesture. "Still, there you were, at that memorial service. I saw pictures on the Gram. So now I don't know what to think. Sure didn't expect you to want to do any heavy lifting."

That was the problem when you lost your App Nerd Friends and your Music Superstar Friend in the same year. Nothing in between made sense. What did *heavy lifting* mean?

Panicking, needing to regain control of this thing, I leaned on Fuse's advice. Made it about the club. "I wanted to talk about Seaside Poets. It meant a lot to Paris."

His head tilted, and sun hit his brown eyes in a way that reminded me of pretty autumn leaves and summer heat at the same time. Did he practice that look?

"You're here"—he squinted, scrutinizing—"to talk about poetry?"

"Yes." Stick to the plan.

He nodded, faced the whiteboard, and added my name next to the number one.

"Fine," he said, loud. "Let's talk poetry. You first." Then, to the room, "Everyone, we got an initiation today, a new voice among us. Come closer and let's hear what New Girl Kya got to say."

A small fire erupted under my skin, roasting my neck, cheeks, and forehead as faces I only knew from class, the hall, and the cafeteria became a zombie horde, closing in around me, hungry.

Escaping the desk I occupied, I rushed close to Shameik, forcing my tone decisive instead of pleading when I said, "No. I don't know any poetry."

"Go off top, then. Freestyle. You'll get good feedback from this group. They'll make your skin thick."

"I don't want thick skin. I don't want feedback." I'd gotten plenty of both when I was much younger and wasn't anxious for more. Yet, my audience waited. Nearly twenty sets of staring, expectant eyes. I'd rather be back in that van with the Dark Nation.

"Well?" Shameik said.

Flashbacks to a different life—a different Kya—came to mind. Comfort and discomfort at once, adrenaline spikes, stepping onstage, the moment just before you open your mouth, and—

Shameik laughed, a deep belly buster. A few others followed suit—Seaside Poets who knew this wasn't the procedure, I guessed—but mostly folks looked confused. A freshman girl raised her hand and spoke without being called on. "Is this not the meeting about the concert?"

"Concert?" I said, nervous all over again.

Shameik, mischievous, said, "SP meeting's been preempted this week. We're using the space to plan a ParSec concert."

He erased my name, then added different words next to the number one. Now it said, "Divide into teams."

Next to the number two he wrote: "Each team drafts a to-do list." And so on.

Bristling, I wrapped my mind around the impossibility of a concert by a dead musician. Unless you were talking one of those hologram things like they did for Tupac that time.

Shameik explained further, his playful demeanor darkening. "That memorial service you went to was garbage. None of her fans were allowed in. None of her *friends*. Those of us who loved her for real are going to do something for real. A memorial concert. I was even able to convince Paris's manager to assist."

"Paula Klein? Why would she want anything to do with this?"

Her heavenly white suit flared in my memory, how proud she'd seemed over that soulless service. If she'd wanted to be involved with Paris's friends and fans, why not open her memorial to the public when she had the chance? Seemed odd.

"Penance, maybe," said Shameik, "or she was worried about her dough. Probably the latter. I contacted her, told her how much of a bad look her event was, and how it could really be bad for her business if the ParSec Nation got it in their head that she wasn't interested in how the fans wanted to honor Paris. I think she saw the sense in my argument. I'm charming like that."

Was *charming* the right word here? *Arrogant?* That felt better.

Shameik said, "You may not be much with the poetry but think you can help with this? I promise we won't put you on front street for anything. You can run concessions or something."

Visions of me selling Starbursts in a half-packed school auditorium while our mediocre marching band did a rendition of "Calm Down, Turn Up!" made me shudder. But even that had to be better than what Paula Klein had done.

Shameik, putting something like this together on his own, was admirable. If such grand gestures were his thing, I got why Paris liked him.

The vibe I got from Fuse suggested maybe there was more to it than affection. That Shameik shouldn't be trusted. She'd yet to tell me why, but no matter what, we needed to know where he was on the night of. Only one way to do that.

"Sign me up."

FUSE

School felt eternal *before* Dad signed me up for solitary confinement. Ever since he made arrangements for me to be isolated whenever I wasn't in class to keep me away from "deplorables," it had become something like psychological warfare. WHY? I wasn't like the other troublemakers in there. I didn't steal any exams. I didn't smack anyone with half of a ham sandwich in the lunch line. Yet, I was being tortured in Cooke High's version of a sensory deprivation chamber. I mean, I could still hear, see, smell, taste, and touch . . . just not with my phone.

All that to say, now that I had my car keys and a moment to myself after a long day in the hole, I wasn't rushing back to the House of Tension and Malcontent.

Also, since witnessing firsthand what ParSec Nation (Dark) had become, there was newly discovered comfort in the over bright halls of Cooke High. Even if mostly deserted.

The school secretary and Principal Corgis sorted paperwork on the other side of the main office windows; I skirted by them quickly, in case Corgis's soul was still bound to Dad's intimidation magic. Didn't need him infringing on this rare bit of school-day freedom.

In the auditorium, musical theater kids goofed around, harmonizing old songs and enjoying their last couple of weeks together before summer. Hovering near the doorway a moment, I enjoyed the tunes. They wrapped up a song I didn't recognize, though it sounded great, then started a poppy rendition of "Started From the Bottom," Drake's hit that I remembered from the days Dad enjoyed tunes too.

When I was little, my dad gave life a soundtrack. From his old-school mix CDs, with Sharpie titles like "Smoove Drive" and "Chocolate City '09," I'd kick my legs to while strapped into my kiddie car seat. Then came "Clean Rap" iPod playlists he fed through a snaking AUX cable into the old car's stereo system, where only half the speakers worked, so we'd rhyme along together to make up the difference. He's the reason I have an ear. Like, I knew ParSec was special before "Calm Down, Turn Up!" when she was posting beats, not yet full songs, for the world to hear, because my whole childhood was filled with special music he supplied.

These days when Dad and I rode together, it was so different. The car was better, the sound system insane, but wasted. Dad only listened to business audiobooks and current-events podcasts. I tried playing some of ParSec's stuff for him last year, when things really started taking off. His response, "Music sure isn't what it used to be."

Of course not! ParSec was the future.

I leaned against the auditorium door, listening with my eyes closed, and dozed off to a doubling of sound. Music from then, and the singing from now, weaved into some nonsensical remix that sounded amazing, if only in my dreams. When someone touched my shoulder, I shrieked awake.

"Whoa!" A girl not wearing a mask recoiled.

Those melodic voices beyond the doorway ceased abruptly. Someone shouted, "Everything all right out there?"

Freaked beyond reason, I went for the exit, and the person who'd scared the crap out of me chased. "Fuse, wait up!"

Spinning, pressing my lower back to the door's push bar, I shoved my way into the late spring heat while tracking this girl, prepared to claw her eyes if needed.

Whatever she saw froze her. She raised her hands defensively. "Hey, be cool. I'm Florian." Only when the door began its backward swing did Florian resume her chase, letting herself outside. "I run the ParSec Love Tumblr."

"So?" The area was canopy-shaded, with a bench no one ever used. Until then. I flopped, and Florian seemed to consider if she should sit too.

"I want to tell your story." She remained standing. It was the right decision.

"Like the one you told Friday?" I'd read the post her and Kya collaborated on, plus the updates after the memorial service. Character assassination of the highest order.

"That's one side of it," Florian said. "I want yours."

"You said I stole from Paris. That's a flat-out lie. I never took one cent."

"I said 'allegedly.'"

"Where do you even get this stuff? What about that nonsense with ParSec's bodyguards having orders to break my fingers if I tried to get near her? She didn't have bodyguards! If she did, then maybe—"

Too close to snapping, I stared upward, asked angels to spare this girl's life. This was stupid. Why was I even talking to this gossipmonger anyway?

She said, "I'm only reporting things as I hear them."

Oh. Okay. That explained ABSOLUTELY NOTHING!

If Florian wasn't a liar herself, then most of her sources were. Kya told me about the parts she contributed to the post. Me being at the warehouse, finding Paris at the same time. Our fight in the police station. Basically, what actually happened. All that other stuff . . .

My phone buzzed. Likely Dad making sure I'd gotten home to my cell safely. Florian kept pleading her case while I glanced at the incoming message. Not Dad.

WINSTON BELL

I'm sorry about what happened to you at the service, but you shouldn't have used me like that.

WINSTON BELL

If you'd been straight with me, we could've worked something out. Maybe made it so you could stay.

WINSTON BELL

You still owe me a real conversation, you know.

My eyes flicked between the messages and Florian's motor mouth. Were these two a tag team?

Florian leaned in as if to read my texts. "Who's that?"

"Yoooo. You are not for real right now." I walked away, secretly daring her to follow. She didn't.

Alone again, I watched the little flashing dots dance on the screen, Winston typing another message. I began tapping out my

"LEAVE ME ALONE, OLD MAN" response, when his next message popped.

WINSTON BELL
If you're ignoring me, I get it. I'm not going to harass you. However, I have been doing some digging into this, and some commentary from you and/or Kya Caine would be nice before I go to print. Your call, though.

One last message came through, a screen capture. Of a poll.

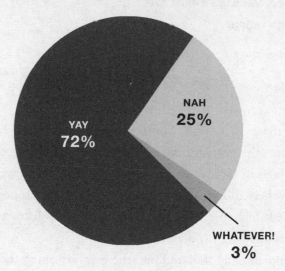

Are #SuperGroupie and #MadScientist a dope murder team or nah?

YAY
72%

NAH
25%

WHATEVER!
3%

Sprinting, I passed Florian, who *seemed to be RECORDING ME, WHAT!?!* I raced up the corridor, swung a wide left, my feet clopping loudly on the way to the Earth Science room, before skidding to a stop just outside the door. The Seaside Poets meeting was still in progress, and I didn't know if me pulling Kya out in front of everyone would mess up whatever plan we had to interrogate Shameik. I needed to talk to her. Immediately.

Pull the fire alarm, a loud and irrational voice screamed in my skull. Followed by one more sensible: *Or you could text her. You could've always texted her.*

Right.

ME

K, get to the gym right now.

KYA

5 mins. Meeting's almost over.
What's wrong?

ME

Everything.

To the gym I went. Sports were done for the year, but the hardcore athletes still managed to find something to sweat over. Some boys in tank tops lifted heavy things by the weight room, while others did push-ups in a row, or jumped rope really fast. I settled into the bleachers, let the view distract me from nervous-gnawing my own fingernails off.

Kya eventually skittered into the gym, scanning the place with frantic, jerky neck gestures, as if checking for snipers. I waved her over. "Why do *you* look so nervous? Did something happen in Seaside Poets?"

"Yes, something did happen, but that's not it. This is just not my favorite wing of the school. A lot of failed chin-ups freshman year. What's up with you? Why the red alert?"

"We have a major problem. Before I get into that, a question."

"Okay."

"On a scale of one to ten, how comfortable are you lying to a reporter if it will save our butts?"

KYA

Back in the passenger's seat of Fuse's cramped car, we navigated afternoon traffic into the next town over. When I last rode with her, we'd survived the Dark Nation, so danger was a relative thing. I'd thought she was a perfectly fine driver then. I was mistaken.

"You're pretty close to that truck," I said. In case she didn't notice.

"I've got plenty of room."

The truck slowed, its lights flaring red, and she jammed her brake, locking my seat belt, then wrenched the steering wheel left, jerking us into the next lane, to the dismay of the Mercedes we cut off. Luxury car horns were very loud.

Somehow we didn't die getting off the highway—to more angry horn play—in downtown Norfolk. The slower city pace didn't improve Fuse's driving, as she maintained something way too close to highway speed, finding every traffic gap and whipping her tiny car into it. Half of me wanted the ride over, but the other half recognized where we were going and quivered.

We were on the same streets from Saturday, traveling in reverse to the same general section of Norfolk where the Dark Nation had dropped us off. I simultaneously could not wait to reach our destination—my knees! God this car was small!—and dreaded being near anywhere I'd been with those masked freaks. Given what Fuse said about this reporter guy Winston, convincing him to stay away from this story—or at the very least exclude us from it—was a necessary evil to keep the Dark Nation off our backs. The warning about exposing them to any extra attention had been clear. A feature article in *MIXX* seemed like *a lot* of extra attention.

Fuse coasted to a curb near the coffee shop where we were meeting Winston. I left her vehicle, started strolling toward the spot. Fuse rushed next to me, linked her elbow in mine, and angled us into the comic book shop that was on the way. The door chime tinkled, and a smiley guy with a full hipster beard greeted us. "Hey, anything I can help you find?"

Fuse greeted his wide smile with a tight one. "We're fine. Just browsing."

We continued into a back corner.

"What are we doing?" I ogled the prices for the intricate action figures, statues, and busts in a locked display case behind her. Two hundred dollars for a Green Lantern Power Battery replica. Five hundred for a full-sized Infinity Gauntlet. Phillip, Simon, and Jim would have, undoubtedly, considered these reasonable prices for such iconic items. My lingering sadness over the missing people in my life notched up a degree.

Fuse said, "I was hoping to talk this over in the car, but you kept distracting me with you whining about collisions and such. We gotta be careful with this dude."

"Already told you I don't feel super comfortable lying about stuff. I twitch." Not the total truth, but my days of plastering on a fake smile greased with fake enthusiasm were long gone.

"That's fine. Just remember this, when we sit down, first thing out of your mouth is 'All of this is off the record.' Whatever he has, we don't want to give him too much more, and we don't want to give him explicit permission to publish any of it. Guys like him are good at getting you all chatty and comfortable. I told ParSec the same thing. She was so caught up with him being from *MIXX*, she didn't listen. Her thinking was if anyone was going to tell all her business, why not one of the hottest music magazines on the planet." Fuse puffed herself up, bobbed her head side to side, and spoke in a gruff manner. *"'Good enough for OGs like Timbaland and Missy, good enough for me.'"*

It was a flawless Paris impression. I clamped a hand over my mouth, cramming back the laugh. So I only cracked up half-loud, and Fuse did too.

Peeking over the shelving, the clerk gave us the "Shoplifters Beware" glare, and I did the thing Mama always taught me. *Buy something, even if it's small. Show them we ain't all thieves.*

Searching the alphabetized display rack, I found the latest issue of Ms. Marvel and walked it to the counter. Relieved, the clerk rang me up, and I paid with the credit card Mama didn't know I had. Fuse was at my hip, eyeing the transaction. When my merchandise was bagged up, and we stepped back outside, she said, "That was an Amex Gold Card."

"It was."

"Why do you have an Amex Gold Card?"

I felt a pang in my chest. "Remind me to tell you about some smart guys I used to hang around. This first, though."

■ ■

Café Clementine was crowded. There were a lot of students in Old Dominion University apparel, either hunched over laptops or open books, studying, or chatting it up with friends. A boisterous party at the back pulled together several tables, and a bouquet of birthday balloons hovered above the midpoint, bopping along as folks talked loudly, laughed loudly, and made the entire place part of the celebration. No one seemed like an obvious creeper, and there were no white masks hovering in darkened corners. As far as I was concerned, this meeting was off to a decent start.

Winston was easily recognizable. The only black man in the place, with gold-framed glasses and long salt-and-pepper dreadlocks falling down his back and shoulders, he pecked away on his MacBook, the Apple logo obscured by colorful band decals. He waved us over.

"Remember what we talked about," Fuse said through unmoving lips, like a ventriloquist.

He'd saved two seats for us, standing as we approached, his hand extended. "Ladies."

I shook and grabbed the seat closest to the window. Fuse greeted him, ignoring his handshake, and took the other chair.

"Order you something?" Winston asked, sitting down.

The chalkboard menu mounted behind the counter listed some tasty-sounding drinks. "A honey vanilla latte, may—"

Fuse cut me off, full-on death stare. "Naw. We're good. And we're off the record. All of this. How do you know about that poll you screenshot?"

Winston said, "Right to it, then. I'm ParSec Nation too."

I clutched the edge of the table, tried to remember if anyone from the van smelled strongly of store-bought musk.

"Since when?" Fuse's tone sharpened.

Winston frowned, confused. "Since I started my original interviews with Paris. Since *you* told me about the enthusiastic fandom that developed around DJ ParSec's songs. There's a sign-up right on her website. ParSec Nation Newsletter." He tapped keys and spun the MacBook so we could see a "Join the Nation" page on Paris's site.

I leaned in. "So if you sign up for a . . . *newsletter*? You get to see them talk about us." Why were those creeps in the van so concerned with secrecy if it was that easy?

Winston spun the computer back, typing new things, and explaining. "No. Joining ParSec Nation is sort of like hearing Wonderland exists. The Dark Nation is kicking it with the Mad Hatter, if you feel me. I'd heard some rumors about a branch of this fandom that's all about wildin' in the name of DJ ParSec's music. Got a tech-savvy friend to get me access to a site on the dark web. Was just planning to use it as a sidebar on my primary story. Then she died, and it sort of *became* the story when I saw that poll."

"That's all you got? The poll? You don't know too much, then." Fuse pressed back in her chair, arms crossed, scrutinizing. "I did say we're off the record?"

"You did. You still owe me a good, on-the-record conversation. Deal's a deal."

"Or you'll publish whatever it is you have?"

"I'd rather not go that route. But a journalist gotta eat, and my ParSec story needs an ending, since we know she's not around for a continuation, I'm sorry to say." He snapped the MacBook closed and looked between us, a silent plea. "We can help each other here."

"How?" I wasn't interested in fending him off the way Fuse was. I'd be careful, yes. I also thought some adult help was a good thing. Better than the two of us against a faceless mob of crazy superfans.

"I'll explain. Tell me this, first . . . are you two trying to figure out who killed Paris Secord on your own. Real-life Veronica Mars? Marses? Whatever the plural is."

Fuse said, "We have strong motivation to find clues."

Winston nodded. "Fair enough. Here's where I come in. I think the story becomes about injustice. The police work on this thing, shoddy at best." He reopened his MacBook, his eyes sweeping back and forth as he read, the screen's ghostly reflection haunting the lenses of his glasses. "I know they brought you two in on the night of. Then, over the course of about three days, they questioned anyone associated with her at the time of her death, that's her grandmother, Paula Klein, a Shameik Larsen"—Fuse stiffened, but Winston kept going—"me, and they made phone calls to some of the regional artists she worked with, though I'm unclear if those leads went anywhere."

"I'm sorry"—I couldn't just sit back clueless—"I don't understand what you want us to do."

"Help me hold the authorities' feet to the fire on this, Kya. It can't be another Tupac, or Biggie, or Big L, or Jam Master Jay, or— You two don't know who I'm talking about, do you?"

"Biggie and Pac, sure." The others, no. Maybe that was his point.

"I bet whoever did this was counting on the exact thing that happened with everyone I named. The police becoming apathetic, the public losing interest. What Biggie, and Pac, and . . . all the rest didn't have was the technology of your generation. The savvy fandoms. Find out what you can about the night Paris died. I'll do the same, we share our information. Worst-case scenario, we get a story that puts more visibility on the killing.

Best case, we do the police's job for them and crack this thing wide open."

"So you want to use us too?" said Fuse.

"You always want to make me the bad guy. I didn't mess up your friendship with her. We both know that."

Fuse sneered, and I could see the clapback bulging up her throat. I said, "The Dark Nation members we've met are insane. You don't know what they did to us this weekend."

He slid his phone forward, the voice memo app cued up. "Care to talk about it on the record?"

"If we do it," said Fuse, "you hold off on blowing up the Dark Nation? Kya's right, they don't play, and you spilling the tea on them is only going to cause problems for us."

Winston made a dramatic swiping gesture across his chest, one way, then the other. "Cross my heart. This story will be at its best with your cooperation. I get that. I need you two on a clock, though. No dillydallying. That's not just for me. The trail is already cold and getting colder. I mean, do you have any ideas, at all, who might've done it?"

Fuse jabbed a thumb at me, then herself. "Ruling us out, right?"

"The police already have. I don't see why I shouldn't. Admittedly, you two are in the best position to identify someone who might've had it in for her."

Reluctantly, with a loud, huffing sigh, Fuse said, "Still off the record, we're looking at her ex, Shameik."

"Ex?" I said. "I thought they were dating. Like, current."

Winston's head bobbed my way, then to Fuse. "She doesn't know?"

"Know what?" To Fuse. "Know what?"

Winston said, "Lord, y'all need to communicate better than that if you're going to be a team." He stood, grabbing his empty cup. "I'm getting a refill while you two work that out."

He strolled away, leaving us, and I said again, "Know? What?"

Fuse wouldn't look me in the eye. "Shameik and Paris. They broke up. And she maybe, kinda blamed me."

PARIS/DJ PARSEC

(14 MONTHS BEFORE)

"This," Fuse said, "is all my fault. Yuck. Should've never invited you for waffles."

"You're a hater," Shameik said, and kissed my neck again. It tickled, but I didn't giggle, because I liked acting as if those kisses didn't affect me so he'd keep trying.

We were in Fuse's room, and I was at her desk, clicking through all the DJ ParSec accounts she'd set up. Seeing how ParSec Nation was living life. Shameik hunched over me, hands on my shoulders, mouth nuzzled by my ear.

"We're supposed to be working." Fuse tried for that stern Mama Bear tone of hers when she wanted things her way. "You could've at least brought a friend if we were going full PDA today."

I said, "You don't like none of his friends. Picky tail."

"I have standards. A boy who puts raw onions on his turkey sandwich every day is not up to them."

Shameik scoffed. "Leave my mans alone. I talked to him about how the appropriate time for raw onions is really never."

"You, sir, are truly making the world a better place with the power of your words."

"Speaking of," Shameik said, his voice high and hopeful. I knew him well enough now to spot his not-so-subtle hints. My stomach sank a little.

Fuse's eyebrows leapt up. "Speaking of what?"

Shameik released my shoulders and turned to her, his hands animated, pleading his case. "I'm trying to get us to do a track together."

Fuse tossed her tablet onto the pastel pillow mountain accumulated at the head of her huge king-sized bed, popped to her feet. "That's a great idea."

I kept clicking through internet tabs. Silent.

Fuse said, "Am I missing something? It really does seem like a good idea. Shameik's nice with the wordplay." To him, she asked, "You got any songs ready?"

He said, "Naw. Not songs, exactly. A bunch of spoken word that would just be fire over her beats. I mean, everybody do songs, right? We could set off something different."

And that was the problem.

The different thing I wanted to set off was mine. Not his. My sound. My tempo. My composition. If he was talking about messing around, doing it for fun, sure, why not? We'd see what we got. Heck, I'd done tracks with Lil' Redu . . . I was only so discerning.

But whenever he brought it up, it was always some grand plan. DJ ParSec was all of sudden DJ ParSec and Shameik. He had ideas for YouTube videos and—

"Maybe you could help me get my online following up, Fuse. I already got the hashtag. #MeikFreaks!"

"Um." I felt Fuse eyeing me for a bailout. Nope, homie, you went down this path with him.

If I focused right, Shameik's ghostly reflection was visible in the MacBook screen. I saw his shoulders slump. "You too, Fuse? How come y'all ain't feeling me on this?"

Fuse said, "I'm not saying I ain't feeling it. I just need to think about it. These plans don't come together instantly."

His reflection tensed in that springy way of his, the posture before he recites a new poem. He was ready to argue, to plead his case. I changed the subject. "Fuse, you wanted to listen to some new tracks for the next set of videos?"

"Yes. Yes, I do." She sounded as grateful as a rescued hostage.

Shameik heavy sighed. Paced to her window, mumbling something I didn't even care to try to decipher. Fuse joined me at the computer, but before we got into it, there was a single knock on her door. Mr. Fallon barged in. "Fatima, I— Oh, you've got guests."

"Hey, Dad," Fuse didn't even look at him, indifferent.

"Mr. Fallon." I couldn't take my eyes off him. Every time I saw her father it felt like I was seeing something exotic—a safari lion.

He pointed at me. "Paris, correct?"

"Yes, sir."

"I don't know you, young man."

Shameik deactivated his pouty mode quick, fast, and in a hurry. He shuffled toward Mr. Fallon with his hand extended. "Shameik Larsen, sir. I go to school with Fuse—I mean, Fatima."

Mr. Fallon shook Shameik's hand and gave us all a look like he was searching for evidence. "You all *are* doing homework."

I expected a lie. Was totally prepared to back Fuse up. But, I don't know, she did this super unpredictable thing and told the truth. "Naw. We're listening to some of Paris's new music for the YouTube channel."

"It wasn't a request, Fatima. You can play mogul when school-work's finished."

Fuse, annoyed, huffed something that might've gotten me the added chore of scrubbing the toilet, or cleaning the baseboards if I ever did that in front of Grandma. "Okay, Dad. We will. Cross my heart."

Shameik and I froze like scared squirrels. How far was this going to go?

But Mr. Fallon simply backed toward the hall. "Leave this door open. I expect to hear some equations, Spanish conjugations, reciting of the periodic table, or something other than music."

"Dad!"

"Or you can take your friends home. No more back talk. Test me."

I knew Fuse and knew she wanted to. I stepped in. "We will, Mr. Fallon. Thank you for helping us get back on track."

"See," he said. "She gets it. I'll have Suzanne make sandwiches."

And he was gone. It was strange how Fuse's pops was cool having so many people over here, even with one of them being a boy. Grandma won't let boys sit on our porch. Like, we literally had to talk in the street. Mr. Fallon was all like, whatever. I didn't know this kind of privacy was a real thing.

"He's so aggravating," Fuse said, louder than what felt safe. Part of me wanted to smack her in the back of the head. I'd give up a limb to know even a little bit about my dad, let alone have a rich, kind-of-cool dad who got a maid to make sandwiches and let you have boys in your room.

Though the boy thing wasn't all that fun right now. With Mr. Fallon gone, Shameik resumed his pouting by the window. He was so stuck on this spoken-word collaboration thing. Me, I liked the kissing more.

I hoped he did too.

Sometimes I wasn't sure.

FUSE

"I was going to tell you."

"When?"

"Eventually. I swear."

"You"—Kya hugged herself, scandalized—"and Shameik?"

"No!" It was overly loud. Some college students seemed frightened. Leaning in, I whispered, "I can't stand him."

Did that sound convincing?

"And she was wrong. It wasn't what she thought it was, not even close." It was painful even thinking about it. "I would never do the things she accused me of."

"Why did she accuse you of anything, though? What was confusing? They broke up for a reason, why would she think the reason was you, Fuse?"

"Right. Look for the logic from the most irrational person either of us knew when she got mad. Am I wrong?"

She considered it. "Okay. Point taken."

"They broke up. He'd been trying to get back. She wasn't trying to hear it. In a lot of ways, Shameik and I were in the same sinking boat. Only he's the one who put us there."

At least that's the way I preferred to remember it.

Winston returned, so I shut this particular conversation down. None of his beeswax. He had three drinks. Kya got her Honey Vanilla Latte. I got a plain black coffee—jerk.

He took his chair, eyebrows raised. "Well? Off the record don't mean we can't talk. Are you going to tell me what went down with the Dark Nation? I need to know how to frame things if and when you give me the green light."

I still felt hesitant. Reporters, man.

Kya seemed ready to burst, and after a sip of honey vanilla whatever—I could smell the sugar in that thing—she went full motormouth. "The other night I was walking home . . ."

She gave him everything, and I sat back, arms crossed, eyes on Winston. He looked like someone told him Christmas Eve got rescheduled to today, and it came with a bulging bag of Halloween candy. He barely looked up from his Mac screen, his fingers dancing to capture whatever he was noting from Kya's story. The typing broken up by the occasional "That's insane" or "Way more extreme than I imagined."

Kya's conclusion was me dropping her off. Then Winston pinned me with his gaze. "So they grabbed you first?"

"Yep. Right after I got booted from the memorial service."

His head tilted. "You were with them for a few hours before they got Kya, then?"

"Sure. My mom says I don't drink enough water, in that instance I think it was the right decision. No bathroom breaks. No snacks." I pumped my fist, playing off the uncomfortable memory. "Hung in there like a trouper, though."

His eager tone shifted, became reserved. "Girls, they didn't hurt either of you, did they? If they did, maybe we should put some energy into tracking them down while we're looking into the circumstances surrounding Paris."

Kya and I exchanged looks. I said, "The worst of it was some pins and needles from being tied up. It wasn't pleasant, but not as bad as it could've been either."

Winston sighed heavy, relieved. "That's something, then. You're kids. You shouldn't be going through any of it."

"But since we are, you're happy to document it."

Kya elbowed my shoulder. "Fuse."

Winston snapped his MacBook shut and waved off my jab. "It's fine, Kya. Me and this one go way back. If she *wasn't* mean to me, I'd know she wasn't okay." He stood and slipped the computer in his bag.

"Wait." I sat up, wondering if we should follow him. "That's it?"

"This is a lot. I could probably spend a month digging into this dark faction of the Nation. They seem organized, tech-savvy. I got people I need to holler at who can maybe tell me how deep the rabbit hole goes. You two keep looking into the ex. We got each other's numbers when we need to link up."

Kya went full butt kiss. "Thanks so much for the beverage, Mr. Bell."

Beverage? Mr. Bell? God.

"It's nice to see some young people still have manners." His gaze was quite pointed. "Pick up if I call. Cool?"

My answer: an eye roll.

"I'll be in touch. Peace." Exit Winston to the sound of door chimes.

Kya sipped the remains of her sweet drink, while I choked down my cool bitter brew. She said, "I think it's good an adult knows what's happening."

"If you say so." I didn't want to admit it did feel kind of good to have one more person in on the Dark Nation secret. Even Winston.

"So, we're on Shameik."

"No." The phrasing just felt wrong to me, and my response was reflexive. "You are, Little Miss Volunteer. We need to find out where he was that night. If he's got an alibi."

"Is that what Veronica Mars would do?"

I nearly snorted coffee. "How old is that guy anyway?"

"He could be our dad."

"Ew."

As if summoned by the mere mention of his title, my phone buzzed. The incoming text was the last thing I wanted to see in that moment.

DAD

I'm home. Where are you?

ME

I'm on my way now.

"You okay?" Kya sensed me reeking of doom.

"Remains to be seen."

KYA

Fuse was quiet on the ride home. No radio or nothing. So I let her be. We could figure our next steps later. Especially since she wasn't the only one stressing.

The closer we got to my street, the sweatier my palms felt, the faster my heart beat. Turning the corner, I already had an angle on our town house. The dark windows. Mama's car gone. There were no nondescript vans on the street, but in my head now, there was always a nondescript van on the street.

I didn't like being in my house anymore. It used to be peaceful, even when it wasn't—like when Mama was really cranky about work, but she yelled about the carpet not being vacuumed so she could "see the lines" or something else that wasn't the real problem. Tuning her rants out was one of my stronger skills. In those moments when I muted her, I thought up ideas, ways to tinker with the SoundChek code, or plans for living in different states with big, famous cities when I went to college. Now I was just waiting for the next mask to pop out of the shadows. If I didn't hate Paris's stupid fans before . . .

"Here good?" Fuse pulled into the same spot the Dark Nation lurked in a few nights ago.

"Sure." It took some internal bolstering to work the door latch and let myself out.

Fuse's fingers grazed my wrist. "Are you sure this is good?"

A jerky nod. "I'm fine. I am."

Then I was out of the car, door closed behind me, tapping the roof so she knew to go.

Fuse didn't move right away. My stomach lurched, thinking she'd watch me until I stepped through my door. Seconds passed and Fuse eventually swung a three-point turn, peered at me one last time while I stood in the street, undecided on which direction I'd be heading. When the brake lights were no longer visible, I craned my neck up at my darkened bedroom window as if staring into the face of a tall bully I had no hope of beating.

Down the street, Miss Elsie's porch light was on, same as when we were kids. Paris used to say it was crazy, like her grandma thought she'd get lost without that light to get her home. I let it guide me.

Her doorbell gonged and echoed, no other sounds to compete with. Maybe she wasn't home, not with the house that silent. I nearly left, but shuffling footsteps getting louder, louder said otherwise. "Hang on, hang on. I'm coming."

A chain clinked. A couple of dead bolts turned. Finally the knob twisted, and Miss Elsie peeked outside. When she recognized me, she beamed. "Oh, child, come in here."

The house was warm as ever. Light sweat made my shirt clammy, but it was still more comfortable than going to my own lonely place. "I'm sorry to bother you, Miss Elsie."

"Ain't no bother." She led me through her front room, flipping on lights as we went. Then into the kitchen, another room she brightened with a wall switch. Had she been sitting in the dark?

Unlike the memorial service, where she'd worn her best outfit, best wig, and best hat, Miss Elsie looked out of sorts. No wig, so her short gray hair was matted. A pale blue terry cloth robe was cinched tight at her waist, pink open-toed slippers exposed unclipped nails. Hunched, more sliding across the floor than walking, she'd aged a hundred years since I last saw her.

"Would you like something to drink?" she asked.

Desperately. The dry heat made my throat feel as rough as an old sock. "I'll pour us some water, Miss Elsie. Please, you go on and sit down."

I filled two glasses from a pitcher in the fridge, then sat at the kitchen table with her. Working hard, I ignored the sickly sweet smell coming from the piled-up dishes in the sink. Back in the day, Miss Elsie wouldn't allow a single dirty fork in the sink—I know because Paris and I washed plenty. Gulping my water, I noticed her watching me, a weak smile flickering. "I wish I had some of that ginger ale you like, Kya. I haven't had a chance to go shopping."

"This is fine. Mama says I need to drink more water."

"Cinda still on you 'bout taking care of your throat? She got some big plans for you, don't she?"

"I don't know about that." I rose, carrying my empty glass to the sink, where I washed it. I began stacking the other dishes to the side, ran hot water with a squirt of detergent into the empty basin, and washed all the dishes I hadn't used. I waited for an objection. It never came.

A baking dish was crusty with some kind of burnt-on sauce. I scraped at it with a spoon beneath the water. While I did, she asked, "Do you watch any of them laser ray movies?"

"I'm not sure I know what you mean, Miss Elsie."

"Paris had gotten in the habit of sending me all these electronic gizmos that I don't know what to do with. Said companies gave them to her for free because they liked her music. Got a closet full of stuff I ain't never open, in case something ever happened and them companies wanted their things back. You know how they do. One of them was some kind of laser ray disc player."

"Do you mean Blu-ray?"

She clapped. "That's probably it. You watch those movies?"

Not really. Mostly we streamed stuff through the jailbroken Fire Stick Mama got from a friend. Netflix, and Hulu, and sometimes movies that were still in the theaters. Mama's friend didn't believe in paying for entertainment you could steal. No point in trying to explain all that to Miss Elsie. I just said, "Not often."

"Well, you should look through all she sent. If you don't want that laser ray player there's surely something in there you do want. Smart girl like you. I remember how you used to take things apart and put them back together. I was afraid you'd crack open my TV if I didn't watch you close." She chuckled.

The last dish was as clean as it was gonna be. Sat it in the drying rack, drained the water, and rinsed down the suds.

"Maybe you can take a look at all that stuff and tell me if it's worth anything?"

The pain in those words, like they came up sideways, was evident. Miss Elsie had always been a proud woman. It was hard to admit she wanted—probably needed—to sell gifts from her dead granddaughter. Why, though? I'd bet almost anything that Paris would've sent her more than a bunch of tech junk.

"Show me where it all is."

There was a closet beneath the stairs full of boxes featuring a bunch of brand names anyone would've known. Samsung. GoPro. Apple. LG. Paris sent enough stuff over to stock a Best Buy kiosk. "There's a lot here."

"Stuff was coming to the house all the way up until a few days ago. Even got a package the day she—"

She didn't finish and didn't have to. I knew what day she meant.

Continuing, voice shaky, she said, "If you see something you want, please take it. She probably would've sent some of it to you if y'all had been talking."

An iPad Mini nearly slipped my grasp. "You knew?"

"I asked her about you. She never gave me no answer I was satisfied with. I knew something had happened. I knew you would've worked it all out. If there'd been more time."

I liked to think that too.

The house phone rang, a shrill sound from an old device. Miss Elsie's head tilted up, toward the second floor. I made a mental note to check the pile for a decent cordless phone.

"That's probably my sister calling from the nursing home. I'mma go take that. Keep looking through that stuff. I won't be long."

She went upstairs, and I sorted the gifts into piles, estimated total value north of five thousand dollars. Miss Elsie was probably taking this stuff somewhere like Wilson's Pawn & Loan, where she'd get crazy cheated because that place was the devil. Be lucky to walk away with five hundred dollars for the whole load. If I put this stuff up on eBay, though . . . I could probably get her close to market value on anything she didn't want to keep.

The smallest box had a handwritten label. Paris's handwriting. Inside it, an envelope. Inside that, a rectangular triple-folded piece of paper. Like the mail version of those nesting dolls.

Unfolded, the paper spilled a thick copper key and a blank white plastic card with a magnetic strip—like a credit card, but not quite—onto my lap. I smoothed the paper, it was some kind of official letterhead, and another handwritten note from Paris.

Grandma, I'm sorry I couldn't get this to you in person, but here's keys to my place. Apartment 14-D. You can come by anytime you want. The view is crazy. You always said if I don't like what I see, change where I look. Advice taken. Love you. See you soon. ~P

This note, plus the key and the card . . . goose bumps puckered along my arms.

Miss Elsie got quiet above me. Then, shuffling, toward the stairs.

I stood, stuffed all I'd been holding in my hip pocket, and tried to smooth the bulge before folding back into my chair.

Miss Elsie reached the ground floor, radiating a better mood than when she'd left. "Find anything interesting?"

"Not much," I said. "Not much at all."

• ■

Mama wasn't home yet. I knew because I texted. She was working and wouldn't be back until close to midnight. This was what you called a dilemma. I couldn't stay with Miss Elsie, the guilt over pocketing that key was eating me alive. I didn't want to take another solo walk to an empty house, given what happened last time. A choice needed to be made, and the key in my pocket felt heavier by the second.

God, I'd burn the whole Nation to the ground if I could. "Miss Elsie, I'm sorry. I have homework."

"You stay on top of your studies, baby." She shuffled along with me, cupped the back of my neck, and pulled me to her for a forehead kiss. "Come back soon."

It was close to eight by then, and daylight saving still had the sun sitting high, that would make the walk home easier. Some kids sat on the army-green electrical transformer at the corner. I knew them all. Remembered when most weren't allowed to leave their yards. They knew me too, so they didn't hesitate warning me.

One boy cupped his hand to his mouth, shouted, "FIVE-OH! FIVE-OH!"

Being home alone wasn't going to be an issue.

Detective Barker waited patiently.

PARIS/DJ PARSEC
(12 MONTHS BEFORE)

Oh my gawd, this can't be life.

There's this bank downtown. I been seeing it for forever. It's all white, with columns like ancient Rome. It doesn't look like any of the other banks on that road. Not the bank with the covered wagon, or the one with the funky American flag logo. It's *the most* bank, dig?

The school bus drove past it every day. In the afternoon, you only saw people in suits coming in and out, cars with the mirror paint. So when I got this check, and my new manager was asking me about the account we were gonna put it in (um, what account, hello?), I knew it was time to pick a place. There was only one choice.

So there I was, trying to get this check in my new bank account for . . . a lot. *A LOT*, a lot.

I'd been keeping the cash from all the parties where I was spinning and local production gigs in a shoebox under my bed. This was the first real money I'd seen. All from a beat—A BEAT—I made. It was a little overwhelming.

When I'd first started, I tried to do it like one of the gods, Kanye West, who claimed he made five beats a day, every day, for three summers straight. I knew I couldn't do five a day, just because that's exhausting. I did the math, though, that comes out to about 1,400 beats over three years. Which was more doable. And I did do.

Averaging about two a day for the last couple of years. Garbage at first, but better and better as time went along. Now that we were posting all these videos and audio clips, I wanted to put everything I had into the world. Why make it if people aren't gonna hear it? Fuse talked me out of that, and not easily.

"We want to keep some of it exclusive. Because when artists come to you—and they will come—you want to be able to play them things they haven't heard. Trust me."

She claimed she was so good at what she did because of her dad's branding and marketing business; he'd pretty much groomed her to be him someday. It's unbelievable, to me. Not that he did that, but when she talked about it, she sounded like she was mad. If I had a kid, I'd *definitely* put them onto all I knew about music, and they'd better appreciate it. I sure would have. Especially if I'd known all this paper could come from it.

Fuse's strategy first got regional artists knocking on the door. Got paid from that (especially from Lil' Redu, who paid double my quoted fee just because he could; I knew better than to ask questions about where that money came from). Then some cats from out of state hit me up. Maryland. Philly. Then I was renting studio time at a spot by the oceanfront, making tracks with them. Got paid from that. Still cash. Still the shoebox. *Shoeboxes*, really.

Word spread. Not just regional *artists* anymore. It became regional hip-hop podcasters. Bloggers. Other music-centric YouTube channels hollered at me about guesting on their programs. Magazines like *Wavelength*, *MIXX*, *Needle Drop*. They all wanted little Q&As, or "The New Hype" articles about me. And then . . .

AND! THEN!

I got the call from a number I didn't recognize. New York. Picked up, and it went something like this.

Me: Hello?

Stranger: Is this DJ ParSec?

Me: Who's asking?

Stranger: I work for Omar Bless.

Me: . . .

Stranger (who was obviously full of it): Hello? Yo, did the call drop?

Me: Stop playing. You do not know Omar Bless.

Stranger (sighing): I swear I have this exact conversation four times a week. Yo, Mar! She needs proof.

Omar Bless: Girl, it's me.

I might've screamed a little. Fuse was right there when it happened, prescheduling tweets or something. I put Omar Bless on speaker so she could hear him; she screamed too. When that was over, we talked about beats. FOR HIS NEXT ALBUM.

How'd that go? Did I mention the fat advance check and the new bank account?

Grandma had to come with me because I wasn't eighteen yet. Also, once all this account stuff got taken care of, I wanted to surprise her by paying off some of her bills. The check was enough for that, and more. When we rolled up, the white lady behind the desk kept looking at us, then the check, then at us, kind of funny. Yeah, I know. It's usually business suits up in this place. Not jeans, hoodie jackets, and fresh Huaraches. The way she kept flicking her eyes at my hair while tapping in info on her keyboard, you'd have thought she'd never seen a twist-out in her life.

Grandma's chin dipped, and her hand fell on my knee. Squeezed. It was supposed to be reassuring, but I figured a long time ago that's the way she reassured herself. She was bothered too.

I wasn't dropping my head. Every time the lady glanced at me,

I stared her straight in the eye. That check was probably more money than she had in her bank account. I belonged here, and the sooner Miss Fidgety Clerk realized it, the quicker we'd both get on with our day.

Only, she didn't finish the job. "Excuse me a moment, please."

We didn't actually excuse her before she spun her desk chair, popped up, and quick-stepped to wherever. She took my check with her.

My phone vibrated. A Kya text. *Another* Kya text.

KYA
So ARE we on for tomorrow or what?

Huh?

Scrolling up, I reread her other texts from this week. Most had come in when I was in the studio with Omar.

KYA
We keeping the tradition alive for my
birthday?

KYA
I hit you up last night, but never heard
back. You okay?

KYA
Are you alive? This isn't like you.

KYA
I'm worried.

ME

ME

I'm cool. Working.

KYA

Okay. Sorry. Didn't mean to bother you.
Just didn't know if the plan was still on.

ME

I'll hit you back.

KYA

So ARE we on for tomorrow or what?

I'd forgotten about the thing we do every year for her birthday. Hit
the movie theater, pay for one movie, sneak into a second one. It had
been a busy week. Good, but busy. Now that I had this dough, we
could really do it up. If this bank lady ever stopped messing around.

ME

Yeah, let's get it.

KYA

☺

KYA

I'm glad.

KYA

It's been a while since I've seen you. I
don't like the way things are between us.
Five Guys after? Talk?

Grandma twisted in her buttery leather seat, tapped my knee, then motioned toward the long counter where Bank Lady had walked my check. She was with two other bank people, huddled up, whispering and glancing at us.

Oh no. No no no no no no.

When she made her way back to us, her bank crew following, I was ready to pop! So what, they think the check fake? A couple of hood rats trying to run game? Should've known better than to come up in here.

Grandma, calmer over crap like this than I could ever imagine, said, "Is there a problem?"

Bank Lady said, "No problem. I was just— Your check's made out to Paris Secord, but the payer is Game Point Records."

"So what?" Say what you have to say. Make it clear we don't belong here so I can snatch those extensions out your head.

"My coworkers and I were wondering if you're DJ ParSec? Because, if so, *we love your music*."

One of her bank buddies said, "Calm down, turn up!" loud enough to echo, startling a security guard.

"Um." My attitude adjusted, although slowly. I guess I'd read this all wrong, but it was hard to come down when I hit critical. Too many times of reading the situation correctly, and knowing you were considered less than, had that effect. I kept my answers short, in case this was a trick. "Yeah. That's me."

They all turned to each other, grinning and gyrating slightly, as if my music was playing at that moment. Wouldn't that be a trip? A DJ ParSec song jamming in a bank?

One of them claimed to be a singer. Another talked about being into old-school hip-hop, R&B, and jazz and how she could pick out some of the influences in the stuff on my SoundCloud. Bank

Lady—you know what, I needed to stop calling her that. It's no way to think of a fan. The sign on her desk said "Madison" and *Madison* said, "I apologize for getting off on a tangent. It's just . . . we don't get celebrities in here much."

Grandma smiled, and there was a brightness to her I hadn't seen hardly ever. Maybe that's what pride looked like. She hadn't had much to be proud of in a long time.

Madison returned to her seat, still holding my check, resumed whatever it was that needed doing while explaining stuff about when I could expect my debit card, how I could make deposits ("small amounts, not a check like this") from my phone through the bank's app, and she asked if I knew other famous musical artists.

Her bank crew hovered to the side but leaned in when she asked that one. I might've mentioned Omar. My phone vibrated a few more times. I barely noticed.

ParSec Nation required my attention.

FUSE

Mental pep talk time. Smile. Speak with certainty. If I believe me, they'll believe me.

All those marketing and motivational book tips came back to me like scripture to a religious person in times of stress. Nothing was more stressful than preparing to deal with whatever overbearing lecture Dad was going to have for me not coming home right after school. I'd just gotten my car keys back. A privilege likely to get rescinded if Dad felt froggy.

Definitely couldn't tell him I was playing Sherlock Holmes over the murder he wants me as far away from as possible.

Okay, okay. I was studying—no. Then he'd be like, with who, and where?

Couldn't claim I went to library solo because I don't go to the library. That much he knew about his little girl.

Excuseless, I trudged inside. No one waited in the foyer with arms crossed and a foot tapping impatiently. That was something. Faint murmurs flitted from the office. A business call, I could tell. He was louder, enunciated more precisely. He was Business Dad, my least favorite version. Also, he was angry, because he spoke fast. Not a great sign, though it gave me more time to formulate a proper excuse.

"Look who finally made it home," Mom spoke behind me.

Dang. I faced her and my fate. "Hi. I thought you had a shift tonight."

"Dr. Fisch asked me to switch. I'm certainly not complaining about a surprise night off." She pinched a full wine glass by the stem. Nope. No problems with her tonight. I attempted to slink to my room.

"Your father wants a word with you."

Nooooooo! "Um, he's on a call, right?"

"Poke your head in anyway. He was adamant." Mom walked her swishing glass into the family room and plopped down in front of the ever-running CNN broadcast, and I was left anxious, contemplating my fate.

As instructed, I poked my head into Dad's office, tried to immediately back out while mouthing, *Sorry, you're on the phone.*

He waved me inside before I could complete the maneuver, motioned for me to have a seat in an empty chair.

"Barry," he said to whoever Barry was, "no excuses. Make it happen. I need to go, and I want good news in the morning. Got it?" He ended the call, rocked back in his chair, squeezing the bridge of his nose as if trying to crush a headache. Was I the headache?

"Mom said you wanted to talk."

"Yeah," he said, "I wanted to tell you the matter with the DJ girl has been resolved. We can all get on with our lives now."

The matter was . . . resolved? I wondered if the Dark Nation got that message. "How? What do you mean?"

"I spoke with Andrea earlier today, and she assured me you'd be involved in no more inquiries. I told her you never should've been involved in the first place, and we briefly discussed litigation options so the OSPD could pay for your time and distress but ultimately settled on dropping the matter if the authorities agreed to do the same."

Andrea was our family attorney. I only knew her name because I scribbled my signature next to Mom's and Dad's on Christmas cards we sent to her and my parents' other associates every December. I probably should've assumed she'd be involved if anything developed. But I didn't know anything had.

I said, "The police wanted to ask me more questions?"

"I know. It's ridiculous." He spun his chair toward his workstation and scrolled through the various Better Businessman–type podcasts he'd become obsessed with in recent years. "They're trying to get children to do their jobs for them. Or find scapegoats. If their seemingly nonexistent evidence compelled them to consider you a person of interest, we'd take a different course. As it stands, you were a good citizen who notified them of a crime and shouldn't have your time wasted for such community service."

The police were preferable to the Dark Nation. Maybe if I'd been cooperating with them—I mean, I got nothing to hide, so why not?—I would've seemed like a less viable target for the Masked Maniacs. Maybe the cops could've found some actual clues and found the killer and I wouldn't be pushing down terror that somebody else was going to throw me in a van and never bring me back.

"Fatima, I expected a more enthusiastic response here."

"Our expectations often differ, Dad."

He craned his neck, flashed his patented Dad-eye, similar to side-eye, but much more annoying. "You know what would've happened if I spoke to my father in that tone you love to use with me?"

"You would've left home and gotten rich and been totally fine?"

He faced me full on, heated. I was skating a line; just couldn't help it sometimes. I'd expected an argument to keep all of my driving and phone privileges even though I'd come home late, and my impulsiveness might have me handing them over for unnecessary sass. Guess I was heated too.

He said, "We didn't raise you to mouth off. I'm cutting you some slack because I don't know what it's like to have gone through what you did. But, understand this, as sorry as I am about that girl's passing, my concern—my duty—is to protect you. I won't apologize to anyone for that, especially a child."

Thing was, he didn't sound sorry about anything. I don't know, I didn't like how he'd used his lawyer and his money to dismiss the police. And ParSec.

Then he dismissed me too. "I've got work to do, Fatima. Don't you?"

"Yes, the child does," I grumbled.

My room felt too cold, and I swapped the day's clothes for baggy sweats and a hoodie. Checked my phone. Several missed—no, ignored—texts from Shameik.

SHAMEIK

Kya Caine rolled through SP today.
Crazy, right?

SHAMEIK

IDK if you heard but we helping plan a
concert for ParSec.

SHAMEIK

You could help too if you wanted.

SHAMEIK

You ain't got to ghost me like this, Fuse. I
know I messed up.

SHAMEIK

She can't forgive me, but I wish you
would.

Sadness and fury and fear rolled up inside me, a big ol' booger
ball of ARGGHHH!

Don't do this, a reasonable voice in my back-brain warned.

But I was still my daddy's Little Short Fuse. Wasn't so much
with the tantrums these days, but a spark could set me off in other
ways. That was the truth, right? Since I wasn't going to be talking
to the police, and I didn't want Kya knowing all my business, I
could admit it to myself . . . there was a spark between Shameik
and me. That was the problem.

Screw the plan.

ME

What were you doing that night?

SHAMEIK

I told you, my head was in a bad place. I
shot my shot, and you shot back, right?
That kiss was both of us.

ME

☹ Not THAT night. The night Kya and I
found her. Where were YOU?

The dancing dots did their thing, kept doing their thing for a solid two minutes. How long was his answer to my should-be-simple question?

Dot-dot-dot

dot-DOT-dot

dot-dot-DOT

The text bubble vanished.

I sat up on my bed, clutched my pillow in my lap. What?

I started tapping out a new message. A demand. Answer my questions, or . . . OR—

SHAMEIK
You're unbelievable. I mean, you trying
to ask if I had something to do with what
happened to Paris?

SHAMEIK
I can't with you right now.

ME
You still haven't answered my question.

SHAMEIK
Here!

The next thing through was a photo. Shameik was in it with what had to be his family—mother, father, younger brother—given the strong resemblances. They posed before a river, at night, with city lights reflecting off the wavering surface. Joyous and a bit goofy. What was I supposed to get from this?

SHAMEIK

My mom and pops been married 22
years. Their anniversary was that
Saturday. We went to Richmond to eat at
the spot where they had their first date.

SHAMEIK

Pops said he wanted my brother and
me to see how real love can start so we
recognize it when it's our turn.

Oh.

I mean, sure, that's what he said, but how did I know the picture
was taken on that night?

That reasonable voice again, *Because you do.*

Winston told us the police talked to Shameik. Given that he was
still among the civilized populace of the city, it stood to reason he
provided an alibi they found agreeable. Like an anniversary dinner
with his picture-perfect family two hours away from the crime
scene.

I started a response, then deleted it. Same with the next, and the
one after that. With each failed attempt, I imagined him watching
those dots dance on his screen, knowing I was inadequate in every
way this time. So I stopped. A few minutes passed, before one last
message.

SHAMEIK

You know what, I get it. You don't want
nothing to do with me. That's mostly my
fault. Mostly. Whatever you're feeling

about all this, I hope you're able to get
right. I'm not gonna bother you again.
Peace, yo.

Nothing peaceful about it. I felt at war on the inside, no victory
in sight.

KYA

My hands shook. I separated my house key from the rest on my keychain. Detective Barker kept his distance while I fumbled with the lock.

"Are you okay?" he asked.

Without looking back, steadily scraping the copper plating *around* the keyhole with a key I couldn't quite control, I said, "Fine."

"Kya. I want to be extra clear here. You don't have to talk to me, and you're under no obligation to let me in. I will not cause you any trouble if you send me away right now."

Finally got the door unlocked, imagined a platoon of white masks hovering in the dark on the other side. "I'd—I'd like for you to come inside. For a little while anyway."

I flipped the switch by the door, aware of how tiny our downstairs space was in a way that only hit when outsiders came here. That wasn't a frequent thing.

I always wondered how it looked to them. The thin carpet with tracks worn in it from years of footfalls. The ancient tile in the kitchen that looked dingy despite me mopping it three times a week. What did the detective smell? Mama's lingering body spray? The fried onions from last night's dinner?

"Um, can I get you some water?"

"That would be great. Thank you." He sat on our couch and

was semi-swallowed by the distressed cushions. Mama called where he sat the Sunken Place.

I grabbed a glass, poured from a pitcher in the fridge, handed the glass over, then sat in the recliner Mama sometimes flopped on after a late night.

Barker said, "I don't know if you're aware that I've been trying to reach you."

I shook my head.

"I called your mother. She referred me to an attorney like she said she would."

My eyebrows pinched together. "Mama got a lawyer?"

"Not exactly. It was that Vito 'the Sledgehammer' guy on TV. The one always yelling about getting you the most from your insurance company after an accident. I think she was just being mean."

Possible. "What do you want to ask me?"

"It's more what I want to tell you. I'm not supposed to be here, this is actually my dinner break."

"I can make you a sandwich."

He stopped me halfway out of my seat. "No, that's not what I meant. There are several cases backlogged with better leads than what we have on your friend. There were two shootings last night that we have a greater chance of clearing than the DJ case. If someone doesn't help us with some real information . . ." He shrugged, sipped from his glass.

"I don't know anything else." Lie. I knew about the music vigilantes extorting Fuse and me. Knew better than to let that slip.

"Are you scared?"

The tremor ran through my hands, hands he watched.

"That's what I thought. Who are you scared of, Kya? I can't help if you don't tell me."

He initiated a staring contest, sincerity in that gaze. A silent promise that he did mean to do right. So I considered telling everything—about the masks, us looking at Shameik, Winston Bell's article—while my phone shimmied in my pocket. Habit had me grab it and glance at the message.

UNKNOWN

Kya, you're going to want to stay quiet here. I hope you know that.

UNKNOWN

We already told you the cops don't care.

UNKNOWN

It would be very bad for you if you involved him in our arrangement.

UNKNOWN

Cough if you understand.

"Kya?"

Terror hit like a thousand invisible spiders skittering along my arms, and back, and legs. Spiders in white masks. I coughed loud enough for the Dark Nation to hear. Then, "Detective, you should probably leave before Mama gets here."

■ ■

Detective Barker drove away. My pulse was a bass drum in my ears, allowing nearly no sound through. The Dark Nation owned my phone. I'd been tempted to hurl it on the asphalt, stomp it with both feet, but they'd warned me about that moments before, while the disappointed detective walked to his car, shaking his head.

UNKNOWN

Don't think of destroying this phone, taking out the battery, or anything else you've seen in the movies.

UNKNOWN

We'll just bring you a new one.

Who did these psychos think they were? Did they treat Paris like this? Was this what came with being a star?

Stomping into my home, I slammed the door behind me. Almost wishing one of them was here.

Rage felt way better than fear.

The house was empty, truly, I felt it. Didn't mean I was alone. I held the phone like I'd taken a call on speaker, the mic angled toward my mouth. "Hey, creeps? Have you been listening twenty-four hours a day? You got someone monitoring my snores?"

UNKNOWN

You should calm down. You'll bust a blood vessel.

"I'll bust your blood vessels! Hello?"

The clapback didn't come. I waited. Thirty minutes passed. Nothing. I paced around the house, phone in hand, not talking and still watching for a return message.

Early evening became late night. Mama arrived home around eleven, smelling of grilled meats. She barely mumbled hello before trudging upstairs. Fatigue hit me by then too. Though my skin crawled thinking the Dark Nation could listen in on me anytime, I mustered a minor rebellion. I left my phone downstairs. In the couch cushions. With a pile of clean towels from the dryer piled on top. All that to manage restless sleep, because there was still the matter of Paris's apartment key, and the mild relief I felt from the Dark Nation exposing themselves when they did. If they hadn't, I would've told Fuse via my phone, meaning I would've told them too. Now that I knew they were up on my devices, I knew how to keep our secrets.

Tomorrow, then.

FUSE

Shameik wouldn't even look at me when we were in class. Which, I guess, I expected. What I didn't expect was it bothering me so much.

We were a complicated mess when ParSec was alive. How's it *messier* now?

At class change, I played his game, strolled right past the newly invisible man. Made a show of not caring.

Instead, I texted Kya. Again.

> **ME**
> Where are you?

> **ME**
> Why aren't you hitting me back?

> **ME**
> You're scaring me, K.

I'd heard nothing, not a word, since I dropped her off. All fifteen messages had the "delivered" confirmation beneath them. All were unanswered. I even tried actually calling her. With my vocal cords. Nothing. We didn't have the same class schedule, so I couldn't catch her in the halls. Didn't know where her locker was, or I would've staked out there. I seriously considered going to the office and asking Principal Corgis to page her over the PA system.

Radio-silent Kya bothered me way more than Shameik.

Did they get her?

Between classes, I checked #ParSecNation mentions for any word on the #MadScientist, but chatter about us had died down in the public channels. Who knew what was happening on that dark website they maintained?

Terrifying visions of Kya tied to a chair flitted through my head, but I pushed those away. If I didn't hear from her by end of day, I'd try Winston. He had a line on the Dark Nation creepy website. Maybe he'd know something. That was third period.

By lunch, I was freaking.

In the ISS room, my tray on my solitary corner desk, I rearranged the fries and made unintentional art in the ketchup while convincing myself that Kya hadn't disappeared because of a group I'd helped form.

"Ms. Fallon," Mr. Deaver, the room monitor said, "you're being summoned."

A twitchy Kya was in the doorway. A familiar pink carbon copy of a Cooke High hall pass fluttered in her fingers.

Mr. Deaver dismissed me with a wave. I fast-stepped to her, thinking, *Prison break!*

Kya didn't wait, moving down the hall like a ghost leading me somewhere I wouldn't like. We turned a corner, and I jogged to catch her. Grabbed her by the elbow. "Kya."

Mute Kya shoved me into the boys' room and plucked my phone from my back pocket.

Facing her, I said, "Hey!"

She shushed me. Dropped our phones into an insulated lunch

bag, then dragged me along. We left the boys' room, rounded a narrow cinder-block divider, and entered the girls' room, our phones left behind. I said, "Am I un-shushed now?"

She nodded.

"Where'd you get a hall pass?"

Finally she spoke. "I work in the guidance office during my free period. There are privileges. Let's not waste time on that right now. We gotta be careful talking around the phones. The Dark Nation hacked them."

"What you mean 'hacked them'?" I pointed in the direction from which we'd come.

"The microphones. Maybe the cameras too. I don't think they have our texts, otherwise . . ." She shivered.

"They're . . . what?" Shameik's messages came to mind. "How do you know that?"

She told me about Detective Barker's visit. How the Dark Nation listened and interrupted. The way they threatened her. Me. Us.

My knees felt watery from the revelation of walking around tagged and monitored like a Nature Channel wolverine. A heart-freezing notion occurred to me. "What about our meeting with Winston? Why haven't they come down on us for that?"

"I thought about it too. Best I can figure, it was loud in the café and neither of us took a phone out until the end. Ambient noise plus being sealed in our bags probably masked anything notable."

"So, luck."

"I'm not taking chances," she said. "They want us near our phones at all times. Monitor our progress. Only, there's some stuff we need to keep close to our chest. Look what I found."

She produced some kind of swipe card and a thick key.

"What are those?"

"Not sure about the card, but the key is for Paris's place." Kya unfolded a squared piece of paper and passed that to me. "I knew she moved a while ago but never thought much about the address. I got this from Miss Elsie's."

"I don't want to know *how* you got this from her grandmother, do I?"

Her lips pressed into a line. Okay, then.

Kya said, "I checked the case file the Dark Nation gave us. The police have already been there. Maybe there's nothing left to see, but I'm thinking we should look there anyway."

I tilted my head, rereading the paper she gave me. Not the handwritten note to Paris's grandma. The stationery it was written on. "The file said they'd been to *this* address?"

"It said—" She looked again. "No, the address was different. It said they'd searched her home."

"Except her home, the one I knew about anyway, wasn't this apartment." I pointed to the "14-D" mentioned in the note. "It was a shabby rental near where Paula Klein lives. She wanted ParSec close at all times, like a therapy animal. I don't know what this is, Kya."

"Shouldn't we find out?"

Yes. Yes, we should.

PARIS/DJ PARSEC

(10 MONTHS BEFORE)

To quote the GOAT, the Notorious B.I.G., "Mo' money, mo' problems." Right?

The government's been messing with my grandma. I don't know what kind of Big Brother Is Watching stuff they got going, but somehow, someway, they got word that DJ ParSec was her granddaughter and making money, and there were questions for her, sent in certified letters. Like, *Dear Miss Secord, is all that cheese being reported to the Internal Revenue Service and applicable state agencies?* Or, *Dear Miss Secord, why are you getting an assistance check from the state if DJ ParSec was a rich and famous producer?*

Never mind that Grandma's assistance check had more to do with all those years she spent putting together carburetors for a stupid car company that didn't take time to invest in asbestos removal. Or that I'm not actually "rich"—I learned real quick that black-folks rich, and *rich*-rich aren't the same thing. That's where my new manager, Paula, came in. She'd taken on a lot of that stupid paperwork for me, so I could focus on the music.

Neither of us saw this thing with Grandma coming. Not the government messing with her, and not Grandma's reaction to the solution I threw out there.

"This my home," she said. "I ain't leaving it, Paris."

"Grandma." I fought not to get loud, not to talk rude to her . . . I wanted her to *get it*. "You don't have to take anything from *them* anymore, and we don't have to live *here* anymore. I already got a place rented. My new manager helped."

"A manager? What manager? How she help?" She crossed her arms and wouldn't look me in the eye. "Lord, child, I don't trust all this you into now. It's coming too fast. Your mama was into that fast life. Running with that good-time crowd, always in them clubs and bars—"

"Stop it, Grandma." I'd heard this too many times.

"—some fine, slick man got to whispering in her ear, talking about fame, promising dinners, and trips to—"

"We already been over this!" I snapped at her. Maybe for the first time ever. Mama and my MIA father, who promised to take her places and meet important people. I'm not her. "There's nothing wrong with fast as long as it's legal."

She switched tactics. "You ain't even going to school no more. What? Why you looking like that? I wasn't supposed to know? They calling every day."

"They're confused. I got a tutor that work with me at the studio." A lie. Paula and I *talked about* getting a tutor. It was probably gonna happen. We just hadn't gotten around to it yet. "Will you at least come look at the new place? It's on the first floor so you're not gonna hurt your knees going up steps no more. There's two bathrooms, so we don't have to share. I won't even be there half the time, so you can turn up *Wheel of Fortune* as loud as you want."

"Where you gonna be half the time if it ain't at home?"

"Spinning. Producing. More work's coming in. Paula says I might even do my own album eventually. She says I'm that good."

Her head was shaking before I got the last word out. "People told your mama things, Paris. You see how it worked for her. Now you repeating her mistakes."

That's when I lost it. "People didn't give my mother cancer! Are you crazy?"

Grandma blinked slowly. Once, twice. I wasn't backing down.

She said, "You're so good at what you do that it got you talking to me—*me*—like that? You always been stubborn, but you ain't never been disrespectful. So tell me again about what's good in this world of yours."

My vision pulsed with frustration. A heavy fist fell on the front door. "Stop banging like you the cops!" I yelled because as furious as I was, I couldn't bring myself to yell at Grandma.

Shameik shouted back, "We're here to move your stuff."

Grandma crossed her arms, kept rocking. I went for the door.

"Yo," Shameik said upon first sight of me. "You okay?"

Over his shoulder a couple of his cousins loafed. One on his phone, the other ogling some chick sashaying up the sidewalk.

"I'm fine. Forget the move. I ain't taking anything from here."

"I brought my peeps and my uncle's truck."

"Then take them back, stupid! I'll call you later." His cousins became alert, a couple of "we cool?" expressions sprouted. I slammed the door.

"If you mean to leave, you should go on. I won't be coming," Grandma said. "I love you, that ain't gonna ever change. It don't seem like you adjusting well to these things you keep claiming so good. When you speak to me, it's with this new attitude. That boy out there seem nice and really like you, you treating him like nothing. I ain't raise you to run over people. What's going on with you? You don't even talk to Kya no more, she's been like family since y'all started walking."

Seriously? What's Kya got to do with this? My concerns are different from hers and her grades and what college she gonna run or whatever.

Paula warned me some people scared of a come-up. They'd fight to stay mediocre and get mad at me for wanting more. I believed her but didn't believe it'd come from my own blood.

Grandma had more stuff to say, but I was on my phone, doing better things with my time.

ME

This is DJ ParSec. Change of plans. I am free this afternoon after all.

WINSTON MIXX MAG

Excellent. I'm still good for today. I'd love to get a preliminary chat in about the piece. We are really excited about the innovative things you're doing with your music.

ME

Nice to know someone gets what this is all about. Where do you wanna meet?

Magazine dude sent a location, and I immediately requested a Lyft. "I'm going. I got stuff to do."

"No."

"Huh?"

She stared me down. "I didn't like any of this, and I let it go on too long. Get to your room, tell this manager woman you're finished. I don't care what kind of money is in it. 'For what shall it profit a man if he gain the whole world and lose his own soul?'"

She'd hit me over the head with everything else. I guess the Bible was inevitable. Enough. "Good thing I'm not a man. I'm out."

She sprang up, faster than I'd seen her move in forever. Grabbed me by the arm. "You wanna act grown, I'm gon' treat you like you grown. If you walk out, don't come back when it goes bad."

"You told my mama that too, didn't you? But I'm the one repeating mistakes? Byc, Grandma."

In the threshold, the bright light of the day—of my future—beamed, casting a long shadow into that dank, old, stifling prison cell of a town house. "A famous music magazine wants to do an article about me. I'll send you a copy when it's done. I'm assuming the address will still be the same. Later."

I left, determined to never spend another night in that house. Felt good about it too. I wasn't even going to miss that roach trap. That's what I told myself.

Sometimes I believed it.

KYA

"The library *sure is* crowded," Fuse said from the driver's seat, her voice too loud and stilted, her hand gestures elaborate. "We'll be *lucky* to find a table. Don't you think, Kya?"

Unbelievable. Whatever talents she had, acting wasn't among them. *Stop being extra*, I mouthed before starting my lines. "I tried to get us a study room, but they're all booked. We'll have to do our research on the main floor."

"You know how librarians are." She pressed her index finger to her lips and ejected spittle as she made the *Shhhhh!* noise. "No talking."

That's not your line, Fuse! Our silence was supposed to be implied. "Yeah, I guess so. Let's go."

In the SoundChek app, I selected the "Quiet Office" mix I created, the closest thing to a "Crowded Library" I could come up with on short notice. The sounds of the occasional cough, rustling papers, a cell phone ringtone going off, then being immediately silenced, all played in randomized patterns that came through the Bluetooth speaker I'd confiscated from my locker last week. I placed our phones and the speaker in Fuse's glove box to, hopefully, convince any Dark Nation listeners that we were too boring to worry about today.

We exited her car as quickly and quietly as we could to make the quarter-mile walk from the public library parking lot to the apartment building identified on the stationery I stole. We didn't speak until we crossed the street to the next block, a safe distance from our co-opted devices.

"Were you trying to win an Oscar back there?" I was grumpy.

"You said act natural."

"If SoundChek doesn't work and the Dark Nation figures we're dumping our phones, there's no telling what they'll do."

"Why you say it like that?" She exaggerated the emphasis. "*SoundChek!* Like you're yelling *Voltron!*"

"It's my audio management app."

"Like one of those noise machines people put on when they want to relax. My mom has one by her bed that plays nature sounds. She likes listening to squirrel coughs or whatever when she dozes."

"No, I mean it's mine. It's an app I built with the Smart Ones."

"The who?"

"The boys from school who died in the car accident earlier this year. They were . . . friends."

"I—I didn't know them."

"Most of the student body didn't either." I walked on, feeling suddenly deserted because Fuse had come to a halt.

"What's wrong?" I said.

"You had a bunch of your friends die in a car accident a few months ago, *then* ParSec?"

This wasn't the conversation I'd planned on having today. Any day. An invisible fist crushed my heart, yet I lived and talked. "We should hurry."

She caught up, less vibrant but just as talkative. "Were they ParSec's friends too?"

"She didn't know them. Didn't know they died." Another sharp pain in my chest, guilt that time. We never got to have that conversation. Not actually. "Can we talk about something else?"

Her head bobbed. "Sure. Absolutely. Tell me more about," she bellowed, "*SoundChek* . . ."

"It's an idea that Paris kind of inspired. You know how she'd sample stuff off old records and use them in her beats?"

"Okay . . ."

"It occurred to me that there might be sounds in real life you wanted to sample, like a school bell. We all got audio recorders on our phone, but it's not the best quality if you're not using some sort of mic attachment. So if you went to record the school bell, and a bunch of people were talking, the playback not only sounded distorted, you probably got more ambient noise—the conversations, the laughs—than anything else. SoundChek fixes that."

"ParSec never mentioned it."

I bristled. "We weren't talking much when it launched."

The crosswalk changed, and we strolled to the next block. It felt weird saying all this stuff aloud. Like joke bait. If some random dude popped out of the trash can on the corner yelling, "Nerd!" I'd feel like I'd asked for it.

Fuse sort of skipped next to me. "Why'd you stop talking?"

"You want to hear more?"

"Heck yeah. That's some intriguing stuff! You built like—what's the bowl thing with the holes you put spaghetti noodles in when you want to drain the water?"

"A colander."

"Right. You built a sound colander."

That was . . . actually an impressive analogy. "So when you record stuff to a digital file, it's ones and zeroes. And serious musicians will tell you there's a mathematical element to music, and music is sound. So Jim, our math whiz, worked up an algorithm that rearranged the ones and zeroes in a recording, to the point where you could separate and enhance noises the app recorded. Once separated, you can sort noises into silos, and mix them back together any way you wanted. SoundChek."

"That's crazy! You sounding like Bill Gates or something. How are you not rich?"

I shrugged. "It makes some money off ads. That's how I float my credit card. But it's not super polished. New bugs pop up all the time, and it's just me fixing them. I don't even know why I bother."

I wish my phone wasn't compromised so I could note that question: *Why bother?*

Unlike my other unanswerable questions, meant for my long-gone friends, Fuse answered right away. "Psh. Same reason we in these streets playing Clue IRL! You care about what you and your people did together."

Maybe there was something to that. I had other concerns right now though. "The Dark Nation are the only people I'm worried about at the moment."

"I'm not." Blustery, with her shoulders hunched, like a small woodland creature making themselves look bigger for an approaching bear, Fuse bounced a few steps ahead of me, spun on her heels to walk backward, so we were face-to-face. "That van stuff and listening in on your conversation with Detective Barker, maybe that's all the Dark Nation has. Two tricks. I'm not trying to spend a lot of time shook over them. I have total faith in your SoundChek plan."

We turned the corner, almost there. I said, "I've been thinking, we need leverage. We crack this thing, give Winston his exposé, and they can be as mad as they want, but we'll be too visible to mess with. They care about their anonymity, and the best way for them to stay anonymous is not messing with us once we're in the spotlight.

Something happens to us, then it makes us more credible, and them more vulnerable. If they think we're a liability too soon . . ."

Even if it was a slim possibility, I didn't want to discuss what their third trick might be.

Fuse said, "I'm cool. I'll try to be less of a method actor next time."

"I don't think that's how method acting works."

Hopefully we were going in the right direction. I looked up the address on the school computers but felt naked without my phone navigation as a double check.

Fuse pointed, her voice light, in awe. "Is that it?"

A new chrome-and-glass tower rose head of us. The tallest building in the vicinity. "I don't see anything else even close to having fourteen floors, so it must be."

We drew closer, and the building got taller. That's how it felt anyway. At its entrance, above a quartet of glass doors leading into a white marble lobby, were six letters spaced evenly above the entryway: SAVANT.

"The building has a name," Fuse said. "Talk about swaggy."

"It also has a doorman." A half-circle desk, also white, provided a workstation for a guard dressed primly in a navy-blue blazer with a V-neck sweater and collared shirt beneath it. "What are we going to do if he stops us?"

Fuse said, "Give me that card key thingy right now."

I did.

"Follow me, laugh like I'm saying something kinda funny, but not really. Don't slow down, and never look at the doorman. Got it?"

She shoved through those glass doors before I was ready. I chased, fought the urge to acknowledge the man behind the desk, though I felt him staring us down.

Fuse said, "There are no good stores here. I so miss Manhattan."

Remembering her instructions, I chuckled uncomfortably. The uncomfortable part wasn't an act.

We passed the desk, stood between four elevators. Fuse hesitated but a second, examining the card. There was a slot above the up button with glowing blue arrows indicating insertion was possible and/or required. Fuse slid the card in.

The arrows flared red. Denied.

"I haven't seen a decent pair of shoes yet," she said, though her eyes said something different. Something panicky.

Stepping up, I removed the card, rotated it so the mag strip inserted on the right side of the slot instead of the left. "Have you ever heard of online shopping?"

The arrows glowed green, and the call button lit on its own. A moment later, an elevator dinged open. We stepped in.

Sailing to the fourteenth floor, Fuse said, "Oscar who?"

"You've really grown as an actress."

FUSE

The Savant's fourteenth floor was as lush as the building lobby. No marble, but thick cream carpet with the slightly plastic smell of newness that gave beneath my feet like firm dough. Brushed bronze sconces lit the corridor every dozen or so feet, and I heard my mom's voice low, at the back of my skull, admiring the art deco aesthetic. The hallway split into a T shape, and placards indicated the general location of this floor's apartments. 14-D was to the right.

We didn't speak. I didn't want to speak. This felt like sneaking into a church after hours. Or a tomb.

Kya slid the copper key into the dead bolt. It turned easily and the door swung inward, wafting us in a sickly scent of decay.

"Oh God," I said, hesitant. That scene from a thousand cop shows flashed before my eyes, the moment of discovering a human corpse, puffy and gray.

Kya winced but didn't linger. She tugged her shirt collar up over her mouth and nose. "Come on."

I followed. Instinctively knew what I smelled wasn't rotted human. Mostly because I'd smelled it before.

Kya angled for the kitchen, visible immediately in the open floor plan, stepped on the pedal at the base of a stainless steel trash bin, and popped the lid. She flinched away from the resulting, noxious cloud. "Chicken wrapper and old broccoli. God."

She yanked the drawstrings of the Hefty bag, tying them into a swift knot, "Get the balcony door."

Crossing the apartment, noting the new, sparse furnishings and stacks of cardboard boxes next to the couch, I worked the latch on the sliding door and unsealed the place. The view was gorge! I could see everything from my car parked two and a half blocks away to the peaks of oceanfront hotels on Atlantic Avenue. A high, cool breeze swirled through, freshening the funk immediately. Kya leaned by me, dropped the rotten garbage outside, then shut us in. "I think it's safe to say we're the first ones here in a while."

"What is *here*, though?" Since my gag reflex settled, I took it all in. Calm. Slow. Even in this barely lived-in space, I felt ParSec's essence. The leather couch still rich with conditioner, the matching love seat still coiled in its delivery shrink-wrap. A flat-screen TV set atop heavy, unpacked boxes with *living room* scrawled in Sharpie on the side. The TV's mounting kit unopened and leaning against the wall it would've likely occupied. Next to that, framed posters from her favorite movies. Her classics: *House Party, The Five Heartbeats*. Newness: *Beyond the Lights, A Wrinkle in Time*.

Music and fantasies. So her.

And neither what it's cracked up to be, her phantom whispered in my ear.

Kya hovered over the movie posters, flipping through the frames. "I watched every one of these with her."

"Same. You kind of had to, right?" ParSec kept a TV on in the background while she worked. One of these favorites in constant rotation. "If you were with her, you did what she dictated."

Kya didn't disagree.

Suddenly it wasn't nostalgia in the air anymore. We weren't here to reminisce.

Kya said, "Now what?"

"Now we turn the secret apartment upside down. I take the back, you look out here? Maybe we start with these boxes?"

We began going through our dead friend's stuff, looking for an important thing with no definitive name, shape, or size.

It wasn't a big apartment. Were hiding places ever big? Dark wood floors over a short corridor led to a single bathroom. I flipped the wall switch, revealing a set of mismatched towels draping the rack, and a clear plastic shower liner that gave full view of the hardly used tub. The mirror over the sink was hinged. The only thing inside the cabinet, a small bundle of Q-tips. "How's it looking out there?"

Kya yelled back, "More spoiled food in the fridge. I'm looking for a knife to cut these boxes open. You?"

"Bathroom's a bathroom. Going to check the bedroom now."

Ninety percent of the room I searched in a glance. The bed was made. I got on my knees, peeled the comforter back for a peek underneath. Loose sneakers and a hard-shell suitcase rested beneath the bed frame. I grabbed the suitcase handle, dragged it out, but could tell from the hollow lightness that it was empty. My eyes flicked to the folding closet doors. Pulling them back, I found more near emptiness. Clothes dangled, not enough to take up even half the closet rack. On the shelf above the garments were stacked shoeboxes, two rows of five.

I rose on my tiptoes, my fingers only grazed a bright orange Nike box on the bottom row. I'd have to jump to tip it, or call Kya. #ShortGirlProblems

Only, Kya called me first. "Fuse. Come here a sec."

She stood over a freshly opened cardboard box. Not one of the moving boxes, one with a shipping label. The flaps spread like wings. Some loose Styrofoam packing peanuts spilled to the floor from Kya freeing cups, a bag of keychains, and T-shirts. Cheap promo swag branded with a logo I recognized—the stylized, interlocking *VSZ* of a company called VenueShowZ. Why was a whole box of it here, though?

Having lost interest in the VSZ swag, Kya focused on a letter slipped into the box.

"Hey, Paris," she read aloud. *"Welcome to the VenueShowZ team, enjoy some promotional goodies courtesy of the marketing team. Here's to world domination over fire beats. First Earth, then the galaxy. We'll be in touch about a press release soon! Much love, the VenueShowZ promo squad."* She frowned. "'First Earth, then the galaxy.' This mean anything to you?"

I'd been stuck on *Welcome to the VenueShowZ team.*

"It means Paula Klein was out. At some point, ParSec fired her. At some point after that, ParSec was killed. I'd say that means a lot."

KYA

Fuse talked fast, with barely a space between words, pacing, explaining to me in not-quite-succinct terms what VenueShowZ was. There were phrases like *one-stop shop* and *top-to-bottom show production* and other things that might require she bust out a whiteboard before we were done. Thankfully this particular continent of the entertainment world wasn't completely foreign to me. I cut her off midway through the monologue.

"They're managers. They manage musicians."

Fuse's mouth became a flat line. "In the way that Apple manages a few small tech stores. If ParSec signed with VenueShowZ, that meant she no longer needed Paula Klein." Fuse chuffed, "If you ask me, she never needed that hag, but you get what I'm saying? ParSec was, by far, the best thing to happen in that woman's career in years."

I said, "Paris would've told Paula she'd no longer need her services."

"Does Paula strike you as the type to take that news well?" Fuse dug through the box I opened, spilling packing nuggets all over the floor while excavating more promotional items. Coffee cups and knit caps for winter. Bumper magnets, and onesies for babies—wow, they really would put a logo on anything.

There were two more boxes beneath it. Fuse toppled the first box, unstacked the second and third, and sliced the sealing tape with the knife I'd located. "Is there a date on the letter?"

"No," I said, rereading. "Check the shipping labels, though."

She examined the flap on one box. "Two weeks ago." Fuse was elbow deep in VSZ promotional hoodies and tote bags. "There's got to be more in here. Something."

While she searched, I kept working it over. "So she got these boxes, brought them in, but never got the chance to open them herself? She might've received these—"

"On the day she died." Fuse punched the side of the last box.

I paced toward the balcony door, thinking aloud. "Paris tells Paula Klein she's fired. Paula snaps, does what she does. Then tries to mislead everyone by planning that memorial service? And helping Shameik with his concert? Why?"

Fuse said, "Make everyone think it's all good. If Paula was grieving too, heartbroken like us, she can't be a low-down, raisin-faced, nicotine-yellow-toothed monster. It's a fake-out."

"Maybe. What about Shameik?"

"It's not him."

Her certainty threw me, and I faced her. "How can you be so sure?"

"I'll show you when we get back to our phones."

Um, okay? I turned back toward the balcony, glimpsed down toward her car, where our phones were snug in the glove box. My blood crystallized.

I slid the balcony door aside, stepped out into the gusty breeze, to be sure.

Three hooded figures circled the vehicle. Still, like robots with the batteries removed. One found some juice, turned slowly in the general direction of the Savant. Even from this height, I could see his mask, a white smudge on his outfit, and on our day.

"Fuse, they found us."

FUSE

Kya barreled back inside, not bothering to shut the balcony door behind her, the greasy stink of that rotten trash following her. She seemed in a full-on panic. I cut off her path to the door, hands raised. "Wait."

She wasn't trying to hear it, sidestepping.

Leaping back into her path, I clapped my hands an inch from her nose. "Wait!" That broke her trance, though I worried another punch was in my future. "Calm down. Tell me what you saw."

Kya talked with her hands. "They're by the car, Fuse. Three of them. They looked in this direction."

"Looked in this direction, or looked at you?"

A slight head shake. "It doesn't matter."

"It does. They can't know where we are. We never talked about this apartment near the phones. Remember?"

If she had a rebuttal, she did not voice it.

"See, makes sense. If we stay put, we can wait them out." My confidence in this plan was paramount.

Someone knocked on the door.

Uh-oh.

We went silent, communicating with SEAL-Team-Six-special-forces-soldiers-type hand signals, except we never discussed or practiced ours, so it looked more like terrified voguing that we still managed to interpret. *You* look. No, *you* look. No, you—

I chopped the air. Fine, *I'll* look.

Creeping to the peephole, I went on tiptoes. The fish-eye lens presented a warped man shape, his back turned toward me. I recognized the close-cropped hair and blue blazer of the Savant's doorman. Tension sloughed off my spine; my fingers grazed the dead bolt, a number of excuses for whatever questions he might have coming to mind. Top dumb thought: Maybe he could help us.

He twisted slightly, knocked again. His distorted profile visible now. As was his mask.

The doorman was Dark Nation. Awesome.

Backing away from the peephole slowly, I detected Kya's reanimated hand motions. She mouthed: *Who?*

I raised a single, halting finger. Calmly approached the kitchen area and retrieved the knife. Her frown deepened when I mouthed, *Get the trash bag.*

She did as told, though, grabbing that funky bag from the balcony. Drawing closer to her, I motioned for her to lean, whispered in her ear, "When I open the door, I want you to throw that trash bag as hard as you can. Got it?"

A ragged sigh and a nod were good enough confirmation for me. I cut a gash along the bag's flank above where a puddle of trash water pooled blister dark and visible through the stretched white plastic.

Leaving the knife on the couch, I returned to the dead bolt latch. The doorman knocked harder, said, "Come on, ladies. We know you're in there."

I raised three fingers on my right hand, rested my left on the lock. Lowered one finger. Kya positioned herself so the door was straight on. Lowered two, turned the lock slow and silent. She got the bag in a two-hand grip, ready to propel. Lowered my third finger and snatched the door open.

"Smart," the doorman said, right before rancid garbage exploded in his face.

Brownish liquid, a color between hot chocolate and horrific baby diapers, splattered his mask and the wall behind him. The man squeed.

I lowered my shoulder, speared him in the gut, knocking him back. Kya zipped past, dipped through the door below a blazing red Exit sign, and I followed her into the staircase.

Fact, it's easier to go down stairs than up. Also fact, *easier* doesn't mean *easy*. By the time we hit the eighth floor, we were wiped, sucking air like asthma pros. Apparently, not a ton of cardio in either of our lives pre- or post-ParSec.

"We gotta"—I gulped oxygen—"keep . . ."

She nodded, forced her legs in motion. I let her be the engine dragging me along.

The final floor opened on a parking garage. Daylight lit an exit ramp, where a bright red Corvette thumped over a speed bump, escaping the Savant like we thought we would.

We were wrong.

As the Corvette's taillights vanished into the street traffic, a couple of Dark Nation members entered the deck from the sidewalk, silhouetted by the sun beyond so their masks stood out beneath their hoods like reaper skulls. Only two of them, but given how exhausted we were from our descent, their appearance was as grim and effective as a steel gate clacking down and locking us in.

We whipped back toward the stairway, but the doorman emerged, garbage stained with flecks of I-didn't-want-to-know clinging to his jacket. There was a third option, thirty yards to our left, a door leading to the building lobby. We started that way, but another mask emerged from the lobby door, cutting off our last escape route.

"Kya"—too winded to fight, I still managed a weak—"Sound-Chek needs some work."

I flopped against the nearest car and awaited whatever came next.

KYA

My body tingled with adrenaline. They'd nudged us into the elevator, a ride back to the fourteenth floor, where three more masks were already inside Paris's apartment. They wandered, plain white faces panning over everything, getting close to Paris's posters and boxes in a way that was skittish, hesitant. I'd seen this sort of thing before.

On a seventh-grade field trip, we'd gone to the Smithsonian. Mr. Montgomery, our teacher, was the same way about the Civil War exhibits—Lincoln's hat and some old rifles.

"Of course he want to time-travel to the Civil War," Paris said, then convinced me to sneak to the hip-hop exhibit. She promised DJ Grandmaster Flash's Kangol cap was way better than what Lincoln rocked. She wasn't wrong.

I imagined Paris's stuff on display in the Smithsonian a hundred years from now, and a sense of awe and possibility dampened my fear, but only for a second. A petite mask made her way from the bedroom, her cartoon-stenciled sneakers squeaking.

Her command: "Put them on their knees."

Rough hands weighted our shoulders. Fuse strained against the force, as did I, but our legs gave at roughly the same moment, and we knelt before her.

"No updates on your progress. Ditching your phones." She

angled on me. "I swear you were about to go running your mouth to that cop, Kya. We already told you—"

"They don't care! But you don't either, right?" I spat, defiant. Tired of being scared. Before, I thought the worst thing ever was being at the mercy of Paris's fans. No. This was relief. They were here, in front of me. Not waiting in some dark parked vehicle. Not lurking in the next bathroom stall, forcing me to speed-pee. Here. Now. I was taller than most of them. "You're a bunch of fake scary-movie wannabes letting us do all the work. You can crack phones and do ninja appearance stuff but won't get off your butts and actually help? Paris would've clowned you."

Fuse said, "Kya. Maybe you shouldn't."

"Shouldn't what? Call them out on their crap? We're in her *secret apartment*. Instead of asking the questions we're asking—why would she need a secret apartment?—they want to mess with us. For all we know, *they* killed her." I elbowed the one holding my left shoulder in the meaty part of his thigh. He yelped and hopped away.

I aimed my venom at Elmyra Fudd, electric with the buzzing release of so much bottled rage. "What? You know I'm right, don't you. Say something!"

Elmyra Fudd pulled a pair of small garden shears from the pouch on her hoodie. Squeezed and unsqueezed the handle, making the blades open and close like chomping teeth. "For that disrespect," she said, "we're going to have to cut your pinkie off."

My electric buzz shorted out.

FUSE

Uh . . . what?

Two goons forced Kya's arm into a stretched position, one roughly pried at her fingers. Those shears kept clacking. Kya's face went slack, the color shifting to a gray that, I'll be honest, I didn't know black folks were capable of.

"Wait!" I shouted, pausing the room. "You're not serious. ParSec Nation—even the Dark variation—always acted in DJ ParSec's interests. For the music. This, hurting Kya, doesn't do anything for her legacy."

Kya's eyes stretched, her chest heaved like she was hyperventilating. A new flash of panic hit me too. I realized, for the first time, how much I cared, genuinely, about Kya. This Dark Nation was a creature of my own making, and that I couldn't control them, that I maybe couldn't stop them from hurting her, was terrifying. Searching all I knew about ParSec Nation, all I'd built them to be before this cell splintered off, I made a gamble. "I'll give you something."

"Like what?" Cartoon Shoes said, her head cresting from side to side, a surgeon puzzled over how to start a procedure.

"Insider scoop. You loved ParSec so much, but what did you know about her? Really?"

The doorman, rank from garbage water, spoke through his

stained mask. "She was a very private person. She only discussed music in her interviews."

"Exactly. Wouldn't it be dope if you knew what she talked about when she wasn't being interviewed? No recorders. No cameras. Kya and I can give you that. Not if you hurt us, though. Right, Kya?"

Whimpering, she nodded. Good. Be smart here. We can get out of this, K.

Cartoon Shoes backed off, lowered the shears. "Fine. Talk."

"Awesome," I said. "Absolutely. Did you know—?"

"Quiet," said Cartoon Shoes. "I want to hear something from her"—she aimed her shears at Kya's eye—"since she's so mouthy."

Kya gathered herself, stuttering at first, "Th-th-there's a cloud account filled with old music. In some cases it's just bass, or a random sample Paris looped. In others, there are whole songs. Pre-'Calm Down, Turn Up!' stuff, when she was just getting good."

All the masks circled Kya, postures relaxed, children hearing a bedtime story.

"You," one of the goons began, his voice airy and reverent, "have access to more music?"

Reluctant, Kya said, "Yeah. I do."

The room erupted. "Ohhhhh!" the masks hooted, hollered, high-fived—their favorite team just scored a touchdown. It was freaky, man. My skin began to crawl right off my body when I considered something horrible.

What if Kya was bluffing? Because I knew what was coming next.

Cartoon Shoes snapped her fingers, silencing her crew. "Fine. Let's hear."

Her tablet was delivered to her hand, and she held it toward Kya. Who said, "Nope."

Now, that was going to cause problems. "Kya."

"I can't get it from here." The shears drew closer, and inch from Kya's hand, snip-snip-snip.

I yelled, "Can't you see she's not lying? If she could, she would. Right, Kya?"

"Yes!"

I said, "We will give you something off the drive, something good. I promise. Only if you let us go right now."

Before I finished, most of the masks became children asking their mom for a toy in Walmart. Pleading through their posture if not words. They wanted new, exclusive DJ ParSec. Music fiends needed their hit.

Cartoon Shoes pushed the others away with palms and forearms, reclaiming her personal space. She stroked her mask's plastic chin with her shears, producing a thin scraping reverb that set my teeth grinding. "You already tried snaking us once with that phone in the car nonsense. How do we know you'll keep your word?"

I said, "Because y'all are some scary, Big Brother lunatics. We've learned our lesson. If we don't comply, you'll do this all over again. Right? So we're going to do what I say"—I hesitated slightly, knowing just how wrong this next part might go, the thought of shears against my skin wringing my insides—"and you'll meet my demands."

Cartoon Shoes's mask canted to the side. "Excuse me? Demands? What makes you think you have any leverage here?"

I was channeling my dad, one of his Business Deals 101 lessons. When they want something from you, ask for something from them. "Not leverage. Mutual benefit. You don't really want to be chasing us and threatening us. You want more DJ ParSec, which we will provide."

"For?"

"We all walk out of here, and . . . none of you ever come back to this apartment again—it doesn't belong to you. You don't get to crawl all over her stuff like lice."

That snatched a portion of jubilance from the masks; knees softened and shoulders slumped. They must've already had designs on whatever was loose and portable.

"What would you rather have? Kya's blood on the floor, or more music from the artist you worship?"

I let it simmer. Masks angled toward each other, shoulder shrugs and hand gestures. Should they or shouldn't they? I was 80 percent confident they would. That 20 percent margin of error made me feel like I was having a heart attack, though I forced my face still, emotionless.

The music was what they really cared about. Not who took ParSec from us. It was all about the legend of her demise and what trinkets they could collect after. Not surprising. I think I've always known fan love was the most selfish kind.

That scathing critique of ParSec Nation—as a whole, not just the Dark varietal—pricked my insides. I'd been a fan first. Been drawn to ParSec off the strength of her music too. Where it could take . . . us. Me *and* her. So I was negotiating terms I would've accepted if in their shoes. "Well?" I said, real boss-like.

Cartoon Shoes said, "New music? By the end of today?"

"I'm not going to say it again." Kya, you better be able to deliver.

Cartoon Shoes dragged it out another few moments, then, "Deal."

She pocketed her shears, and with a nod, the goons released Kya and me. I stood slowly, while Kya kind of crab-walked to me on hands and heels, putting comforting distance between her and her would-be surgeon.

"Let's go," Cartoon Shoes said. "All of us."

We exited the apartment and building, the Dark Nation operatives escorting us all the way back to my car. If anyone was paying attention—and no one seemed to, people were very good at turning away from what might be strange and/or dangerous—we'd have looked like a twisted coven of friends wishing each other farewell after an awesome BFF gathering.

Cartoon Shoes's hood cinched tight around the moonshine oval mask as she tapped contact info into her tablet. The swoosh sound of her sent message was barely audible over the cross-street traffic. "Send whatever you have to the address I just provided you. One hour. We'll be waiting."

The Dark Nation dispersed. Each in a different direction. Until we were alone. Managed to get my door open, slid into the driver's seat with the adrenaline shakes. Kya was a moist-cheek mess in the passenger's seat, her chest heaving as she tore the glove box open. The Bluetooth speaker was still going, though the sound was wrong. The office noises she'd mixed together weren't randomized. There was a single sound from the compilation, a sneeze, repeating like machine-gun fire. *Achoo-Achoo-Achoo-Achoo.*

Kya killed the speaker, shook her head at her malfunctioning app before swiping it away, then powering down both of our phones. She thudded her skull against her headrest a few times, went still. "Thank you for stopping that back there."

"Dude, it was for my benefit as much as yours."

Her eyes were squeezed shut, her lip quivering.

"Hey, you're welcome." I gently rubbed the hand that would've been a digit short. I sat there awhile, letting her come back to some form of normal, before I asked the critical question. "Is there really a cloud drive with unfinished ParSec music?"

She sniffled. "No."

Craaaaappppp. "Why did you say there was? You think it's going to go well when they learn we lied? I'm really partial to my fingers." She didn't respond. I found her lack of concern disturbing. "Kya."

She snaked a hand into her collar, tugged out a plastic, pastel pink nub hung from a string. "I took it all off the cloud. Put it on this drive. There are about twelve gigs of music here."

My pulsed quickened all over again. How did I not know about this? "ParSec knew you had it?"

A tight nod. "You wanted to know why me and her weren't cool at the end. Turn on the car."

I did. She unclipped the drive from the nylon lanyard and plugged it into the USB port in my center console. On the audio display, file folders appeared in alphabetical order. Kya twisted the search knob until she highlighted a folder called "Everything, I'm Not." Her hand fell away from the knob, as if her arm gave out. She was incapable of going the final step. "Play that one if you want."

Of course I wanted to play it. I jabbed the control on my steering wheel, and a guitar melody spilled from my speakers. No thumping bass line, definitely not the party songs ParSec Nation—or I—was used to. A classical piano riff joined the guitar. "A ballad?"

Kya didn't respond. Instead a voice on the track answered, falsetto at first, stretching a note, before settling into full-voice, throaty lyrics:

All of me doesn't fill this space.
All of me is all out of place.
A part of me is all, do I stay?
And all you do is take away . . .

It was simple, and beautiful, and I stopped it because I had an ear, recognized the incredible singer by her tone alone.

"Kya," I said, "that's you."

PARIS/DJ PARSEC

(6 MONTHS BEFORE)

It wasn't a good day. The landlord left this stupid note on my door about keeping my music "to a respectable volume" or there'd be some kind of fine on next month's rent. Which was a problem because when I checked my bank account for last month's rent, I only barely made it. The numbers hadn't improved much since, meaning Paula, who was supposed to be managing my money as well as my gigs, and me were going to have another talk. I didn't want any more tech toys—my landlord made if very clear he wouldn't accept a GoPro as partial payment. I didn't want to hear about unexpected expenses and slow paperwork. Funny how there was never any delay in Paula getting paid.

I still had shoebox money, but that wasn't going to last forever.

Living on my own was way harder than I thought it would be. Someone always want something. Some payment always due. It's like everybody's taking little bites off you all day, every day. My big fat advance check had dwindled. It maybe wasn't as big as I'd thought, all things considered.

"Is there anything else I should take out with these pizza boxes?" Shameik asked, folding old grease-stained cardboard into a heavy-duty garbage bag.

Gawd. "I don't know. Maybe."

I was hunched over my notebook, trying to write a song. He could, literally, see me working on the hook. So of course he needed me to supervise his Mr. Clean activities at this exact moment. Like I didn't have enough to do already.

The seal broke on the refrigerator, followed by, "Bae. Seriously. It's nasty in here."

I let my pencil fall on my notebook and took three deep breaths before answering. Still wasn't sure I kept my tone in check. "Did you come over here just to nitpick everything?"

Then he was beside me, agitated, not doing a good job of keeping his tone in check either. Our normal lately. "I came here to roll with you to the studio. Since you were working, I figured I'd give you a hand because your crib is crazy right now. You're welcome."

"I was going to clean this weekend."

"You said that last weekend."

Forget this. I grabbed my earbuds, prepared to drown him out with my latest beat.

This dude—who really must've lost his mind—*snatched them out of my hand*. "You're trippin' now, Shameik."

"Me? I'm—" He stalked from my tiny hand-me-down desk, rounded my beat-up couch, and began plucking up various debris littering my coffee table, TV stand, windowsills, and any other available flat surface. He tossed it all into his bag that was starting to bulge like Santa's sack. "Soda cans. Dirty Tupperware. Burger wrappers. Beer bottles!" He lingered on the dark green long-necked bottle in his grip. "Who was over here drinking beer, Paris?"

"November Mobb." Not that it was any of his business who comes to *my* place.

"Those rappers from Maryland? You brought them here?" The way his mouth tightened, and his eyebrows drew together, he had many more questions now, and I already knew I wasn't in the mood to entertain his stupid jealous streak.

"Yeah. After the studio session, we felt like celebrating some dope successful work. One of the guys brought the beer."

"Those cats are, like, grown men. What you bring them here for?"

"I feel like you're trying to imply something. You should stop."

He threw the bottle into the bag hard enough to break it. "My girlfriend's alone with some drunk old guys and I'm not supposed to be concerned?"

"I wasn't alone. Paula was here—still talking business. So were the girls the Mobb brought down to sing on the track."

His posture shifted, he glanced away, lips moving as if doing math in his head. "So, basically, a party? That you didn't invite me to?"

I sneered and took some minor joy in delivering this particular answer to his interrogation. "You had school the next day."

He grinned, bobbed his head. It wasn't good-natured. "About that. I guess it's taking Paula longer than expected to find that tutor that's supposed to help you graduate."

"Now you're my maid and my guidance counselor."

"Man, what's wrong with you?"

He had the exhausted look I'd gotten used to seeing on people who just can't seem to grasp what this music thing takes. Kya for not going to the movies on her birthday, and not texting her back instantly, and not hitting Five Guys anymore. Grandma when I told her I actually had a say in what my life should be. Shameik because . . . I don't even know, my place wasn't all OCD neat like his meticulous bedroom? Or I had guests I didn't inform him about?

Shameik set his bag down, seemed to be thinking about his next words carefully. I waited, wondering if I needed to throw this guy out. It wasn't lost on me that I rarely thought of him as my boyfriend anymore.

He said, "Paris, I'm worried about you."

For what? I was about to ask when he added, "So is Fuse."

I blinked rapidly, like he'd shined a bright light in my face. "You and Fuse been *discussing* me?"

He cursed under his breath. "It ain't like that."

I pushed from my chair and went to him, chest to chest. "You just said."

"This is what I'm talking about. Your mood's all over the place these days."

"What do you expect, Shameik? I got mad work to do. And bills to pay. And Paula talking about trying to get me out-of-state gigs, so I need new material. This isn't easy!"

"We know."

"We. You and Fuse. Who haven't been talking about me."

He backed away. Defensive. "You know what, forget I said anything. Let's just go to the studio. I'll keep Redu's crew occupied so you can actually finish up at a decent hour, and we'll talk about it later."

"No."

"Huh?"

"I said no."

He threw his hands up, defeated. "Fine. Point taken. I will not bother you anymore. The *artiste* must focus. I'll do my homework while we're there."

"You're not hearing me, Shameik." Was I really going to do this? I'd thought about it. Dismissed it as just being frustrated about my money. But even skirting close to it gave me a feeling of weightlessness, like something heavy falling off my shoulders. "We gotta take a break."

He shook his head, scowled. "We have arguments like this all the time."

"I know. What's okay about that?"

"I'm sorry, Paris. I could be more chill. I know."

That may be true. Probably, we both could, but I liked that weightless feeling. It was nice dealing with something unpleasant head-on, one of the few unpleasant things in my life I could deal with head-on. "Me and you, we're in real different places right now. I'm not saying I don't like you, but I just need to focus on my music. I can't do that if I'm thinking about whether you're mad."

"I'm not mad, though. Couples have fights."

"I don't want to have fights. Or be a couple. You gotta understand that."

He didn't understand. Didn't take my sincere effort to do this quick and painless well at all. "Yo, you're acting like a real—"

He caught himself, stopped just short of something nasty. Too late.

"What? Like a real what?" This was part of why we couldn't work. His little outbursts when he didn't get his way. Fine, I could be nasty too. "Don't come to the studio. I'll be fine with Lil' Redu on my own. And we both know you keep wanting to hang around because you hope I'll break down and do a song with you. It's not going to happen. Your sound ain't my sound. So stop pouting and get out of my crib. We're done."

"Wow." He seemed stunned. Confused. "Tell me how you really feel, Paris."

I said, "Did you forget where the door was?"

"You're serious."

"Shameik, we already arguing. Don't make me start yelling. Just go."

He grabbed his backpack off the couch, skulked to the exit, and hovered at the threshold. "I know you going through some stuff right now. But be careful you don't let the music be the only thing you have left when—"

I slammed the door on him and got back to work.

■ ■

"Mic check, mic check!" Winston spoke into his phone, the display spiking with the sound of his voice, ensuring the recorder captured everything. Like always, he flipped the mic toward me, and I said, "One, two. One, two."

"This is how . . ."

". . . the ParSec crew do!"

He laughed, but I didn't. My mood was still bad no matter how hard I tried for a different vibe. The recorder levels jumped with his high cackle. It was so corny, and the first time he ran it down for me, I hit him with some vicious side-eye. He explained it was a ritual. Every time he started a piece on an artist he was getting to know, they'd put together a few bars of something special. He didn't write about it, no one else ever heard it. Just for him.

"It's good luck," he'd claimed. "Every time I've done it, the artist became a future *MIXX* cover story. I'm talking J. Cole before *The Come Up*. SZA before the *S* EP."

Well then. Who was I to break the tradition?

We were on our fourth session, in the studio I rented by the beach for Lil' Redu to work on his—sigh—mixtape. Written by him—double sigh—and produced by me. It wasn't going well.

Mostly because Redu's a lazy artist. Repetitive rhyme schemes, played-out subjects. But his money spent well enough, and more important, he paid in cash, something sorely needed since the pay for all of my other work took forever and a day to actually get to me. Every time I asked Paula why that was, her answer was the same: "Proper accounting isn't quick work, dear."

There was time before Redu and his messy entourage showed up, so I leaned in my rolling chair, back to the soundboard, while Winston sat wide-legged on the couch. His thick canvas bag filled with legal pads, his laptop, copies of old *MIXX* issues. He wasn't all stiff and about business the way he was in our first Q&As. We'd gotten to know each other better, and he knew something was wrong.

"You okay? You seem distant tonight," he said.

Fuse was always on about how I shouldn't ever relax around journalists. Some advice she picked up from one of her books, or blogs, or wherever else she got those tips she always threw at me. Fuse, who was, apparently, chatting up my boyfriend (ex now, gotta get used to that) about me. Maybe it was her I shouldn't relax around. "Just don't know who's real and who's fake anymore."

"Something happened."

"I mean"—I was mindful of his phone, the recorder app—"off the record, all right?"

"Sure." He snatched the phone up, tapped the screen, set it facedown.

I told him about some of the things going on. The money, Shameik and Fuse, Grandma and me not seeing eye to eye. Our previous conversations kept my personal life vague, but I was happy to be talking to Winston again and not thinking about publicity— even though it was kind of the same thing. I don't know. *MIXX* magazine was about the art *and* the artist. Winston was good at focusing on that. On me. I liked him.

When I stopped talking, he said, "Wow, that's a lot. Good that you vented . . . you gotta do that sometime. I'm glad you felt comfortable doing it around me."

"You cool for listening."

"You're dealing with something very few people ever experience. Overnight success."

I willed my jaw to unlock. "It didn't happen fast for me."

"Of course, that's the reality," he said, understanding. "But that's not how the world sees it. You drop a song—pieced together in your grandma's house on rudimentary equipment. It blows up on the strength of the sound and this wild social media blitz by a fandom that rivals artists who have been around over a decade. You're ascending fast, and it's rare that the people you left on the ground can ever catch up."

My cheeks warmed, and I spun my chair toward the soundboard, messed with the levers for no reason. "I'm not that big."

"You will be by the time my article drops. I've seen this kind of thing before."

He joined me at the board, recorder in hand. "You mind if we go on record again? We'll only discuss what you want."

I nodded.

"Seriously, how do you pull off a thing like that? Tell me what made you rewire old laptops and keyboards. How'd you even know to make that stuff work? How'd you pull together ParSec Nation from your grandma's living room? Who was your support system? The friends who believed in you? The family that nurtured you? Time to fess up."

The mic hovered in my face, inches from lips. Waiting to

immortalize my truth. What was that? Grandma holding me back. Kya wanting no part of the success. Shameik nagging. Fuse running her mouth when she shouldn't. I said, "It's all me. I'm determined. Sort of knew how to put the pieces in place to make it happen. Guess it's in my blood."

"Your blood?" Winston pressed. "What part would you say your parents played in all of this?"

I shrugged that one off same way I had my whole life. "Moms passed when I was young. Pops won't ever around." Leading to his most uncomfortable question yet.

"How'd you do with that?"

"Fine. I mean, look." I swept an arm around the state-of-the-art studio we currently occupied. Having one parent, or no parents, wasn't totally strange. Fuse was one of like three people I knew whose mom and dad stayed together.

Winston leaned in, intense. "What I mean is, is there any feeling behind those missing components in your life. Does it drive the music?"

A couplet played in my mind, almost a whisper. *All of me doesn't fill this space. / All of me is all out of place.*

"Naw. I make party music. Nobody trying to turn up on mommy and daddy issues."

He didn't ask another question. I focused on the board but didn't fill the silence with music. "I mean, okay, I knew I didn't want to be like my parents. I didn't want to—poof!—vanish like him, or slowly fade away without having left a mark like her. I wanted to exist. Loud and proud. So, yeah. Maybe something in that drove me. I'm not dwelling, though." I perked up, mashed the play button. "I'm excelling!"

The bass dropped on my latest project. Working title: "Quasars."

"Ohhhh, is that track for me?" Lil' Redu and crew filed into the studio, loud and raucous. They bounced to the beat. Party up in here. Redu said, "That better be for me."

It wasn't. My no—a word he didn't like and never took graciously—plus the sudden silencing of the beat that he'd never rhyme on, cut him like a knife. His crew laughed, likely knew what it was. This beat was too good for his barely mediocre rhymes. The way his eyes narrowed and jaw set made me think he knew too.

Bad blood now flowed between us. It didn't stop.

KYA

We made it back to Fuse's house—past the fancy gate guard, up the winding hill bordered by manicured lawns and expensive landscaping, into her cobblestone driveway. Evening traffic slowed us down, getting us dangerously close to blowing our one-hour deadline. So close, Fuse didn't bother taking me to her room. We entered a foyer that was three stories high and detoured into her dad's home office, where she snatched the drive from my hand and got the file cued up as an email attachment.

She said, "Yo. Demands?"

"You really think they're going to do what we say?"

"If we threaten to wipe this drive"—she spun the chair, faced me—"they gotta give us some room to work. This is an arrangement that can make everyone happy. So tell me what you want."

"No more kidnapping."

She typed it up. Along with "stop hacking our phones" and "no visits to Paris's apartment in the Savant." Satisfied, Fuse clicked send, and the email disappeared with a whooshing sound effect.

"What song did you send them?" I asked.

"The one you played in the car."

I leapt forward, bug-eyed. "What? Why? I played that for *you*. Can we recall that email?"

"Uh, no. Plus, we're out of time. That song was fire, and a dope song will probably satisfy them more than some unfinished beat. What's the problem here?"

"There's no problem. I guess." I tried settling the butterflies in my stomach. It's not like they'd know it was me singing. I'd done a good job putting all that behind me.

With our end of the bargain met, Fuse pressed into her dad's chair, eyes squeezed shut. And I took in the opulence of the room, preferring to catalog my environment than think any more about my voice, or how I'd almost gotten some minor surgery without anesthesia.

The room had custom cabinetry throughout and bookshelves packed with everything from cracked-spine paperbacks to leatherbound, gold-lettered volumes. Mr. Fallon's desk was translucent black glass, his machine an iMac Pro—the most expensive kind. Even the pens protruding from the decorative TED Talks coffee mug seemed made of fine wood and precious metal. This was what money was like.

Fuse opened her eyes, her thoughts in a totally different place than mine. "I cannot believe you've got pipes like that!"

I shrugged.

"You're always so quiet. I mean, you sound like—" She popped from the chair and flung herself to a floor-level polished walnut cabinet running the length of the back wall. Crammed inside were cardboard sleeves protecting actual vinyl records. Not the hipster rereleases you could buy in drugstores now, but original pressings. I recognized the smell from Mama's much less impressive collection, stored in a single box at the back of her closet.

Fuse pulled a specific album, dropped it on the desk next to her dad's computer. "You sound like her."

Whitney. The album title and the name of the legendary R&B diva. May she rest in peace.

"You know her stuff?" Fuse said.

A slow nod. "From the time I was strong enough to hold a mic, it was drilled into me. I sung her songs at parties, in pageants, in studios, at parks, on day cruises. I could sing this album end to end without you even dropping a needle."

Not just her album either. Karyn White. Jody Watley. Evelyn "Champagne" King. Lisa Fischer. Some En Vogue from Mama's failed attempt at starting a girl group. She had me learning the music of her childhood, her classics, before I knew my ABCs. When I got old enough to pick my own performance pieces, it was Beyoncé, Ciara, Keyshia Cole, even a little Carrie Underwood if the crowd seemed into it—that country girl could go. Mama stayed stuck on power ballads of the '80s, but she conceded on modern tunes because the freedom of choice kept me a willing participant in my own torture, if only for a hot second. By the time I was twelve, I'd grown tired of the weekend shows, the long drives to singing competitions, music that preceded me by twenty years. Mama didn't like it, but I was getting too old and big to force.

Fuse didn't ask about all that. I wasn't volunteering it. Singing was a thing I used to do.

I sat at the desk, checking the files on my drive in the Finder window. "We can ration the music to the Dark Nation. A song a week if they leave us alone, stop tapping our phones, stay away from Paris's apartment."

"Why don't you sing more? What you did on that track was like a superpower."

I fought a groan. Maybe it was a mistake letting her know about my past, and how Paris and I collaborated before "Calm Down, Turn Up!" Fuse, apparently, wasn't going to let this go. "Focus. There are more important things to worry about."

"Agreed"—her voice high and hopeful—"but I want to focus on this right now. It's been a rough day."

"Fuse— You know what, fine, here it is: Performing sucks. Maybe not for everyone, but it did for me. I hated it. Every time. But Mama was a singer who never made it, and my voice was better than hers ever was, so for me to not do the thing I hated—get up in front of all those strangers, dancing and crooning even if it meant I needed to vomit in a bucket backstage right before my cue—I was somehow betraying her and every little girl in the world who wished for a special talent. It was like that until I was big enough to say no, and when no didn't work, I'd go out onstage and just wouldn't sing. When you feel like I felt up there, cheers and boos were the same. I could take the shame of flubbing performances just to make a point. Mama couldn't, though, and finally the forced show-dog routine stopped. So there. Happy now?"

Fuse's head bobbed a bit, processing it. "I wouldn't say happy."

I nearly growled at her.

"You said that track, or your singing, or whatever, was the reason you and ParSec weren't vibing. Why? I mean if you weren't performing, what did you have to do with the music?"

"Paris had been a writer since I could remember. It took her longer to develop the ability to make songs. You know what I mean? I knew what sounded good, because, well, I sound good. I helped record the words she wrote. We made a bunch of demos together. Thus, this." I motioned to the files on-screen. "She's a good learner, so her voice got stronger. Her style is more like talking on the track than singing, but every so often you hear—"

"Her get singsongy," Fuse interjected.

"Not exactly a technical term, but yes. We worked on that. That little bit of vibrato that comes through, it took time, but she got it."

"Wait." Fuse frowned. "She was mad at you for helping her become a better singer? That doesn't make any sense."

Because that wasn't the reason. "I took our music. I wouldn't give it back."

"Why?"

Someone should throw you away.

I didn't know if I would tell her. Or could. That conversation with Paris was still my greatest regret and might be for the rest of my life. I deflected, maybe in a mean way. "How about you tell me what went down with you and Shameik first. I still don't have that whole story."

She flinched. "Wow. You go hard when cornered, huh?"

"Seems like we'd both rather keep some things to ourselves."

Whether or not we'd drag those skeletons out of the closet became a moot point when the robotic voice of the Fallons' alarm system announced: "FRONT DOOR OPEN."

Fuse panicked. "Get that drive out."

I ejected it, tugged it from the USB port, and reattached it to my necklace a second before Mr. Fallon rounded the corner, his face tight, his eyes scanning. "Fatima, what are you doing in my office? Who is this?"

"Dad, this is Kya. From school."

His expression became more suspicious. I felt compelled to say something studious. "We were working on coding an app for our CS class, and Fatima said your machine was better equipped for the work."

"What kind of app?" He wasn't letting us off that easy. Fair enough.

I logged into my cloud account and opened up earlier versions of SoundChek code. "It's an audio management platform."

Mr. Fallon rounded the desk, examined my work. "Elegant."

Fuse went bug-eyed. "It is?"

Mr. Fallon said to me, "Obviously, you're the architect of this particular technical marvel."

"Obviously." There was more than a little chill in Fuse's voice. "Is it okay if we get back to it, Dad?"

"Forty-five more minutes. I'll need the room for a conference call after. Good to meet you, Kya. Thanks for helping Fatima with a useful skill."

He closed the door, and Fuse mockingly mouthed, *Thanks for helping Fatima with a useful skill.*

I felt embarrassed. For her. For myself. Mama was a lot of things, but she never ever praised anyone else's kid over me, as far as I knew. "I'm sorry," I said, apologizing for being a weapon used against her.

"For what? Showing him you're a better student than me was genius. He might've kicked you out if you hadn't. I'm glad you made that play."

Though the dullness in her tone suggested otherwise.

FUSE

We perpetrated the coding-for-class fraud for another half hour just to cover our bases, before I ushered Kya to my car to drive her home and finish our real discussion. We didn't start talking until we cleared the neighborhood gate, as if we secretly suspected anything spoken inside my community's walls was susceptible to my dad's eavesdropping.

Once on main roads, I said, "Okay, next steps."

Kya didn't answer, twisting in her seat. "Should we talk about that? Back there."

"What?"

"Whatever that was with your father. I'm pretty good at reading tension."

"You'd have to be emotionally illiterate not to read the tension between me and my dad. It's all good, though. We're good."

"Seems like a contradiction to me. When things are tense between Mama and me, there's definitely nothing good about it."

I tapped my steering wheel, thinking on the best, most succinct way to approach this and move on. "My dad's a sellout. Eighty percent of our conversations are him telling me why I need to be a sellout too. So there."

"What does that even mean, Fuse?"

"Look, my parents have money. I guess that's obvious."

"Yeah."

"Mom has always been science girl. Art and music and movies, none of it registers with her beyond a background aesthetic for wine tasting. And that's cool. Do you, Mom. Dad wasn't like that. I got my love of music from him. You saw all that vinyl in his office, right?"

She nodded, that puzzled look still on her face.

"He used to be down. Black music, black movies, street gear. I remember sticking my little kid feet in his big, old Tims and stomping around the house. I remember when he first started his digital marketing and branding company, he'd leave for work in jeans and a basketball jersey. He'd go pitch to clients like that. He was a cool dad.

"Then, the more successful he got, the more he started looking down on stuff he'd loved—stuff he got me to love. It was weird. He'd go to some dinner with Mom and her medical colleagues, the next day he's bringing a tailor by the house to measure him for custom suits and the jerseys were on their way to the Goodwill. He'd go to some retreat with other local business owners, then have us listening to self-help books whenever we were in the car. No more music.

"He made it seem like it was all about self-improvement. Personal presentation. Respectability. Naw, though. He got shamed out of his roots. Everything we loved was bad now. He got so different so fast, I felt like we were in *Get Out*."

Kya tread carefully. "As you said, your family has money."

"Yeah but—"

"And you have your dad. Some people would consider that lucky."

Some people. "Is your dad—the situation—like ParSec's, er, situation?"

"No. I know exactly who and where my dad is. Raleigh, North Carolina. With his new wife, and his other daughter. He sends me Applebee's gift cards on my birthday."

"I'm sorry."

"The ribs are actually pretty good at Applebee's."

I laughed and felt horrible about it until Kya laughed too. "I'm okay with it," she said. "Maybe it's one of those grass-is-always-greener things. A sellout dad sounds better than a gift-card dad. To me."

I recognized I sounded ungrateful, or spoiled, or something. I wanted her to understand that I didn't hate my dad, I just wanted him to remember what we used to have. "It hurts to see someone you love change, and then tell you the things you are, and the things you love, should change if you're ever going to be something in the world. I hate it. I wanted to show him he was wrong. You can be yourself and succeed."

Kya lurched forward quickly, stretching her seat belt to the limit, some realization making her spasm. "That's why you showed up? I always wondered where you came from, and why you were giving Paris all that help with the videos and the social media."

"I mean, above all else, I liked ParSec and the music was hot. But, yeah, I saw an opportunity. I knew a lot about marketing because of Dad's company. I wanted to show him you could do what he does and still be true to self. It was like a philosophical exercise or something."

"I thought you were just some kind of bandwagon leech."

"That is so flattering, Kya."

"I'm sorry. I'm being honest. It's like you appeared one day and you were her universe."

"Then you know part of what I feel. When someone close to you switches up for reasons you can't understand. And I know some of what you felt, because it was clear my dad loved hearing about your coding and your app. You're the kind of friend he wants me to have."

"Your sellout dad approves of me. Now who's flattering who?"

"If honesty feels this great, makes you wonder what's so bad about lies."

We were on the highway, my phone rattled in my cup holder. An incoming text. I said, "Check it."

Kya said, "Winston wants an update."

Of course he did. "Tell him no news. You and me still have things to discuss."

"VenueShowZ."

"I've been thinking about that a lot too."

Kya responded, and he hit us back almost instantly. Kya said, "One word: *disappointing.*"

"Tell him his hairline's disappointing."

That should've gotten a laugh. Good joke, if I said so myself.

But Kya was on task, focused. "If VenueShowZ manages artists, and Paris signed some kind of deal with them, where did that leave Paula Klein?"

"Out on her butt would be my guess."

"Yet, she goes in on that weird memorial service. She wants to help Shameik and the Seaside Poets organize a concert. Why?"

"It's not altruism, I'll tell you that. I once saw her haggle with a Girl Scout over a box of Thin Mints. She's still maintaining an online presence for ParSec. The VenueShowZ deal never went public. So she's trying to stake a claim, probably scheming on a way to keep getting paid off ParSec's work."

"How's that even possible?"

I shrugged. "You'd be surprised. Paula helped ParSec get emancipated, meaning she was able to legally sign binding documents. Immediately after that, ParSec signed a bunch of forms that gave Paula control and access to all sorts of stuff. Bank accounts, booking contracts, music ownership, and royalty payments. It went deep. ParSec was never happy with her money once Paula took over."

Kya said, "When I was singing, a bunch of people approached Mama about managing me. She always said we had to be very careful about who we dealt with if we didn't want to get robbed."

"That's real. My dad says signing the wrong piece of paper can cause any businessperson major problems, but nothing's above being reversed with the proper legal team. I'm thinking VenueShowZ had the players to make Paula irrelevant." We got off on Kya's exit, a low buzzing desperation trembling throughout my body.

Kya said, "Are we saying that . . . we think Paula—?"

"I think we're saying it needs looking into. But how?"

"Oh, oh." Reaching around to her back pocket, Kya freed her own phone. In my periphery, I watched her tapping and scrolling. She said, "Shameik emailed everyone about a concert planning meeting Friday. Guess who's going to be there."

"Paula's coming to the school?"

"Yep."

Possibilities began to churn, I turned into Kya's neighborhood. "Okay. There's an opportunity here. Let me think on it a little bit."

I wasn't sure she heard me, her attention was on Paris's grandma's place as we coasted by. Kya said, "I should probably get her that key back."

"No you won't." The Savant apartment had been on my mind quite a bit since our run-in with the Dark Nation.

"Why? What's wrong?"

"Nothing's wrong. We just might have use for it." I stopped at her place, my brakes squealing slightly. "Super teams need lairs."

KYA

The next couple of days were mundane, more so than any week in recent memory. Summer crept closer, each day hotter than the last. In school, a joyous vibe radiated from the seniors getting ready to take on the world soon. From the juniors, ready to take their places as the kings and queens of the school. From the faculty, just ready for a break.

I kept expecting the song I gave the Dark Nation to hit the web, make the rounds among Paris's fans, or even go viral. #NewMusic

Didn't happen. So the Dark Nation wasn't all about sharing the new music love. Fine by me.

There was enough to deal with. Class, homework, Mama only annoyed over her hostess job and the young singers snatching summertime gigs at the oceanfront bars. "Jobs you could be getting," she'd snark at me under her breath. Her pestering about performances didn't bother me the way they used to. At least she wasn't wielding garden shears.

Online, the #ParSecNation hashtag slowed significantly, with most mentions centering around someone playing a Paris song and others chiming in on whether it, or another, was their favorite. Based on the loose chatter, it was hard to tell she was dead, not the way her music lived on.

Fuse kept in touch via texts, nothing earth-shattering there either. The concert planning meeting was still our way to Paula.

Once we got to her, then what? Instead of working out an answer, our texts mostly devolved into exchanges like this:

FUSE

Did you know Cap'n Crunch has a
for real whole name?

ME

Huh?

FUSE

It's Horatio Magellan Crunch.

ME

How do you even . . . what?

FUSE

It was the answer in this trivia app I play
sometime. Here's another good one: How
much you think Judge Judy makes in a year?

ME

The mean lady with the doily collar on
TV? IDK. I guess it's a lot.

FUSE

45 mil. Per. Year. Kya! I NEED that job.
I can talk slick to dudes suing their
landlord over defective doorknobs just as
good as her.

ME

Wow. Now you've got me considering
law school.

FUSE

Do TV judges need law school?

ME

They gotta be a judge before the TV part.
Right?

FUSE

Searching. Hold, please.

There were more conversations like that, mostly in the evenings. Sometimes random ones in the middle of the night. The phone vibrated next to me, where it rested beneath my covers. It never woke me because it was hard to count what I did these days as actual sleep. I didn't mention it to Fuse, because I knew—I think we both did—that if she texted me trivia at three in the morning, and I hit her back, neither of us were sleeping easy. Though we soldiered on.

On Thursday, I thought Fuse found a solution. She texted right after final bell, catching me before I boarded the bus home.

FUSE

You got somewhere to be this evening?
Can you roll with me?

ME

Mama's working. I got time.

FUSE

Meet at my car.

She didn't tell me where we were going. She didn't have to. "We're driving toward the Savant," I said.

"You still got that key?"

"Yes. Why?"

"Trust, K. Trust."

Fuse drove us straight into the parking deck beneath Paris's apartment building, and pulled directly into the space designated for apartment 14-D. She grabbed her bag, and I joined her outside the car. "Is this a good idea?"

She said, "It's the best idea. You'll see."

We took the garage elevator to the fourteenth floor and let ourselves into the apartment. We'd left the balcony door slightly ajar, and the breeze had aired the place out, leaving behind the scents of rain and salt. I closed the door, cutting off a draft. Fuse plopped her bag on the couch, snatched the zipper open, and rummaged inside.

"Do you think there are more clues here? Are we opening more boxes?"

"Nope." She tugged slim plastic Blu-ray cases from her bag. I recognized the cover art immediately. *Beyond the Lights. Love & Basketball. The Five Heartbeats. House Party. Girls Trip.* Each movie still shrink-wrapped.

Fuse said, "I'm sure her copies are in one of these boxes, but I didn't feel like searching, so I just bought these from Best Buy last night." She pulled one more thing from her bag. A miniature disc player. "Since you're tech support, wanna hook this up while I get the plastic off these movies?"

"Why?"

"Because we can't stick unopened DVDs into the TV, Kya."

"No. Why are we here? Doing this now?"

She seemed genuinely confused. "Because they don't get to dictate what we do in her honor. Not the Dark Nation. Not Paula. Not even Shameik. When ParSec wanted to chill, she didn't make beats or go to parties."

"She did this." I held the mini player in my hand, a smile coming so hard and fast it made my cheeks ache. I worked, as did Fuse. I got the proper cables connected, she crinkled plastic wrap into a clear pile on the floor. With the Blu-ray player's menu screen displayed on the TV and five awesome movies spread on the couch cushions, Fuse said, "Which one first?"

Without thinking, I said, "The one she'd pick."

"*Love and Basketball*," we said at once.

At the start menu, just before Fuse pressed play on the remote, I said, "Wait. Wait, wait, wait!"

Fuse hiked an eyebrow. "What's wrong?"

I hadn't contributed. She was right, we chose how we grieved for Paris. Only, the movie idea was all Fuse. I needed a fingerprint on this, and I think I knew how to make that happen.

I checked a frequently used app on my phone. "Yes! Five Guys is on Grubhub, delivery in forty-five minutes. If we're going to honor her, we have to go all out. What do you want on your burger?"

■ ■

On the couch, blinds closed, huddled over empty burger wrappers and abandoned fries, we were crying way before the epic one-on-one game between Sanaa Lathan and Omar Epps at the film's climax. We'd both shared tears with Paris over this film and others. We both missed the good times we'd never have with her again.

When the credits rolled, we took a long moment to gather ourselves. In the quiet, a new question came to me. *Will I ever be able to do any of the stuff I used to do with any of you and not feel sad?*

I opened Notes, added it to my list.

"What are you writing?" Fuse asked, sniffly.

I'd forgotten she was there.

"What?" she persisted, sliding closer.

"They're just questions. Stuff I can't answer because they're for the people who aren't here anymore." That it came out so easily surprised me. Maybe I hadn't forgotten Fuse was there, I'd just gotten comfortable with her.

"Like what?" She didn't wait for an answer, butting up against my shoulder and peering at my screen. She read aloud, *"How much grief, on average, does it take to break a person? Oh, Kya."*

My comfort level eroded. I turned my phone down. "You think it's dumb."

"I don't. I was just pondering. My thinking is, it doesn't take much grief at all to break a person, and nothing's wrong with that. Broken things can be fixed. What else you got?" She pawed for my phone, which I transferred to my other hand and held at arm's length.

"You're Iyanla Vanzant now?"

"I've had a therapist since I was, like, eleven. Picked up a lot of good advice. It's nice to have someone to talk to. Tell me it's not just you and that phone."

I didn't want to lie.

"Oh my God, Kya. Not even the grief counselors at school?"

Again, no lies here.

"I'm here for you, kid. Let me see those other questions."

I put my phone in my pocket, not quite ready for all that.

"Fine, fine," Fuse said, unoffended. "But my therapist told me if you keep all that stuff bottled up too long, it leaks in unexpected ways. You could be cool one minute, raging the next." She palmed the eye I punched at the police station a million years ago. "I'd rather not be on the receiving end again when it does."

"Noted. What now?"

We decided we could do one more of Paris's favorites—*Girls Trip*—before the parents got too antsy about our whereabouts. I left it to her to swap the discs while I took a bathroom break. When I returned, what was on the screen was far from funny.

Fuse stood before the TV, pale light flickering over her body. "I switched back to cable while I was waiting for you. This was on the news."

It was a story about long-missing Adelaide Milton.

5:47 p.m. on a random weekday, and someone was shining a beacon over the airwaves for a kid who went missing years ago. Paris died less than two weeks ago. Who was telling her story?

I mashed the TV's power button and a cheesing, gap-toothed Adelaide winked out of existence.

Fuse said, "It's really just us. Isn't it?"

"Feels that way."

The movie marathon would have to continue some other day. Neither of us had to say it. We cleaned up our mess, locked the Savant apartment, and in the elevator down to the parking deck, Fuse said, "I might have an idea on how to deal with Paula."

The counter decreased and dinged through several floors. "Are you going to tell me about it?"

"Probably best if I don't."

"Well, this is unexpected. I trust you enough now to let that go."

"You're going to make me cry again."

The ride home was relatively quiet. We didn't talk, but while I rested my head against the cool window and watched the world zoom by, I hummed a DJ ParSec song.

Someone had to.

FUSE

Sleep did not come easy after we left the Savant, so I was on the struggle bus at school the next day. I'd downed my second Red Bull by the time final bell rang and considered the third I'd brought along, but Kya looked like a wild-eyed demon when we met in the science hall, so I gave my fix to her. She bucked the can like she was practicing for a college party. Three gulps and the crumpled empty was in the recycling bin, ready.

"Now what?"

But the question required no answer. Shameik rounded the corner, escorting Paula, dressed in one of her casual, trade-marked all-white outfits—jeans and a breezy blouse, clutching her plastic water bottle filled with this week's liquid diet, like I knew she would, like I'd been counting on. Their slaphappy conversation ceased when she spotted Kya and me loitering out-side the meeting room.

Never one to let awkward silence be awkward on its own, I said, "Hey, Paula. Nice hat."

She flinched and reflexively reached for her awful platinum wig. Upon realizing the punking, she said, "Always a pleasure, Fuse." Motioning to the room where early gatherers murmured, she said, "That your group?"

Shameik nodded with the vigor of a puppy wagging its tail. "Yes, ma'am."

Pre-vomit rose in back of my throat but settled quickly.

Paula dipped into the room. I jerked my head her way, and Kya only hesitated a moment, eyes bouncing between Shameik and me, before she followed. Leaving us alone. So.

"You're here," he said.

"I am."

"To help?" He took a step closer to me. Leaned in. Spoke low. "I know things got heated when we were texting the other night. I've cooled down since then. Thought about this a lot. There's no reason we can't . . . try, Fuse. She's gone."

I shuffled backward, fast, like I was hooked to a retracting bungee cord. "That's all the reason I need, Shameik."

His gaze darkened, and he threw his hands up, exasperated. "I got a meeting to run." He brushed past me, his shoulder catching mine.

Oh, no this dude didn't!

"Hey, everybody," his voice boomed, the room quieted. "We're gonna get started because there's a whole lot to do. This is Paula Klein. She was DJ ParSec's manager, and she's got awesome news about the memorial concert. Can you tell them about it, Ms. Klein?"

Shameik slid into an empty desk, eyed me lurking in the doorway. His eyebrows arched, like, you're still here?

I stepped in, closed the door behind me, and had a seat. The weapon in my bag clanked as I dropped it on the floor.

I had bigger jerks than him to deal with this afternoon.

KYA

Fuse still hadn't explained the when/what of how we'd crack Paula Klein, but she took a desk close to Paula, though she clearly despised her. Civility *could* be part of the investigation, I guessed.

Paula clasped her hands together. Her bloodred lipstick made her mouth a half-healed gash across her powdered face. "Such a bright, vibrant group of young people. Coming together in the face of tragedy. It gives me great hope for the future." She sipped from some nasty-looking broth. "This initiative is close to my heart and exemplifies the PK Music Group brand. Our vision, 'Changing lives through good tunes,' is not just talk."

Fuse coughed loudly, drawing death stares from Paula and Shameik. She waved away imaginary particulates. "Something foul in the air. Apologies."

A hand popped up in the middle of the room. Florian, who'd frantically been taking notes on her laptop, said, "Ms. Klein, would you be open to an interview for my Tumblr after the meeting?"

Paula produced a business card from her back pocket and got the closest student to pass it along. "Today may not be so good. I've got appointments into the evening. Email me and we'll see what we can do."

Florian grabbed the card greedily. "Thank you."

"As I was saying . . ." Most of what she expressed was a dull history of her own musical accomplishments. Her short-lived career as a drummer, signing her first act back in the '90s, managing groups whose names she said with a showman's emphasis, expecting gasps of recognition. No one here knew Sonic Spaceship or the West End Dolls—pop groups most representative of her roster's sound before she found a foothold in urban music. Her droning tested the potency of my Red Bull. We should've all gotten credit toward partial completion of a school year by the time Shameik stepped in.

He was smiling, charming, and insistent. "Ms. Klein, I think they'd like to hear the news you shared with me in the email."

"Yes. Of course. DJ ParSec was more than a beloved artist to me. She was"—dramatic pause—"like a daughter."

Fuse gripped her desktop with force. That it did not shatter was a testament to its solid construction.

"Shameik made a passionate case regarding my misstep in limiting access to her memorial service. He was right. Her classmates and fans need closure. I made some phone calls. Pulled in some favors. I'm happy to announce that the First Annual DJ ParSec Memorial Jam will take place at the Ocean Shore Amphitheater."

Excitement crackled through the room. A couple of woot-woots! We weren't talking a cheesy talent show–level venue. The Amphitheater was where big acts performed summer shows.

"Not only will it be at the Amphitheater, but it's going to feature performances by local artists like Olivia Merrick . . ."

Cheers. I knew Olivia from my singing days. She'd released some indie songs and was solid. The group was pleased.

". . . Clutch Boyz . . ."

Skateboarding brothers with a rap-rock kind of flow. A lot of the boys in the room nodded and grunted their approval.

". . . Lil' Redu . . ."

The reception was lukewarm. Did anybody like that guy's music, for real?

". . . and"—another dramatic pause, this one earned—*"Omar Bless!"*

Insanity. The room exploded. Omar Bless wasn't from VA, but that was okay considering he was the heir apparent to monster acts like Kendrick Lamar and Future. Partially on the strength of his DJ ParSec–produced track "Smoke Screen." The Grammys were over half a year away, and there was already talk of him crushing the awards show next go 'round.

This was shaping into something that Paris would've been proud of. The room knew it, even if most people here didn't know her. Making it harder to share their enthusiasm. Paula Klein's "daughter" had fired her, so why go all out like this?

"It's happening fast, people, a little over two weeks from now. I've taken the liberty of producing radio spots to get the word out, and tickets will hit online vendors Monday morning. By Monday afternoon, I expect all seats filled. With your help spreading the word, of course."

Florian's hand went in the air again. "How much will the tickets cost?"

"Varying prices, depending on section."

A portion of excitement seeped from the room. Some of the people here probably got lunch assistance, so purchasing concert tickets wasn't realistic.

Paula, reading the disappointment in the room, saved this bit of news for last. "One arrangement I made personally . . . first five hundred attendees showing a valid Cooke High School ID get through the door free of charge."

Florian rushed forward and flung herself at Paula with a full embrace. Others joined. A mass of black and brown children hovering around the woman in white like she was the sun. Shameik kept his distance. Fuse and I didn't leave our desks. Something about this just felt wrong.

Could it be that she might've been the one who had created the demand for a memorial concert by killing our friend?

"Everybody, chill." Shameik forced the group to simmer down, an uncomfortable expression sagging his face. "Give her some air."

Some remained standing, most returned to their seats. Fuse flicked disgusted looks at me, with one hand buried in the folds of her bag.

Paula continued with a few more logistical things. How we could help spread the word, how early Cooke High students should plan to arrive if they want a crack at the free seats. Her speech was faster, almost urgent. She bounced foot to foot, and Fuse grinned.

Shameik said, "Let's thank Ms. Paula Klein for dropping in with such fantastic news, everybody."

Paula accepted the ovation like a veteran performer, kissed Shameik's cheek, then left. Fuse mouthed, *See you in a bit*. And pursued.

Wait! What?

I left my desk too, vaguely aware of Shameik giving me the stink eye as I chased my friend into the hall.

"Fuse," I hissed, "what are we doing?"

She was annoyed, dismissed me with a pushing motion. *Back off!*

"Fuse!"

"*We* aren't doing anything. Remember, you trust me now. You should hang back on this one."

"We're in this together. I really want to know the plan now."

She spun on me, scary. I backed into a wall of lockers, the thin aluminum bins clashing like weak cymbals. "When the Dark Nation first started and they were wildin', I told ParSec to steer clear of their videos, comments, and low-key dry snitching about the borderline illegal things they did in her name. Plausible deniability."

"What's that got to do with me?"

"That we're in this is my fault. I built the monster that's got us running around like buddy cops. This should've never fallen on you. Not in the slightest."

"But it did, and I'm here."

"Listen. I'm out of this school one way or another. My dad's seen to that. Any trouble I get in probably won't be the same as trouble you get in. Let me do this on my own in case it goes bad."

Oh my God, what was she going to do? "After what we've been through, I'm not letting you take the heat for anything done on *our* behalf."

Fuse backed off. "Final warning, then. I don't need you in there for this."

"*I* need to be in there, though."

She raised her hands in submission. "Those fad diet drinks she sips, they make her pee like she's pregnant. She makes a pit stop when she enters and leaves a venue. I watched her do it like clock-work for months. I knew she'd have to go before she left the school. Knew I'd get a crack at her."

Fuse snaked one hand into her bag, stalked into the bathroom. I followed, just as a roaring flush sounded. Paula Klein undid the latch on her stall and clutched her chest when she saw us. "Jesus, Fuse. What now?"

Yanking her hand free of the bag, wielding a device I'd only ever seen on TV, Fuse said, "Now we have a real conversation. No bodyguards protecting you here."

Paula's eyes bugged. I imagined mine did too.

Fuse depressed the trigger, and blue lightning sparked between the prongs of the stun gun.

So much for civility.

FUSE

The stun gun was a relic from the back of Mom's closet. These days she preferred pepper spray and the spiked keychain her self-defense teacher gave her to this heavy, takes-a-full-day-to-charge fossil. She wouldn't notice it gone. Unless I got expelled and/or arrested for having it on school property. Even then, I felt confident a self-defense argument would play since I wielded it against a possible murderer. I was standing my ground.

Paula's feet scrabbled. She squeezed in a narrow space next to the paper towel dispenser.

"Make a noise and I'll light you up." I said. Paula clapped a hand over her mouth. Terrified.

Good.

I wasn't actually going to use the stun gun on her. Who knows what would happen given the weapon's age and Paula's penchant for cheap fabrics. Fireball? Eh. No, Paula wasn't in any real danger today, but I liked letting her believe she was. In my experience, bullies were more afraid of the world than anyone they preyed on. My plan was to leverage that fear into useful info. Best-case scenario: a confession. Worst-case: Disney World–level fun for me.

Kya—just as terrified as Paula—said, "I'm going to wait outside."

Too bad I couldn't let her in on the fine details at that moment. "Told you that'd be best."

She scurried away, leaving Paula and me alone in a long-overdue reunion.

I said, "You threw me out of my friend's memorial service. You did it smiling."

"Fuse"—her eyes followed the business end of my mom's stun gun—"may I speak?"

"No."

With my free hand, I slipped the VenueShowZ letter from my pocket and placed it on the counter near her. "Pick it up. Read it."

Her bony, shaky, liver-spotted hand plucked it up. "I don't have my glasses."

"It's a letter from ParSec's new management company. She fired you. Seems real suspicious that she tried to move on from your company and ended up dead. Somehow I bet that got left out of whatever statement you made to the police, right?"

"There's been a mistake here!" Her voice trembled with the lie.

"Did she fire you or not? A lie or the truth will make me happy in vastly different ways. I promise you'll only enjoy one of them." Energy sizzled between the gun's prongs.

"Yes! We'd come to an agreement to terminate our partnership. But it's not what you think."

"I think you, or one of those goons from her memorial, needed to teach her the consequences of double-crossing you. Right, Paula? You've already admitted you're petty. Why not cop to petty enough to murder your former meal ticket?"

Her chest hitched. "I didn't hurt her, Fuse."

"Hurt and kill aren't the same thing, Paula."

"I promise you it wasn't me. It wasn't *me*." Her head dropped, she cupped her face in her hands. Enough hot tears spilling that they leaked between her fingers and dripped to the floor.

"If not you, who?"

Her face tipped up, she was a sloppy crying mess. "I knew where she was going to be. That night."

"And?"

"I'm telling you I didn't go there, and I didn't send anyone there. Not on purpose."

I leapt forward. "What's that mean?"

"He was mad, and I was too. I knew about the pop-up party she was throwing, and I only mentioned I wouldn't be going. That's all I said. He said, 'Going where?' and I suppose I let it slip."

"He who, Paula?"

Barely a whisper, as if saying his name would summon him in a cloud of fire and black smoke. "Lil' Redu. I told him where to find her."

PARIS/DJ PARSEC

(4 MONTHS BEFORE)

"Redu, you're mumbling again." I toggled the talkback button, muting my side of the conversation so he couldn't hear me curse under my breath. This was our ninth take.

Even though he was unaware I was calling him every name but his own, I, unfortunately, could still hear him making excuses inside the recording booth. "That's how I want it to sound."

If I didn't need his money . . .

Annoyed, I played back what he'd just done, then unmuted my mic. "Do you understand yourself, Redu? I guarantee the average listener won't. You sound like the Swedish Chef from the Muppets. Don't he, Fuse?"

I waited for her to chime in, but her face was in her phone. Again.

"Fuse!"

She jerked alert. "Huh? Sorry. What?"

"Redu's verse."

Dazed and distracted, she was like, "Yeah, it's dope."

"See!" Redu shouted from the booth.

I smacked my forehead.

Thank goodness he'd come to the studio alone tonight. No rowdy, constantly shifting entourage to make the process more painful with their unwanted input and feedback. Crazy that in their absence, *my* one-woman entourage was the session's problem child.

Fuse's eyes were on her phone again, and she left her seat. "I gotta step out for a minute. This is important."

With a wave, I dismissed her. She'd made tonight's work harder by ego-boosting this clown. Whatever been going on with her lately had her off her game. No new ideas on the social media front. My followers and SoundCloud plays had been stagnant. Paula been on me about bringing in some more "seasoned branding talent," a suggestion I shut down, of course. Never told Fuse, but maybe I should. She been slipping lately and hadn't said why.

"Run it back!" Redu demanded.

We started again. Did three more mush-mouthed takes that had me wondering if he'd gotten dental work done before coming here. Fuse had the right idea. I needed a break. "Take five. I'm going to get some air."

I bundled up, because Ocean Shore cold could feel like ice water misting you from all directions, and stepped out the studio expecting to see Fuse in her car, doing whatever. I didn't see her, though. I heard her. And him.

Around the corner, the conversation quick and desperate in tone. I snuck closer to make out words, and I didn't feel the cold anymore.

"—told you that you have to go," Fuse said.

Shameik wasn't trying to hear it. "Is that what you want, though? For real?"

"What I want doesn't matter. You can't be here. This can't happen."

"*Again.* You mean it can't happen *again.*"

"It should've never happened. It was a moment of weakness. I've regretted ever since. I should—I should just tell her. I'm going to." Crunching gravel footsteps, and rustling fabric. "Let go of my jacket, Shameik."

"Seriously, though, me and her ain't together no more. You don't have to tell her anything. We should be able to do what we want."

"I don't want, Shameik. Maybe in the moment, I did. But it was wrong. You shouldn't have kissed me, and I for sure shouldn't have kissed you back."

No way. Seriously? This was what they've been up to? How stupid did they think I was?

I rounded the corner. He towered over her, both of his hands were on her hips, gripping hard through her jacket. Her head was turned away, avoiding his gaze like she'd stumbled upon Medusa. So he saw me first. Startled, he released her and backed away. The sudden shift in demeanor drew her attention to me, and her face went slack. She said, "ParSec—"

One finger, the signal my first-grade teacher used when the classroom needed to quiet down. Fuse must've realized it was in her best interest to heed my direction here.

Shameik, however, "Well, now you know."

"There's nothing to know," Fuse countered, and took another step closer before rethinking her safety.

"Sounded to me like there's a bunch to know, Fuse. You kissed him?"

"No. Yes. I mean, it was an accident."

"A kissing accident?"

"Why do you even care, Paris?" Shameik stuffed his hands in his pockets and bounced his shoulders. He did that when performing some of his angrier poetry. "You got the studio. And Lil' Redu.

And your famous clients. Since when do you concern yourself with us peons?"

"Excuse me?"

Fuse said, "Shameik, stop! ParSec, don't listen to—"

I'd lost all my chill. "Whatever scheming you two been doing is my fault because—what? I have a job? A life? Responsibilities? I'm out here on my own now, and because I couldn't hold your hand or take some corny picture at the homecoming dance with you, you got the right to hook up with my so-called friend."

Shameik scowled, but Fuse shrank. Like she was trying to get small enough to sail away on the wind. Still, she tried it, she opened her mouth. "I'm sorr—"

"Don't you dare apologize," I said. "The two of you never could get enough of talking about me behind my back. So keep on. When I get a platinum album, when I'm rolling into the Grammys, when I get a big house on a hill, talk about me. Because that's all you'll have."

I turned, heard Fuse's shuffling footsteps. "You don't want to come back into this studio, Fuse. I promise you don't."

And she didn't.

Back inside, at the board, I hit the talkback button. "We're going again."

I started the track, but he missed his cue. Instead, saying, "You good?"

"Rap!"

I started the track again. We got through the session, I collected my money and went back to my cold, dark, lonely place. Success never felt less valuable.

••

Three days later, it was 7:00 p.m., winter dark out, and I should've been at the studio.

I couldn't leave my bed.

It was freezing outside but hot in my room. An oscillating fan on my dresser fwump-fwump-fwumped back and forth, creating a cone of cool air I wanted to live in. My phone buzzed, and my first instinct was to throw it across the room. Considering how crappy this place Paula had me renting was, the impact would probably collapse the whole structure and kill me.

The phone buzzed again, and I made a guessing game of who it might be. It wasn't Fuse because I'd blocked her number. Certainly, it was someone with an urgent need because on top of making hot music, I was also a genie. Everybody wanted something. Everybody's mad if they don't get it. But I'm just one person. This was supposed to be living the dream. Living the dream didn't feel much different than living with the roaches at Grandma's house. Except lonelier.

Two buckets in the kitchen plinked with random drops from a leak the maintenance man didn't seem real motivated to find. There was a hornet's nest in the guest bedroom closet, so I'd been contemplating having the whole room sealed up like an Egyptian tomb. Paula said she'd talk to someone about it. That was two weeks ago. Maybe Fuse wasn't the only person on payroll who needed replacing. The more I lay here, the longer that thought lay with me.

On buzz three, I flipped the phone over. Saw a name I hadn't heard from in a while and my heart skipped.

KYA
I don't know if this is even your number
anymore.

KYA

I need to see you. Please.

KYA

I miss you.

My eyes prickled with fresh tears over that last text. I missed her too. Even if I didn't know it until that moment.

ME

Five Guys? In an hour?

KYA

Yes.

KYA

Thank you.

▪ ▪

I got to the burger joint fifteen minutes early but didn't order. I'd wait for Kya, and we'd get our usual. My treat. Brought cash because Paula hadn't fixed my bank account situation yet. That sizzle from meat hitting the grill and that savory oily smell that made fresh oxygen feel inferior was thick. My mouth watered. How long since I was last here? I honestly couldn't remember.

The table we usually copped was occupied by a dad and his two babies. One was in a carrier thing, like a picnic basket for infants. The other looked like he was ready for kindergarten. While the dad helped the infant hold its bottle, the big kid played in his fries, humming some tune that seemed nursery rhyme-ish.

Lately, in the studio with Redu, or with Paula breathing down my neck about some future gig, thinking about music felt like I had a bad milkshake. I'd forgotten moments like *this*. Pure, old-school inspiration.

All of a sudden I was happily thinking of piano chords. *Ting-ting-ting-ting*, then some kids—like a choir!—on vocals, laid over a sample from something Disney. I'd been feeling *The Lion King* lately, probably something from that would work. It was all messy in my head, and I broke out my phone to get some rough sounds down in the GarageBand app so I wouldn't forget.

The door chimed. I recognized Kya by height alone. She was all bundled up in a bubble coat with the fur-trimmed hood shadowing her face, had the puffy cartoon gloves. I absently waved her over, then made sure to save my new song file. She'd get exactly where I was coming from with this, she knew my vibe. Even though she claimed music wasn't her thing anymore, since we were talking again, it might not be that hard to get her in the studio for one session. Then, another. Then . . .

The possibilities of getting the team back together again. We'd had our problems, yeah, this dinner, though . . . that had to mean we're all good. Just as those piano chords chimed in my head, hope blazed in my chest.

She sat, flipped her hood back, and I knew whatever this was, good was nowhere near it. "Kya? What?"

Her eyes were puffy, nearly swollen shut. Snot crusted her nostrils. She mopped her damp cheeks with those puffy gloves, succeeding in nothing but smearing tears.

"Did something happen to your mama, Kya?"

A head shake. "No. Not her."

She seemed dazed almost. Rambling. "Phillip wanted to be a millionaire. He had all these plans. The app was making money, and I started thinking, yeah, yeah we could—"

Who the heck was Phillip? "Kya. You ain't making sense. What app?"

She sobbed into her fist, and the only thing I kept thinking was, *why* did you text me?

Salty, I slid from the booth, kept it chill, though. Food would help. "I'mma get you something to eat. The usual?"

She waved me off. "No thank you."

"I got it."

She was insistent. "I can't eat right now. I just needed to talk to someone. Mama had a gig, and I don't think she'd care that much anyway."

But I would? I haven't seen you in months, Kya, and I got out of bed for all this me-me-me crap? More problems laid at my feet.

She said, "Simon was all about the math and sometimes didn't care about the other stuff."

"I thought his name was Phillip."

If she heard me, I couldn't tell. Then she mentioned some other dude—Jim—and I needed a break from the drama.

At the counter, I ordered, paid. My burger sizzled, and so did I. I mean dang, Kya, a "Paris, what's up with you?" would've been nice. Or a "Paris, are *you* okay?" Why did no one in my life give a crap about me anymore? Them, them, them. All the time. What can DJ ParSec provide today?

The worker dropped my burger in its paper bag, topped it with greasy fries. I wasn't hungry anymore.

That family from before was packing up to brave the cold, the older kid still singing his nursery rhyme. What was inspiration minutes ago was now a sonic irritant, the audio equivalent of hot sauce in your eye. How in the world did I think I could spin a song from that? Such a stupid idea. Right up there with coming here in the first place.

Back at the table, Kya looking all sad and heartbroken pissed . . . me . . . off. Still, I tipped my bag toward her. "Take a fry."

She shook her head. "No. I can't."

I grabbed a handful myself, jammed some in my mouth to keep from cussing her out.

Kya managed to squeeze more words through her sloppiness. "I talked to Simon right after last bell. That wasn't even six hours ago. How could it happen so fast?"

The fries were Cajun style, too much seasoning. I almost gagged swallowing, and with those fries went my patience. I threw the whole bag of food into the trash can a few feet from us, a shot as impressive as a Diana Taurasi three-pointer.

Kya stiffened, surprised by the move.

I said, "I really didn't come to hear about your boy troubles. That crap is juvenile to me. I been making these money moves, and this, frankly, wastes my time."

"Boy trouble?" She had the expression of someone trying to interpret a difficult problem. "I'm talking about my coding club? Phillip is a member of the Smart Ones. You don't remember them?"

"Naw, I don't remember no coding club." Truth. Some of the stuff from Cooke High felt twenty years gone, so much has happened.

Her tears dried instantly, like I'd blasted her with oven heat. Her watery red eyes became just red. Almost demonic. Some of our childhood fistfights started this way. If that's what it was, that's what it was.

"I've tried to text you, Paris. Tried calling, even. You blew me off on my birthday, and every other time I reached out. You're a star, and it hurt, but I gave you space. Tonight's not like those other things. I came here desperate."

So did I!

But I didn't say that. I didn't tell her that I'd been so, so low lately. Instead, "So you called me here to read me over missing a movie and some calls. If you knew half of what I been going through, you'd feel stupid mouthing off about your club and your app. News flash, Kya, there's more important stuff happening in the world than the dumbness you're doing to pad your college applications."

She flipped her hood back up, snapped the button at her collar, prepared to leave. Everybody leaves, right. "Go on, then," I said, faked a laugh. "Tell your friends you got to hang with a legend in the making tonight. Put that in your college essays! Want a selfie before you go?"

Her hood angled toward me, so big and floppy, only her mouth escaped the shadow it created. She said, "No. I don't want a selfie. I do want you to listen. For once."

"What?" How was she going to whine now?

"You're rotten on the inside, Paris." Her voice was as clear and steady as I'd ever heard it. Better than when she sang. "You've always been a little bit. Selfish, and demanding, and hardheaded. Whatever that foulness in you before was, it's spread. Somebody should throw you away."

On that, she left. A gust of icy wind swept the restaurant when she shoved her way outside.

Stunned, I was unable to process her words, despite replaying them over and over. Must've been an hour I sat there, long enough for Kya to get home and to a computer. The notification on my phone broke my trance:

CHANGES HAVE BEEN MADE TO VAULT CLOUD FILE "MUSIC AUTOSAVE."

It was an old cloud account, where Kya uploaded stuff we did. Before.

Wait. Wait. Wait.

I tapped the notice. The app opened automatically, navigated to the folder. It hadn't been *changed*. It had been *emptied*.

All our music was gone.

KYA

I'm going to get expelled. I'm going to get expelled. I'm going to get expelled. Unless . . .

Posted outside the bathroom, only catching vague murmurs of whatever information Fuse pried out of Paula Klein, I played sentry. The best I could hope for was no one came along, so no witnesses to back up whatever Paula told the cops later, because, for real, two black girls assaulting a white woman in a bathroom—she was *definitely* going to the cops. We'd lie, deny, cry . . . anything but admit to what would surely mean jail time on top of the certain expulsion. A lot of jail time. Even if Paula had killed Paris. That's the way things worked. We don't get to stand our ground.

It was after school. The hall was empty. I'd only have to keep things that way until Fuse finished. Simple, if she hurried.

"Kya, hey!"

No, no, no!

Florian rounded the corner. Her backpack straps cinched tight on her shoulders, a single white earbud cable snaked from her ear to the phone she held before her like a compass. From the bathroom, I caught something that sounded like "There's been a mistake here!"

Fuse, *please* don't electrocute her right now.

Quickstepping, I met Florian halfway and hoped sound didn't travel. "What?"

"You and Fuse Fallon left that meeting in a hurry." She leaned sideways, inspecting the empty hall. "Where is Fuse?"

"Um, she . . ." I made a show of rubbing my abdomen. "Her stomach . . ."

Florian grimaced but remained on-mission. "'Cause you two seem real buddy-buddy now. That's a story I could run, and the ParSec lovers would eat it up. Enemies to friends in the wake of tragedy. That's good enough to get picked up by some bigger music sites."

"So, publicity for you."

"Just sayin'. You obviously haven't been checking the feeds. Some folks in ParSec Nation still hatin' on y'all. A little positivity could go a long way."

"I don't know if anything you're saying right now could be classified as positive."

"You two keep acting like I don't want to help. Stubborn for no reason."

Any other day, I would've walked away, but if this kept her from getting closer to that bathroom . . .

"Ask your questions. I'll give you three."

She wouldn't have smiled bigger if I was her mom saying she could have pizza *and* ice cream. She fiddled with her phone, stretching the cord taut on her earbud. "Awesome. Let me set up my recorder?"

All sorts of bad things occurred to me in a microsecond. Fuse's warnings about staying off the record with reporter types (even wannabes like Florian), the high possibility of the Paula Klein bathroom maneuver getting loud at the exact wrong moment.

"No recording!" Fear and self-preservation are what made me snatch her device like I did.

The earbud cord popped loose from its jack. Her music app controls appeared on-screen, and my thumb brushed the play command, resuming the song she'd been listening to, loud through the speakers.

A part of me is all, do I stay?

And all you do is take away.

Florian snatched the phone back, silenced it. Too late.

Of course I'd already recognized my voice—mine and Paris's song. The song no one else on earth should've had . . . unless they also had a fondness for creeper masks and custom sneakers featuring old cartoons.

Paula was sobbing, alarmingly loud. It drew my attention when she lurched from the bathroom before spotting me and stumbling away in the opposite direction. Fuse emerged next, yawning like she was bored. "I think I'm crashing off all that caffeine. What? What's the matter?"

"Florian! She's . . . she's—" I turned toward the unmasked monster who'd been terrorizing us.

The hall was empty.

FUSE

Google Maps took us to the address Kya obtained with her guidance office access. Ten minutes from the school, putting us twenty minutes behind Florian's head start. Given the capabilities her and her merry band of masked crazies had displayed thus far, I feared what she might do with that time. "What if she's not there?"

"We wait." Kya brooded. "She's got to come home eventually."

That felt . . . dark. Grim in a way that scared me a little, and I still had Mom's stun gun.

"Turn right on Edwards Street."

We cruised into a suburban neighborhood near the Ocean Shore city limits. Detached, single-level ranch homes, mostly. Faded asphalt and patchy lawns. There was no outlet. The street became a wide turnaround. Someone's basketball hoop, weighted down with a couple of sand bags, marked the end of the cul-de-sac.

"Your destination is on the left."

Thanks, but the confirmation wasn't necessary. I recognized Florian's car—an old, well-kept forest-green Honda Civic—at the curb in front of her house. I circled the b-ball hoop, pulling right up to Florian's bumper.

Kya said, "Give me that stun gun."

I'd seen this look, a second before I got real acquainted with Kya's fist. I spoke in the calm, cool tone of my therapist, "K, chill.

Remember what I said about you keeping stuff inside, and how it might leak out in unexpected ways? I think we may have reached that point of the program."

"Give me. That. Stun gun."

Okay, she'd snapped. Best to comply. Fished the weapon from my bag, and she snatched it from my hand, was stomping across one of the best-kept lawns in the neighborhood on a beeline for the door.

I hurried behind her, anticipating chaos. She triple-jabbed the doorbell, the stuttering gongs loud from my position at the bottom porch steps.

"Kya, be cool!" said the person who just held an old white woman captive in a school bathroom.

The door opened, a dark-haired lady—petite, with round red cheeks like two apples—revealed herself. Florian's mom, given the resemblance. "Can I help you?"

Okay, so I expected Kya to kick the door in, snap this woman's neck like Jessica Jones, and tear Florian out the house through a load-bearing wall. Alas, she took my initial advice and was kind of chill about the whole thing, concealing the stun gun in the back waistband of her pants like a real G, going to her standard scholastic fake-out tactics.

"Yes, ma'am. We go to school with Florian. She told us to come by and talk about the final project that's due Monday."

Flo-Mom beamed. "Of course, come in. She's in her room."

Kya didn't hesitate, disappearing into the shadows of the house. I followed while Flo-Mom called, "Florian! Your friends are—"

The thud of running footsteps, a panicked Florian yelling, "Ma, you didn't—"

She saw us, and maybe reconsidered voicing any concerns she might have.

"Your school friends are here about your project." The way Flo-Mom put it, not a total lie. She left us, attending to something delicious-smelling, though I doubted we'd be invited to stay for dinner. Kya stalked down the hall, fists clenched.

Florian backed into her room. Kya followed, as did I, closing the door gently behind us. The click from me turning the lock sounded final.

"I'm sorry." Her twin bed caught the back of her knees, forcing her to sit-fall on the squeaky mattress. Her *Rick and Morty* sheets were a snarled ball beneath her.

"Are you now?" Kya asked. "Where are your shears?"

Florian whimpered.

A huge monitor lit up the desk by the foot of the bed. On the floor next to it, a tall computer tower hummed and glowed with alternating purple and green light shining through transparent side panels. A custom job, much like the items perched on shelves that rimmed the room's perimeter.

Those sneakers she wore when she'd terrorized us were on display with other—admittedly dope—shoes. All redone to some animation aesthetic. One pair featured *Dragon Ball Z* characters. Some Justice League Chuck Taylors sat toe-to-toe with some Avengers Jordans. There was *Steven Universe* on some Huaraches, and *DuckTales* on a pair of Adidas shell toes. I kept skirting back to the Air Force 1s I'd come to know intimately in the moments where Florian made me believe I might die. Elmer chasing Bugs, barrels raised. Probably thought you were so meta with that, didn't you, Florian? Tables have turned now. Her face quivered, terrified.

I said, "It's not so fun when the rabbit's got the gun, huh, Flo? Would it help if we put on masks?"

"You're not going to hurt me. You're . . . you're better than that."

"Wow," I said, "she actually tried it."

Kya hefted the stun gun appreciatively, depressed the trigger so it crackled with blue fire. "Good weight."

"I know, right?"

Florian hugged herself.

Kya triggered the electricity again, an inch from Florian's face. "Who are you to twist Paris's name and legacy so you can run around like a bad Batman villain? *We* knew her, *we* were her friends, and you think you can weaponize her memory against us?"

Florian squirmed. "Kya, I really never meant you any harm."

"You threatened to cut off my freaking pinkie, you psycho!"

"No, no. I wasn't going to really *do it*. I promise. It was this thing that came up in one of the Dark Nation forums, like an inside joke."

I said, "Y'all joke weird."

Kya's muscles shook with the strain of, I don't know, wrestling with her sanity. I wagered Florian had a fifty-fifty shot of not getting cooked today. When I got up this morning, I didn't realize how many jail-worthy events I'd be involved in before sunset.

Sane Kya won this initial bout, as she tore herself away from Florian and stepped toward the massive computer. "Is this where you listened to our conversations? Made your little polls about us?"

"You better answer," I told Florian, leaving off "for both of our sakes."

"Yes! I am sorry. I understand that, maybe, I crossed a line."

I said, "Maybe? Who else was in the van that night? Were

they the same guys at ParSec's apartment? They go to Cooke High too?"

Again, Florian attempted to maintain some fading tough chick facade like she wasn't going to talk.

"Okay. Kya, fry her."

Kya lunged, stun gun extended like a spear.

"Wait, wait!" Florian cowered. "Keep it down. My mom doesn't know about any of this."

"That's what you're worried about?" Kya scoffed.

"There's no one else at the school that I know of. We don't even know each other. The masks aren't just for scaring you two."

Kya glanced my way, I returned a slight nod. I believed the part about the masks at least. Whenever #DarkNation popped up with one of their ratchet videos or online photos they were masked up too. It's something they did from the start, though I never knew why. Till now.

Still. "Aren't you the leader?" I asked. "They took orders from you."

She made an "eh" face. "Only because I handled the tech. They treated what I did with my iPad like sorcery. *Here be dragons!*" Florian snort-laughed at her own bit.

Kya was deadly serious. "No more jokes. Nothing's funny."

"Alls I'm saying is the Dark Nation is a bunch of splinter cells. Mostly in North America, but there are members on at least four continents. Second-heaviest population is Asia. ParSec's music bangs in Japan."

"I'm aware," I said. "So you felt okay rolling with a bunch of masked dudes you knew nothing about?"

"I think the guy with the van is from Portside. The two that snatched you, Kya, I believe they're brothers. Don't know where from."

Kya leaned in, jaw set, stun gun in a death's grip. "How did the brothers from nowhere get my address?"

I touched Kya's shoulder, guided her back with a light grip. "Florian, as you can see, Kya is prepared to hurt you. You'd deserve that. I might let her do it. But we have other concerns at the moment."

Kya's mean expression communicated a clear question: *We do?*

In the race to Florian's, I hadn't had a chance to fill Kya in on what I'd learned from Paula. I'd need to be careful how much I let slip here. Just because Florian was caught didn't mean she was defanged. Horror movies had taught me vampires were most dangerous when they're cornered.

Motioning to her computer setup, I said, "How good are you with that stuff?"

Florian answered carefully. "Good-good."

"If I gave you a name, could you do all your spy hacker stuff to get us info on that person?"

"Depends on the name."

"Lil' Redu."

Florian grimaced. "His rhymes are so stupid. In my opinion, 'Calm Down, Turn Up!' succeeds in spite of him. Contrary to what he'd have the world believe. That whole Lil Wayne vibe meets—"

Kya ignited the stun gun.

"Let me see what I can do."

PARIS/DJ PARSEC

(2 MONTHS BEFORE)

"I'm sorry about the way I been acting. Okay? I've been stressed out, everybody been on me about stuff. I know it's not an excuse. Still, I hope you'll accept my apology."

Winston swiveled his chair and patted my knee. Quick. Two taps, then pulled away. He'd been my only comfort lately. He said, "You haven't mistreated me. At all."

Absently, I tapped the pads on my drum machine, alternating between a bass and snare. The only sound in the studio. The booth was empty. No one in the place except the owner—asleep in his back office—and us. These days I preferred the empty studio to home.

I hadn't worked on any new music in a couple of weeks. No energy. The love was absent.

But that crap with Fuse and Shameik, then the blowup with Kya, things ain't been feeling right since.

Was my only friend really a reporter? "You're probably the last person I should be telling this stuff to."

Winston lifted his phone, showed me a black display, set it back down. "We're off the record. No one ever has to know about this. Believe it or not, I recall some of what you're going through."

"All your friends turned on you?"

"Don't know that I'd put it that way. At different stages in life, you grow apart from people. The break can be a subtle drift, or a quake fracturing the world. It's almost always for the best."

I triple-tapped my snare. "That could be a song." I was only half-kidding.

"I dabbled a bit in my youth."

"Yeah?"

"Don't sound so surprised. I could jam. Write, sing, play a little guitar. I saw myself as a Lenny Kravitz type."

"Who that?"

"Guy who made Katniss's costumes in the Hunger Games movies."

"Oh."

He picked up his phone, tapped the screen. "Here, listen. This one is called 'Again.' He won a Grammy for this."

The drum intro, plus the accompanying guitar, had me immediately. Winston closed his eyes, reclined as far as his chair allowed, mouthing along to lyrics about someone Lenny Kravitz loved and hoped to see again. Simple, really. And devastating.

"Can you"—I cleared my throat—"turn it off, please?"

He hunched forward, recognizing that I wasn't feeling whatever he thought I'd feel, and rapidly tapped at his phone, allowing for another half verse before he got it paused. "Tell me what happened, Paris. I'm not a journalist right now."

It all came out. My beef with Grandma over leaving home. My money not being what it should be and Paula with the excuses. Kya getting brand-new on me and saying I was rotten trash or whatever. Fuse and bum Shameik sneaking around.

"The way my so-called friends flipped was the worst. Adults are adults, y'all don't get how anything is. No offense."

"None taken."

"Fuse and Kya backstabbing me like they did. It felt beyond betrayal. I would've trusted them with my life—now I know that would've been the absolute wrong move. Jealous heifers. They were just waiting to step on my throat." It felt good to say it out loud.

"Wow. Better you found out sooner than later. Believe it or not, I've been through this sort of thing. It hurts now, but a year from now, two years from now, when you're traveling the world and being the star you were born to be, you'll barely remember their names."

That lit up something in me. An ember, so warm. He sounded like a TV dad, the only kind I ever knew. "You got kids, Winston?"

He took his time answering, flipping the phone in his hand like an oversized coin. "Yeah. We're not as close as I'd like. That's my fault. This business has a way of straining relationships. As you know."

"They don't want things better between you and them?"

He spun his chair so he wasn't facing me. I panicked, afraid I'd crossed the line, pushed him away. "My bad. It's not my business."

He didn't correct me. "Speaking of business. If you're really unhappy with Paula—from what I've turned up in my research, you wouldn't be the first—you're not obligated to stay with her."

That I knew. When I wasn't in the studio, I was researching other, better managers. Maybe I'd need a lawyer. Maybe Winston would help. "How would I break away? Who would I need to talk to?"

He jabbed his thumb toward himself. "You've started in the right place. First, you gotta be serious about exiting the PK Music Group. We don't want to roll on this if you're not sure."

"Say I was. What'd be next?"

"If you were certain, really certain, I'd ask you this question: Have you ever heard of VenueShowZ?"

KYA

I lay in my bed, weary, still not sleeping well, and texting while a Nat Geo science program about uploading consciousness into the cloud played low on my TV. It'd been six days since Fuse talked me out of cooking Florian with that stun gun. Six days of nowhere leads from that little tech witch. No one's seen or heard from Lil' Redu, like he never even existed.

FUSE
Wanna set phasers to stun, go back to Florian's house, and see if we can motivate her into some better results?

ME
As tempting as that is, I'd like to believe she's smart enough not to jerk us around given the amount of pain we could easily visit upon her, if we so choose.

FLORIAN
Guys, you do know I'm still on this group text?

                                                    ME
                        Shut it, Flo. Fuse—are we kidding
                        ourselves here? It's going on a month.

FUSE
I don't have a good answer.

Aside from her trying to track Lil' Redu, part of our deal to not beat Florian down involved her running interference with her other masked colleagues, so she wasn't totally useless. She continued to hang out in their secret forums, keeping their expectations low and, essentially, not spearheading further harassment since she appeared to be the local boss. The Dark Nation was finally off our backs. But finding Paris's killer was never solely about them, and we were running into a wall.

Winston told us the police had already questioned Lil' Redu. If they let us go because obviously we didn't do it, *and* let him go, didn't it stand to reason there was nothing there?

FUSE
And you believe Paula?

                                                    ME
                        We've been over this. She didn't
                        snitch on us, and she
                        could've.

FUSE
Yet. Doesn't mean innocence.

ME

She's coming through on all her promises
for the concert. The buzz is getting
crazy. All the tickets gone. That's a lot
of visibility if you're trying to distance
yourself from the murder you committed
in a fit of rage.

FUSE

Or it's misdirection

FLORIAN

Guys . . . I think I have something.

We'd been here before. I didn't bother getting my hopes up.
Florian thought she had something when she'd gotten into Lil'
Redu's SoundCloud account and discovered some metadata pointing
to a computer in Hampton. It'd been an internet café. She'd thought
she had tracked the tricked-out Range Rover he was known to ride
in. It'd been a rental from a sketchy place that kept horrible records.
She'd thought she'd found one of his girlfriends, but that'd been
some Instagram model whose pictures he'd stolen and reposted. The
more we looked, the more fictional Lil' Redu became. A rap ghost.

Florian had seemed so bad at this, during that long ride back
from Hampton the other day, I had to ask how she'd gotten into
our phones.

From Fuse's cramped backseat, she'd said, "You use the school's
Wi-Fi. It's not very secure at all."

Fuse had said, "What's that even mean?"

"Kya, open your phone."

I did.

"Swipe left until you can't anymore."

I'd swiped my index finger through the three screens of apps that normally occupied my phone. It should've been three screens only.

One lone app had been present on that fourth screen. Something called Hack in the Box.

I'd wrenched in my seat, grilling her. "You put this on here? How? It can't be just unsecure Wi-Fi."

She'd responded slowly. "You'd be surprised how much a public hotspot opens you up to."

I'd grabbed Fuse's phone from the center console, swiped to her last screen, sighed.

Fuse had said, "You do this to everyone in the school?"

"Just the interesting people. High-profile couples. Athletes. No one ever notices."

"Not even when you blast their personal business for the whole world to see?"

Florian had the nerve to sound indignant. "My sites wouldn't be so popular if people weren't so hungry for—"

Fuse had jammed the brakes, locking my seat belt and throwing Florian forward so she bumped her head on the back of my seat. "Ow!"

"Sorry," Fuse had said, resuming speed. "My bad. What were you saying?"

"My sites are—"

Fuse had jammed the brakes again.

"Ow!"

I'd said, "Take it off, Florian. Both of our phones."

"You can do it yourself. Just delete the app, then do a hard reset. I'll be locked out, so long as you don't log on to the school's Wi-Fi again."

Even after that, I'd found I couldn't delete my paranoia. I checked my phone constantly in case Hack in the Box reappeared while I wasn't paying attention.

"Hey, Kya!" Mama opened my bedroom door without knocking. She brushed the hair on her left side away, inserted a large hoop earring, and squinted like her contacts were irritating her. "What you doing?"

"Nothing. Nat Geo."

"You and your science shows. Ever since you was a little girl." She smiled when she said it, not a criticism.

"You're in a good mood."

She went to work on the other earring, sashaying in place, near giddy. "Mr. DeVan Jamison is going to be in the audience tonight at Drift Bar. He's in town for his niece's birthday or something, and wants to see what sort of talent Ocean Shore got to offer."

The name wasn't familiar, and her good mood wouldn't survive until morning. We'd been here before. Without knowing a thing about him, I understood he was someone involved in the industry—a producer, or a manager, or an A&R for some label. Someone who'd half-listen to her set, accept a copy of her demo, then vanish until she saw him in the audience during the American Music Awards broadcast before she drank herself to sleep.

"Break a leg." She didn't need me to crush her.

"You know how I do!" She wiggled a little in her pencil skirt and exited, a cloud of lavender body spray dispersing in her wake.

Her heels clacked down the stairs, the door slammed. I was alone. Something that was easier—not easy—the more I put the Dark Nation behind me. I'd never forgive Florian for the discomfort I felt in my own home. So she better have something. Another wild-goose chase wouldn't go well for her.

FLORIAN

You know the music videos Lil' Redu put on YouTube? Supposedly he has a crew called the Velvet Vendetta Gang.

FUSE

GROAN—yes, I know about the VVG.

FLORIAN

Every video starts with this zoomed in shot of a burgundy velvet chair. The chair has a crest embroidered in it. I decided to look for it, see if I could link it to a graphic designer or something. Here's what I found online.

The link she sent opened the home page of the Bay Breeze Country Club, where the crest was featured prominently.

FUSE

How does this help?

FLORIAN

Look at these screen caps of his videos.

What came next was no surprise. Bikini girl in the pool. Bikini girl in the hot tub. Bikini girl in the sauna—

The guy was married to his aesthetic.

ME

Get to the point.

FLORIAN

Now look at these pics from the country
club's photo gallery.

I sat up then, kicked my comforter away as each new image
came in. A pool. A hot tub. A sauna. The same one's from Lil'
Redu's videos.

FLORIAN

Guys, this club is private. You can't just
shoot a video there.

ME

We think Lil' Redu—Mr. Street Game
Poppin'—belongs to Country Club?

FLORIAN

Worth checking out. Right here in town.

ME

How we gonna get in if it's private?

FUSE

Easy. I'll get us in. My dad's a member.

                                                  ME
                                             For real?

FUSE

For real.

FLORIAN

Can I come?

                                                  ME
                                             Shut up.

FUSE

Saturday. We drove past the Bay Breeze Country Club. Fast at first, because I missed the turn. Dad's membership was a family membership, but he'd never brought me here. Mom didn't go because of the club's "history of discrimination." I never knew—or cared about—what she meant. Leave it to Kya to come through with the stellar research.

"This club didn't have a black member until 1986. The year after their centennial."

"Okay."

"There was a big news story about it. You can find old local broadcasts on YouTube in the 'You Knew This Was Gonna Be Racist' playlist."

"Okay."

"That doesn't bother you?"

"Of course." My second and third pass was more creep mode, really inspecting the marble columns bordering the entrance, and those hedges on steroids blocking the view of anything beyond that paved, intimidating inlet.

Kya said, "So Florian's gotta be wrong again. Places like this don't let someone who raps about 'buckshot spray the VA way' join their ranks. Right?"

"You would think so."

My fourth pass wasn't a pass. We turned onto the blue-gray asphalt drive, and the manicured forest swallowed us. Sunlight broke through foliage gaps, projecting blotchy silhouettes of leaves and branches over us for what felt like an hour before the driveway opened into a looping arch swooping up a hill. At the peak sat a clubhouse, wide enough where you could classify the opposite ends as wings, and built of pale bricks. There was a central entrance with gargantuan double doors and a canopy offering shade where crusty old dudes offloaded their golf clubs, I guessed. Beyond that, the drive had an offshoot to a parking lot at least half-filled with cars celebrities boasted about. Benzes, Beamers, Jaguars, and one royalty-like Maybach with silk curtains blocking anyone's view into the backseat. My tiny economy vehicle might get bullied here.

Still, I parked (a few spaces away from a futuristic-looking butter-yellow sports car that might transform into a robot at any second). We got out, and the clubhouse loomed.

Kya said, "No one's stopped us yet."

She wasn't wrong.

No doorman greeted us as we walked into the frigid lobby. It was warm today, but the AC here would've been suitable for a two-hundred-degree day. Gotta keep the money crisp. I shuddered and hugged myself. Kya took it like a champ, only raising the zipper on her thin hoodie jacket to her chest. A blond man—six three, in a polo shirt that hugged his toned chest, and bulging calves visible thanks to his pleated khaki shorts—emerged from a nearby corridor, his attention on the clipboard in his hand. When he glanced up and recognized he wasn't alone, he flinched. "Oh, hey. I didn't hear you come in."

"My dad's a member!" I blurted, fumbling the never-used Bay Breeze ID card from my pocket. "This is my friend. She's not a member, but the rulebook says I'm allowed one guest."

Kya elbowed me, whispered, "Fuse." She didn't say, *Stop being extra*. Still, message received.

The blond dude said, "Awesome. I just need to scan your card and have you sign your guest in."

An unoccupied podium stood off to the side of the foyer. He took my card and passed the bar code beneath an infrared scanner, triggering a quick confirmation bee-doop noise, then passed me a sheet. "Sign your name, her name, and the current time."

As I scribbled the particulars, Kya leaned over me, squeezed my arm, and the hairs on the back of my neck raised. Were we in danger? My head swiveled, expecting masks.

She jerked her chin toward the sheet I'd been signing. Took a second before I saw it. Two lines above my signature, signed in less than a half hour before. I jabbed my index finger on the sheet, pointing at the member's name. "You know him?"

Blondie said, "Of course. Everyone knows Redu!"

"Where is he? We're friends and I want to say hi."

Blondie blinked rapidly, surprised or confused. I couldn't tell which. "Last I saw, he was enjoying brunch in the dining room."

"Thanks."

We moved with purpose, following placards displaying the direction and turns to the dining room. Kya said, "First, Lil' Redu's a legit member here . . . which is *amazing*. Florian got something right."

"Second?"

"Dude got weird when you said we were friends with him. Did you notice?"

"Maybe it's because I'm not a video girl in a bikini. I don't know. Here."

A sign over the door read "Hubert and Diane Payne Dining Hall." Beyond, round tables arranged like islands, rimmed with mostly unused place settings, and decorated with lush floral arrangements in center vases. I scanned the room for brown skin, took like a half second. Seven of the ten waiters were people of color, three were black. Of the thirty or so sporadically seated diners in the room, only two were black. Just one male. He wasn't our rapper.

That guy was older than my dad. Plump, clean-shaven, with ashy gray hair, dressed for golf in a lavender shirt and beige pants. He laughed heartily at something his pink-faced dining partner said.

"What the heck, Kya?"

She shrugged.

The dining room was washed in natural light beamed through floor-to-ceiling windows looking over a recreation area. Teal water lapped the edges of a pool. Children of various ages participated in, or played spectator to, an in-progress Ping-Pong match. A patio door opened, granting access to a third type of black person. Not a waiter, not a diner. I almost didn't recognize him.

"Fuse." Kya pinched me again.

"I see."

A scrawny, smiling, young guy in a V-neck sweater and pressed fitted jeans approached the older black diner. Sound carried, and they were close enough to make out the affectionate, "Hey, Pops!"

What Lil' Redu talked about with his pops, we didn't know. It ceased abruptly when his eyes cut our way and recognition dawned, the "oh no" look on display.

Oh yes.

We delved deeper into the dining room and could just about smell the anxiety on Lil' Redu when we rolled up on him. "Hey!" I said.

"Hey." He positioned himself between us and Pops so the old man wouldn't see all the complicated things his face did. Twitched. Sweated. Ticked.

Pops said, "Who are your lovely friends, Reggie?"

I said, "Please. Introduce us. *Reggie.*"

Reluctant but playing the role, "Pops, this is Fatima Fallon. A friend from school."

And what school was that, Reggie? "Hello, sir. My dad is a member here." I still had manners, shook the man's hand.

"I don't know you," Lil' Redu told Kya through a sneer.

She maintained the pleasantries. "Kya Caine."

Pops's fellow diner gave us polite nods. Then Pops let us in on Lil' Redu's earlier request. "Tell the desk to sign the theater room key out to you under my account. Enjoy your movie."

Pops's dining buddy said, "What fine piece of cinema will you all be indulging in?"

"Don't know," I said. "I'm kind of in the mood for a good mystery. How about you, Reggie?"

He walked away, jerked his head for us to follow.

KYA

No loud, tacky fashion labels now. His clothes were visual Muzak, pastel and wrinkle-free, soothing. He wore glasses, round lenses with barely there frames. His grill was gone. His *tattoos* were gone. What was happening here?

We followed him back to the blond, where he acquired a key like some video game quest, then to a room in a separate wing. He unlocked the door, pawed in the dark for an LCD remote requiring both hands, tapped some commands, and amber sconces flared at intervals along the wall. The color scheme was burgundy (the walls, tiled floor, and ceiling) and cream (the plush leather recliners, love seats, and couches sitting at an incline before a screen). A projector was suspended from a ceiling rod, shooting ghostly blue light.

Lil' Redu plopped on the nearest seat, and scrolled through an extensive on-screen movie library. "What y'all haters want?"

Really. Dude was like Jekyll and Hyde.

Fuse popped him across the back of the head. "Use our names. And we'll use yours. *Reggie.*"

While he growled at her, I gently removed the remote from his hand, undividing his attention. "The older man. He's Redu and you're Redu. How is that?"

"Reginald. DuPree." He patted his chest. "The Third."

Fuse said, "You can't make this stuff up."

"He's my grandpa. He doesn't know about me rapping, and I'd like to keep it that way."

Fuse was giddy on this. "You mean fake rapping! I knew you weren't street."

"I *am* street."

"Wall Street?"

One of the dining room servers poked her head in. "Mr. DuPree, would you and your guests like popcorn? We have regular and caramel."

"Caramel. Thank you."

The server disappeared while Fuse laughed into the back of her hand. It wasn't funny to me. "The stuff you rap about, slinging, gangsters. There are people who really live that life. Some *have* to live that life. You're okay taking their stories and pretending they're yours. How?"

He sat forward, indignant. "My money real. One hundred percent. That's all people really care about."

Fuse was on her phone, googling. "Ah yes. Got it. Reginald DuPree the First, partner in Saunders, Vivendi, and DuPree, Attorneys-at-Law."

"Vivendi?" Visions of a stout, angry man screaming and pointing at me through my TV screen while horrific car accidents spooled behind him came to me. "Vito 'the Sledgehammer' Vivendi? The personal injury guy with twenty commercials a day?"

"He's part of the firm, but no one likes to claim him. Too gaudy."

Fuse said, "About as gaudy as a gold grill and face tattoo of a tiger's mouth, right. Let's get to it. When you threw your little studio tantrums, you threatened to kill ParSec. Nobody believed you, but she's dead anyway. So we gotta ask. How invested were you in this whole gangster image?"

His face twisted, lips spread showing spit-slick teeth, some approximation of the eternally tough scowl he wore in his videos. "You two got to be messing with me. You're trying to say I offed her."

I said, "Maybe all the murder you rap about is as real as your money?"

From me, to Fuse, to me, his gaze bounced. His face smoothed, no longer acting or amused. "I didn't *kill* anybody. Yes, I wanted my music back. She was holding my tracks because some dummy in that day's entourage spilled sweet tea on the soundboard."

Fuse said, "About that. Who were those people you're always with? As fake as you are, you rolled with some intimidating folks."

"I found them at the mall. I'd go in, wait for some people to recognize me. Then ask if they wanted to hang. All part of the costume."

Fuse scrutinized that. "No one saw through you? I mean, besides me?"

"You bought it. They did too. All they saw was a credit card and free food."

Fuse said, "So you were paying for studio time with your allowance?"

"Pretty much. Grandpa's big on personal growth. So he gives me and my cousins an annual stipend to pursue stuff we want. So I used my fifty thousand to—"

"Fifty thousand!" I might've shouted. My voice went into a different register for sure. "You got fifty thousand dollars and used it to make garbage trap music."

"Garbage? The world would disagree, string bean. I got eighty thousand followers on SoundCloud, two hundred thousand subscribers on YouTube. You don't even want to know what I'm doing on the Gram. My fans hold me down, and I don't worry about fools. Like you."

"Fair enough," I said. "Since you brought up your social media, worry about this: The night Paris died you were offline the entire time. No new pics, no new posts for a solid eight hours. We checked. The next time you posted, you were offering condolences plus some shade." I held my phone like badge, the screenshot tweet on display.

Don't Make Me Chin Check You @LilReduDaGod
Heard @DJParSec caught a bad one. Wack yo! Done lost
too many in these streets. Know her fans gon miss her, tho.
Somebody got to, I guess. #RIPParSec #ParSecNation

"I wasn't being shady. Yes, I wanted my music. And no, we didn't get along. I didn't want her *dead*."

Fuse said, "So why were you mysteriously absent from the internet at the time she was killed?"

He groaned and twisted to reach his own phone in his back pocket. He woke it, tapped open his Photos app, and swiped to an album called "Hello World." Then said, "I was here at Bay Breeze that night."

Fuse took the phone, held it so I could see too. A series of pictures flickered by. Redu—*Reggie*—in a classic tuxedo, with a pretty girl in a froufrou ball gown at his hip, their elbows interlocked. More pictures showed more black boys and girls in formal wear. In some pics, they lined up, as if being inspected. In others, spread out and caught mid-motion in some sort of group dance. We waited for his explanation.

"It's my beautillion."

I thought he'd stuttered. Our confusion must've a showed.

"It's a ball, you classless scalawags. An introduction to society. Like a cotillion, but for guys. My granddad's fraternity organizes it every year for the urban kids they mentor."

"You're not urban," I said.

"My stipend doesn't come free, whoever you are. Grandpa wanted me in it, so I participated, hung with the guys from time to time. They have some hard lives."

"That you probably lifted for a track," Fuse said.

"Judge my music all you want. That alibi is the same one the cops got. You can't dispute it."

At the top margin of each picture was a date and time taken. Learning what a clown he really was, I had no reason to think he'd doctored these somehow. No way he was anywhere near the warehouse with Paris.

"I would never have hurt ParSec because, for real, she made my stuff better. What you don't know is we'd squashed that beef. No need for either of us to go into a new situation with baggage."

"New situation?" I asked.

"We both signed new management deals with VenueShowZ. Messing with Paula Klein was counterproductive."

I'd stopped listening after VenueShowZ.

Fuse said, "When and how did VenueShowZ approach you?"

"Maybe three months ago."

"Who was your new manager going to be?"

He shook his head. "It don't work like that. VSZ a big company. They have *teams*. The marketing team. The booking team. The travel arrangements team. You got a problem, it's not one person's problem, so no one's ever more valuable than the other."

"That sounds like the formula for incredible once-in-a-generation music, for sure," Fuse said drolly.

"Some assistant put me on the phone with a guy and another guy. We emailed back and forth, I let one of the paralegals at Grandpa's firms look over the paperwork. It wasn't messy like dealing with sketch-queen Paula. I had money in the bank and show dates booked for the summer"—he snapped his fingers—"like that."

"How'd they find you?"

"Assumed they knew about me because of ParSec, since they signed her first."

"Did you mention that to the police?"

"Why? So they can mess up the deal?"

I couldn't believe this guy. "*That's* what you're worried about?"

"She's gone. You don't think she'd want one of us to go on and keep the music alive?"

Fuse slow-nodded. "Here's your phone back."

Reggie reached and she let the device fall off his fingertips a good two inches shy of his hand. It cartwheeled to the floor, smacked tile with a flinch-worthy crack.

"Yo!" He was on his knees, flipped it over. The screen was black, with a spiderweb crack orbing out from its center. He mashed the wake button. Nothing. "It won't even turn on."

Fuse said, "Use your stipend to fix it. Let's go, Kya."

With that, we left. Destroying a bit of that poser's property was only a small consolation. We sat in the car but didn't move. Where was there to go when we'd reached another dead end?

"This mean we're back to Paula?" I asked.

"No. Maybe. I don't know." She tapped her own phone screen. "What you doing now?"

"Give me one second." She jabbed her tongue from the corner of her mouth, like a painter deciding the right color and stroke for a troublesome work in progress. Then she tapped some more. This went on for two silent minutes, then she chuckled and poked the screen with one final tap. "Check this."

She showed me a tweet. Before I'd read the whole thing I was grinning.

"His phone's broken," Fuse said. "No notifications. He's going to be so surprised by how much the true Lil' Redu fans love him."

Fuse Is Determined @FuseZilla14
People saying @LilReduDaGod is throwing a pool party at Bay Breeze Country Club. Free to all #ReDuvenators. Ask for Reggie at the door. #popupparty #RIPParSec

It was at fifty-four likes and thirty-two retweets when I passed it back to her. Unless he could change into his costume like Superman, Lil' Redu's getting exposed.

Our consolation just got bigger.

Fuse thumbed the engine start button and took us off the swank country club's property. We rode high in the moment. Didn't notice the car tailing us until its emergency lights flared and we heard the siren.

FUSE

Hidden lights flashed behind the grill of the unmarked police car. The sun backlit it, all we saw was alternating red-blue, red-blue. Like lewd winks from a creeper you didn't want to be left alone with. It sped up, tailgating. Close enough that if I slammed on my brakes, there was no way it wouldn't slam into us. Riding my bumper, almost connected, it hit the siren again. A short burst—*whoop-whoop*—that translated to *pull over*.

I rarely drove with both hands, but I went to the driver's manual mandated ten o'clock–two o'clock involuntarily, my eyes darting from the road to mirror. Kya's hands went flat on the dashboard. She was as still as those passenger dummies solo drivers used to cheat the HOV lane.

We'd been searching for the person who killed our friend. Searching for a legit murderer. Through the entire ordeal—the Dark Nation, Shameik, Paula, and Redu—I wasn't as scared as now. "Where should I pull over?"

If was never on the table. I wanted to drive to Dad's office, park in the lot, and call him down to be with us. Then dragged the idea to the trash, imagining him bursting out of his building worked up and drawing a cop's attention in the worst way.

"Ahead," Kya said, "the gas station."

Yes. That was the right answer, I'd have thought of it too if I wasn't concerned with not swerving into a ditch. Apparently, Kya had gotten the same instruction I had. I doubt there were many black kids who didn't.

Not after Sandra Bland. Not after Philando Castile.

Not after the dozen other names I could list from memory because they'd been seared there while me, Mom, and Dad watched the same news stories on different dates and in different states.

Black person dead because cop got scared. Or angry. Or felt disrespected.

I turned into the lot and parked in an empty space on the side of the station. It wasn't crowded. The only other person present was a white man at the pump, filling his pickup truck. He left the pump on automatic and leaned against his truck, stared our way as if watching a show. The prominently flown Confederate flag in the truck bed got me thinking we'd picked the wrong gas station.

The unmarked car parked at an angle behind us. Blocking us in the space.

Kya freed her phone from her back pocket and started recording. She pointed the camera at me, spoke crisp and loud. "I'm Kya Caine, and I'm with Fatima Fallon. We've been pulled over by an Ocean Shore police officer in an unmarked vehicle for reasons unknown. I will continue to record the stop to its conclusion, and if this recording is interrupted in any way, it is not voluntary."

Staring straight ahead, hands in plain sight, the only movement I dared make was another glance at my rearview mirror. I heard the cop's door open, caught his midsection in the mirror—plain white button-up, dark slacks, a huge pistol on his hip. My grip tightened, threatening to tear the steering wheel off its column.

Kya was sideways in her seat, going for the best shot. Her shoulders dropped, relaxed. Relieved. "Oh."

Oh?

My side mirror offered a better, full-body view of the approaching officer. His hands were raised, far away from his gun. In one he gripped his badge, its golden glow magnified by the sun. "Kya, Fatima. It's Detective Barker. Don't be afraid, girls."

I didn't release the wheel, though my grip relaxed. "Detective."

He stood at my window, blocking the light. "I need to talk to you two. Not here."

Kya said, "What's going on, Detective?"

"Oh, I think you have a strong inkling. If you don't mind, let's do this over lunch. I'm going to get in my car, and I want you to follow me. Are we clear?"

Neither of us answered quickly.

"You could run," he admitted. "But I know where each of you live, so let's just keep this cordial." He took a step toward his vehicle, then returned. "Kya, you shooting all this right now?"

"Yes, sir."

"You kept recording? Even after you knew who I was and I told you not to be afraid?"

Kya was defiant. "Yes, sir."

He tapped my doorframe lightly. "Good girl."

• •

We followed the detective to a place called Evangeline's Kitchen, where he got us a corner booth close to the window and away from the other lunchtime diners. He let us order what we wanted, did most of the talking between bites of his patty melt.

"Let me tell you what I know so far," he said. "You two have been reinterviewing persons of interest in Paris Secord's murder. You've been running into dead ends. Whatever trail you pick up stops cold. How close am I?"

We were in so much trouble. Kya wouldn't look up from her pecan waffle.

Barker chomped more sandwich. "You don't have to answer that one. I understand if you're feeling queasy about all this. My next question I'm going to have to insist you answer. Have you two lost your minds?"

"No," Kya said, frowny and mean.

Barker peered at me.

I said, "Someone's got to do something."

"Someone is doing something. The police."

I laughed. Didn't mean to and promptly said, "Sorry."

"Don't worry."

"I mean I'm sorry we're not sitting on our hands and trusting this to you. We know who the police prioritize, and ParSec was no Adelaide Milton."

Kya jumped in. "It's been almost a month, Detective. We've heard nothing about any new leads, or suspects, or anything."

"Girls. I want you to think about what I'm going to say really hard. Why would you hear anything? Seriously? You're high school kids. It's routine for us not to go blasting every detail of an investigation for the world to see. Like that Reggie DuPree kid you dropped in on—I'm guessing he told you about his beautillion. Rock-solid alibi we knew about weeks ago. I guess our mistake was not posting it on Twitter and tagging you, right?"

Kya leaned forward, matching his intensity. "How did you know we were at Bay Breeze?"

"You led me there. Last we spoke you'd acted so strange, I became concerned. I swung by your school one day and saw you leave with this one." He pointed at me. "Considering the last time you two were together in my presence it was a UFC fight,

I found the whole thing curious. I've kept an eye on you, off and on."

Kya squirmed. I made myself *not* squirm. What did *off and on* mean? Did he know about the secret apartment at the Savant? It got worse.

"Tell me about ParSec Nation," he said.

My appetite vanished.

"Let me elaborate. Tell me more about the kooky online fan base that was more than obsessed with your friend and known to pull sometimes violent pranks when they didn't get what they wanted."

I said, "You don't think—"

"I think a lot of things, Fatima. The idea that an obsessive personality in a horror movie mask dropped in on your pal and acted erratically is something I think about often. Particularly once we ruled out the most obvious people closest to Paris."

"They're unstable and stable," Kya said.

"What's that even mean?"

"You shouldn't lump them all together. It's not fair. ParSec Nation is like any other group, anywhere. Some are well-meaning, casual listeners. Some take it too far, the ones who do call themselves the Dark Nation. We don't know much about those more extreme members. Do we, Fuse?"

"Nope."

It was mostly true. We only knew Florian, and she was a straight-up coward without her mask and muscle. The last thing I wanted was police blindly coming down on Paris's fans with nothing to go on other than their use of a hashtag. If the police had something there, they wouldn't need us to start a witch hunt.

Barker sat the last third of the sandwich on his plate. "I hope you're telling me the truth. You're only making it more likely we never get to the bottom of this thing if you're not."

Kya got bold. "Have you searched Paris's place?"

"Yes. We were made aware of the apartment by Paula Klein early on. I hope you haven't been there, since there's an evidence seal on the door. That's a crime, girls."

"No, we haven't been to that place at all." Kya was 100 percent honest. We hadn't been to *that* place. Now we knew he was unaware of the Savant.

"Why shake us down now, Detective?" I said.

"I wouldn't classify this a shakedown. I do want you to stop. You're just retracing our footsteps, and if anything comes from our previous interviews, your interference muddies things. So here's what I'm offering, and it's a final offer: Ask me what you want. I'll tell you where we are, on the condition it stays between us. Then you start acting like kids close to wrapping up a school year. Plan for the summer. Go to this memorial concert everyone's talking about. That will be good closure for you."

Closure. One last song, one last dance, one last turn-up! Before we act like ParSec didn't exist. For a millisecond, I disliked Detective Barker.

Kya took him up on his offer. "Have you interviewed people we don't know about?"

"Depends. I haven't tailed you twenty-four/seven, so what you got?"

"Reggie, we know."

Barker was back to eating his sandwich, confirmed with a nod. "Miss Elsie?"

Another nod.

Kya went rapid fire. "Paula Klein. Winston Bell. Shameik Larsen."

In the middle of a big chew, Barker raised his hand. "Say that name again."

"Shameik Larsen—"

A head shake. "Before that."

Evangeline's Kitchen got a few degrees cooler. I said it for her. "Winston Bell."

Barker's head cocked, he abandoned his sandwich altogether. "Who?"

KYA

Fuse said, "You don't know Winston Bell? But he—"

I pressed my heel into her sneaker, right at the toes, shutting her up. "He writes music articles. He was writing a piece on Paris."

Barker got inquisitive, pulled a tiny pad with a tinier pencil from his shirt pocket. "Local reporter?"

The question burned. Barker knew *nothing* about Winston, so none of the police did. Carefully uncertain, I said, "I think he maybe worked for a magazine. *MIXX* or something."

"I know the publication. Either of you ever speak to this fella?"

"I saw him at her memorial service. Fuse, you?" I kept pressure on her foot, felt her fighting the wince.

"He was around the studio sometimes."

Barker jotted his notes. "Should be easy enough to run down. Anything else I need to know?"

"Nope," Fuse said with a fist pump. "You really *scared us straight*, Detective Barker."

Why, Lord? Why was she so awkwardly dramatic?

Barker's eyes narrowed. "This was my nice warning, girls. I can see where you're coming from. I've lost good friends. This ain't your job, though. Next time your loyalty's going to get you in trouble. We clear?"

"We are." My hip nestled next to Fuse's, I nudged her from the booth. "Thank you for lunch, we're going to go home and think about what we've done."

His suspicious stare didn't drop, but nothing could be done about that. I shoved Fuse toward the door. We didn't speak again until the yellow Evangeline's Kitchen sign was well behind us.

Fuse said, "Winston told us the police questioned everyone she'd been close to. He said they'd questioned *him*. I didn't imagine that."

"You didn't."

"Why—"

"He played us, Fuse. I bet he played Paris too. More than played her."

Fuse mumbled under her breath, accelerating on a straight stretch of road. Ahead, the light flicked yellow, but she didn't slow down. When it went red, she still hadn't noticed. "Fuse!"

She jammed both feet on the brake, bringing us to a screeching stop. Her chest heaved. "He was around her for months! Around *after us*, Kya. When we were all bitter and bickering, and she didn't have anyone—"

"She had him. He used her up."

Despair sank in, shaking me. Fuse went full tantrum, smacked her wheel over and over. I let her have her moment until the light changed, and the driver behind us leaned on their horn, reminding us our pain was limited to the confines of this compact hybrid. Fuse didn't go right away, and that driver swerved around us. The world moved on.

"Go," I said. "To the Savant." I shot a text to Florian, told her to meet us.

Fuse put us in motion. "Why?"

My flash drive necklace with all the music Paris and I did

together still hung beneath my shirt. I squeezed it. "Someone once said super teams need lairs. We've got work to do."

• ▪

By the evening my voice mail icon was lit with a red *1*. I played it on speaker for Fuse and Florian.

"Kya, this is Detective Barker. Just checking on that name you gave me. Are you sure it was 'Winston Bell'? I've found a music journalist named Winston Zaius, and another one named Anthony Bell. Both did some work for MIXX, *even collaborated on a few cover stories, but nothing under the name you gave. Call me back."*

Not yet. We were hunting ghosts too.

The sky shifted from bright blue to the color of a bruise, and we left the balcony door open for the salt-seasoned breeze. Florian stretched her legs across the couch, her back on the armrest, and her laptop balanced on her thighs. After every short typing burst and dead end, she shook her head. "All his social media is janky. No selfies, or any other photos with him in it. Concert shots of crowds and random music magazine covers. He doesn't have a ton of followers. Doesn't really post. This is bad catfish stuff." Her tone turned accusatory. "*Nobody* checked this guy out? If I'd known it was that easy to get next to her, I would've said I was from *MIXX* too."

Fuse said, "He had credentials."

"Obviously fake," I said.

She recoiled.

"I'm not blaming you. Just saying he worked to fool you, and Paula, and anyone else who didn't dig deep enough. It's con man stuff, he played the long game."

"Why?" Fuse said, almost a plea. "What was in it for him?"

The question hung between us for a while. Florian caressed the couch, awed, occasionally mouthing, *She sat here.* The girl was still a fan, still slightly disturbed. Fuse paced, up the hallway to the bedroom, back to us. Me, I stared beyond the balcony railing. Knowing I couldn't guess what Winston wanted from Paris. What he wanted from us, though . . .

"He'd gotten onto the Dark Nation sites," I said, hovering over Florian, motioning for her to do her thing. She accessed the sites that used to poll the Dark Nation's feelings on Fuse and me. No pie chart now, only a sound widget for playing and downloading the song I'd given Florian. "Fuse, when did you last hear from him?"

She checked her text. Told us a date and time. As I suspected.

"It was an hour after that sound widget posted," I said.

Fuse leaned over Florian, checked for herself. "He's watching, and he's worried."

"Right. He was working so hard to get in tight with Paris, he would've weaseled onto the ParSec Nation sites—regular and Dark—long ago, for all the insider info he could get. When the police never came to him, he would've thought he was golden."

Fuse resumed the pacing. Balcony to kitchen, hands dancing the whole time. "Oh, oh. The Dark Nation started messing with us. Posting about a murder team and forcing us to dig deeper. He got spooked and—"

"Decided to feed us this garbage about helping get our story out there."

Fuse came to an abrupt stop, locked eyes with me. "We were his direct line. We told him every lead we had. He knew they'd be dead ends. As long as we weren't questioning *him*, it meant he was still clear."

Florian watched the back and forth like a tennis match. "You two are a little scary."

"What?" we said simultaneously.

Florian focused on her computer.

Fuse, wary, said, "Should we call Detective Barker back? Tell him what we know?"

The detective had been correct about some things. We should've been thinking of summer, and the end of school, and the concert. We should've been allowed to be just high school kids.

The possibility of such a mundane existence was taken from us the minute we saw our friend gone too soon. Covered in blood. We had a right to see this through. "He's not wrong about us running into dead ends. So let's try it his way for now. We tell Detective Barker what we know. But we won't let him keep us in the dark either."

Fuse said, "How?"

"That's where Florian comes in."

She perked up on the couch. "Yeah?"

"That Wi-Fi hack you've been running at the school. I'd like to hear more."

FUSE

We all have our strengths. Mine included savvy thoughts on social media platforms, hot outfits, some pretty mean dance moves, and pro-level snark. Kya's strengths were her STEM-minded practicality and sort of emotionally detached zombielike demeanor (except when she's really mad . . . watch out then) that allowed her to make sound decisions, with purpose. When she and Florian started in with the techspeak, and Kya began formulating, then explaining, her plan, I realized another of her strengths.

Evil genius.

The #MadScientist moniker I slapped her with may not have been too far off. That became clear over the next few days as we went through the motions of giving Detective Barker a crack at Winston Bell. First thing's first, our return to the OSPD precinct for another chat with Barker.

He was wary when he greeted us, then had us follow him into an interrogation room for privacy. "Didn't expect to see you two again so soon."

Kya held up her phone. "I got your message."

"You could've called."

"We know," Kya continued, "but we wanted to give you more information on the reporter we told you about. After our talk yesterday, we felt more comfortable doing it in person."

I said, "And there's nothing suspicious about that."

Kya tensed beside me, and I could fully admit my weakness there. I was not built for covert operations.

Barker, more interested in possible leads, had his full attention on Kya, though. "What you got?"

"I wanted to point you to some of his social media." She was, very obviously, having trouble getting to the info she wanted to share. She tapped her screen, tried opening several apps, then her web browser. Nothing worked.

Having the phone in airplane mode didn't help, of course. Barker didn't need to know that, though.

Kya said, "I can't get a signal. Could I have the Wi-Fi password here?"

Barker didn't think twice about it. "Sure."

It was "c0p$R0ck."

I laughed. Kya tensed again. Sorry.

She deactivated airplane mode, logged on to the station's network. Kya supplied all of Winston's useless social media and the phone number he'd sent his texts from. Maybe the detective would have better luck than we did. Who knew? That was never the point of the visit.

Barker escorted us from the station, and as we stood in the sunshine, Kya asked, "Will you bring him in?"

The detective said, "It might not go that way, Kya. We don't know who he is, or if he was even in the state the night your friend died. Right now it's just a conversation."

Kya nodded. "Thank you."

On our way back to the car, I asked, "Why'd you even go there with him? Does it matter?"

"Just confirming that even with his good intentions, we can't count on him. So I feel less bad about what we're doing."

Florian waited in the backseat of my car, her laptop balanced on her knees. Kya said, "You got it?"

Florian tapped a key, and Detective Barker's voice flitted through her weak speakers, a direct feed from his phone's newly co-opted microphone to us. "*—told you guys when you empty the coffee pot, make another batch!*"

And we were off.

KYA

We mostly kept our promise to Barker. We attempted to focus on school and the upcoming memorial concert. We didn't try to track down Winston ourselves, leaving it up to the detective and the OSPD. But our monitoring of the situation didn't leave much to be encouraged about.

From what we could tell, Barker was working a lot of cases, old and new. Florian compiled the audio, and we were at the Savant every night listening for progress. Nothing. Winston hadn't returned his calls, and he didn't seem super stressed about it. That didn't sit well. But we agreed to give patience a try. For a while anyway. Plus, I was plenty busy otherwise.

With the concert rapidly approaching, Shameik had planning meetings every day after school. Fuse hung around for me to finish but steered clear of Shameik. By then, I knew the details of what went down between them, so I got it.

Midweek, I was assigned the job of creating a looping, Paris-centric slideshow meant to run on the venue's big screens between sets. Easy enough. Shameik said he wanted as many photos as possible. Recent, childhood, baby, whatever. Most of that I could handle on my own and with Fuse's help, but for way back in the day, there was only one source.

On the Thursday before the concert, I met Fuse at her car and asked, "Do you mind if we skip the Savant tonight? I want to put the final touches on the slideshow, and I need to go by Miss Elsie's and scan some baby photos."

Fuse tapped her phone. "Fine by me. I'm letting Florian know she's got the night off. I don't think I could sit through another thrilling episode of the audio play I've come to think of as 'Barker Farts' anyway."

The detective was rather gassy.

Fuse pulled up to the curb in front of Miss Elsie's but kept her engine running. I said, "You should come in. You can help me pick the best photos."

Her hands wrenched the steering wheel. "You think I should? I never met her grandma. Won't it be weird?"

"You're helping people remember her fondly. It will be fine."

She killed the engine and joined me on the porch. Miss Elsie was dressed in actual clothes today. Jeans and a flower-print blouse, with a good wig. That made me happier than I'd been expecting.

"Hey, sweetie!" She kissed my cheek. "Who's your friend?"

I said, "This is Fatima Fallon. She knew Paris too."

"How are you, ma'am?" Fuse shook Miss Elsie's hand.

"Is it still okay for me to take a look at your photo albums?" I asked.

Miss Elsie wrung her hands, nervous. "You're going to be careful? Those photos are all I have."

I raised my phone. "No worries. I'm basically taking pictures of the pictures. I won't even have to touch them."

She visibly relaxed and pointed us to a hutch beneath one of her end tables. "They're all right there. I'll make y'all some sweet tea while you look."

"Thank you, ma'am," Fuse said, while I freed three separate albums as thick as dictionaries at the public library.

We went to work flipping pages, looking for the best shots. I needed maybe eight to ten solid pics, but we didn't move with urgency. We marveled at not just pictures of Paris in her infancy, but her mother when *she* was young. A late '90s teen with finger waves in her hair, big hoop earrings with her name—"Tracy"— suspended in the center. Designer overalls, with one strap loose.

"They looked alike," Fuse said, her voice airy. Maybe a little awed.

She wasn't wrong. Teen Paris could've impersonated Teen Tracy if she'd ever hopped in a time machine and went back to the prior century. I always thought Tracy Secord looked so fun and healthy in those photos, much different than the frail woman shuffling through my, admittedly vague, memories.

We switched albums, immediately found Paris's baby pictures. She couldn't have been more than two months old when someone decided a sailor outfit, hat and all, was the move for picture day. Her raised cheeks and toothless grin said she didn't know enough to mind.

I aimed my phone and snapped the photo to my cloud account. "That one is definitely making the cut."

We found more, an equal mix of sweet, goofy, and outright hilarious. Maybe enough to call it a night. Then I flipped to a new page, prominently featuring a photo of Tracy—emaciated-looking now, her hair unkempt, the signs of her long, arduous sickness just starting to show—holding an eight- or nine-month-old Paris on the porch of this very house. I was about to turn the page again, when Fuse grabbed my wrist.

"I've seen that shirt before." Her voice shook.

"What shirt?" There were five smaller photos on the page, and I didn't understand the gravity of what Fuse was saying.

Fuse snatched the whole album up and left her seat for the kitchen. "Miss Elsie!"

I chased.

Miss Elsie said, "Tea's just about done, sweetie."

"I had a question, actually. Do you know anything about this photo?" The heavy album clapped thunder when it fell on the kitchen table.

Miss Elise paced over, examined the picture, eyes narrowed in confusion. "Yes, I took that one myself."

"Do you know what that shirt is about? Where it came from?"

At that, Miss Elsie rolled her eyes, and I mistakenly thought Fuse had offended her. But no. It wasn't Fuse. Not even close. "I do," she said. "That is what a no-good deadbeat thinks passes for support. Like a baby can eat a T-shirt."

Huh?

Miss Elsie said, "Paris's daddy was good for that nonsense. Sending shirts and expensive baby shoes and records to Tracy. Never money. Then when Tracy passed, it wasn't even that."

Miss Elsie shrank, and I was a little mad at Fuse for sapping her energy. But when I glared at her, Fuse was shrinking too. "I'm sorry, Miss Elsie," Fuse said, then, to me, "I need to go to the car."

She walked out. Really, it was more like a jog. Miss Elsie said, "Is that child all right?"

"Sure," I lied, because I honestly didn't know. "I'm sorry to run like this, but, the slideshow."

Miss Elsie's "these kids today" look was unmistakable, but she didn't seem offended. "Just come back soon because I can't drink all this tea by myself. It'll mess with my sugar."

Before I left, I put away the albums, still trying to figure why a T-shirt in a photo had Fuse acting so strange. It was just a concert souvenir.

The Fugees. Europe. 1997.

FUSE

Cupping my face in my hands, with the AC blowing full blast, I still felt too hot and flustered. Information overload.

I tried to make sense of it. What I saw was too specific to be pure coincidence. Also too crazy to be what I thought it was.

Kya fell into the passenger's seat, bug-eyed. "What happened in there?"

"I've seen that Fugees shirt before, Kya."

"What's a Fugee?"

Her ignorance jarred me from my panicked state momentarily. "Seriously, you know all that old R&B but not the Fugees? Lauryn Hill?"

"If they didn't make a song I had to sing in a talent show, why would I? Why, do you?"

Mostly, it was from Dad's History of Hip-Hop lessons. But I'd been reminded of the group more recently. "Winston Bell wore that exact same shirt the day of ParSec's memorial service. The. Same. Shirt."

Kya opened her mouth. Closed it again. Sat with it a few seconds, and I waited for her rational explanation to counter my irrational one. All she said was "No."

"No what?" Tell me what I'm missing here, Kya. Tell me I'm wrong. Please.

"It's a T-shirt. A lot of people could have it. What if it's one of those retro shirts they sell at Hot Topic in the mall?"

"That specific? That obscure?"

"Fuse—what you're suggesting . . ."

"The thing is I haven't suggested it yet. But you're thinking it too, aren't you? *Why* would Winston fake being a reporter to get close to her? What was in it for him?"

"I just assumed he saw a meal ticket. Like Paula."

"Could be. Could be more personal. Much more."

She finger-combed her hair, stared back at Miss Elsie's like she'd left something there. Perhaps sanity. Sanity was definitely missing in this car, at this moment. "It can't be," she said, slightly above a whisper.

It needed to be voiced, and considered. One of us had to stop dancing around it. As horrible as the possibility was.

I said, "I think Winston might be her dad."

PARIS/DJ PARSEC

(THE LAST DAY)

My new condo was on a high floor. Movers brought my stuff up while a maintenance man fixed my leaky showerhead. He packed up his tools and mentioned if I'd gone for a higher floor, I'd see the ocean. "There's always more, if you can get it."

Missing that view—and the extra rent it would've cost me—wasn't a huge loss. I wouldn't be here much anyway. The press team at VenueShowZ planned to announce our partnership next week, and to celebrate they sent me a bunch of promotional crap as a welcome present. (I think they were probably just cleaning out a storage closet, but whatever.) After that, it's "Hurricane ParSec." I'll be all over. New York, Chicago, Denver, LA. Then Europe and Asia. All while recording and working with other artists. Someone on the booking team—Megan or Michelle, I couldn't remember her name—said a lot of people were excited. I should've been one of them, right?

Inside, I cast a cold gaze over all my luxury living. I shut the balcony door behind me, stepped into my kitchen for water, and saw my reflection, fuzzy and warped, in my refrigerator door. There was only a half-full gallon jug of spring water in it, a pack of chicken (close to the expiration date), broccoli, and an orange. I drank from the jug because I didn't have cups and sat my one skillet on the range, heating it for the meat.

My chicken seared, and I checked my feeds. I'd dropped a new track overnight, my last chance to do so before the VenueShowZ release team began dictating when, where, and how my music got distributed. The response was . . . not what I wanted.

What Are THOSE?! @SneakerHead1213

This track feels rushed.

#ParSecNation

I Got Bars for Days @RhymeFam52

It's fire. You just need to listen a few times to absorb it.

#ParSecNation

Diva Life @TonaeBanks15

Feels amateur. None of the layers of her usual work.

#ParSecNation

Sherry Is on Hiatus @SherBear227

Y'all crazy. This is dope. True music fans would get it.

#ParSecNation

Wakanda's Best Barber @CutMaster98

IDK. Something's changed.

#ParSecNation

That last comment, it lingered. Something's changed. Look around, Paris, what hasn't?

There were more posts of course. Praise, harsh critiques, and straight-up trolls. More than a few DMs. One in particular stood out.

Fuse Is Getting Her Life Together @FuseZilla14
Love the new track. Playing on repeat right now. You haven't
blocked me on here yet, so I know you're at least getting
these messages. That being said, STOP SLACKING ON YOUR
SOCIAL MEDIA POSTS! Fans like an engaged artist.
Hope you're doing okay, even if you're still mad at me.
#ParSecNation #Forever

This chick got some nerve. She always had. Couldn't help but laugh a little.

I'd seen the other DMs. A strangely Fuse-appropriate mix of apologies, ALL CAPS YELLING, and unsolicited advice. She was right, I hadn't blocked her on Twitter. *Why* hadn't I blocked her?

A scorched whiff tickled my nose. I ran to the smoky pan, flipped the chicken too late. One side was black-burnt, inedible. I deactivated my stove and dumped the whole messy overcooked chicken and its bloody pink packet in the garbage, along with the broccoli. Dinner was ruined, but I had an idea.

A pop-up party. Unsanctioned, unannounced until the last minute. Like a good engaged artist.

There was a warehouse Fuse had found, like, a year ago. It could work. Just my turntables, my laptop, a mic, and some speakers. Stuff I could fit in my new ride, to bring this all full circle. Closure.

Monday I would be on an early flight to New York. Winston said VenueShowZ wanted to give me that NBA free agent treatment. Packed conference room, customized presentation on a big screen, all the important people there.

There were still important people here too. Very little time to make things right with them. I'd felt it more than ever over the last few weeks. When the deals were coming together, and I saw dollar figures bigger than what really made sense for folks from where I'm from. There were holes—people-shaped holes—in me, in the world, that the money and corporate promises couldn't fill.

I missed my friends. My family.

Fuse, in spite of our fight. She was wrong for keeping whatever happened between her and Shameik from me, but the further we got from it, the more I understood she was scared. She LET ME KNOW IN SEVERAL DMs.

I hadn't *loved* Shameik. Really, he got on my dag-gone nerves and I barely thought of him after we broke up. Why be mad over their barely-a-kiss? Even if more than a kiss happened, so what.

Time told me I could get over Fuse messing up. It's not like I'm above dumping all over a friend in the heat of a misunderstanding.

Just ask Kya.

The things I said to her. Sure, she gave as good as she got. Stealing our music had me salty for a minute. But Kya was meek. Grandma always said so. She only clapped back when cornered. I'd forced her hand because . . . what? She'd called me out on how I was tripping? Letting this fast life get away from me?

I could fix things with Kya, though. With all of them. Before I go.

Flinging myself on the couch, phone in a two-handed grip, I sent separate texts to Kya and Fuse—I didn't even want to think about getting those two together on a group text, the phones might melt.

Kept it simple. Told them to meet me tomorrow, an hour before my pop-up. It was time to squash the bad vibes between us. On Sunday, I'd go by Grandma's. Do church with her. Dinner. Maybe just stay the night and have the car to the airport pick me up from there Monday.

In the middle of my spontaneous planning, I got a text.

WINSTON

I hope you're all settled. Can I swing by?
Some important things to discuss before
we start the new adventure. Long overdue.

ME

Not tonight. Pretty tired.

White lie. As my new manager, he wouldn't approve of my impromptu party. He probably wouldn't approve of my plan to meet with my old friends either. Totally my fault. I'd only shared the bad and the ugly with him, so that's all he knew about them.

Besides, he'd been keeping a secret from me—one that bugged me a lot, if I was being honest—so I didn't feel much guilt about playing this close.

WINSTON

Look, it won't take long.

ME

We'll be together 24/7 come Monday.
Can I please get a little sleep before
things get crazy?

WINSTON

Fine. Call me in the morning when you're
up. I'd like to have a chat before we fly.
It'll be worth it.

Sorry, Winston. You'll be talking my ears off about business details when next week hits. I wanted one last weekend just for me. We'd get to whatever he had to say.

We had all the time in the world.

■■

It was exciting to be excited, something I hadn't felt in a minute. Anxiety. Pressure. Frustration. All of those sensations had been present and accounted for during most of the last year, but this pop-up had me amped. My going-away party.

I'd slept little that night, so the day of the party there were plenty of nerves over Kya and Fuse, I can't lie. Like, I made peace with it maybe not going well, but I had to try before I left. They'd both agreed to meet before the party, though—a good sign. I'd dropped the particulars of the event into the ParSec Nation forums, so even if we didn't end in a great place, I'd be too busy spinning for my extended music family to dwell on it.

The warehouse we'd be partying in used to store raw metal and engine parts for navy ships. Fuse explained it to me when she first scouted the place months ago. An anchor insignia was faintly visible on the wall opposite where I'd be setting up. I stared at it a long time when I got there. The only sign anything had ever filled this wide empty space.

A chill ran through me, but I shook it off. Got my equipment arranged.

I'd finished setup. My turntables were ready. The LCD displays glowed aqua blue. My laptop rested on its stand, playlists galore at my disposal, a fire Metro Boomin track played low through my headphones, making the EQ levels jump. Found myself staring at that anchor again when my first guest arrived way early.

"Hey, what are you doing here?" Winston crossed what would become a dance floor in a little under two hours, smiling but not happy. I knew him well enough by now. "I expected to hear from you today, but I see you're busy."

Busted. "I knew you wouldn't approve."

"You gotta stop doing free shows," he said. The aggravation in his voice was slight, but there.

"This the last one. You're still going to get your fifteen percent on everything else I do." It came out a little slicker than I intended, and got slicker still. "Plus your finder's fee."

I wanted him to know I knew.

His neck snapped, swung his dreads like whiplash. "Who told you about a finder's fee?"

"Someone on the contracts team. Their name is only important if it's not true."

He smirked, tried to make it a small thing. "There was a finder's fee involved for local artists I sent their way. Once I made the acquisitions team aware that Paula Klein wasn't serving her clients properly, there was a certain amount of in-house gratitude."

My heart dropped like a broken elevator in a short building. Winston getting a percentage for connecting me with VenueShowZ wasn't the worst thing in the world. It just felt that way. More self-serving secrets, and I was about to go on the road with this man.

He stepped onto the dais with me, grabbed my shoulders, and wouldn't let me pull away. "I never took a finder's fee for you. They offered, but I turned it down."

"You turned it down?" That was unexpected. "Why would you do that? I think you should've told me, but that was money you're entitled to." There were no favors in this business. If I'd learned nothing else over the last two years, it was that. Everyone wanted their cut, now or later.

"Partly because I'll make that cash back as your road manager. Mostly because some things you don't take money for. Me finding you is one of them. *I* should be paying somebody."

He said it like I would understand. Like it was obvious. We played a waiting game, and I won.

"This was something I'd hoped to speak with you about last night, let you get right with it before we got on the road."

"Get right? What you mean, Winston?"

"That, for one. Winston ain't the name I grew up using. See, I used to make music like you, and my given name wasn't a sexy stage name. I was born Onell Davis, in Richmond."

"You're from Virginia."

"Right."

Where was he going with this? "You were Onell, but took the stage name Winston?"

He pushed his palm toward me, like he was shoving words back in my mouth. Irritated at my interruptions it seemed. "Not exactly, let me get to it! My stage name was Pickk, with two *k*'s. I played guitar. We recorded some, traveled more. Never broke through, though. You're lucky and don't know half of that luck you were born with."

I stepped back. He didn't like my interrupting, so I didn't. But I didn't like how weird this felt.

He stepped closer. "Winston Bell is new. Been going by that a little over a year."

As long as I'd known him. From the time he stepped in the studio, flashing his *MIXX* magazine covers, talking about the famous people he knew.

"Don't look like that," he said. "I see you getting nervous."

Not nervous. Scared. "Hurry up and say what you got to say."

"About a year and a half ago, I was in Vegas, at the lowest I ever been. Down to my last hundred dollars in this big fancy casino. Dice in hand, a roll away from losing that too. All of a sudden this fight breaks. Craziest thing I ever seen. There were teenagers, and bikers, and someone throwing a big animal head, the kind people in mascot costumes wear. I don't know, that's just Vegas, I suppose. Everybody gets escorted off the casino floor when the police arrive.

"So I cash out my hundred-dollar chip, hit a buffet, and do what I normally do—look for music on my phone. I go to SoundCloud, and guess what their algorithm spits at me? Your song. I listen because it's catchy, and I click your profile because I'm impressed. When I saw your last name was Secord, and where you were from, it was a sign. You get what I'm saying?"

"No, I don't. Why don't you just say it, then?" Though, everything in my body screamed I didn't want to know. Not really.

"You're my little girl," he confessed finally. "You're named Paris because of me."

I might not have believed him if not for that last part. How many times had I heard that I was the Paris my mama got, not the one she was promised.

I didn't cry, never have. Instead, I got mad. "Get away from me!" Slapped him, and he stumbled off the dais, rolled his ankle, collapsed. Maybe he was telling the truth, because the anger that flared behind his eyes was like looking in a mirror.

He massaged his cheek. "You're right to be upset, I expected some of that. Don't hit me again, though. That's not proper."

"You've been gone my whole life? I've never been to Vegas. Where else did you go when you weren't reminded of me by SoundCloud?"

"Never said I was a perfect man."

"Perfect? You're barely a distorted bootleg of a man, *Onell*."

He climbed back on the dais, his pointer finger poked the air shy of my nose. "Watch it. Be mad, but show some respect. Don't matter how long I've been gone, I'm still your—"

I kicked him in the thigh the way Shameik showed me when he wanted his monthlong YMCA self-defense class to seem like kung fu monk training. The connect was meaty and reverberated to my hip, throwing me off balance into my turntables. The loosely secured mic fell off its stand onto my mixer.

He winched, cursed, hopped backward on his good leg. Whatever patience and wishful thinking he'd stored for this confession was no longer present. Onell, my father, looked like he wanted to—

We were alone. In a warehouse far off a main road. No one would be here anytime soon. He came closer, playing peaceful. "Paris, you're not thinking. Take a breath and—"

I swung the mic stand at him like a club, tried to knock him over with the weighted base. He jerked back like a bad dance move, and I missed. It was an overswing, spinning me with it, until I was off balance, and he snagged me by the waist.

"Stop it, Paris! I'm ordering you to stop."

Who was he to order anything? I had no memory of this man in my life, he'd done nothing when my mother was in the hospital in so much pain she didn't want to be hugged, or even touched.

Never helped when I was sick, or hungry, or scared from bad dreams. Had Grandma comparing me to Jesus just to make me feel better. "Not even the Lord saw his father in this world."

His forearm grazed my chin, and I bit into his denim jacket sleeve. There were layers between my teeth and his flesh, didn't matter. I bit down with all the force in my jaws. He howled, tried to fling me off. He succeeded.

I twirled from his arms like a dancer, spinning, my head low. The stand my laptop sat on was made of heavy aluminum so it wouldn't vibrate or fall in a crowded party. The corners were sharp.

My temple connected with all the force generated from me and Onell's combined pain.

A solid thunk, then my legs wouldn't work.

I lay on my board, and one of my limp arms fell, knocking my headphone jack loose. My playlist thumped through the speakers, echoing throughout the warehouse. My face was wet. But, how?

"Paris!" Onell yelled from far away. "It was an accident, girl. Get up!"

Didn't want to. This music was too good. A rest might be better.

"Paris! Paris! Baby, I'm sorry."

This might be better.

This might be

This might

This

KYA

It was full dark, no stars. City lights sprinkled the view from Paris's balcony like glitter, a sight that would've been pretty even a day ago. Now it was pinpricks of light in an ugly stain. Everything was.

We'd come to the Savant after Miss Elsie's because where else was there to go? The horror of what we'd surmised—the gigantic nature of it—couldn't be in close proximity to any other people, like toxic waste.

Fuse had folded herself onto the couch for the last hour, her eyes squeezed shut, as if concentrating to banish our new knowledge from her brain. I chose the balcony, where my thoughts darkened with the night sky.

Winston Bell was Paris's father. I tried to poke holes in it but couldn't quite convince myself. You didn't always need evidence to know something was true.

"We could go to Barker," Fuse yelled from the couch. Her first words in a while.

Sure. We could. I didn't think Fuse's T-shirt connection would wow him, considering he hadn't even found Winston yet.

"Or not," Fuse said, taking my silence as the answer it was. "Feel like sharing your master plan, then?"

"When they get here."

She hinged up off the couch, unenthusiastic about the guests I'd invited. "You're asking for a lot of faith, Kya."

"I know. It will be easier to explain it once, when we're all together."

The knock came soon enough. I went for the entrance. Hand on the knob, I said, "You're okay."

"I will be. Let them in."

Florian entered, followed by the Savant newbie I'd asked her to pick up on the way. Shameik. His neck craned taking in the space. His examination stopped when his eyes landed on Fuse.

I said, "Sit down you two. A lot to discuss."

Florian plopped on her usual spot, and Fuse sat next to her. I sat on a stack of sturdy, unpacked boxes in the corner. Shameik lowered himself to the floor, opposite Fuse. Kept flicking glances her way.

"Thanks for coming," I began. "I—"

Fuse interrupted, "Hold up, K. I need to do something real quick."

She bounced up, grabbed Shameik's hand, reeled him to his feet, then led him to the back of the apartment, into Paris's bedroom, and closed the door.

Not the most shocking thing today, but surprising enough.

Florian said, "If you made me leave my crib so they could make out, I'm going to need some gas money."

FUSE

"Sit down," I said.

His annoyed expression shifted into something close to disgust. "Here? This is her bed."

"It's not what you think." Though his response to that wrong assumption being distasteful instead of hopeful was admirable. He was a decent guy. "Sit."

Obedient, he lowered himself onto the mattress, and I remained standing. He was tall enough that we were still nearly eye-to-eye. I said, "There is no us. There's never going to be."

"Fuse, wait a minute—"

"I'm not saying the puppy dog eyes you were giving me out there meant that's what you want. I'm not trying to embarrass you, but I need to be absolutely clear. We kissed in a heated moment. I liked it. But I don't want it anymore. I didn't want it anymore after that night. You can't finesse me into wanting it again, your anger's not going to make me feel guilty or obligated. You shouldn't want someone who feels guilty or obligated. We're both better than that."

The annoyance vibe was back. I got it. If our roles were reversed, I wouldn't enjoy hearing stuff like this either. He was about to hear worse, though, and we needed this over and done with so Kya could talk without distractions.

He bobbed his head, that clapback attitude of his revving up. Before he could start, I said, "We know who killed ParSec."

His mouth snapped shut.

"We're going to do something about it. Kya's got a plan. She thinks we need you, but I understand if you don't want to be around me after this. If—IF—you can be okay with what I'm saying, then maybe we both get the chance to do right by ParSec in a way we didn't before. Up to you."

I turned, let myself out, and closed the door to give him a moment.

Back in the living room, Florian said, "Are *you* giving me my gas money?"

I looked to Kya. "What's she talking about?"

All I got was a head shake. Then, "Is he coming? I don't want to have to say this twice."

Shameik emerged from ParSec's bedroom, trudged up the hall. I waited to see if he'd continue through the door, to the elevator, and out of my life forever. He reclaimed his space on the floor, gaze leveled on Kya.

"Tell me who did it, and what we're going to do about it." He gave me a tight "we're cool" nod.

I believed him and returned the gesture. "The floor is yours, Kya."

She began, "We have a little over a day to make this work, but if we play this right, I think, maybe, we can do what the police can't. We can take down Paris's killer at the concert."

KYA

It took an hour to walk them through it, and none of it meant a thing if this very first part didn't work. With time slipping away from us (Mama had texted twice about my whereabouts), it was now or never.

"We're really doing this?" Fuse asked.

I said, "We're going to try. Anybody want to back out?"

Florian said, "He took away the music. He's gotta feel some pain."

"She was more than music," I said, still strongly considering the joys of doing this girl physical harm.

Shameik said, "I'm good."

Unclipping my music drive from my lanyard, I handed it over to Florian, who plugged into a USB port on her laptop. She uploaded two tracks to a Dark Nation site, with a message:

#SuperGroupie and #MadScientist making progress but still owe what they owe. They might be off the hook soon, so enjoy these while they last. Deal's a deal.

"It's done," said Florian.

I said, "Now we wait. If he's as predictable as I think, it won't take long."

It wasn't a half hour before Fuse's phone buzzed with an incoming text.

WINSTON

Hey, Fuse, what's happening? Checking in on your progress. My editor's really on my back about solid leads. Do you have something yet?

ME

Maybe. We think so. Have you ever heard of a company called VenueShowZ?

WINSTON

Of course. What about them?

ME

Paris was involved with them somehow. Paula Klein wasn't happy about it. We think we should let the police know. It seems shady.

As I suspected, everything Winston's done so far has been about keeping an eye on anyone looking into Paris's death. To redirect— like when he co-signed on Paula and Shameik being suspects—or get a warning if we ever got close to him.

What he'd do if he thought we were a threat . . . I was hesitant to guess.

Ellipses pulsed as he tapped a return response. Fuse said, "He's thinking really hard about his answer. He might be spooked."

I shrugged. "Doesn't matter. Push through. If he doesn't bite, we go directly to Barker. It's all we can do."

The dots vanished. Several minutes passed with no activity on the exchange. I thought we'd lost him. Then . . .

WINSTON

Sorry, I was driving. Stationary now.
You should send me what you have on
VenueShowZ. I can do some digging on
my end.

ME

I don't think so. Texting about it feels
dangerous with the way the Dark Nation's
been on Kya and me. Can we meet?

WINSTON

I'm in New York. Email would be better
for me.

ME

Sorry. That just feels risky. You're in New
York. We're here with the same nutjobs
that snatched us up.

WINSTON

I'm back tomorrow. Coffee shop?

ME

Can't. My parents are taking me to visit
the school I'll be attending next year.

WINSTON

What about Kya? Get her to do it.

                                          ME

                              She doesn't have a car. What about the
                              memorial concert Saturday? You going?

WINSTON

Yes. Big, public. The Dark Nation can't
make a move there. Smart.

                                          ME

                              Glad you think so.

WINSTON

Excellent. In the meantime, let's keep
that VenueShowZ thing between us. No
telling where that rabbit hole goes.

Yeah. No telling.

Fuse ended the exchange. "Well?"

I said, "I'm going to reach out to Detective Barker tomorrow. Shameik, you let us know as soon as possible if you can't get what we need. Florian, you're on standby. Everybody get home. Sleep if you can. If we're lucky, we've already done the hardest part."

Nobody bothered to remind me that, in our little group, luck wasn't an abundant commodity.

FUSE

Friday was uneventful and perfect. That right there should've been an omen. But we rode the wave.

School was school, the real work starting after final bell. Everyone doing their parts. Kya informed Detective Barker that the man known as Winston Bell would be at the concert, and he should be waiting with, like, a SWAT team, or whatever. Shameik did his part so we wouldn't have issues at the venue. Florian kept playing tech support, just in case.

All our ducks in a row and I was still up at the crack of dawn Saturday morning. I was dressed and ready by nine, even though the concert wouldn't start until one, pacing around my house in a denim skirt, pixie boots, and a cropped tee. All cute and stuff even though I was fidgety and anxious, I hit Kya up. Surprise, surprise . . . she was awake too. Trying to put out the day's first fire.

KYA
Come over. I could really use your help
with an outfit.

ME
Firing up the Batmobile!

Kya's clothing situation was distracting enough to calm me down and dire enough to warrant my intervention. We were truly helping each other.

While her mother snored like a grizzly in the next room, I salvaged all the best pickings from my girl's closet and weighed options. "We're going to have to MacGyver this situation, K." I channeled my mom in the operating room requesting clamps or suction. "Scissors!"

Over the course of a ninety-minute triage session, I strategically slashed her jeans, did her nails with three different polishes, applied some makeup, got that hair poppin', and as a final touch, removed the bottom third of a NASA hoodie to show off her totally ripped abs. "Where you been hiding this six-pack, Kya?"

She hugged herself, bashful.

"Girl, look!" I spun her toward the mirror on the back of her door.

She twitched, startled, but then couldn't hide her grin.

"Bet you haven't looked this good since you were singing in tiaras, am I right?"

No confirmation, though she spun sideways to check out her profile.

"Who's the master?" I said. "Give. Me. My. Props!"

She said, "Should I go like this? I mean, all things considered."

"You should. Call it a celebration outfit. When the police get their hands on Winston, we're going to turn up the way ParSec would've wanted. Trust me."

So, of course, I was extra wrong.

■ ■

At the Ocean Shore Amphitheater, we stood in the rapidly filling gravel lot, the two major entrances crowded with people and security. Guards passed a metal detecting wand over everyone who walked through the gate. Anyone with a bag opened it, while an attendant sifted through the contents with a stick. Any prohibited items—weapons, unauthorized recording devices—would either be confiscated or the owner would not be allowed in.

That just wouldn't do. "Come on," I said, leading Kya, and her bag that would never have made it past those prying guards, away from the primary entrance.

There was a third way into the venue. The VIP entrance near the loading docks, behind the stage. It's where the performers entered. Where security would be much more lax for us. Thanks to Shameik.

A guard roughly the size of a small city sat in a strained folding chair next to the VIP doors. He dabbed his sweat-moist forehead with a handkerchief and wheezed orders when we approached. "Lemme see some badges."

I held up a finger while texting with my other hand. "One sec, please."

Shameik appeared in the doorway, two blue VIP lanyards dangling, obtained thanks to his hands-on involvement with planning today's event. "So this thing is really on?"

Kya hung her lanyard around her neck and slipped by Shameik. I took my lanyard and followed her inside where freestanding, cordoned-off walls represented dressing rooms in the open-air facility. Behind those walls were stars—like Omar Bless. I guessed his dressing room from the abundance of loiterers and black-shaded guards. In less-occupied corners, soon-to-be stars, like the open dressing room for up-and-comer Olivia Merrick, who leaned in her doorway, sipping tea while a makeup artist flicked her neck and collarbone with a brush.

Everyone rocked their color-coded lanyards. Blues—like us—were VIPs hanging out. Greens, workers or performers. Red were press. I saw a couple of recognizable local reporters primping while their crews set up lights and cameras. Kya lingered a few yards ahead, clutching her precious satchel. As I moved to join her, Shameik grabbed my arm. "Hey, wait a sec."

"I don't have time, dude."

"This won't be long," he said, hushed. "You're going through with this?"

"You got these lanyards for us, even after we told you why. You have to know we are."

"All I'm saying is I can still come too. Paula Klein is handling all the artist particulars. I can be, like . . . muscle. If necessary."

"Shameik, you're skinny. If muscle is needed, we've done this wrong."

He let me go, tucked his chin to his chest. "Call if you get in trouble."

"Thank you." I squeezed his fingers and joined my friend, who looked traumatized.

"Bad memories?" I asked, comfort hand on her back. I thought this was about her singing days.

"You could say that." She pointed a shaky finger at a group of eight dancers, stretching and warming up. They all wore white Dark Nation masks.

Now, that's not what I wanted to see. Those weren't Dark Nation operatives, not in the open like that. So that mask nonsense was catching on with regular ParSec Nation supporters? The inmates really were taking over the asylum, then.

Tugging her along, I angled for the path leading back to the public spaces. We passed through another security gate without

issue, now that we had credentials, and emerged into the bear
sunlight of the amphitheater grounds.

The performance area began several dozen yards to our left. A
pale concrete path ran between a green knoll that served as "cheap
seats" for anyone partial to a picnic blanket, their personal folding
chair, or cool grass brushing their backsides. Closer to the stage was
the pavilion hovering over several hundred traditional seats, let-
tered and numbered. From where we stood, most people hadn't
moved down to the ticketed area. Opting to roam in the open spaces
while the DJ bumped a mix of old- and new-school hip-hop.

Kya still seemed skittish, like the crowd was too much for her.
So I kept angling her to the agreed-upon location. A place not
much less crowded, and certainly not soothing. The ladies' room. It
wasn't line-out-the-door bad yet, but it required a bit of twisting
and turning to reach the last closed stall. There, I hesitantly said,
"Florian?"

The door swung open, and a hand emerged. "Just give me
the bag."

Kya tugged the satchel strap off her shoulder and passed the
heavy sack inside.

"We good?" I asked.

"No. It's gross in here. If you're asking about the equipment,
give me five minutes."

My phone was buzzing with an incoming text while she spoke.
"Can you make it three?"

WINSTON
I'm here.

The DJ stopped spinning. Horns and a slow drummer's intro played under an announcer's voice.

"Put your hands together for Portside's own dynamic duo . . . thhhheeeeeeeee Clutchhhhhh Booooyyyyyzzzz!"

Amplified vocals mixed with cheers as the sibling rappers began their set. Fans who'd lost track of time scrambled at concessions or the souvenir stands, picking up last-minute sodas, T-shirts, or—why?—Dark Nation masks. One vendor held a long pole, at least ten feet high, with masks hung on each side in vertical rows, like a many-faced demon judging us. He wore his own mask atop the crown of his head so not to obscure his voice while he yelled, "ParSec Nation! Turn up here! You too can dress like a lunatic for just twelve ninety-five."

He didn't actually say that last part, but he might as well.

Winston and Fuse did the thing people do when they're trying to find each other in a crowded space. "I'm over by the thing" or "I'm standing under the other thing" except Fuse kept texting lies so he *couldn't* find us, while I tried calling Detective Barker and his reinforcements.

"He's not picking up!" I said.

Florian sent us a group text that told us why.

FLORIAN

Guys, I'm still pulling audio off Barker's
mic. He's not here yet.

ME

Where is he?

FLORIAN

Stuck in traffic. There's a line of cars
trying to get into the lot.

ME

Is his backup stuck too?

FLORIAN

I don't think there is any backup. He's
on the phone with his wife complaining
about how he's the only one at the
precinct who takes us seriously.

"Panic," Fuse said, "will not help anyone. I'll just keep stalling
Winston, until—"

"Too late," I said, feeling especially exposed in a way that had
nothing to do with my bare midriff.

As the meandering crowd spilled toward their seats for the
opening act, there was less camouflage and opportunities for misdirection. Thirty yards away, Winston stood by a pavilion support
column. Low-key in black boots, dark jeans, white shirt. A thin
hoodie jacket was tied around his waist by the sleeves. And a red

press badge dangled from his neck even though we knew he wasn't really the press, because he was a con man till the end.

He didn't see us—yet—going for this fake cool aloofness as he glanced up from Fuse's fake messages. I tried not to make eye contact with him. I failed.

"Fuse," I said. "He sees me."

She faced me, her back to him. "What?"

"Wait!" I hissed, all too aware that we weren't really supposed to come in contact with him at all. Knowing what we knew about him—who he really was—we had to be sure not to tip him off in any way.

And Fuse was a notoriously bad actor.

I said, "We can't spook him. He's probably already nervous, wondering what we got. We need him comfortable until Barker gets here. Like nothing's changed."

She rolled her shoulders, bounced on her toes. "I understand."

"Nothing at all."

"I got this."

"Okay," I said, feeling the old showtime anxiety. A mix of butterflies in the stomach, spaghetti in the knees, and helium in the head in that hot minute before I stepped into a spotlight. The crowd between us and him thinned further, this was our window. I waved, polite as I'd always been to him.

Fuse turned, and I watched the whole thing go wrong in slow motion, too stunned to stop her.

In all their previous interactions, she'd been a Snark Queen to him. Rude enough that he'd joked about it the first time I met him, almost like he admired it.

In a typical bad-acting moment, Fuse played the emotion wrong.

She smiled and waved.

Oh no.

A uniformed security guard passed between. Winston's eyes followed the man a moment, some assumption or deduction forming. His face became as emotionless as a Dark Nation mask. His chin bobbed, a slow the-jig-is-up nod. He folded himself into the diminishing crowd as smoothly as a wizard stepping into a vanishing cabinet.

"Kya, he—"

"I know." I rushed forward, surprised by how quickly he disappeared. Dude was a serious ninja. "Do you see him?"

"I'm short. All I see are shoulders."

I spun in place. Was anyone moving toward an exit, or backstage?

Fuse had her phone out. "I'mma text him."

"What are you going to say?"

"Hey, we don't think you're a killer. Come back."

There was no time for her sarcasm. I broke out my own phone too, intending to shoot a message to Florian. We got the notifications at the same time.

Our Twitter accounts were pinging. Some tweet about us—or for us—blowing up. Hesitation. A hot breeze blew across my neck. Fuse looked first.

The Truth Is Out There @X211ABE

#ParSecNation shocking new audio from the maestro

herself. Did she name her own killers? @KCAppWiz

and @FuseZilla14 more dangerous than we knew?

You be the judge! #RIPParSec #CalmDownTurnUp

#ParSecMemorialConcert

There was a link. Fuse snatched earbuds from her pocket, uncoiled them, and gave me one to plug in, while she wedged the other in her ear canal. She tapped the audio widget and maxed out the volume. It was still tough to hear it over the performers onstage, just not tough enough to prevent the damage.

Paris's voice. She had very pointed things to say:

"Fuse and Kya backstabbing me like they did. It felt beyond betrayal. I would've trusted them with my life—now I know that would've been the absolute wrong move. Jealous heifers. They were just waiting to step on my throat."

Who knew when she'd said it, or when Winston recorded it in those long, fraudulent times with her. He'd saved it for an emergency. His weapon of mass destruction. The link to that file had been retweeted seventy-eight times already. There were two more tweets threaded to the damaging audio link, both featuring the #ParSecMemorialConcert so there was no confusion. He wanted this crowd to know.

Oh, Winston and his sentimental goodbyes.

The second tweet in the thread was our pictures. Snatched from our other social media.

The third was a call to action:

The Truth Is Out There @X211ABE
#ParSecNation #ParSecMemorialConcert
Get them.

FUSE

I snatched Kya's hand, pulled her away from the performance area, toward the exit. "We gotta get out of here."

Moving swiftly we cut through a crowd distracted by the things all people were distracted by these days. Their phones. A blessing and a curse in that instance.

Our window of opportunity would close soon.

We turned a corner by the concession and vendors, followed a sloping path toward the gates. I skidded on my heels, and Kya crashed into me, knocking me a few steps farther. At least four mask-wearing members of ParSec Nation hovered in a loose cluster by the exit, scanning phones, then the surrounding crowd.

"Back, back, back," Kya said, and tugged me into retracing our steps on to vendors' row.

If one person recognized us, it'd be over. If we couldn't get out, we needed some way to hide our—

"Kya, you got money?"

"Ten bucks. Why?"

There was fifteen dollars in my purse, plus a debit card. I went to the closest seller that had what I needed. "Excuse me, sir. I need two masks."

KYA

No. I wasn't going to put one of those things on. Not ever.

Even as I shouted the declaration in my head, I trailed Fuse and didn't argue. Gut reactions and smart decisions were rarely the same thing.

The vendor plucked two masks off his post, said, "Twenty-six fifteen with tax."

I chewed my bottom lip, the math easy and bad. "Do you take cards?"

"Cash only."

"Who doesn't take cards these days?" Fuse said.

He did not seem open to her constructive feedback.

I said, "Sir, we got twenty-five."

The vendor moved one mask to his far hand, away from us. "Well, that gets you this and some change."

"Seriously, dude?" Fuse said. "You can't cut us some—"

"Fuse." Three masks moved from the performance area in a line. Eyes up, their heads panning.

"Fine," she said, taking the mask and the money she was owed. Money that would do neither of us any good if Paris's committed fans had their way.

We took the one mask and slid between a soda stand and a food truck that sold exotic personal pizzas. Fuse pressed the mask into my chest. "That's all you."

"Why me?" I'd yet to take it.

"I did my job a little too well. You look like a supermodel. Everyone sees you right now. I can stay low, tuck my head."

Was she complimenting me or manipulating me?

"Take it, Kya!"

She was like a terrier puppy barking, and I wanted her to shut up. I took the mask, stretched the elastic strap, and pulled it on. Became one of the Nation. Regular or Dark? Didn't much matter anymore.

"Now," Fuse said, "we're splitting up."

"No!" My voice was muffled, and I caught a whiff of the mint gum I'd chewed earlier. My forehead was sweaty already.

"It's not a horror movie," Fuse said. "We split up because it's easier for one person to move through the crowd. Use the mask to get to VIP. I'll have to be a little stealthier about it, but I'll meet you there. Should be easy to get off the property through the way we came. We'll sort all the Winston stuff later."

"How are you this scary calm? You're like a master strategist."

"One of my business books was called *PR Is War*. It crossed up all these marketing principles plus *The Art of War* book by that Sun Tzu guy. I'm finding it all very handy. Go!"

She shoved me from our nook, so I went. Waded into the crowd, praying there wasn't some Dark Nation secret handshake I'd be asked to give. The mask did its job, I blended in with so little effort, I almost forgot about the friend I'd left behind, vulnerable and alone.

FUSE

Awesome, Kya. This Dark Nation monster I created can be good for something. At least one of us might make it.

I stepped deeper into the shadows between concessions, tapped a message to the team.

ME

Flo, where are you?

FLORIAN

Still in my office. Bathroom stall number
ewwww.

ME

Kya, you?

KYA

Almost to VIP.

FLORIAN

You two are still here? I've seen the Dark
Nation chatter. Monumentally bad idea,
guys. Just going on the record with that.

ME

Can you do something about them?

You're like their CEO, right?

FLORIAN

I've already tried. No one's even paying

attention to me. They're rabid.

ME

Oh joy!

KYA

How's your setup looking? Were you able

to do what I asked?

FLORIAN

Yes, I did the thing. Worked perfectly.

Also, most of the facility is on the

network. I've got cameras, the engineer's

soundboard, lights, and effects. I don't

know what good it's going to do you

now. All things considered.

KYA

Fuse, where are you?

ME

I might be hiding behind the soda tanks

where you left me.

KYA

I'm coming back.

ME

No you are not! I'm fine. I can make it.

KYA

You better.

Okay, okay. What was it? Fifty yards, seventy-five, until I got to VIP? At least there'd be a limited amount of people back there. The Clutch Boyz set was halfway done. Olivia Merrick would be next. All attention would be on her and the headliner, Omar Bless. Little old me shouldn't even pop on anybody's radar in midshow frenzy. Just had to get there.

Slowly, I ventured from my hiding place, visualizing my path and identifying all threats. The good thing about those creepy masks . . . they stood out. I spotted eight hostiles with cyborg-like vision and mapped a course between them.

Fast, head down. Focus on the objective.

Go!

You know those really good sportsball runners that caught the thing on one side of the field, and got all the way to the other side of the field despite there being like fifty heavily padded gladiators between where they started and where they finished? I was like one them! (Even if I didn't know the proper terminology.)

People loaded down with snacks were my cover. I sidestepped groups of girls that never looked up. Stuck to the shadows of people larger than me.

I almost made it unnoticed.

"Hey," someone roared, "there she is."

There was no need for confirmation. I saw white masks angling my way like ghostly sharks breaking the surface for a feeding frenzy.

Screw it. I sprinted, swerving around people with nimbleness that had my social media nerd lungs straining. The guard at the VIP barrier seemed oblivious to the mini mob chasing me, simply waving me through as I held up my badge.

Inside the cordoned off area, I finally looked back. Five masks had reached the threshold, all without the proper credentials. Safe for now.

Though not for long. I made for the exit, but there was no clear route. Masks here. Mask there. Masks everywhere.

Blending in with the backstage chaos kept me safe in the immediate, but I needed another pit stop. Some place to chill, contact Kya and Florian.

At the stage steps, watching the Clutch Boyz going into their finale songs, Olivia Merrick and all her dancers stood in a prayer circle. Hands clasped, heads joined, Olivia, undoubtedly, doling inspiring words. With the Olivia Merrick entourage in that good, holy headspace, I slipped past them into the unguarded dressing room she'd occupied previously. Gently, I closed the door and rested against it, gasping. Eyes squeezed shut.

Think, Fuse. Think.

My phone buzzed with incoming text. Kya or Florian, for sure. I stepped deeper into the harshly lit dressing room, snatched a handful of pretzel sticks off a table of mangled meat-and-cheese trays, sad-looking salsa, and a bowl of all red gummy bears.

KYA

Tell me you're not still stuck behind the
concession.

ME

Nope. Made it back here. Had to dip into
Olivia Merrick's dressing room. Too hot
near the exit.

KYA

I know. I think we'll have to wait until
Omar Bless goes on. I heard some
stagehands talking . . . he's going to do
his last collaboration with Paris first. That
should draw the masks like a bug zapper
draws flies.

ME

IDK if I can wait that long. Olivia's gonna
come back after her set, and

That's as far as I got with that message. The dressing room door
opened and closed, fast enough for one mask to join me. We faced
each other. His hoodie cinched tight around his plastic face like a
Dark Nation pro. He loosened the string, peeled back the cloth.
Then flipped the mask up so it sat atop his dreads.

My pretzel sticks fell from my suddenly slick and trembling
hand, clattering on the floor.

Looked like Winston Bell and I were going to have a little chat
after all.

KYA

Fuse, answer your freaking texts!

She hadn't responded. She started to, I saw the flashing ellipses that meant she was typing. Then, nothing.

This area filled with more and more people repping the Nation. Maybe it was because Omar Bless's set was supposed to be some special tribute to Paris. Maybe they smelled us back here. Even hidden behind one of their masks, I felt exposed. We needed to be gone like yesterday.

I wasn't leaving without her. That was starting to look like neither one of us was getting out of here. Not unscathed.

More masks came.

FUSE

He removed the mask clumsily, his dreads tangling in the elastic strap, so he had to break it to free himself. My feet scrabbled on the concrete as I backed into a corner, bumping into several stacked crates. Nowhere else to go.

Rummaging in my bag, I grabbed the stun gun. Tried forcing my hand not to shake when I wielded it. "Stay back, or—" I depressed the trigger. A weak spark, something like static electricity, flickered and died. I jammed the button again and again. I never recharged it.

He observed my weapon, almost sad for me.

"I'll scream!" I said. "Don't come closer."

"What do you think you know?" he asked.

I spoke loudly. Enunciating. "You murdered ParSec. Care to tell me the rest?"

"That's not what happened. You always had a poor opinion of me. Believe it or not, no one murdered Paris. It's the last thing I'd want to do to her."

"So you were there when she—"

"Fell. Accidentally. Sure."

My fear tapered, anger cresting over it. "She fell? Accidentally? And you left her there for Kya and me to find?"

"It was for the best." His voice cracked, like he meant it. "It would've been too confusing if I'd stayed. It wouldn't have changed anything."

"Maybe it would've changed the trash fire set to mine and Kya's lives over an unsolved mystery that was perfectly solvable. Maybe if you'd been honest about who you were to her, she might've kicked you to the curb before you'd done any real damage!"

Winston crumpled his mask in one fist, took three quick steps forward. Roared, "What do you know about who I am to her?"

I whimpered then. All that was between us was the beat of a Clutch Boyz song. Their big hit, "Do Not Pass Go." The finale.

A few bars in, he confirmed what we'd suspected and feared. "I didn't hurt my little girl, okay? What happened to Paris was an unfortunate accident that will haunt me forever. Maybe I should've been gone, but I thought my sudden disappearance would arouse more suspicion. I planned to wait until things had cooled. You and your friend wouldn't let them. I hope you'll be able to move on now."

"You think that's it?" Fury tempered my tongue. "That I'm just going to let this go?"

"I'm a ghost, kid. With one more thing to do." Winston fished his phone from his pocket, tapped it with his thumb. Seconds later, my phone vibrated with a notification.

The Truth Is Out There @X211ABE

#ParSecNation #ParSecMemorialConcert

@FuseZilla14 is in Olivia Merrick's dressing room.

Happy hunting.

Awesome.

He backed away, keeping his word. He didn't plan to hurt me. He didn't have the guts to do it himself.

Winston dropped his phone. Stomped it dead. Then slipped out of the dressing room. I rushed to the door and turned the dead bolt I'd neglected earlier. Trapped myself inside. Mere seconds before the pounding started. Heavy fists like drumbeats, playing a song I didn't like. A danse macabre.

KYA

My angle on Olivia Merrick's dressing room was good, though I didn't like a thing I saw. Fuse still hadn't texted back, and when Winston Bell stepped out, my heart lurched, expecting the worse. While he walked away from the dressing room, a platoon of Nation masks swarmed the door, pounding like zombies. He slipped through them all, and my first instinct was to tackle him in front of everyone. Would've done it, if I didn't finally get the text I wanted.

FUSE

In a bit of a pickle here, gang. Barbarians
at the gate.

ME

I see you. What do you want me to do?

FUSE

Tell me how many are out there.

ME

Ten or twelve. They're going to break
down the door.

FLORIAN

I see both of you on the security feed.
This looks pretty bad.

ME

Captain Obvious, where's Barker?

FLORIAN

He's inside and hooking up with venue
security. They're all coming to you. Just not
in time.

Nothing at this venue was constructed to withstand a mob assault; both ParSecNation and the Dark Nation were angry enough to do real damage if they got to Fuse. Someone needed to distract them.

The crowd cheered as the Clutch Boyz finished their set. The brothers bounded down the stage steps shirtless, sweaty, and high off the adrenaline. Olivia Merrick waited to go on, bouncing nervously on her toes. Near her, a rolling cart with a bunch of powered-down wireless microphones. I walked over and grabbed one. Red tape circled the handle and the number twenty-five was written in marker.

I sent my last text.

ME

Florian, if you still have access to the
soundboard, keep mic 25 hot as long
as you can.

The dancing ellipses appeared; I couldn't wait on the response. Before Olivia's intro music began, before the announcer attempted welcoming her to the stage, I tossed my mask aside and sprinted up the stage steps to a chorus of surprised gasps and shouts for security.

I caught a flash of white—Paula Klein—in the wings observing and yelled to her, "Help me if you can."

I was out there. Looking over the monitor boxes and the footlights at an uninterested crowd that didn't seem to think I was more than some stagehand prepping for the next act. I flipped the mic's power switch, thumped it twice, sending a percussive one-two throughout the venue. Raised it to my lips, like I was kissing an old friend.

"I gotta talk fast because they're going to shut me down soon. I'm Kya Caine. My friend Fuse Fallon is backstage about to get wrecked over lies."

Someone booed. A few sporadic followers joined. Most didn't care. This wasn't going to work if they didn't care.

"We did not kill Paris Secord!" My shout reverbed throughout the venue. Snatching attention. Not everyone. Enough. I kept going. "But we know who did."

I glanced back the way I came, security guards barreled up the steps.

"A man who goes by the name Winston Bell killed Paris, who you may know better as DJ ParSec."

Paula Klein blocked the guards. It seemed. At first.

Then she sidestepped, swept an arm in my direction with a show woman's flourish, as if to say, "Be my guest."

Classy, Paula.

I backpedaled to the far end of the stage while three burly security guards closed in on me. I needed more time. More time.

There was one thing I knew how to do that always stopped a show.

"New DJ ParSec music, right now," I said, and put everything I had into a high C note that wasn't quite Mariah Carey's level (whose was?) but close enough for government work, as Mama said.

The guards froze in place. A slow clap started in the audience the longer I held it. Five seconds. Ten. I was running out of air.

I stopped, lowered the mic, and gathered myself. Only one shot at this. "Paris was our friend, but we weren't always friendly. That's what happens. We had peaks and valleys, but we weren't ever without love."

In the wings, next to Paula Klein were the Clutch Boyz, curious enough to return. Olivia Merrick who looked rightly pissed—sorry. And, most surprising, Omar Bless himself. He was a stark contrast to Paula in his black-on-black ensemble. A yellow diamond chain hung from his neck, nearly to his navel. He peeled off his designer shades to watch my show. Expressionless.

"This is a song she wrote. It's called 'Everything, I'm Not.'"

And I did the thing I'd never thought I'd do again. Gave them a show.

All of me doesn't fill this space.
All of me is all out of place.
A part of me is all, do I stay?
And all you do is take away.

At first, I was skittish, expecting any number of things to happen. My mic would go dead. Security would rush me. The crowd's boos would drown my vocals.

Except if someone was scrambling to kill my mic, Florian scrambled better. If the security wanted to tackle me, I'd entranced them like sirens did to sailors in nautical legends. And the crowd, they bought into my a cappella performance because I was good at this. Always had been. Would've made Mama proud.

Halfway through the second verse, my mic cut out. I knew it was coming. But as I went mute and the security approached to get me off the stage, the crowd began booing. Hissing. When a guard grabbed my arm, a water bottle rattled by our feet. Then another. Then more assorted trash.

The guards hesitated, allowing a chant that had started in the back to amplify and reach me.

"LET HER SING! LET HER SING! LET HER SING!"

As much as the spectators cheered me on, and as special as this moment was because it was one of Paris's song, I still didn't love this. I only hoped that my gift was enough of a distraction to save the one friend I had left.

I allowed myself to be escorted offstage, despite the demands of the audience. Past Paula, and the Clutch Boyz, and Omar Bless, who said, "You killed it, shorty."

Olivia Merrick—visibly angry—did not compliment me. I got it.

I was going to be a tough act to follow.

I always was.

FUSE

Once the pounding stopped, I heard it all.

Kya's play drew the attention of the masks on the other side of the door, but I didn't dare step outside. Only listened to it all. She told the truth, and she sang. For ParSec, and for me.

I love you too, Kya.

Her voice was beautiful, until it wasn't. Her mic went dead, and shortly after, more pounding on the door.

The wood would buckle, splinter, and a horde of masks would have their way.

Resigned, I palmed a handful of red gummy bears, shoved them in my mouth. Why not?

"Fatima," a familiar voice called, "if you're in there, open it. It's Detective Barker and amphitheater security."

Sticky, half-chewed gummies cascaded off my lips. Scrambling, I opened the door. The detective had two large men in Security T-shirts with him. All masks had dispersed. I hugged him like he was my favorite uncle.

Gently, he pried me off, embarrassed. Maybe a little mad. "You've got a lot of explaining to do. Come on."

Detective Barker escorted me through the VIP entrance, where a distraught Shameik gave me the "what's up?" shrug.

I mouthed, *Later, man.*

A lot of phones were out, snapping pics. Recording.

We ended up at Barker's car, the same one he'd pulled me over in. In the backseat, my friend. I leapt across the seat, throwing my arms around Kya.

When Barker got behind the wheel, he twisted, had the Big Mad face. "You girls . . . I don't even know what to say. What happened here? Where's Winston Bell?"

Kya did not appear to be listening, her eyes on her phone.

Barker said, "Are you not hearing me? Did he get away?"

"Not for long," Kya said happily.

"It worked?" My head nuzzled beside hers, watching her phone.

"It worked."

"*What* worked?" Barker demanded, flustered.

Kya, prim and proper, placed her phone in her lap. "We should go to the station now. Best you're not driving when you hear this."

KYA

"Start from the beginning," Barker ordered.

Symmetry was always my preference. While I should've been quaking over the repercussions—known and unknown—of what me, Fuse, Florian, and Shameik pulled off, I was comforted by the location of our confession. The same interrogation room I'd occupied the night we'd found Paris. Instead of me and two scary cops, it was Fuse and me, facing down the adults in our lives. Together. It was becoming our thing.

Mama came, smacking her nicotine gum and threatening murder telepathically. Fuse's parents were present, her mom in hospital scrubs and her dad with his tie tugged loose. All mad, but a little awed too—even if they wouldn't admit. Five minutes into our story, Barker held up a hand, cutting us off. "Don't say anything else. I need to talk to the chief and maybe an assistant district attorney. I don't know where any of this stands legally. Jesus, girls."

He stomped out of the room, leaving us with the parents. I'd have rather dealt with an angry police chief.

They all blew at once. An eruption of:

"What the—"

"Are you crazy, stupid, or a little of—"

"I'm going to strangle you when there are no cops around—"

Beneath the table, Fuse's fingers curled into mine, and we took the onslaught. We'd been through worse.

FUSE

We were *not* on stable legal grounds. Barker, his chief, and a frazzled man from the district attorney's office decided they *didn't* want to hear another word about what happened before, or during, the concert. Not without some thought, and other lawyers present—really, not without their butts covered. District Attorney Office Guy was all, "This is so unorthodox. You girls are minors. We need to tread carefully."

Fine by me. I knew plausible deniability when I saw it.

Since we were never officially under arrest, by midnight we were released to our parents, which was worse than being under arrest. They marched us to the cars silently, took our phones, effectively severing any communication between us, then drove us in separate directions, to our separate homes. Though I imagined the reckoning was similar for us both.

I only saw Kya in passing for the next week. At school, an entire army of educators prevented one-on-one contact. Principal Corgis would not suffer any more of Dad's wrath. The bridge in our forced separation was Florian, who remained on the outer rim of the memorial concert debacle while benefiting the most from it. (More on that later.)

Knowing how treacherous digital waters could be, we went analog in a series of passed handwritten notes through Florian the courier (who probably read every single one despite explicit instructions not to . . . desperate times).

I was fine. Kya was fine. My parents threatened to send me to stay with cousins for the summer. Kya's mom didn't have that option, so she yelled a lot, according to Kya's many, many notes.

We couldn't meet after school, not even for a moment, because Dad had one of his corporate underlings waiting with a car five minutes before final bell.

Five days of that. With occasional reminders by way of a Detective Barker phone call to our parents, and parents yelling at us, about how we'd made everyone upset.

The tone changed when Detective Barker called the Thursday after the concert.

That morning, sometime between 1:00 and 2:00 a.m., a package arrived on the gray concrete steps of the Ocean Shore Police Department. A tied, gagged, and slightly bruised Winston Bell.

Courtesy of the Dark Nation.

KYA

I'm smart enough to have known better.

I thought the apprehension of a rising music star's alleged murderer, who might also be her estranged father, by what was, essentially, a fan cult, would've been more newsworthy. Not so in Ocean Shore.

The local stations ran the equivalent of their daily black criminal briefing. Winston's—real name Onell, but he'd never be that to me—mug shot with a vague "being held in connection to the death of a local musician." He might as well have been accused of robbing a 7-Eleven.

They didn't even say Paris's name.

In other news, two Hollywood studios announced different versions—authorized and unauthorized—of the Adelaide Milton story were going into production, and there was a rush for one to beat the other to theaters. The casting call had thousands of little girl actresses across the country getting blond wigs or dye jobs for auditions, hopeful that adopting Adelaide's look got them noticed; they weren't wrong. It made me so, so angry.

Paris mattered too.

She mattered enough that I needed to do something more. Something we talked about many times when we were younger, during late-night sleepovers, when we comforted each other over our MIA fathers.

It wasn't going to go over well with Mama, or Detective Barker, or the district attorney.

I proposed what I wanted to Fuse in a furious exchange of notes via Florian. Fuse was apprehensive but agreed to play it my way on one condition: She got to go too.

Detective Barker was the first adult I approached thanks to a burner cell phone, courtesy of Florian. As expected, he said no, almost a reflex. I had a bargaining chip, though. The thing all of the adults in the equation pushed for from the moment Fuse and me told them everything we'd done: our silence.

Withholding the details of our "interference in the investigation" was actively encouraged. Detective Barker said it was to not jeopardize the case against Winston. Mama theorized OSPD didn't want it getting out that children did the police's job for them. Mama's never been a dumb woman.

So my proposal became a demand. To which Barker replied: "You're really going to extort me?"

"It's a conversation. With one person. Isn't that better than me having conversations with lots of people? Don't we all get what we want?"

"It might not even be possible, Kya." The detective was distraught, whiny. Strange to hear a grown-up talk that way.

"I'm sure you'll find out. Soon." I hung up, wishing Fuse could've been there to hear me, really, channel her.

It took a few days. Then Barker had to talk it over with our parents, who also rejected the idea . . . at first. They weren't too different from the DA's office, pushing for the particulars of it all to be buried. They wanted to move on from Paris in a way that just wasn't possible for Fuse and me. They wanted this over.

To comfort them, we said it would be done after this. We said we'd be safe, and Detective Barker would be there the whole time. We said a lot of things to gain an audience with a monster.

Fuse and I were going to visit Winston Bell.

FUSE

Jail had a smell. It was strong, burned my nose. Like generic mouthwash . . . not mint or spearmint, but that brown Listerine Mom's great-aunt Dorthea kept a lifetime supply of, plus a little bit of pee underneath. The smell was a distraction from my totally irrational fear that once the doors shut behind me, I'd never be allowed to leave this place.

It was early, the arrangement dictated we go at the butt crack of dawn and Barker wouldn't leave us alone, not for one second. Through the metal detector, past the lockers where we had to store our phones and keys and any other "contraband we might have on our persons," through heavy doors that had to be unlocked by some unseen force watching us through not-subtle cameras.

We were directed toward a row of visitation stalls, to two dull aluminum stools that sat at a low counter. On the wall, an orange phone that communicated directly with the orange phone on the other side of thick glass with mesh wire running through it.

Something like an air horn sounded, a short blast. Then a heavy lock clacked on a door beyond the glass. A guard walked Winston in. He moved freely, though with a new limp. No cuffs or shackles, and he politely thanked the guard for showing him to us. He offered a weak smile, his bottom lip crusty and scabbed. What should've been the white part of his left eye was a scary, demonic red from broken blood vessels. The Dark Nation really worked him over.

He scooped up the phone receiver with a shaky hand. Kya did the same on our side, holding the earpiece in the general region between Barker and me. We all leaned in.

The guard on Winston's side said, "These conversations are recorded."

It sounded like a low-quality radio broadcast on our end, but we understood. It wasn't a problem.

Winston said, "Thanks for coming, girls." Like he'd initiated this.

"Thanks for being in jail," I replied.

Kya moved the receiver away from me. "Did they tell you why we're here?"

His gaze flicked from me, to Kya, to Barker, and back. "To give me a quote for my memoir? I'm going to have a lot of dedicated writing time, it seems." His laugh was weak. That he had it in him to joke at all was disturbing and had me shuddering over the time I'd been alone with this unhinged man.

Kya sneered. "Did Paris know you were her father? Before it happened?"

He looked away and lowered the receiver. Nothing funny now. He returned the phone to his ear, gave two quick nods.

Kya's breathing quickened. I know why she asked, and understood the impact the confirmation had on her. I took the receiver, gave her a moment to gather herself. I had things to say too.

"You know where you messed up, right?" I began. "How we got you?"

His eyes narrowed, became inquisitive.

"That's what I thought." Given how he'd left me to be devoured by the Dark Nation wolves, I was so going to enjoy this. "It was the venue Wi-Fi, Winston. Or what you thought was the venue Wi-Fi."

I broke down Kya's plan—maybe more simply than she had explained it to me, Florian, and Shameik that night at the Savant, but I captured the essence. Shameik, in his concert-planning mode, got us access to the amphitheater Wi-Fi a day early, enough time for Florian to spoof the login page like she'd done at the high school. On the day of the concert, anyone in the amphitheater who tried to access the Wi-Fi found what seemed like a strange glitch, forcing them to log on twice. The first time was our fake page, giving us access to their phones if we wanted it. The second time was the real venue page. Florian had Winston's phone number from our many texts, making it easy for her to identify him the moment he logged on.

Barker leaned close, hearing the extended version of this for the first time.

"To be honest, we never trusted the police to get this right— sorry, Detective."

Barker didn't seem amused.

I focused on Winston. "We also didn't expect you to go nuclear option and sic the entire Dark Nation on us, so our plan wasn't flawless. You actually might've gotten away fine if you didn't follow me into Olivia Merrick's dressing room."

This was the part I was looking forward to most. I let it hang.

He bit. "What are you talking about?"

"See, when we got access to your phone, we put an app on it"—I cocked a thumb at Kya—"one she designed. SoundChek." I made sure to give it the same gravitas Kya did when she spoke of it. "Inspired by ParSec, which is fitting. We thought if you got away, we might bug you and listen to your conversations for any clue that might lead us to you later. But you talked and talked and talked while we were together."

"I broke that phone," he said, slightly incredulous.

I pointed up. "The cloud, bro. Even with the concert being loud, and chaos happening all over, the app did a great job of recording you, and separating your voice. Then we played your game, by giving the recording to the Dark Nation. Once they heard what you said, and we provided a detailed description of you, they did the rest. Heard they found you in Canada. A lot of DJ ParSec fans there."

I was ready to rub more salt in his wounds, but Kya tapped my shoulder, motioned for the receiver. "Can I?"

Knowing what was coming, the joy of bragging wore off quickly. "Yeah. Cool."

She gripped the receiver, pressed it to her ear, and delivered a message that Paris, maybe, never got the chance to.

KYA

The nerves I felt were more than any I'd experienced stepping onto a stage, or grabbing any microphone. Maybe because this wasn't for me. "I don't know how long you lied to her. I don't know how she reacted when she found out who you really were. I can't imagine how you told her, if you were compassionate or ashamed or indignant. I don't know anything about you, because she didn't. You were never there, and Paris told me, more than once, what she wanted to say to you, if she had the chance."

As he'd done for Fuse, he leaned even closer to the glass, his undamaged eye widening in a way the bloodied one wouldn't allow. I sensed a desperate anticipation in him. So, no, Paris hadn't had her say. He robbed her of that too.

"Paris told me, that if she ever met her dad, she'd say"—the words caught in my throat like a fish hook, forcing them up felt like tearing something, but I did it anyway—"'I did fine when my mom died. I did fine when I got my first drum machine. I did fine when those girls from down the block wanted to beat me down. I did fine when . . .'"

"What else?" he said, tears glistening. "What else?"

"Mostly, that was it. See, it was like a song she'd been working on for years. She added to it when new stuff happened. 'I did fine when school was hard. I did fine when Grandma's sugar got bad. I did fine. I did fine.' The coda was always going to be the same, though. 'I did fine without you.'"

No blinking, no tears, no fear. Not from my side of the glass. Not anymore. I put every bit of venom into my final words for Winston Bell. "She wasn't wrong. The only good thing you did was her, and you took that from the world. I hope you rot here."

I laid the phone on the slim lip of the stall, in case someone else had something to say. We were done. At least I thought so.

Winston's voice sounded tinny and far away as it crackled through the receiver. "Wait, one of you."

Fuse picked up the receiver and held it so we all could hear. "What?"

"The recording, from where you hacked my phone, is that the strongest piece of evidence you have?"

Fuse glanced to me, shadows darkening her face.

Barker leaned into the receiver, speaking quickly, and sounding afraid. "We're not at liberty to discuss our evidence." Pointedly, he told us, "Don't say another word, girls."

Winston said, "Because I've already spoken to a lawyer, and he doesn't think you have a ton of admissible evidence. A lot of what you described sounds less than legal."

What was he saying? I couldn't tell because his voice was flat, his face emotionless. If he was threatening us, he lacked the malice. If he was taunting us with the possibility that he might walk, he lacked the supervillain-esque glee. Honestly, his vibe reminded me of my days with the Smart Ones, when a tough equation halted progress and ruined an afternoon. What math was Winston working here?

He twisted on his stool, announced to the guard, "We're done."

"Hold on a sec," Fuse said.

The response: a click as Winston dropped his receiver in the cradle, severing the connection.

"Wait." I pounded my fist on the glass as he joined the guard at the door.

What just happened? What had we done?

The lock released on his side, opening a portal. Winston stood, and I dropped the receiver, letting it bounce, then dangle on its cord. Before Winston vanished into the guts of the jail, Fuse saw what I saw, what hadn't been visible because his body blocked the view of his right hand when he'd entered the room. She squeezed my arm, likely more freaked by the visual than his ominous last words.

The hand was heavily bandaged.

A splotch of red seeped through, bright and blotchy.

His pinkie was gone.

FUSE

Three days later, Detective Barker asked my parents to bring me to the station to speak in person. Apparently, he'd heard something recently that made him extra cautious about talking over cell phones. Ahem.

Mom wanted to bring our lawyer, but the detective assured her that wouldn't be necessary. At the station, we found Kya and her mama waiting. My stomach did flip-flops. What had Winston done now?

Barker didn't take us into an interrogation room. We took a different path through the police station, upstairs, into a conference room. A monitor sat at the end of a conference table surrounded by a dozen leather chairs. The detective motioned for us to sit down.

"What is this about?" Dad said, voice echoing.

"Yeah," said Kya's mama, "I don't like all this secret squirrel mess."

Barker said, "Trust me. It'll be worth it."

So we took our seats. Me and my parents on one side. Kya and her mama on the other. Kya sat directly across from me, sporting her skittish look.

I feel it too, girl. Whatever this is, we can handle it.

Barker sat, and I braced myself for the inevitable tsunami. Had Winston escaped? Were we going to have to go into witness protection to hide from him?

Barker said, "I wanted to give you the good news myself."

Good news?

"There won't be a trial. Your questionably obtained evidence won't get ripped apart by some sleazy defense attorney. You girls will never have to sit on a witness stand. The man you know as Winston Bell is pleading guilty to his involvement in your friend's death. He told his lawyer the day after we met him. He's been deposed. The paperwork is being finalized. You got him."

Both Kya and I shifted to the edge of our seats. I didn't know if I'd heard him right. "He admitted he murdered ParSec?"

Barker mouth twitched. "He confessed to involuntary manslaughter."

Kya said, "That's not murder. That's way different than murder."

Barker showed his palms, as if trying to push any disagreements we had away. "He's going to jail, girls. That's a win. Something that doesn't happen if you didn't do what you did at the—"

"How much time is that monster going to get?" The question was unexpected, coming from my dad. His hand fell on my shoulder, and a part of me melted. I wrapped my hand around his fingers, felt five again.

"The max sentencing for the crime is ten years," said Barker.

Kya's mama grabbed Kya's forearm, said, "But how much time is he going to get?"

Barker said, "Because he's cooperating, it will be significantly less."

"How much?" Kya snapped, startling the room.

"Maybe as little as a year if he behaves in jail."

The room became airless. I had to stand, get some oxygen

from somewhere. One year? How many years did he take from ParSec?

Kya doubled over in her chair. Sobbing. Her mama rubbing slow circles on her back.

As I paced, I noticed the arrangement on the far side of the room. A chocolate-frosted cake and bottles of sparkling cider. Barker brought us here to celebrate. I said, "You thought this was going to be a party, didn't you?"

Barker said, "You may not see it this way, but there's good news here."

Kya said, "But not justice." She got up and left the room.

Suddenly all eyes were on me. Her mama said, "You're probably the only one she's going to talk to right now."

I followed into the hallway where Kya had pulled her ever-present flash drive from her beneath her shirt, clutching the plastic in her fist. Her phone was in her other hand, and she was scrolling.

"I know you're not okay," I said.

She grunted, kept looking at her phone.

"So, what are you?"

Kya met my gaze. "Patient. #ParSecNation is still lit."

I'd seen this look before, when she was ready to slow-roast Florian. "Kya, you've got the crazy eyes. What are you thinking?"

"I'm thinking a year works."

"What?"

"There's enough unreleased Paris music on this drive for us to keep the Dark Nation satiated for that long. Then, whenever Winston's back on the street. Maybe they take him for a ride he deserves."

Images of his seeping red bandage flashed behind my eyes. What acts might the Dark Nation evolve toward in a year's time? Yooooooo. "Um, Kya . . . you're terrifying right now."

"No. I'm hungry. Let's go get some of that cake."

And we did. It tasted better than I imagined.

KYA

I returned the Savant key to Miss Elsie. To make up for stealing it in the first place, I offered to escort her to the building and show her around Paris's place. She accepted.

Through the lobby, past the doorman, up the fancy keycard-controlled elevator we went. The unhidden gleam of awe in her eyes. She spent a lot of time touching the things in the apartment.

"What was you and that other little girl doing here, Kya?"

The Blu-rays Fuse bought still rested on a cardboard box by the TV. "We came here to remember her. We watched some of her favorite movies together."

Miss Elsie only nodded, then drifted into the bedroom. She stretched herself across Paris's bed, pressed her head into the pillows.

"I'll go wait out front," I said.

"No, baby. Stay." She sat up, dabbed at the corner of her eyes, before focusing on the open closet. "Paris always did love them shoes. Never knew why anyone needed so many pairs."

She approached the closet, and I already knew what she wanted. She was Fuse-level short.

I said, "I'll help you get them down."

Three Nike boxes came down easily enough, but the weight felt weird. There weren't shoes inside. I sat them on the foot of the bed and Miss Elsie popped the lid on one.

"Good Lord," she said, then immediately began pulling stashed stacks of five-, ten-, and twenty-dollar bills free.

Opening the next two boxes yielded the same results. I went back to the closet because seven more boxes remained on the shelf. When we pulled them down, we found one more box of money. The rest were actual shoes, but still.

Miss Elsie backed away from the piles of money. "What should we do about it?"

"*We* shouldn't do anything. *You* should keep it. She would've wanted you to." Nothing in me doubted the validity of that statement.

She hemmed and hawed some more, and I decided arguing was futile, so I grabbed one of Paris's pillows, peeled off the pillowcase, and began sweeping cash into the improvised money bag. An unstuck Miss Elsie followed my lead, filling her own sack.

We left the Savant—through the parking deck exit since we looked like comic strip bank robbers. In the Lyft home, Miss Elsie rubbed my knee and said, "I'm glad she had you. Even for a little while."

The feeling was mutual.

FUSE

School ended. As did my illustrious career at Cooke High. My senior year would be spent at Coral Oak Academy, which just sounded dumb to me. Were coral and oak ever even in the same place? Also, I didn't love their whole khaki pants and sweater vests vibe. Ugh. I shall endure!

During that first week of summer, Dad had Suzanne summon me to his office. We hadn't had a conversation since the concert. There was plenty of him yelling, and me zoning like some out-of-body experience, but not conversations. I was certain this sudden need to use his indoor voice meant terrible things, like when the water recedes all calm and stuff before a tidal wave.

He'd been behind his ridiculous huge monitor; headphone cables snaked from the audio jack. I took a chair that kept the monitor between us, hoping to avoid his judgmental eyes. He rolled his chair from its nook, around to me. No obstructions to save me.

"Has Andrea been in touch about something? Am I in more trouble?"

"No. Nothing like that."

What was it like, then?

He said, "I have some questions." He rolled back to his desk, tapped his space bar, and music spilled from his speakers. A custom mix. A sped-up version of the *Star Wars* "Imperial March" with "Ladies First" by Queen Latifah and Monie Love.

I was out of my chair and around his desk in an instant, watching the footage—my footage—of ParSec mixing on YouTube. Anxiety hit when I imagined the ways he'd find to be mad at this.

"This is good stuff," he said. "I looked at most of the videos on this channel. All you?"

"I—I came up with the concepts. Suggested some things musically, but once ParSec got the hang of it, it was more like a true collaboration."

"Your friend seemed very talented."

"You have no idea."

He clicked away from the video, pointed at the different rows on the channel's main page. "You've divided these videos into different silos. Entertainment, educational, then straight promotional. Why?"

"I wanted to attract a variety of viewers. Some would be interested in hot music, others in actually doing the things that ParSec could do. Two kinds of sticky content. The promo stuff is more of a necessary evil, but I wanted it available. If someone came to the channel and clicked on a bunch of videos, they might be interested in spending money. I hoped it would create a sort of loop that kept ParSec on a lot of people's minds all the time."

"Wow, kid. There are guys with master's degrees working for me who I gotta yell at to get this much thought and effort."

"I pay attention," I said. "So you don't have to yell at me."

"Yeah. Perhaps I don't." He shifted in his chair, opened iTunes, and queued up a song. "You loved 'Ladies First' when you were tiny. Two years old, in your car seat singing the hook like you wrote it. Took it to heart, I suppose."

Mild irritation prickled my skin. "You loved it first. Then you didn't. What's up with that?"

"You've got it wrong, Fatima. Still love all those songs we used to sing, and all the stuff we used to do, but you make room for new things in life. New passions. No one is the same person they were even five years ago. Not even you."

I scoffed, prepared to counter.

He cut me off. "Your braces are gone. You started having boyfriends. All of a sudden you and your mom talk about stuff I have no clue about."

"That's not true." Was it?

"Right. You barely talk to *her* anymore. You're almost an adult, and it's cool. For the most part. I know it has to happen, and I made my peace with it. But, if I'm not preserving my little rapping two-year-old in amber so she never evolves, might I get the same courtesy?"

I never thought of it that way. Never considered having anything close to this conversation with him. Why is this happening now?

He said, "I don't know if I have all the story about what happened to your friend, but this thought's been nagging me ever since the night she died, when I picked you up from the police precinct. What if it had been you?"

My throat was suddenly dry. "Dad, I'm fine."

"I know, but understand. Even with that thought in my head, I didn't do anything to change the way things were between us. Because you were fine. Then, it happened a second time, and I hear all about how you've been around this man who killed his own kid"—his voice seemed scratchy—"and I knew I couldn't wait any longer to fix whatever's broken between us."

He stood, hugged me. I hugged him back. For a long time.

His phone went off, not a call, but an alarm. I had the ugly, fleeting thought that he'd set a timer on our emotional moment. Glancing at his screen, he cursed softly. "Always a meeting, I gotta hop on a call in a few minutes."

"It's fine." It was, the intensity here was a little much. "We'll talk later."

"We sure will. Think about this in the meantime . . . interning at the office this summer."

"Seriously?"

"Sure. You've got solid ideas and a better grasp on modern social media than some of my senior staff. It will be good for everyone."

"Can I switch up some of that boring elevator music y'all crank through the building?"

He mulled it over. "Maybe on Fridays."

"Then I will consider it."

On my way out, he called to me. "Fatima, you're forgetting something."

I turned and spotted my phone and car keys on the desktop.

"If you're coming to work for me, you'll need all your tools, right?"

I snatched up my things. "I haven't said yes yet."

Dad pulled on his telephone headset, switching to business mode. "You will."

Cocky, bold, yet cool. Good strategy, Dad.

The odds were in your favor.

■ ■

Having my phone returned felt like I found my way back to civilization after a decade on a desert island. So much to catch up on.

Like Florian's trifling tail. Her ParSec Love Tumblr had gone quiet after one last story about Paula Klein mismanaging DJ ParSec's money. That story got picked up by other interested parties—like more gossipmongers and the authorities. That wasn't the trifling part. *How* Florian managed to snag bank records from Paula was.

Since the concert, Florian started several sites that seemed to scoop every major tabloid site when it came to news on some very specific artists. The Clutch Boyz. Olivia Merrick. Omar Bless. Her smaller sites still dealt in local gossip—but they were popping too with her spilling the tea on everyone. How?

That whole spoof the amphitheater Wi-Fi thing . . . our big way to get Winston . . . well, Little Miss Gossip Blogger must've retained access to more phones than we told her to, since we told her to only access one.

One particularly juicy piece of gossip involved Shameik and Olivia Merrick, who got to know each other a little better the day of the concert. #ShOlivia was a thing and the #MerrickMob was on board with it, for now. Olivia's fandom was already showing some of the rowdier traits that eventually birthed the Dark Nation. Shameik would be smart to treat that girl right. Or else.

I wish them the best, though.

Still, how long could we let this ride? I consulted with my partner.

ME

Florian!

KYA

You've noticed too? She's Lois Lane all
of a sudden.

ME

What are we going to do about it? Don't
say stun gun.

KYA

Well . . . I don't really have any other
good options right now.

                                    ME

                 We can't just let it go, right?

KYA

No. We'll deal with it. It should be a
simple matter really. I'll promise not to
strangle her. She'll stop spying. Easy.

                                    ME

           I'm finally free to leave the premises.
                 Should we do it today?

KYA

If you're off house arrest, I actually have
something that's a little more pressing.
Come get me?

                                    ME

                 Should I be scared?

KYA

Not even a little bit. You'll see. I think
you're going to love this.

She wasn't wrong.

KYA

Fuse drove a familiar route, to a familiar place, for the last time.

We parked in the Savant deck, in the space that was legally still Paris's through the end of the month. Though, it would be emptied by movers tomorrow. Miss Elsie told me these things, just before handing me the keys.

"Go there," she'd instructed, "take whatever she would've wanted you to have."

"I don't know what she would've wanted me to have."

"I'm sure you and that other little girl can figure it out."

Inside the apartment, we weaved around the same old boxes, rummaged through all that VenueShowZ swag, and decided we were all set on keychains, water bottles, and cheaply stitched sweatshirts. They'd be better used at the Goodwill.

Fuse opened the balcony and let the breeze in. It was salty, the ocean felt close. "Now what?"

"You know the list I kept, all those questions about grief and stuff?"

"Sure." Her tone was soft, ready to console.

"Sitting in my room while the parent cooled down gave me some thinking time. I realized all those questions were pretty much asking the same thing. When is it all right to move on?"

"I take it you have an answer."

"I think. You move on whenever you can, however you can."

Fuse closed the balcony door, lopping off that breeze. "Is that what we're doing here, Kya?"

"It's a first step." I took my spot on the couch and tucked my legs under me. "We never watched *Girls Trip*."

Fuse settled in next to me, close, snuggle distance. "This was your plan the whole time. Wasn't it, Mad Scientist?"

"My machinations are too complex for you to understand, Super Groupie!"

"You going to order the Five Guys?"

My phone was already out. "On it."

While waiting for the food, we sat listening to the distant sounds outside. Traffic. Squawking gulls. Wind gusts between buildings.

Abruptly, Fuse said, "I have an idea."

FUSE

This was our last day in the last space that was ever hers. We'd honor her with the movies and the food, but we couldn't forget the most important thing. The thing she'd lived and died for. I tapped through screens on my phone until I reached it. I showed Kya. "You do the honors."

KYA

My hand seemed a separate thing from me. Floating out, finger extended. I love you, Paris. I will miss you always.

I pressed play.

PARIS/DJ PARSEC

That VA sound, comin' 'round again!
We 'bout to take you for a spin!
Bom-bom-ba-ba-ba-tah! Bom-bom-ba-ba-ba-tah!

ACKNOWLEDGMENTS

To quote the late, great Notorious B.I.G., "And another one . . ."

As always there are so many people to thank. Adrienne, Mom, and the family: love you all, thanks for every bookmark you've handed out, every impromptu book talk you've given in grocery lines, and every other low-key marketing thing you do weekly to make sure others know there's an author in the clan.

Jamie Weiss Chilton and Eric Reid: Thank you for being such strong advocates of my work. Big things ahead.

Jody Corbett: You are so good at your job, you're getting shouted out twice. So well deserved.

The Scholastic team: Phil Falco, Josh Berlowitz, Elisabeth Ferrari, Tracy van Straaten, Lizette Serrano, Emily Heddleson, Danielle Yadao, Jasmine Miranda, Rachel Feld, Julia Eisler, Alan Smagler, Elizabeth Whiting, Alexis Lunsford, Sue Flynn, Jacquelyn Rubin, Jody Stigliano, Charlie Young, Terribeth Smith, Nikki Mutch, Roz Hilden, Tracy Bozentka, Dan Moser, Meaghan Hilton, Randy Kessler, Besty Polti, Chris Satterlund, Barb Synder, Jana Haussman, Ann Marie Wong, and Preeti Chhibber . . . thank you all for all you do!

The subject matter experts and the beta readers (DISCLAIMER: if it's right, it's them; if it's wrong, it's me): Ruta Sepetys, Jed Deaver, Andrew Shvarts, Dahlia Adler Fisch, Tiffany Jackson,

Olugbemisola Rhuday-Perkovich, S. Craig Jackson, and Melando Brown Jr. (aka Junior Beatz).

Finally, the remaining crew: Meg Medina, Ellen Oh, Dhonielle Clayton, Sona Charaipotra, Nic Stone, Jason Reynolds, Jeff Zentner, Tracey Baptiste, Kwame Alexander, Aisha Saeed, I. W. Gregorio, Marieke Nijkamp, Miranda Paul, Sara Farizan, Lilliam Rivera, Dapo Adeola, Daria Peoples-Riley, Gretchen McNeil, Jennifer Wolfe, Mitali Perkins, Leah Henderson, Shadra Strickland, and all the rest.

Rock on!

LAMAR GILES is the acclaimed author of *Overturned*, a YALSA Top Ten Quick Pick for Reluctant Young Adult Readers and a Kirkus Best Book of the Year; *Fake ID*, an Edgar Award finalist and a YALSA Top Ten Quick Pick for Reluctant Young Adult Readers; and *Endangered*, also an Edgar Award finalist, as well as the editor of the anthology *Fresh Ink*. Lamar is a founding member of We Need Diverse Books. He resides in Virginia with his wife.